His hands tightened on her shoulders...

"What is it?" she asked wonderingly. For once, she sounded like a bewildered young girl, not the woman whose actions tormented him with questions and whose presence shattered his sleep.

"You want to kiss me?"

"No," she said quickly, then less certainly, "yes."

She struggled to keep up the pretense of girlish adoration. Except that after she'd kissed him, he'd caught arousal stirring in her eyes.

"Which is it?"

She bit her lip and before he could stop himself, he bent to kiss her, to stop her torturing that luscious mouth. Her shocked gasp was a glance of warm breath across his face.

His hands slid around her back, holding her as a lover holds a woman he intends to kiss. Thoroughly.

Knowing he'd pay, knowing this was absolutely the last thing he should do, he brushed his lips across Miss Trim's...

Praise for

Anna Campbell and Her Novels

"Truly, deeply romantic."
　　　　—Eloisa James, *New York Times* bestselling author,
　　　　　　　　　　on *Tempt the Devil*

"Anna Campbell is an amazing, daring new voice in romance."
　　　　—Lorraine Heath, *New York Times* bestselling author

"Regency noir—different and intriguing."
　　　　　　　—Stephanie Laurens, *New York Times*
　　　　bestselling author, on *Claiming the Courtesan*

"No one does lovely, dark romance or lovely, dark heroes like Anna Campbell. I love her books."
　　　　—Sarah MacLean, *New York Times* bestselling author

What a Duke Dares

"Romantic fireworks, the constraints of custom, and witty banter are combined in this sweet and successful story."
　　　　　　　　　　　　　　—*Publishers Weekly*

"4½ stars! Top pick! Campbell's vibrant voice rings out in another touching, humorous, and utterly delightful story. Her multidimensional characters' dialogue sparkles with wit, and the sensuality blazes across the page."
　　　　　　　　　　　　　　—*RT Book Reviews*

"This book is engaging, sometimes heartbreaking, but thoroughly enjoyable . . . *What a Duke Dares* is a winner."
　　　　　　　　　　　　　　—FreshFiction.com

"A beautiful love story with an unforgettable hero. This is a must-read story for those readers who enjoy darker historical romances and beastly heroes."

—RomanceNovelNews.com

Midnight's Wild Passion

"4½ stars! It isn't just the sensuality she weaves into her story that makes Campbell a fan favorite, it's also her strong, three-dimensional characters, sharp dialogue, and deft plotting. Campbell intuitively knows how to balance the key elements of the genre and give readers an irresistible, memorable read."

—*RT Book Reviews*

"Readers beware: do not start reading *Midnight's Wild Passion* late at night. You'll stay up, as I did, telling yourself you'll only read one more chapter before putting it down for the night. Next thing you know, you've finished this marvelous book and discovered that it's nearly dawn."

—JoyfullyReviewed.com

My Reckless Surrender

"4½ stars, Top Pick! The enthralling story is complex and passionate...Quite a book!"

—*RT Book Reviews*

"Prepare yourself for Anna Campbell's most sultry, tempting tale yet! *My Reckless Surrender* wraps itself around readers like the most sensual of silks, Ms. Campbell's gorgeous writing a true thing of beauty."

—JoyfullyReviewed.com

Captive of Sin

"Smart Regency romance...Readers will cheer for these lovable and well-crafted characters."

—*Publishers Weekly*

Tempt the Devil

"4½ stars! Vibrantly refreshing and sizzling with sensuality and a depth of emotion that takes your breath away."

—*RT Book Reviews*

Untouched

"Reminiscent of early Laura Kinsale. Her flair for sensuality and darkness, wounded heroes, and strong women appeals to readers yearning for a powerful, sexy, and emotionally moving addition to their keeper shelves."

—*RT Book Reviews*

Claiming the Courtesan

"4½ stars! This fresh, vibrant novel launches an exciting new historical voice: a don't-miss author whose talent...ensures her place as a fan favorite."

—*RT Book Reviews*

ALSO BY ANNA CAMPBELL

THE SONS OF SIN SERIES

Seven Nights in a Rogue's Bed
Days of Rakes and Roses (novella)
A Rake's Midnight Kiss
What a Duke Dares

A Scoundrel by Moonlight

ANNA CAMPBELL

FOREVER

NEW YORK   BOSTON

Copyright © 2015 by Anna Campbell
Excerpt from *What a Duke Dares* copyright © 2014 by Anna Campbell

Forever
Hachette Book Group
1290 Avenue of the Americas
New York, NY 10104

www.HachetteBookGroup.com

Printed in the United States of America

First Edition: April 2015

10 9 8 7 6 5 4 3 2 1

OPM

Forever is an imprint of Grand Central Publishing.
The Forever name and logo are trademarks of Hachette Book Group, Inc.

The Hachette Speakers Bureau provides a wide range of authors for speaking events. To find out more, go to www.hachettespeakersbureau.com or call (866) 376-6591.

The publisher is not responsible for websites (or their content) that are not owned by the publisher.

ATTENTION CORPORATIONS AND ORGANIZATIONS:
Most HACHETTE BOOK GROUP books are available
at quantity discounts with bulk purchase for educational,
business, or sales promotional use. For information,
please call or write:

Special Markets Department, Hachette Book Group
1290 Avenue of the Americas, New York, NY 10104
Telephone: 1-800-222-6747 Fax: 1-800-477-5925

A Scoundrel
by Moonlight

Prologue

Mearsall, Kent, May 1828

A venge me."

The raspy whisper stirred Nell Trim from her grief-stricken haze. She straightened in the hard wooden chair beside the narrow bed. Around her, tallow candles guttered. Outside the cottage's mullioned windows, the night was dark and quiet.

She rose to smooth her half-sister's covers. "Shall I fetch Father?"

"No." Dorothy grabbed Nell's hand. The late spring air was warm and Dorothy's fever had raged for two days, but the fingers that closed around Nell's were icy with encroaching death. "Listen...to me."

Nell stared helplessly into the girl's ashen face. Once Dorothy had been the village belle. Now her skin was gray and dry, and her large blue eyes sank deep into their sockets. She was eighteen years old and looked three times that. "Dr. Parsons said to rest."

Dorothy's cracked lips turned down. "There's no time."

Nell's heart cramped with futile denial. "Darling..."

Her half-sister's hold tightened, stifling the comforting lie. "We both know it's true."

Yes, they did. Dr. Parsons had relinquished all hope after Dorothy had lost her baby. Nell still shuddered to remember the sea of blood gushing from her half-sister's slight body.

Since then, Dorothy had lingered through agony. Looking into her drawn face, Nell knew that lovely, vivacious, heedless Dorothy Simpson wouldn't last the night. "I'll get you some water."

Irritation shadowed her half-sister's face. "I don't want water. I want your promise to take up my cause."

Nell frowned. "But you don't know who assaulted you."

For months, Dorothy had hidden her pregnancy, until even her unworldly schoolmaster father had noticed. In tearful shame, she'd confessed that a stranger had attacked her.

Dorothy's bitter smile was out of keeping with the frivolous girl Nell knew. But of course, frivolity had brought disaster, hadn't it?

"It wasn't exactly...assault."

Horrified, Nell snatched her hand free. "What do you mean?"

"What do you think I mean?"

Ever since hearing that Dorothy's pregnancy resulted from violence, Nell had been angry. This hint that the story wasn't exactly as presented—hardly surprising, Dorothy was often unreliable with the truth—left her bewildered. "You went...willingly?"

Dorothy's expression conveyed a strange mixture of shame and pride. "I loved him."

"Was it one of the village boys?" Nell felt queasy. Had someone they knew taken advantage of Dorothy? It seemed the most obvious answer, yet Dorothy had always scorned Mearsall's lads as yokels.

A grunt that might have been a dismissive laugh. "Don't be silly."

"Then who?"

Dorothy's gaze fixed on some distant horizon. Unbelievably Nell heard a trace of her sister's old conceit. "A great gentleman. A man who could give me everything I wanted."

"Everything except a wedding ring," Nell said sharply, unable to reconcile Dorothy's boasting with this pain and disgrace.

Tears filled Dorothy's eyes. "I knew you and Papa would scold. That's why I said I'd been forced."

Despairingly, Nell stared at this wayward girl she loved so much. Dorothy was seven years younger, more child than sister. When Nell was five, her soldier father had died fighting the French. Widowed Frances Trim had then married the considerably older William Simpson, as much to provide security for her daughter Nell as for companionship. Since Frances's death ten years ago, Nell had cared for her halfsister like a mother.

"Oh, Dorothy," Nell said, a world of regret in the words. She could hardly bear her guilt at failing to keep a closer eye on her sister.

Convulsively Dorothy clutched Nell's hand. "Don't be cross."

"I'm cross with the man who did this to you." That was an understatement. She'd like to see the wretch hanged.

Before this unknown blackguard had got his filthy paws on her, Dorothy had been an innocent, although easily flattered. A man wouldn't need much town polish to convince Dorothy, who'd never been past Canterbury, of his credentials as a lord.

"Good," Dorothy said with venom, her face as white as the pillowcases.

For a terrifyingly long time, Dorothy lay still. Nell's heart slammed to a stop, only to resume beating when Dorothy drew a rattling breath. She was alive. Just.

"I want you to..." A coughing fit interrupted. Every word sounded like her last.

"Don't talk," Nell said, although she was frantic to know who had wronged this beautiful, vibrant girl.

Dorothy's words emerged in a breathless tumble. "Find him and expose him to the world as a villain."

"But who—" Nell began.

"Promise me." Dorothy struggled up on her elbows, the effort draining what little strength remained. "He said he'd marry me. He said he'd take me to his house and set me up like a queen."

She started to cough again. Nell released her and poured some water, but drinking only made Dorothy choke. "Rest now."

Petulantly Dorothy struck away the glass, spilling water on the sheets. "When I told him about the baby, he laughed. Laughed and called me a brainless slut."

Nell winced at the language, even as her anger focused on this devil. "I'm so sorry."

"He has...a book." Dorothy closed her eyes, gathering herself. This time, Nell didn't interrupt. For the peace of her soul, Dorothy needed to speak. "A diary of his seductions. Girl after girl. All set out neatly as stories in a newspaper."

"Oh, my dear..." This spiteful betrayal horrified Nell. "Why on earth would he show you that? That's needlessly cruel."

"He was proud of it. Proud of all the women he'd ruined." Her voice thickened with tears. "If you find that book, you can destroy him."

"But how?"

Dorothy became agitated. "Just don't tell Papa. Please."

"I won't, darling." Grief split Nell's heart at this fleeting glimpse of the sweet child she'd once been. "But where can I find this book?"

Dorothy breathed in shallow gasps. "Go to his house."

"His house?" Was Dorothy delirious? "Where is his house?"

"You'll find it." Dorothy drew a shuddering breath. "You're clever, too clever to believe a man's lies." Lower still. "If only I'd been as clever."

Acid tears stung Nell's eyes. Over recent years, Nell's cleverness had inspired Dorothy's resentment rather than admiration. If Nell or William mentioned propriety or prudence, Dorothy had flounced away, convinced that her family was hopelessly hidebound. "Who did this to you?"

Dorothy opened glazed eyes and her grip tightened to bruising. "Swear you'll find that diary and expose this monster for what he is."

Her half-sister's desperation sliced at Nell. "Of course I swear. Tell me the man's name."

Hatred sharpened Dorothy's face. "The Marquess of Leath."

Before Nell could respond to this astonishing claim, Dorothy began to shake and gasp. Nell surged forward to enfold her sister in her arms, but it was too late.

Pretty, reckless Dorothy Simpson had breathed her last.

Chapter One

Alloway Chase, Yorkshire, late September 1828

Finally he was home.

James Fairbrother, Marquess of Leath sighed with relief and whipped off his heavy topcoat as the footman fought to close the massive oak door against the blustery night. This year, winter came early to the moors. Most years, if Leath was honest. When he'd left London, lovely, golden autumn had held sway. The further north he'd ventured, the less lovely and golden the weather became, until he'd arrived at his family seat in a freezing gale.

"Go to bed, George. I can manage from here." At three in the morning, he wasn't selfish enough to keep the man at his beck and call. Knowing that he'd beat any message he sent to Alloway Chase, he'd left London in a rush. He'd considered putting up at an inn before the final desolate run across the heath, but the moon was full and the night was clear, if brutal, and his horse had been fresh.

"Thank you, my lord." The young man in crimson livery took the coat and bowed. "I'll light the fires in your apartments."

"Thank you."

As George left, Leath collected his leather satchel of documents, lifted the chamber stick from the Elizabethan chest against the great hall's stone wall, and trudged down the long corridor toward his library. Against the looming darkness, the candle's light seemed frail, but Leath had grown up in this rambling house. The ghosts, reportedly legion, were friendly.

Physically he was exhausted, but his mind leaped about like a cat with fleas. The roiling mixture of emotions that had sent him hurtling up to Yorkshire still warred within. Anger. Disappointment. Self-castigation. Confusion. A barely admitted fear. He wasn't ready to seek his bed, although the good God knew where he did want to go, except perhaps to blazes.

Usually when he reached Alloway Chase, the weight of the world slid from his shoulders. Not tonight. Nor any time in the near future, he grimly suspected. There was a difference between visiting the country at one's own prompting and having one's political advisers demand a rustication for the nation's good.

Outside his library, he paused, puzzled.

A line of faint light shone beneath the door. At this hour, the household should be asleep. Stupid with tiredness, he wondered if at the grand old age of thirty-two, he'd finally encountered one of the ghosts. The most active specter was Lady Mary Fairbrother, murdered during the Civil War after her husband caught her in bed with a Royalist.

As the door slowly opened before him, the unreal sensation built.

Flickering gold filled the widening gap. Leath found himself staring into wide dark eyes.

The apparition gave a breathy gasp of surprise. A stray draft extinguished both candles, and then he heard a dull thud as the girl lost her grip on the light.

Instinct made him drop the satchel and reach for her. It was as dark as a thief's pocket, and something told him that she'd use the cover to flee. His hand closed around a slender waist. This was no visitor from the spirit realm. The body he held was undoubtedly human. Warm. Lissome. Taut with outrage or fright. Perhaps both.

"Are you a burglar?" she asked in a low voice, wriggling to escape.

"Isn't that what I should say?" he asked drily.

"I don't understand," she hissed back.

She sounded young. Before the candles went out, he'd merely glimpsed her features. He wondered, although it could have no importance, whether she was pretty. "Damn it, stop squirming."

Uselessly she pushed him. "Then let me go."

"No." He caught her more securely and back-stepped her into the library.

The thick darkness was confoundedly suggestive. He was overwhelmingly conscious of the curve of her waist and the brush of her breasts against his chest. The soft, urgent rasp of her breathing indicated fear, but sounded disconcertingly like sexual excitement. Hell, he could even smell her. Her intentions might be murky, but she smelled of freshly cut meadows and soap. If she was a burglar, she was a dashed clean one.

As he kicked the door shut behind him, she released a soft yelp and made a more vigorous attempt to break free. "I'll scream."

"Go ahead." He dropped his candle to the carpet and reached behind him to turn the key in the lock. When he rode up to the house, he'd been mutton-headed with weariness. This riddle of a female in his library stirred him to full alertness.

"You've locked us in," she said accusingly. "Who are you?"

A snort of laughter escaped him. She was a direct wench. This encounter became more bizarre by the second. Perhaps he'd fallen asleep in the saddle and he was dreaming. If not for the living woman under his hand, he might almost believe it. "More to the point, who are you? And what are you doing in my library after midnight?"

A bristling silence descended. "*Your* library?"

"Yes." Unerringly he approached the high windows and flung back the curtains. Moonlight flooded the room. He turned to inspect the woman, but she lurked in the shadows by the door and he discerned little, apart from her slenderness and unnaturally upright posture. Her hands twined nervously at her waist.

She piqued his curiosity. A welcome change from the bitter dissatisfaction that had dogged him this last year. Using the tinderbox, he lit the branch of candles on the table under the window.

Briefly Leath caught his reflection in the glass, outlined in gold light. Large, looming. If he'd made the girl nervous in the dark, she'd be terrified now that she saw him. He didn't look like a welcoming, easy sort of man. Recent trials had added sternness to a face not blessed with charm at the best of times.

Slowly, he turned. And his heart slammed to stillness.

His mysterious lady was a beauty.

Ignoring the way her lips tightened with resentment, he raised the candles to inspect her. A plain gray dress with white linen collar. Silvery blond hair drawn severely away from her face. No trace of curl or ribbon to soften the austerity. Her face was austere too, as perfectly carved as an angel on a cathedral doorway. High forehead; long slender nose; slanted cheekbones; pointed chin. Assertive brows darker than her hair above widely spaced eyes that regarded him with impressive steadiness. Few men could withstand the Marquess of Leath's intense stare, yet this girl didn't even blink.

Her mouth provided the only hint in that pure, calm face that she was more than a beautiful marble statue. Her mouth was . . . marvelous.

Full. Lush. Sweetly pink.

He was so big that most women seemed tiny in comparison, but the repressed energy radiating from her made her appear taller than average. His eyes lingered on the delightfully rounded bosom beneath her demure bodice.

Her gaze turned frosty and despite the uncertain light, he saw a flush on those high cheekbones. Good God, whoever she was, she had spirit. He reduced most young ladies to blushing silence. This girl—and she was little more, mid-twenties at the most—might blush, but she was far from intimidated.

When she bloody well should be.

The childishness of that last reflection had his lips twitching. He'd feared months of boredom ahead, but his return started in a most intriguing fashion. If he'd known this odd, fascinating creature waited in Yorkshire, he might have visited more often, instead of burying his head in parliamentary business in London.

"Just what are you up to?" he asked softly, placing the candles on a table and stepping closer.

Ah, she wasn't totally foolhardy. She retreated toward the door, eyes widening. He wished he could see their precise color. The light simply wasn't good enough. "You're trying to frighten me."

"Perhaps I'm seeking a little respect," he said smoothly.

She curtsied, but he could tell that her heart wasn't in it. "Your lordship."

He folded his arms and surveyed her under lowered brows. "So you know I'm Leath."

"You said it's your library. And her ladyship has a portrait in her room. I recognized you when you lit the candles."

The world toadied to his wealth and influence, but the spark in this girl's eyes looked like hostility. A challenge sizzled between them. Or perhaps the beginnings of attraction.

"At last a straight answer," he said wryly. "Now can you bring yourself to tell me who you are?"

"Will you let me go if I do?"

Her audacity stole his breath. Nobody defied him or denied him or bargained with him. Most people tripped over themselves to do his bidding before he'd even worked out what his bidding was. "We'll see."

Her eyes narrowed, confirming his impression that she didn't like him. He wondered why. "You have a reputation for keeping your hands off the housemaids, my lord."

"What in Hades?" Her meaning smashed through his burgeoning interest. "Are you saying that you're a...housemaid?"

A fleeting smile tilted her lips. His wayward heart jolted at the promise of other, more generous smiles. "Yes."

"You don't look like a blasted housemaid." Nor did she speak like any housemaid he'd ever known. She sounded like a lady.

"You...you caught me at a disadvantage."

"I'll say I did."

He waited for some retort, but her expression turned blank. For the first time, to his disappointment, she looked like a servant. Although this sudden docility meant that he might discover why she was in his library. Housemaids started work early and generally didn't have the energy to run around after bedtime. "What's your name?"

She dipped into another curtsy. He could have told her she overdid the meekness, but he held his peace.

"Trim, my lord."

Trim? He couldn't argue with that. "Trim what?"

He thought she might smile again, but she'd leashed her rebellious spirit as tightly as she tied back her hair. He wasn't a man who experienced profound and sudden sexual urges. But he'd give this girl every sparkling diamond in the family vault if she'd take down her hair. If she let him touch it, he'd throw in the damned house as well.

"Nell Trim, sir."

"Helen or Eleanor?"

"Eleanor." Her voice retained its curiously flat quality and she stared somewhere over his shoulder.

Eleanor. An elegant name for an elegant woman. An elegant woman who was his *housemaid*.

"Very good." Except Eleanor wasn't a suitable name for a junior servant. Eleanor was a queen's name. It brought dangerous, powerful women to mind. "What are you doing in my library, Trim?"

By rights, he should call a housemaid Nell, but with her slender neatness, Trim suited her so well.

"If I tell you, you'll dismiss me."

He kept his expression neutral. "I'll dismiss you if you don't."

She leveled that direct stare upon him. "I couldn't sleep, and I wanted something to read. I always return the books, my lord; you have my word."

A housemaid who rifled his bookcases and offered her word? She became more extraordinary by the minute. "You can read?"

"Yes, sir." In a show of deference that didn't convince, she lowered her eyelids. Years in the political bear pit had taught him to read people. He was sure of two things about the trim Miss Eleanor Trim. One was that deference didn't come naturally. The other was that somewhere in this odd conversation, she lied.

"So what did you choose?" She hadn't carried a book when she'd run into him at the door.

"Nothing appealed. May I go, my lord? I'm on duty early."

"Do I need to search you to see if you've stolen anything?" She could be a master criminal bamboozling him into complacency. Except he didn't feel complacent. He felt alive and interested as nothing had interested him in months.

Temper lit her eyes. She didn't like him questioning her honesty. "I'm not a thief."

Ah, the false docility cracked. He hid his satisfaction. "How can I be sure?"

"You could check the room for anything missing, my lord."

"I might do that." Abruptly his sour mood descended once more. What the hell was he doing flirting with a housemaid in the middle of the night? Perhaps his political advisers were right about him needing a break.

He bent to pick up the candle the girl had dropped when he'd barged in on top of her. He lit it from the branch and passed it across, then unlocked the door. "You may go, Trim."

She raised the candle and surveyed him as if uncertain whether this dismissal was good news or not. Her curtsy this time conveyed no ironic edge, then she backed toward the door. "Thank you, my lord."

"For God's sake, I'm not going to pounce on you," he said

on a spurt of irritation. It niggled that for a different man living in a different world, the thought of pouncing on the delectable Miss Trim was sinfully appealing.

Her eyes flashed up and he saw that beneath her drab exterior, she was fierce and strong. He awaited some astringent comeback. Instead she dragged the door open and fled.

Wise girl.

Chapter Two

B last, blast, blast.
   Exhausted, angry, disgusted with herself, Nell collapsed onto the narrow bed in the small room that had become hers a month ago. She buried her head in her hands.

Why, oh, why did the depraved marquess have to catch her searching his library? And when he did, why on earth hadn't she behaved like a proper servant? Until now, she'd managed to hide any rebellious impulses under a subservient mask. If she'd been humble and silent, he'd have sent her away, instead of finding her of surpassing interest.

But she'd just been so furious to see him alive and well, when her beloved half-sister had died in such shame and misery. Caught by surprise, she'd forgotten to play the circumspect domestic.

And now she'd attracted his attention.

She didn't want to arouse James Fairbrother's curiosity. She wanted to find the diary that proved his offenses, then leave Alloway Chase and pass the matter of Leath's destruction over to the Duke of Sedgemoor, his sworn enemy. A woman of her humble background would get nowhere, taking on such a powerful man. But the duke could use the book to blackmail Leath into behaving himself, or publish the details and expose the marquess to trial by public opinion.

Nell hoped he chose the second course. Lord Leath deserved general condemnation.

In her bedroom at Mearsall, the plan had appeared straightforward, once she'd come to terms with the exalted status of Dorothy's lover. A check of her stepfather's old newspapers had confirmed his lordship's presence at a house party in Kent, around the time Dorothy fell pregnant. Leath had been near enough to seduce Dorothy. Given her death-bed confession, that was enough evidence to convince Nell to pursue the marquess's downfall.

As Dorothy had promised, discovering the location of the marquess's family seat had been easy. It had also been surprisingly easy finding employment as a housemaid.

She'd set herself a daunting task, but she'd made a promise to someone she loved—and she was angry. The idea of this devil ruining more innocent girls like Dorothy made her want to scream with rage. She'd left Mearsall to seek the diary and other evidence of Lord Leath's sins. If she failed in Yorkshire, she'd find work in his house in London and continue her quest there. However long it took, she'd make him pay for his crimes.

But now that she'd met the marquess, nothing seemed so clear-cut. After that oddly charged encounter downstairs, her heart still galloped like a wild horse—and her mind whirled with bewilderment.

Dear heaven, when his wicked lordship had locked the door, she'd nearly collapsed with horror. She was alone in the middle of the night with a lecherous monster. She'd never imagined that her quest might involve physical risk.

Cursing her naivety, she'd prepared to fight off the hulking brute.

Then the marquess had confounded every fear. Apart from catching her to stop her escape, he hadn't touched her.

Which was...puzzling. And troubling.

She'd sensed his interest. At twenty-five, she wasn't a green girl, and she knew what it meant when a male leveled that prickling, intense concentration on a woman. Yet he'd kept his distance and remained remarkably polite, given her barely concealed insolence.

In her mind, Lord Leath had always been a caricature of a villain. But tonight, once she'd realized that he wouldn't leap on her—and she'd realized quickly despite that unwelcome awareness—he'd proven much more real. And much more alarming.

Immediately she'd noted his cleverness, his calmness, his confidence. All worked against her. The man in the portrait in his mother's apartments was big and powerful, with a personality that threatened to burst from the frame.

In the flesh, he'd been...more.

He wasn't a pretty man, by any means. But there was beauty in that tall, strong body and that craggy, individual face with its beak of a nose and heavy black brows. No wonder Dorothy had been smitten.

Still, Nell had expected more overt charm, a Lothario from a play, all smooth words and false compliments. She couldn't picture this man filling a girl's head with nonsense until she spread her legs.

These riddles gave her a headache. And she faced a day's work and, if she could evade the marquess, a night's searching.

Hope staged an uncertain return. Perhaps Leath's unexpected arrival was more blessing than curse. Perhaps Nell hadn't yet found the diary because this dedicated seducer kept his record of ruin with him.

If so, the diary was now at Alloway Chase.

"Darling, I didn't know you'd come home." From the chaise longue, Leath's mother extended her hands toward him.

He hated to see his mother's health deteriorate to a point where she spent most days in her apartments. At least his rustication meant that he could devote more time to her. Guiltily he realized that he hadn't been home since his sister Sophie's hurried wedding last May. Parliamentary business had been pressing, as had his need to rise above the scandals engulfing his family.

"I got in late last night." He took his mother's hands and pressed a kiss to her cheek. "You look well."

It wasn't true, but it was less of a lie than last time they'd met. The gray morning light through the large windows was stark on her thin body. But her cheeks held a hint of color and her eyes were brighter than he'd seen them in years.

"I'm feeling better." She indicated a chair, inviting him to stay. "How long are you here?"

"Until people can say the Fairbrother name without a sneer," he said flatly. He supposed that he'd learn to accept his exile, although at least with his mother he needn't hide his bitterness.

She frowned. "I'd hoped the brouhaha about your uncle might blow over by now. After all, it's a year since he shot himself to escape a hanging."

A year in which everyone had eyed Leath as if afraid he might resort to violence and larceny the way his odious Uncle Neville had. A year in which Leath's every political plan had fallen foul of some opponent mentioning the Fairbrothers' infamous criminal tendencies. A family flaw only widely recognized since his uncle's exposure as a thief and murderer. Thanks to Camden Rothermere, the damned meddling Duke of Sedgemoor, the whole world knew about Neville Fairbrother's crimes.

For months, Leath had been furious at Sedgemoor and his cronies. Only gradually had he admitted that ultimate blame for the family's straits lay with Lord Neville.

That was little satisfaction when another snide comment in the House of Lords topped one of Leath's speeches with jeering laughter. For years, the Marquess of Leath had been the most powerful personality in parliament, his progress to the premiership taken for granted. The gossip now dogging him gratified his enemies—and a disappointing number of people he'd counted as friends. He was cynical enough to recognize that the world loved to witness an ambitious man's fall. But recognition made it no more pleasant to be that man.

"You forget Sophie," he said grimly, rising and prowling toward the window, too restless to sit when reviewing his recent disasters.

His sister had set tongues wagging afresh when she'd eloped with a penniless younger son who happened to be Sedgemoor's brother-in-law. Sophie's timing had been calamitous for Leath's political hopes. The whole world now considered Fairbrother a synonym for flibbertigibbet. Or scoundrel.

Neither adjective befitted a future prime minister.

His mother looked troubled. "She's safely married now, and you and Sedgemoor united to approve the match."

Much against Leath's inclination, he'd offered the runaways what countenance he could. He and Sedgemoor had even patched up their feud, at least in public. They were never likely to be friends, but Leath no longer itched to punch His Grace's supercilious nose.

Whatever measures both families had taken, they couldn't contain the scandal. Especially as it followed so closely on the heels of his uncle's disgrace. Even worse, Sophie had jilted Lord Desborough, one of England's most powerful men, and as a result his lordship had shifted from Leath's greatest ally to his implacable foe. "My political career still hangs in the balance, Mamma."

He turned to see her raising a frail hand to her lips. "James, I'm sorry."

Damn it. His chagrin got the better of him. Upsetting his mother was the last thing he wanted. He wasn't himself this morning. And he knew who to blame. A housemaid! He had bats in his belfry.

"At the moment, the party powerbrokers consider me more hindrance than asset. I'm to retire to my estates, keep my head down and my nose clean, and reappear once the world has had time to forget the gossip."

"That's unfair. None of this is your fault. Your uncle was an out-and-out rogue. Your father banned him from the house after he got that poor girl into trouble."

Leath had been a boy when his uncle had raped a maid. "Perhaps Uncle Neville's crimes aren't my responsibility, but Sophie was," he said heavily.

"At least she's happy."

Her voice indicated that Sophie's happiness hardly counted, compared to the damage she'd done to her brother's career. His mother had married the late marquess, expecting to be a political hostess and eventually wife to the prime minister. After a carriage accident crippled his father in his forties, her hopes had focused on her then-twenty-year-old son. For the final eight years of his father's life and the four since, Leath had devoted himself to fulfilling his parents' political dreams. He'd loved his father dearly. The possibility of failure now when the prize hovered so close made him grind his teeth in frustration.

"Your exile isn't all bad." His mother had clearly decided to take the news stoically.

"Isn't it?" he said gloomily, wandering to the dressing table and picking up a delicate Meissen shepherdess. The simpering expression mocked his pretensions to taking on his brilliant father's mantle.

"I'll see more of you."

He sighed and replaced the figurine. "Yes, and my tenants will be pleased I'm home."

"There's no substitute for the lord of the manor."

"Perhaps not," Leath said shortly. "But I can't angle for influence in London and be here at the same time."

"No," Lady Leath said without offense. "But a period of reflection won't go astray. It's time you thought about a bride."

Startled, he bumped the crowded dressing table, setting the china figures and glass bottles rattling. "What?"

His mother regarded him patiently. "Don't pretend it's an outlandish suggestion, James. You need an heir. Right now, you need more than an heir; you need allies. If this mess hasn't taught you that a man can't stand alone in politics, nothing will."

"With the stink surrounding the family name, who would have me?"

"Don't be a fool. You're the Marquess of Leath. Anyone with a scrap of acumen knows that you'll return stronger than ever."

"So nice that my private requirements count in this decision," he said with a hint of sarcasm.

His mother didn't smile. "You're not an amorous shepherd in a poem, James, free to bestow his heart and hand where he likes. Fairbrothers marry for advantage, not because they fancy a pretty pair of blue eyes."

"You loved my father."

Her face softened. "I did. But even if I didn't, I'd have married him."

Leath struggled to contain his surprise. And disappointment. He'd always thought his parents had married because they were soul mates. Yet it seemed that they'd married for the same cold-blooded reasons as most other aristocrats.

"My wife and I will enjoy a mutual regard." He must marry to continue the line—and a woman from an influential family was the obvious choice. While he mightn't pant after neck-or-nothing passion, nor could he be completely pragmatic about his choice. He was a man before he was a politician, however ambitious he might be.

This time his mother smiled. "Of course, that would be ideal."

Ideal but not essential, he noted. His mother continued, "What about Marianne Seton? She behaved perfectly when Sedgemoor got entangled with that dreadful Thorne woman. You might balk at Camden Rothermere's leavings, but her father would make a valuable friend."

Poor Lady Marianne, jilted when the Duke of Sedgemoor fell in love with the notorious daughter of a scandalous family. A love match that had only caused trouble. Just as Sophie's love match had. Still some hitherto unsuspected part of Leath's soul revolted at the idea of marrying without affection.

"Mamma, I can choose my own bride," he protested, even as he pictured lovely, sedate Marianne Seton in the Fairbrother sapphires. They'd match her eyes. Which seemed a dashed stupid reason for proposing to a chit.

"What about Desborough's sister? An engagement would heal the rift between you. Honestly, I could box Sophie's ears for ruining that match."

A chill slithered down Leath's spine. "Lady Jane is forty-five if she's a day, not to mention a dedicated spinster."

His mother sighed. "Pity she's too old to bear children." She paused and Leath hoped the discussion was over. A hope quickly shattered. "If only Lydia Rothermere hadn't married that penniless libertine. She was a marvelous hostess, and a Rothermere match would silence talk of a feud."

"God made a mistake when he created you female, Mamma," he said drily. "You'd make a capital prime minister."

She laughed and dismissed his comment with a wave, although it was true. "I'm a mere woman, James."

He smiled, hoping that she'd stopped listing possible marchionesses. "And clever as a fox."

"You flatter me, darling." Briefly he saw the beautiful girl who nearly forty years ago had captivated the brilliant marquess with the glittering political future. Fate had played his parents some cruel cards.

"Not at all." He sank into one of the frail chairs near the blazing hearth. The chair creaked beneath his weight. He was a large man and the furnishings in his mother's apartments were decidedly dainty. "Let me establish my credentials as a respectable landholder before we plot my walk down the aisle."

"You've always been a solid, reliable, thoughtful gentleman. People will eventually remember that. You'll be back in London before you know it."

He smiled, while his vanity bucked at the description. What a dull dog he sounded. "Ever the optimist, Mamma."

"I have every faith in you."

Sometimes he wished she didn't. Each step of his life, he'd carried the weight of his father's unfulfilled promise and of his invalid mother's hopes. No wonder he'd never kicked over the traces like his less burdened colleagues.

Now he faced a solid, reliable marriage. The prospect was depressing. "I thought to find you all cast down with your own company," he said. "You're in better spirits than I expected."

"I was lonely at first. There's no denying it."

"So what's happened?"

She looked almost mischievous. "Aha, I must reveal my secret."

Whatever she was up to, he was in favor if it lent her this spark. "Do tell."

She rang the bell on the side table. The door to the dressing room opened and a neat, fair-haired young woman entered, head lowered and hands linked decorously at her waist.

Leath's gut tightened with a premonition that the alignment of his planets changed forever. Of course, the girl was the mysterious Miss Trim who had kept him restless and intrigued past dawn.

Chapter Three

"My lady?" The girl's curtsy conveyed considerably more respect than she'd granted him a few hours ago, Leath was piqued to note.

"Nell, let me show you off to my son." The fondness in his mother's voice troubled him, although only moments ago, he'd been grateful for whatever had brought about this positive change in her. His mother turned to him as if she presented a huge treat. "James, Miss Trim is my companion."

The girl poised in the doorway. She wore the same plain gray gown and her hair was still wrenched back. She looked biddable and competent. Why, then, was he so convinced that she was up to no good?

During his sleepless hours, he'd wondered if his imagination exaggerated her attractions. Daylight didn't lessen her physical impact. There was nothing flashy about Miss Trim, nothing vulgar. The purity of her features struck him even more strongly now than in candlelight. And that miracle of a mouth still made his skin itch with unwilling sexual response.

"Good morning, Miss Trim," he said calmly.

Her gaze shot up to meet his. With a satisfaction completely out of kilter with the fact, he noticed that her eyes were a coppery brown, striking against her pale hair. "Welcome home, my lord."

"Thank you."

What the devil was she playing at, calling herself a housemaid? What the devil had she been playing at in his library at three this morning? The revelation of Miss Trim's position in the household raised more questions than it answered.

"Nell has become indispensable." His mother's voice was warm with affection. Which made him uneasy on so many levels.

"I'm sure." Leath mustn't have contained the irony in his tone because his mother cast him a puzzled glance.

"She's transformed my life," his mother said, in answer to his unspoken criticism.

"You're too kind, my lady." Miss Trim's voice was low and melodic, like a cello.

"You didn't mention Miss Trim in your letters," Leath said neutrally. Given his mother wrote most days, the omission had to be deliberate.

"I wasn't sure you'd approve," his mother said.

"I'm not sure I do," he said. "When I've offered to arrange a companion, you've always declined."

His mother grimaced. "You'd saddle me with some destitute relative. Bores, every one."

"A little harsh."

"But only a little." His mother reached for Miss Trim who, blast her, took her hand. "Nell does me perfectly, especially since Sophie left. I need someone young and bright to talk to."

Leath had no right to resent the implication that he wasn't

young and bright. Miss Trim cast him a nervous glance under thick lashes, dark like her brows. She must expect him to betray her midnight wanderings. He wondered why the hell he didn't.

"Perhaps. But I would have liked to help you find someone suitable."

The girl's lips flattened. His mother looked equally unimpressed. He realized that he handled this as badly as a parliamentary novice with an unpopular petition. He must be wearier than he'd thought. Or Miss Trim's silent and subtly hostile presence unsettled him.

"Nell is completely suitable. You'll see."

He'd see something, that was sure. He wasn't letting the manipulative Miss Trim out of his sight.

"My lady, perhaps it would be better if I finished ordering those embroidery patterns." The girl shifted uncomfortably. Obscurely it galled him that her manners proved better than his. He and his mother should hold this discussion in private.

"If I'm going to quarrel with my son, perhaps you should," his mother said.

"No, stay. I want to talk to you, Miss Trim."

"Bully her, you mean," his mother sniped.

Leath ignored the jibe and focused on his mother. "Where did you discover this paragon?"

"In the kitchen, my lord," Miss Trim said with a hint of challenge.

"Nell, don't bait my son. He doesn't like to be crossed," his mother said as if describing a fractious toddler. "James, Nell came to us in July as a housemaid. I was suffering… megrims and she was drafted into my care. It was immediately apparent that her talents extended beyond dusting and scrubbing."

Leath fumed under his parent's tolerant glance, even

as guilt assailed him. He well knew his mother's courage. "Megrims" meant she'd been prostrate with pain. And he'd been in London and ignorant of her suffering. While this encroaching maidservant took advantage. "A housemaid is no apt companion for the Marchioness of Leath."

"She is when the marchioness so decides," his mother snapped. "If I can no longer choose who serves me, it's time I moved to the dower house."

Leath endured a meaningful glance from Miss Trim, as if to remind him that his mother's health was poor and this disagreement must try her nerves. Damn it, he knew that. In frustration, he ran a hand through his hair. If they ever allowed women into parliament, every man there was doomed.

"Mamma, this is your home. There's no need for this."

"If it's my home, I should be allowed to select my servants," she said stalwartly.

Miss Trim shifted to a table covered with bottles and vials and poured a cordial for his mother. "Your ladyship, perhaps I should return to my former place in the household."

Leath's eyes narrowed on her. "Capital suggestion."

His mother accepted the small crystal glass with a grateful smile. He couldn't help noticing the glitter in her eyes. She didn't look ill. In fact, she looked better than she'd looked in recent memory. But the doctors had insisted that too much excitement could exhaust her.

"I will not countenance you dismissing Nell just because you've got some bee in your bonnet." She handed the half-empty glass to Miss Trim, who returned it to the table without glancing at him.

He sighed. "It's a pity to start our reunion with an argument."

His mother regarded him with a less militant light in her fine gray eyes. "Perhaps I should have told you in a letter."

He doubted that would have changed his mind about Miss Trim's suitability, although he might have had a clue about the identity of last night's moonlit wraith. "I'm willing to give the girl a chance."

He waited for his mother to insist that he had no say in the matter, but it seemed she too regretted their disagreement. "You'll soon see how good she is for me and you'll be as grateful as I am that she came to us."

Somehow he doubted that. "I would still appreciate the chance to interview her."

Miss Trim glanced up quickly and he saw that she was as reluctant to be interviewed as his mother was to allow the interview to take place. Too bad. He was master here and it was time he took control. His mother had always been an excellent judge of character and he had a large and capable staff. But even so, things at Alloway Chase were not as he wished.

"Don't let him browbeat you, Nell," his mother said with an encouraging smile.

"For heaven's sake, Mamma, you make me sound like a tyrant."

His mother arched her eyebrows. "If your guilty conscience prompts that thought, perhaps you should examine your behavior."

He flushed, he who stood firm under the most concentrated parliamentary attack. His mother always knew how to best him, devil take her. "I'll be gentle."

The girl clearly didn't believe him, but his mother took the statement at face value. "Thank you. I won't have you upsetting someone who is so kind to me."

Miss Trim hovered near the sideboard, looking as guilty as sin. Interesting.

"Miss Trim, if you please, we'll adjourn to the library."

He knew she caught the faint edge as he mentioned the scene of their nocturnal encounter.

"You promise not to browbeat her?" his mother insisted.

He muffled a growl. He wasn't in the habit of badgering the servants. At this rate, the girl would be in such a state by the time he questioned her, she'd be in hysterics.

"Do you need anything, my lady?" she asked with a calmness that belied that prediction.

"Just my book and spectacles," his mother said and accepted them with a smile. "Don't stand for any nonsense from James."

Miss Trim's smile was faint as she curtsied and preceded him from the room with a poise that wouldn't disgrace a debutante at Almack's. As he followed, Leath couldn't help thinking that she was the damnedest housemaid he'd ever seen.

Nell's heart hammered with dread by the time she reached the library. She knew Leath chose this room to intimidate her. Goodness, after his tiff with his mother, she might yet face dismissal. It was clear that he wanted to get rid of her. If he did, how would she gather the evidence against him?

Before she was summoned, her eavesdropping had been enlightening. The newspapers were right. Leath's political career was in trouble. Good. When Sedgemoor used the diary to expose him as the villain he was, all hope of public office would evaporate.

Nell had arrived at Alloway Chase despising Lord Leath. But that was before she'd listened to him battle with a mother he loved over something he considered important for her sake, not his own.

Mentally Nell kicked herself. His kindness to his mother didn't mean anything. With his family, the marquess might act the civilized man, but at heart he was a monster. If she forgot that, she was lost.

She stood straight and quiet in the center of the library as he prowled across to sit behind the desk.

"It's too late to pretend humility, Miss Trim," he barked, making her start.

When he'd spoken so tenderly to his mother, the beauty of his deep baritone had struck her. Now his voice was like a gunshot. Of course it was; she was a lowly servant. And he didn't like her, despite those disturbing moments last night when she'd sensed male interest. This morning he'd regarded her like a cockroach in the castle's pantry. Should the Marquess of Leath ever condescend to visit that prosaic location.

"Yes, my lord," she said meekly, intending to needle him.

She succeeded. He growled and gestured toward the chair in front of the desk. "Sit down."

"It's inappropriate for me to sit in your presence, sir."

"It's inappropriate to answer back, my girl."

He had a point. She sat and concentrated on her lap to avoid those intense deep-set eyes.

Last night, his size had struck her as remarkable. Since then, she'd told herself that nervousness alone had painted him as such a powerful physical presence.

It wasn't nervousness. He was tall and broad and dauntingly muscled. Clearly he found time for plenty of exercise away from his parliamentary activities. The portrait in his mother's room was of a young man, long and lean and with a touch of innocence in his face. When she dared to glance up, there was nothing innocent about the man studying her over steepled fingers. He clearly awaited her full attention. She shivered and prayed he didn't notice her disquiet.

"Tell me about yourself."

The mad urge rose to announce that she was Dorothy

Simpson's sister and she was at Alloway Chase to ensure that he never ruined another woman.

"Well?" he asked when she didn't answer. "Cat got your tongue?"

She licked her lips in uncertainty and suffered a jolt when his eyes focused on the movement. Immediately she was back in that strange dance of hatred and fascination. She'd been mistaken to think he'd conquered last night's sensual awareness.

Oh, dear Lord, this was an unholy mess.

"I'm a little frightened," she admitted.

"Rot." He arched those formidable black eyebrows. "How did you come to work here?"

She straightened in the chair, which would have put any of the furniture in her stepfather's cottage to shame. "I'm an orphan."

"Is that so?"

Her lips tightened. When she'd told his mother that her parents were dead—well, it was true, however kind her step-father was—the marchioness had overflowed with sympathy. Lord Leath studied her as if reading the layers of deceit beneath every word.

"Yes."

"And how long have you been alone in the world?"

She couldn't restrain a faint sharpness. "You speak as if my bereavement is a matter of choice, my lord."

He bared his teeth. "My apologies."

She shifted uncomfortably under his unblinking regard, before she reminded herself that betraying her fear gave him the advantage. "My father was a sergeant major under Wellington in Portugal. He died when I was a child. My mother remarried and died when I was fifteen."

All true. So why did she feel like she lied?

"Where did you grow up?"

"Sussex." Her first lie. If she mentioned Kent, he might connect her to Dorothy, although he'd shown no recognition when she'd told him her name last night.

"You don't sound like you're from Sussex. You sound like a lady."

William Simpson had been an unusual man, educated on a scholarship at Cambridge despite his humble origins. He'd made sure that both girls in his charge spoke with educated accents. "Are there no ladies in Sussex?" she asked sweetly.

His lips quirked. "None that I've met."

That was another surprise. In her imaginings, Dorothy's seducer had possessed no sense of humor. Nell had expected evil to seep from his very pores. But unless she'd already known his wickedness, she'd see nothing to despise and much to admire. It was odd, the more she saw of Leath, the less she understood why flirty, flighty Dorothy had found him appealing. Perhaps on the hunt, he adopted a different style.

"How did a woman from the gentle south end up here?"

She'd prepared a plausible story. The marchioness had swallowed it without question. She had a nasty feeling that the marquess wasn't nearly so trusting. "I was to take employment in York, but the lady was called back to London unexpectedly and shut the house. One of the other servants told me about Alloway Chase and I decided to try my luck."

His face didn't lighten. Her stomach sank with the certainty that she hadn't gulled him. "So you crossed an inhospitable moor, came miles from the nearest civilization, on the off chance of finding employment?"

She kept her voice positive. "Indeed, sir. Fortunately there was a vacancy for a housemaid."

That had been lucky. Although if there hadn't been a place, she'd have sought work in the area and waited until a job opened up. Staff at big houses were always coming and going. She'd have found a spot eventually, especially with the excellent references she'd written in the guise of a wholly fictitious employer at a wholly fictitious Sussex manor. Of course there was a risk that someone might check her background, but hopefully by the time anybody discovered her ruse, she'd be far away with the diary in her possession.

Under that level gaze, she battled the impulse to fidget. No wonder Leath had such a reputation as a shark in parliament. If she were the opposition, she'd roll over and give him anything he wanted.

"I find it puzzling that you accepted such a junior position. Surely if you can read and write, you'd find work as a governess."

Perhaps she should have adopted a rustic accent. The problem was that she couldn't see herself keeping up the pretense. "I was desperate, sir."

She should have known that an appeal to his compassion would fail. "Is that so?"

When she didn't answer—she wasn't a skilled liar, which was why she stuck to the truth as far as possible—he went on. "And now you're my mother's companion."

"It's a preferment beyond my wildest dreams," she said quickly.

For an uncomfortable moment, she wondered if he'd try to shake the truth out of her. Surely only her guilty conscience persuaded her that he recognized her lies.

"I'd like to hear more about your wildest dreams, Miss Trim," he said slowly.

She clutched her clammy hands together to hide their unsteadiness and stared directly into those unfathomable eyes. "Do you suspect that I'm not who I claim, my lord?"

To her surprise and considerable discomfort, he smiled.

This was the first time she'd seen his smile and she wouldn't describe it as nice. It was the sort of smile a wolf gave a chicken before he tore it to pieces. Flashing masculine attraction and straight white teeth that looked ready to snap at her.

"Outlandish fancies, I'm sure, Miss Trim."

Dangerously, she forgot her meekness. "Do you put all your domestics through this inquisition?"

"Only the ones I discover raiding my library in the middle of the night," he said affably.

Curse her blushing. "I told you, I wanted something to read."

"Yet in all those volumes, nothing caught your interest."

Oh, dear God, he was a devil. Why wouldn't he leave her be? She'd been overjoyed when the marchioness had promoted her. She'd soon discovered that housemaids had no privacy and little time to search a house the size of Alloway Chase. As a companion, she had a lot of free time—the marchioness wasn't demanding—and a room of her own. Not only that, she had access to the family's apartments.

The disadvantage of her new status was that she'd hoped to pass through Alloway Chase without attracting notice. Even before last night's encounter with the marquess, her ladyship's favoritism put paid to that idea.

"Perhaps I could advise you on purchasing some novels, my lord," she said with cloying helpfulness.

If she'd thought his smile was astonishing, his laugh made her sit up like a startled rabbit. It was warm with appreciation. She liked it so much that she had to struggle shamefully hard to remember she despised him. She stopped wondering why Dorothy had found him appealing. Even she, with every reason to loathe him, couldn't stifle a prickle of attraction.

Dorothy hadn't stood a chance.

"Perhaps you should." The watchful light returned to his eyes. "Do you enjoy your post, Miss Trim?"

"Yes, sir," she said, only partly a lie. The marchioness was a darling. Her kindness had gone a long way to helping Nell cope with her grief over Dorothy's death. Nell winced to think that her vendetta against the marquess would ultimately hurt Lady Leath.

"I need hardly say that I take great care for my mother's happiness."

Given that he hadn't visited his mother in months, she could disagree. But even if she'd been his social equal, it would be impertinent to say so. "As do I, my lord."

His eyes glinted as if he saw every prevarication. "Then please don't imagine that your attentions will go unremarked."

"No, sir." She took the words as the warning they were.

"You may go, Trim."

Trim, not Miss Trim, she noticed. Clearly he'd indulged her delusions of importance as far as he intended. That suited her fine. She couldn't help feeling that if she lingered, that searching dark gaze would winkle out every secret. Then where would she be? Out on her ear. And he'd be free to continue on his nasty, seducing, ruinous way.

Strangely she was angrier now than when she'd arrived. And more intent on bringing this brute down. Even after a short acquaintance, she recognized that the marquess was a clever, perceptive, interesting man. Yet still he chose to wreck innocent lives.

Taunton, Somerset, early October

Hector Greengrass settled his considerable bulk into the oak armchair in the cozy little tavern's inglenook. It was a bloody chilly night, but in the month that he'd been in the area, he'd trained the locals to leave the room's best spot for him.

He raised his tankard, took a deep draft and smacked his lips with satisfaction. The ale was good. Even better was this lark he'd set up over the last year since leaving the late Lord Neville Fairbrother's employment. Sodding pity that the man had shot himself. Sad waste of a fine criminal mind.

Greengrass knew that most people saw him as hulking muscle, but he possessed a fine criminal mind too. And he wasn't a cove to let an opportunity pass. When he'd realized that things in Little Derrick had gone awry, he didn't hang around to share his master's fate. He'd kept his eye on the main chance and survived.

He'd more than survived; he'd thrived.

Before abandoning Lord Neville, he'd taken what cash he could find and a few trinkets. Best of all, he'd nicked his lordship's detailed record of debauchery. Since then, that diary had bought Greengrass's mighty fine life. Not to mention his fancy clothes.

Even poor women paid to keep their sins secret. Luckily for Greengrass, Lord Neville had indulged his lusts up and down the country. Greengrass had plenty of bumpkins to hit for a shilling here and there, in return for suppressing the record of their ruin.

The sluts whose fall had resulted in pregnancy were no use to him. Their disgrace was clear for the world to see. But thanks to Lord Neville's yen for silly virgins, the diary listed hordes of girls desperate to keep a good name in small, gossipy communities. They'd give up their last penny to escape public shame. After all, if their families disowned them as wanton trollops, the likeliest outcome was a hard life on the streets. Something well worth digging into the housekeeping money to avoid.

Greengrass still marveled at the diary's salacious thoroughness. His lordship couldn't bear to hold back any detail of his illicit encounters, and the pages were well-thumbed with use. A sane man would have hesitated to keep such a complete record of his sins, but clearly Lord Neville enjoyed reliving each affair over and over again.

Still, Greengrass had good reason to be grateful to Neville Fairbrother for his nitpicking record keeping, as though the chits he seduced formed part of his famous collection of pretty baubles. Lord Neville could never get enough women to slake his appetite. The only pity was that he'd limited his depredations to the lower classes. It made sense—anyone further up the social scale wouldn't believe that Lord Neville was the Marquess of Leath. They had access to newspapers and London gossip that would expose the lie before his lordship got into their drawers.

Poor and stupid, that was how his late lordship had liked them. And poor and stupid in large numbers kept Greengrass in ready cash and easy bedmates.

Aye, it had been a bonny twelve months or so. A false name and constant traveling kept him out of the magistrates' hands—there was a warrant out for him, thanks to his crimes last year in Little Derrick. And it was grand how eager a lass became when disgrace was the alternative. In a lifetime of fiddles, this blackmail fiddle was the best.

The landlord thumped a brimming plate of roast beef and gravy on the table. Fast as a striking cobra, Greengrass's massive hand shot out to crush the man's wrist. "I'll have a bit more civility, my fine fellow," he said cheerfully, closing his grip until the bones ground together.

Hatred flared in the man's eyes. But stronger than hatred

was fear. Pale with pain, the man bobbed his head. "Your pardon, Mr. Smith." He struggled to smile. "Enjoy your dinner. And of course, it's on the house."

"Better," Greengrass grunted, releasing him and picking up his knife and spoon.

Aye, being cock of the walk was fine and dandy.

And when he'd tired of catching tasty little sprats in his net, he had a bloody great mackerel of a marquess ready to take his bait.

Chapter Four

Lord Leath's return soon had Nell seething with frustration. Until now, she'd found Alloway Chase a surprisingly congenial location. Perhaps because unlike Mearsall's schoolhouse, there was no silent, reproachful ghost reminding her that she'd failed to watch over her half-sister. Her stepfather had seen her unhappiness and hadn't discouraged her when she'd suggested finding work away from home. He'd have been appalled if she'd told him why she really left Mearsall.

Under the marchioness's relaxed supervision, she'd found ample opportunity to seek the diary. So far she'd concentrated on the library. It was a huge collection, but she had time and patience. Or at least she'd had both until the marquess started working there. And after their early hours encounter, she hadn't worked up courage to wander the house at night again.

Now he'd brought a secretary from London. Even when his lordship was absent, Mr. Crane occupied either the library or the small adjoining room. A room he locked every evening.

As subtly as she could, Nell had quizzed the other servants about the marquess. Some of the maids had hair-raising stories about lecherous employers in other households, but nobody had a bad word to say about Leath. She'd failed too in all attempts to obtain evidence of his lechery from women living on the estate.

It was decidedly annoying. And a little unsettling. Nell had imagined that the people who knew him best would despise him for the monster he was.

His lordship had been home nearly a fortnight and he was yet to spend a night away from the house. For a heartless seducer, he was a diligent worker. Reams of correspondence came in and out, and he also paid conscientious attention to the estate.

Clearly his licentious impulses were under control. So far, she'd only seen him behave inappropriately with one woman. When he'd caught Nell Trim about the waist that first night. When he'd spoken to her as his equal. And more, the shameful awareness that hummed endlessly between them.

When they were together, dislike set the air sizzling. It must be dislike. She refused to admit that she found the man who had ruined her half-sister attractive.

His lordship's presence was impossible to ignore. The air buzzed with energy, the staff were on extra alert, the marchioness glowed, the gardens bloomed with extra color. Goodness, even the sun shone more brightly, now that the master returned.

If Nell had remained a housemaid, avoiding his lordship would have been simple. For his mother's companion, it was impossible. With every day, maintaining her loathing became more difficult. And each moment felt more like a betrayal of Dorothy's memory. Nell could almost believe that there were two Lord Leaths. One despoiled innocent girls and abandoned them to suffer the consequences. The other was kind to his mother and considerate of his staff and careful with his tenants.

She couldn't believe Dorothy had deceived her—her half-sister's dying words had rung with anguish and burning sincerity. But still Nell couldn't match the Leath she came to know with the man who so callously had destroyed an innocent girl.

Her desperation to find the diary built to a frenzy. Hatred alone gave her courage to carry out her scheme. She didn't want to think how Leath's sternness softened when he smiled at her ladyship. She needed instead to remember Dorothy lying quiet and unmoving after breathing her last.

Wariness—and awareness—deepened every time that enigmatic gaze settled upon Nell, as if the marquess added up all he knew about her and found the total wanting.

As Leath approached the library after his morning ride, he heard the unexpected sound of laughter. Frowning, he opened the door and paused, observing the tableau before him. A tableau that didn't please him at all.

He was used to everyone snapping to attention. He wasn't by nature a vain man, but how irritating that neither of the people sharing a jolly chat noticed him. Paul Crane, his staid-as-a-maiden-aunt secretary, poised halfway up the library stairs, passing books down to a beautiful woman who smiled at him as if she enjoyed the most wonderful time.

Of course it was Miss Trim. Miss Trim who never looked so animated nor so happy in the company of the man who paid her wages. Morning sun poured through the tall windows to light her graceful figure. She looked unassuming in one of her ubiquitous gray dresses. Her hair was scraped back in its severe style. She made a most unlikely seductress, but something in Leath stirred to savage resentment that she smiled at Crane in a way she'd never smiled at him.

"*Clarissa* will keep her ladyship busy," Crane said.

"It's rather dour," Miss Trim said. "What about something by Miss Austen?"

"At least they're shorter."

Who knew his secretary read novels? And what other housemaid discussed books with such familiarity? She was an unusual one, Miss Trim. So unusual that Leath felt like grabbing those straight shoulders and shaking her until she confessed her secrets.

"Here's *Pride and Prejudice*. That's a favorite in my family."

"Mine too."

Family? She claimed to be an orphan. Leath tensed like a hunting dog on a fox's scent.

"Her ladyship might have read it."

"His lordship needs to get something more recent for his mother," Miss Trim said, making Leath bristle at the implication of neglect. "It's odd that she doesn't get a standing order of the latest books from Hatchards. Surely Lady Sophie wanted to read something published in the last ten years."

"Lady Sophie wasn't much of a reader," Crane said. "If I can assist with making a list for the marchioness, I'd be happy to oblige. My sister is always mentioning some book or another in her letters."

"Clearly I'm not keeping you busy enough, Crane," Leath said acidly.

Silence crashed down. Crane wobbled on the ladder and dropped the leather volume onto the carpet. "My lord..."

Miss Trim turned more slowly. "Your lordship," she said coolly, curtsying and lowering her eyes.

Damn it, Leath already regretted the loss of that glorious

smile. It was possible he made her uneasy—God knew, his constant physical yen for her made *him* uneasy. But he didn't think she was frightened. Instead, he felt like she watched him, waiting for some slip. He had no idea why. But his skin prickled when she was in the room, and not just because of his inconvenient interest.

"My lord, Miss…Miss Trim wanted some reading for her ladyship. I didn't think you'd mind if I helped her." On unsteady legs, Crane descended and bent to retrieve the book. "I can only apologize most sincerely if I've overstepped the mark."

Damn it, Leath had reduced his obliging and efficient secretary to a stuttering wreck. He hated feeling like the specter at the feast. Illogically, he blamed the girl whose gaze was focused on the floor. The girl who looked as if she'd never permit an insubordinate thought to cross her mind.

He believed that like he believed in fairies building bowers in his parterre.

Despite his guilt, his voice was stern. "I'd like that report on draining the Lincolnshire property today."

"Yes, sir," Crane said miserably. He passed the book to Miss Trim. "I'm sure her ladyship will like this."

Leath's grumpiness deepened as she bestowed a glimmer of a smile upon Crane. "Thank you. I'm sorry I kept you from your work."

"Not at all," he said, and Leath's eyes narrowed on the young man's besotted expression. Crane had always struck him as a sensible fellow. Leath would hardly have employed him if he wasn't. Clearly the marquess wasn't the only man at Alloway Chase susceptible to wide brown eyes.

"Crane," Leath said curtly.

"Immediately, my lord." He glanced nervously at his employer, swallowing until his Adam's apple bobbed, then disappeared into the office.

"Not so fast." Leath caught Miss Trim's arm as she edged toward the door. The contact slammed through him, demanded that he kiss the impertinence out of her. Pride alone steadied his grip. "I'll thank you to stay away from my secretary."

Brown eyes could be warm as honey. They could also flash with disdain. After a blistering moment of communication that had nothing to do with lord and housemaid and everything to do with male and female, she glanced away. "Yes, my lord."

He stared at her, willing her to look at him properly. Even, heaven save him, smile the way she'd smiled at that stupid boy Paul Crane. "See that you follow my instructions."

"Yes, sir."

His hand tightened. Through her woolen sleeve, he felt her strength. He was used to society ladies. Miss Trim felt real and earthy in a way no woman of his own class ever did.

The silence lengthened. Became awkward. Reminded him of those charged moments the night they'd met. He still woke from dreams with her citrus scent filling his senses and his arms curling around a fantasy Eleanor Trim. In his most forbidden fantasies, he did a lot more than hold her in his arms.

He hadn't panted after the maids since he was an adolescent. Even then, he'd recognized the essential unfairness of pursuing women who worked for him. How could a woman freely give consent to the man who paid her wages?

Despite Miss Trim's outward docility, he knew that she'd have no trouble denying him. Blast her.

"May I go, sir?"

He caught a faint edge of mockery. He hated to think that she recognized his lust. He didn't trust her, he didn't much like her, but dear Lord above, she set him afire as no woman ever had.

"No."

This time when her eyes flashed up to his, he was delighted to see trepidation in the coppery depths. So far, they'd played a game where she knew the rules and he didn't. That disadvantage ended today.

He'd tried ignoring her. Much good that had done. Now he'd try a direct challenge. "Sit down. I want to talk to you."

A frown crossed her face. "Her ladyship will wonder where I am."

"I won't keep you long," he said coolly, releasing her with a reluctance he hated to acknowledge and gesturing toward a chair.

He moved behind the desk, hoping that the authoritative position might lend him some desperately needed gravitas. How ludicrous that he'd faced down the greatest men in the land without a qualm, yet this one humble girl, who worked for him, goddamn it, made him as unsure as a boy with his first sweetheart.

Not that he was naïve enough to imagine anything romantic happened here. He had a bad case of blue balls for an unsuitable woman. Given that satisfying his craving was out of the question—not least because if word got out about him tupping his mother's companion, he'd rusticate in Yorkshire forever—he needed to control himself.

Easier said than done.

Miss Trim had a subtle, enticing beauty. Every time he saw her, he thought her lovelier. Right now, with her chin set and a flush on her slanted cheekbones—perhaps embarrassment, more likely vexation—she was delicious. Like a cranky goddess.

The silence extended. And extended.

"We weren't doing any harm," she said eventually, without looking at him.

"Crane has work to do. Too much to waste time flirting with pretty girls."

Hell, he'd better watch his tongue. At the compliment, the pink in her cheeks deepened delightfully. She had lovely skin, smooth and creamy. It looked as soft as velvet and his fingers curled against the blotter as he beat back the urge to touch her.

"It was only a few minutes, and he was being kind."

Leath hid a wince at the unspoken criticism that he, in contrast, wasn't kind. She had a point. Crane hadn't deserved the reprimand. "My mother doesn't like novels."

"She does now. I suggested something more entertaining than those dry-as-dust treatises you send her."

She was definitely criticizing him, the baggage. "She's satisfied with my choices."

At last Miss Trim raised her eyes and looked at him properly. As he expected, there was no fear in her expression. Instead more watchfulness. "That's what she'd tell you, I'm sure."

"She likes to keep up with my political career."

That lush mouth quirked with a faint derision that made him feel like a gauche schoolboy. "Yes."

An ocean of implication in one short syllable. Because Miss Trim must be aware that just now he had no political career. And if he didn't keep his nose clean until they invited him back, he'd never have a political career again. Good enough reason, even if he forgot that he was a gentleman, to keep his hands off her, however beguiling she was. And now she'd stopped pretending to be a dutiful domestic with no will beyond her master's, he found her very beguiling indeed, bugger it.

She was a puzzle. He didn't like puzzles. But however closely he'd observed her over the last week, he couldn't work out her scheme. Perhaps she was what she claimed to be, a woman down on her luck.

Perhaps.

"You're a very unusual housemaid, Miss Trim," he said and was intrigued that his remark made her uncomfortable. Every instinct shrieked that she hid something.

"Because I suggested that your mother might enjoy a novel?"

"I doubt many of my housemaids could recommend a lady's reading," he said neutrally, steepling his fingers and regarding her.

She raised her chin with un-housemaid-like hauteur. She tried to play the self-effacing servant, but she wasn't much good at it. Something else that made him question her background. Girls went into service young and were trained to become obedient ciphers. There was nothing of the cipher about Miss Trim, and while she wasn't exactly disobedient, there was an edge to her that indicated she cooperated only so far as she was willing.

"Have you asked them?" she said sweetly, regarding him as unwaveringly as he watched her.

His lips twitched. "No, I haven't. But I'd still like to know where you developed this extensive knowledge."

More discomfort. For a woman who lied so often, she was dashed bad at it. "The lady who was my last employer encouraged me to better myself."

"Is that so?"

"Yes, sir."

"So she read you the latest books while you polished the silver?" He didn't bother to mask his skepticism.

To do her credit, she hardly flinched, although in her lap she gripped the Austen like a lifeline. "Yes, sir."

"I'm surprised you left this paragon." He could come

right out and accuse her of lying, but where would be the fun in that?

Her lips tightened. "Needs must, sir. Why don't you believe me?"

He leaned his chin on his joined fingers and regarded her. "Should I?"

"Yes." She sucked in an annoyed breath and he felt a strange little tug in the vicinity of his heart. The housemaid shell became thinner by the moment. He still didn't trust her, but he'd lay money that she was closer to her real self now than she'd been since their encounter on his first night home. "My lord, do you find my work unsatisfactory?"

"My mother likes you." Both of them knew that was no answer.

Her expression softened and he realized that whatever else he doubted, she was genuinely fond of his mother. "I'm most grateful to her ladyship for her kindness. There's no conspiracy in asking Mr. Crane to help me find something to ease her cares."

He frowned. "Is her health worse?"

Miss Trim's gaze became shuttered. "She doesn't complain."

So she was loyal to his mother. Perhaps the marchioness's favor wasn't completely misplaced. "She wouldn't."

The girl's eyes narrowed and he remembered what had made him mistrust her motives from the first. Whatever lip service she gave to his title, she didn't like him.

How bizarre.

He muffled a wry laugh. What an arrogant coxcomb he was. He'd never before wondered if his employees liked him. They did a job. He paid them—generously. Most of the time, he hardly thought about them.

He thought about Miss Trim far too often.

"She's looking better for your return, my lord."

Ha, another barely hidden accusation of neglect. He ought to put this presumptuous chit in her place and tell her that if anyone wanted him in London fulfilling his father's dreams, it was the marchioness.

The girl shifted restlessly, behavior unacceptable in a well-trained domestic. It was clear that Miss Trim would dearly love to finish this conversation.

Too bad.

"You will tell me if my mother's health deteriorates." More order than request.

Her shoulders went straight as a ruler. She didn't like being told what to do, yet domestics were accustomed to having every move regulated. Whatever Miss Trim had done before coming to Alloway Chase, he'd lay money that she'd been nobody's household drudge.

Which begged the question—just why was she here?

"Perhaps you should ask her yourself, sir."

"I doubt she'd tell me."

A faint smile lightened her expression. "You're probably right. But I suspect a man of your cleverness could get an answer."

"Lately I've lost all confidence in my cleverness," he said with a sigh, thinking how little he'd managed to glean from this interview. Miss Trim's ability to evade a straight answer put his parliamentary colleagues to shame.

Briefly he thought she might respond to that, but another of those damned evocative silences descended. Into the quiet, the clock outside chimed eleven. He'd kept her too long. Too long for his peace of mind. Too long for her reputation with the other servants.

Just . . . too long.

He gestured dismissal. "That will be all, Trim."

After a brief curtsy, she disappeared through the door

with a speed that betrayed her eagerness to escape. He stood and stared unseeing through the window at the flat gray disk of the lake. A premonition that he invited danger by singling out this girl weighted his belly.

He wondered about his strange affinity with Miss Trim. He wondered about the hunger she aroused. He'd never felt anything like this before. If he wanted a woman—and he made sure he only wanted women who wouldn't cause trouble—he made arrangements, scratched the itch, and moved on to more important issues.

He couldn't dismiss the delectable Miss Trim as unimportant, whatever he tried to tell himself. The thought of tumbling her thundered through him like an earthquake. His head might insist that he'd recover from his inappropriate interest. His ravenous senses told him that he had to have her soon or go mad with it.

That edgy, roundabout conversation just now had been a mistake. He was more intrigued than ever. And more convinced that she concealed secrets.

Even worse, he knew that he wouldn't leave her alone, whatever the risks. ·

Nor was his mood improved when he checked the mail piled on the desk to find two more of the sad little letters that had haunted his past year. The revelations of his uncle's crimes seemed never to end, but for Leath, the most pathetic results of Neville Fairbrother's activities were the begging notes from women raising children in poverty and disgrace. Letters addressed to Leath because Lord Neville had assumed his nephew's identity when he'd seduced these girls.

For most of his life, Leath had done his best to ignore his odious relative, so he had no idea how long the swine had played this particular game. From the timing of the letters, Leath guessed at most a few months before his uncle's suicide.

Why had Neville Fairbrother stolen his nephew's name? The answer had died last year with his uncle, but Leath could guess. Some spiteful attempt to destroy his nephew's reputation. A way of diverting blame from where it belonged. Perhaps even an attempt to impress the women with a marquess's title.

Whatever his uncle's motives, the scheme couldn't have continued indefinitely. While it was clear that the man had threatened his victims to keep their mouths shut, he must have known that his deceit would emerge. Perhaps he thought that family pride would keep Leath complicit, even after the masquerade was exposed.

The women who had written to Leath had all been so desperate that they'd braved his uncle's wrath to ask for help. His heart ached for these innocents. The scale of the devastation Neville Fairbrother had left behind beggared imagination.

Leath had employed a confidential agent to locate the women and offer aid. Otherwise he'd kept the letters private. Good God, if this got out, especially if people believed Leath rather than his repulsive uncle had fathered the children, all hope of high office would disintegrate.

His confidential agent could help him with something else. Miss Trim had arrived bearing glowing references. Perhaps it was time someone investigated her background.

Chapter Five

From the corridor, Nell watched Leath entering his mother's rooms. She hadn't seen his lordship since that nerve-racking interview yesterday when he'd expressed his distrust. His expression this morning portended trouble. She had a premonition that the trouble concerned Lady Leath's lowborn companion.

Nell slipped into her small office. She set down the ink she'd got from Mr. Crane—who was young and handsome and eager to help, and forgotten the moment she left his company—and crossed to close the door to the marchioness's sitting room.

"...Miss Trim isn't suitable." Leath's deep voice carried to where she stood.

Nell couldn't see mother or son, but she guessed that the marchioness was in her accustomed place on the chaise longue and his lordship paced the floor as he did when he was impatient.

"James, we had this argument when you arrived a fortnight ago." The marchioness's voice was softer.

"I thought I'd give her the benefit of the doubt before my final decision."

"*Your* final decision?" Lady Leath asked sharply.

"Mamma, you know I'm considering your welfare."

"I know you've taken an unreasoning dislike to Miss Trim."

"She doesn't deserve your confidence."

"I grieve to think I raised such a snob. Your father took people on their own merits."

"Well, my father was clearly a better man in every way."

Despite everything, Nell felt a twinge of sympathy. Something in his weary tone indicated that he didn't appreciate the comparison to his brilliant father.

"Nell is from a respectable family. Poverty isn't a crime."

"I don't know anything about her background, and when I ask her, she's remarkably noncommittal."

"Only because you bully her. Frightened people always look shifty."

A contemptuous snort escaped Leath. "She's not at all frightened of me, Mamma."

"And is that why you want to dismiss her? Because she doesn't cower at your merest whisper?"

Brava, your ladyship. The talent for political debate wasn't confined purely to the male Fairbrothers.

"I want to dismiss her because I don't trust her."

"She's worked as my companion for well over six weeks and the more I see of her, the more I like her."

"You're missing Sophie."

"You're here now," the marchioness said with spurious docility. "Still I like Miss Trim. And you forget how long Sophie was in London before she married Harry Thorne."

"Exactly."

"James, stop this." In her mind, Nell saw the marchioness

glare at her son. "I mightn't be able to run from Derby to York, but there's nothing wrong with my mind."

"I'm not implying that, Mamma."

"Yes, you are."

"I'm trying to do what's best. That girl puts herself forward in a most unbecoming manner."

Dear Lord in heaven, why hadn't Nell been more careful around Leath? Dismay left a foul taste in her mouth. She'd tried to disappear into the background, but something about his lordship goaded her. Nell swallowed to dislodge what felt like a rock stuck in her throat and leaned forward to hear the rest of the conversation.

"What's best is that Nell continues to keep me company in her delightful fashion."

"I insist you dismiss the girl."

"Why?"

"She's sly."

"No, she's not."

"And she doesn't show proper respect."

"Her manners are excellent. I won't have you interfering, James." The marchioness paused and when she resumed, a husky edge indicated that her son had upset her. Of course he had, the insensitive toad. "I'll pay her from my pin money if you're unwilling to cover her wages. I'm hardly at your mercy, although you're acting like I'm a charity case."

"Mamma," he protested, "I can't be easy with that girl in the house."

"Then that's your problem." The husky note persisted. "I can't be easy if you banish someone who is my friend as much as my employee."

Nell's fists closed at her sides, even as her conscience chafed at what her plans meant for the marchioness. Her lifelong loyalty to Dorothy clashed painfully with her newer loyalty to Lady Leath.

"I could arrange for one of Aunt Sylvia's girls to come."

The marchioness's delicate sniff was a feminine version of Leath's snort of derision. "Not a brain between them. Anyway, it's cruel to shut a young girl up with only a decrepit old lady for company."

"You're not decrepit."

"I'm too decrepit to put up with those silly chits and their constant chatter."

"What about Cousin Cynthia?"

Another delicate expression of disdain. "She's even stupider than Sylvia's girls. And she'd read me sermons. She's becoming odiously preachy in her old age. One would think she'd never kissed an undergardener in the maze at Hampton Court."

"Did she, by God?"

Nell could tell that this glimpse of his staid relative in her salad days had momentarily distracted Leath. Pray God he stayed distracted.

"She was quite the hoyden before she became so holy. Although she wouldn't thank me for remembering."

"Speaking of people reading things to you, when did you develop a taste for novels? You've never picked up anything frivolous in your life."

The marchioness laughed. "You can thank Nell for that."

"I'm sure," Leath said, and his displeasure oozed down Nell's backbone like ice.

"Don't be so stuffy, James. After Sophie married, life became dull until Nell brightened my days. I can't imagine why you've got yourself in a twist about the girl." She paused. "One might think you're jealous that I'm so fond of her."

"A masterstroke, madam. But sadly one that's gone astray. You won't get me to retreat in a fit of pique. I don't like that girl and I want her gone."

"Well, I do like her and I want her to stay. Will you insist?"

"I'd like to."

"But you won't."

Nell couldn't be nearly as sure as the marchioness. She braced to hear Leath pronounce the fatal words, but he laughed with a mixture of chagrin and fondness. "You've won. Temporarily. But I'm watching your dear Miss Trim."

"You won't see anything to her detriment."

Nell took a moment to appreciate the marchioness's trust. Trust she didn't deserve. Her whisper of guilt swelled to a clamor. She might be grateful that her ladyship won this battle, but Leath was right to be wary.

"You're an obstinate wench."

"Of course I am, darling. Where do you think your stubbornness comes from?"

He laughed with genuine humor, and began to speak about someone they both knew in London. Very quietly, Nell shut the door.

For the moment, she was safe. But only for the moment. Leath wouldn't let the matter go. And he'd do his best to discredit her with the marchioness. From now on, she must move carefully. She also needed to resume her search for the diary, no matter the danger.

The marchioness made no mention of her son's attempt to dismiss Nell, but her manner became if anything, more affectionate. Nell tried to steer clear of Leath, but it was inevitable that they should pass in the corridor or encounter each other when she slipped into the library to select a book for the marchioness.

The lady's taste for novels grew apace. When Nell had started as a companion, her duties had involved conversation, playing cards, and writing letters. Occasionally she assisted with treatments during the marchioness's bouts of ill health. Now they'd rushed through *Pride and Prejudice* and had just finished *Sense and Sensibility*. Apart from the dreary *Clarissa*, Nell had no idea what to choose next. The Alloway Chase library was crammed with dispiritingly worthy volumes.

Nell enjoyed reading aloud and the activity was undemanding, welcome when she managed so little sleep. The last three nights, she'd devoted fruitless hours to searching the library. Fear goaded her to haste. If the marquess caught her, he'd dismiss her for sure, whatever his mother said.

"Shall we continue with *Don Juan* this morning, your ladyship?" Nell had started Byron's poem yesterday and the marchioness was enjoying the change.

"Yes, please, my dear. Such a wicked fellow."

"Byron or Don Juan?"

The marchioness laughed, although a flat note in her amusement worried Nell. Blast Leath for harrying his mother.

"Both. Help me to sit up, if you please. I'm feeling a little tired."

Her request didn't surprise Nell. The fair, delicate features, so different from her son's saturnine intensity, were drawn. She settled the marchioness more comfortably and opened the morocco-bound volume where she'd left off, with the youthful philanderer seducing the virtuous but hot-blooded Lady Julia.

Settling the parcel he carried more securely, Leath paused on the threshold to observe the two women in the sunny room. Capricious autumn offered up a few perfect days before winter descended.

With a tenderness that he couldn't mistake, Miss Trim was arranging his mother's pillows. It was possible, even probable, that the girl was a self-serving schemer, but at this moment when she thought herself unobserved, he couldn't mistake her affection for his mother.

When he'd tried to have the chit dismissed, he should have expected to fail. He was honest enough to admit that his reasons for wanting to banish Miss Trim extended beyond her influence over his mother. He wanted her out of his house because he wanted her out of his mind. She was far too distracting. Hell, she was far too tempting.

Her veiled hostility didn't douse his sexual interest. It fired him up. There was something exciting about a woman who didn't fawn over him and imagine herself either his marchioness or his mistress.

With a turn of her graceful body that made his heart leap, the girl reached for a book. She sat in profile, so he saw the delicate nose and resolute chin so incongruous on a housemaid. His hands itched to tear away the pins torturing her bright hair. He mightn't trust her, but by God, she was a pleasure to behold.

Whereas his mother didn't look well. He frowned, hardly hearing Miss Trim begin to read. Then, like his mother, he found himself caught up in the racy tale.

> But who, alas! can love, and then be wise?
> Not that remorse did not oppose temptation;
> A little still she strove, and much repented
> And whispering, "I will ne'er consent"—consented.

On the line's sting in the tail, Miss Trim noticed Leath in the doorway. While the duchess snickered, the girl's cinnamon eyes widened. Fleetingly he saw no trace of dislike.

He wished to Hades he did. Instead he was astonished to discover that his reluctant attraction wasn't one-sided.

Like wanton Lady Julia in the poem, Miss Trim's expression spoke of resistance—but also desire. If they were alone, he'd sweep her into his arms and kiss her until she yielded to what they both wanted.

This was a bloody disaster.

"Go on, Nell. This is so delicious."

"My lady, Lord Leath is here."

When his mother glanced toward him, her weary face briefly brightened. "Darling, come and listen. Nell's reading me a naughty poem."

"You're too young for Byron." Leath deposited his brown paper parcel on a gilt and marble table, then kissed his mother's cheek.

"Nell is," his mother said with another smile. "It's most shocking what that libertine got up to. I remember all the gossip, of course. This adventure must be based on real life."

"Byron was a rake, mother."

"And you didn't like him, I know."

"I didn't." He remembered the brilliant, troubled, troublesome man he'd met briefly as a youth. "He was an entertaining fellow, and clever with it, but he left a good many ladies the worse for knowing him. I can't admire someone so addicted to selfish pleasure that he was cavalier about the harm he did."

The blaze of heat in Miss Trim's eyes had cooled to curiosity. He couldn't imagine why she cared about his opinion of the notorious poet. Leath certainly wasn't the only person in England to frown upon his activities.

Hell, he needed to stop staring moonstruck at his mother's companion. He turned back to the table and lifted the parcel. "I've brought you a present."

His mother tried to sit up and Miss Trim rushed to assist

with a gentleness that Leath couldn't help noting. "Oh, how wonderful. I love presents."

He held the box out. "Careful. It's heavy."

"Not diamonds then?" she asked playfully.

"Not today."

Miss Trim fetched scissors to cut the string. "I'll finish those letters, my lady."

"No, stay, Nell. This looks intriguing."

His mother tore at the paper, as excited as a child at a birthday party, then reached inside the box. "James, and you pretended to disapprove."

"How could I disapprove of anything that gives you such enjoyment?"

She drew out a beautifully tooled volume in dark green leather. "*The Fair Maid of Perth*. How wonderful."

"I asked Hatchards to send their most popular books. There's now a standing order each month. If you find that doesn't meet your needs, they'll increase it."

"How can I thank you?" His mother's eyes sparkled as she looked at him.

He often sent her gewgaws, jewelry or scarves or trinkets for her rooms. But he couldn't remember her getting such pleasure from a gift. And it had been so simple to arrange. He felt like a fool that he hadn't thought of it earlier, and unreasonably nettled that he'd needed Miss Trim to point out how a good book or two might brighten his mother's restricted existence.

"What fun we shall have, Nell."

"Indeed, my lady," the girl said neutrally. Leath cast her another glance and was surprised to see that she studied him without her usual reserve. Instead, she regarded him as if he was a puzzle she couldn't put together. He wondered why. The mystery here was Nell Trim, not the Marquess of Leath.

"Can you stay, James?"

"Of course," he said, although now he paid closer attention to his estates, he was surprised how much work it took to run them. Even more surprising was how he enjoyed meeting the challenge of his vast inheritance.

"Lovely. Perhaps Nell will read on. She's most entertaining."

He stifled a groan. The last thing he needed was that low, husky, damnably suggestive voice describing seduction.

"I'm sure his lordship doesn't want to listen to me," Miss Trim said.

She'd avoided him recently. Was she still smarting after their talk in the library? Or had his mother told her that he'd tried to send her away?

"You should read James some of those agricultural reports that arrived yesterday," his mother said drily.

"How did you know about those?" he asked, although he shouldn't be surprised. His mother remained mistress of the house, despite rarely leaving her rooms.

"I have my spies," she said. "They tell me that the ghosts are back."

"What nonsense."

"It's not nonsense. As a new bride, I saw Lady Mary on the battlements."

"On a foggy night, Mamma."

"I'm not the only one."

"At least you were sober."

His mother's jaw firmed. They'd had this argument before. She fancied that the castle, parts of which dated to the fourteenth century, was haunted. "Lady Mary's visiting us again."

"On the battlements?"

"No, in the library. For the last three nights, lights have been seen after midnight."

He thought he heard a strangled gasp from Miss Trim,

but when he glanced at her, she'd lowered her eyes in her perfect servant pose.

"Who the devil's skulking in the gardens at that hour?" he asked.

"Garson was watching for poachers."

"And drinking to pass the time," Leath said with grim amusement. "I'll have a word with him. If my gamekeeper has taken to the bottle, he's not safe wandering the property with a gun."

"You mock, James, but you know it's true that Lady Mary's husband strangled her."

"I know that's true. I don't know it's true that she lingers to keep an eye on her descendants. And if she does, I doubt that she's developed a taste for literature. Especially as I have it on good authority that my library is full of boring books."

He didn't look at Miss Trim. But his brain worked, even as he argued with his mother's conclusions. Despite his joke, Garson wasn't a drunkard. If he said he saw lights in the library, odds were that he had.

A determination to catch Miss Trim in the act gripped him. If he could prove to his mother that the girl meant no good, he could send her away.

And conquer this inconvenient itch to bed her.

Chapter Six

Nell had read every thought that crossed the marquess's mind when his mother told him about Lady Mary's ghost. He'd known immediately who was flitting around his library. Fear had twisted her stomach into knots as she waited for him to denounce her. Then she'd realized that he'd take this as a golden opportunity to catch her prowling about.

Her suspicions were confirmed that evening when she saw Mr. Wells, the daunting butler, delivering a tray to the library. Obviously refreshments for his lordship's watch.

For once, she was a step ahead of Lord Leath.

The diary wasn't in the library. The next likely place—in fact always the most likely place—was his lordship's bedroom. After all, the scandalous document would hardly be shelved alongside *Fordyce's Sermons* where anyone could lay their hand upon it. The problem was entering the marquess's rooms unobserved. His vigil in the library provided the ideal chance.

Now as she crept along darkened hallways, only a candle to light her way, the house seemed twice the size it did by day. And by day, the sprawling pile stretched for miles. Thick carpeting under her feet muffled her passing, but she remained preternaturally alert.

His lordship's valet lived above his rooms, but last week Selsby had been called away to his sick mother. Everything conspired to allow her to search Leath's apartments.

She prayed that she'd find the diary quickly. She desperately needed to escape Alloway Chase. The longer she stayed, the flimsier became her resolution. Every moment she spent with the marquess left her more befuddled. Witness today when he'd surprised his mother with those books. Hardly the act of a thoughtless cad. And was he hypocrite enough to denounce Lord Byron for sins he himself had committed? She wouldn't have thought so.

If she'd been ignorant of the marquess's offenses, she'd like him. Oh, who was she fooling? She'd more than like him. Even knowing his wickedness, she found him breathtakingly attractive.

However dirty that made her feel.

How could she yearn after the man who had destroyed Dorothy? Was she victim to the same fatal weakness as her half-sister?

Carefully she inched open the door to the marquess's apartments. Although he was safely ensconced in his library, her heart skittered with fear that somehow he was in two places at once.

She stepped into dark, cavernous space. She closed the door and raised her candle to reveal a sitting room, as masculine in décor as the marchioness's was feminine. Flickering light glanced across a leather couch and two armchairs beside a cold hearth. Piles of books teetered on heavy mahogany tables. She'd lay money there wasn't a novel among them. Light glinted off decanters on the sideboard.

James Fairbrother's presence was palpable, as though he stood right behind her. The muscles across her neck and shoulders knotted until she told herself to settle down. He was downstairs. She was safe, at least for now.

She pushed open the door from the sitting room and entered a short corridor. Shelves lined the first room off the hallway. She inhaled to calm leapfrogging nerves, then wished she hadn't. When had the marquess's scent become so familiar? Her senses expanded with pleasure as she recognized sandalwood soap and clean, healthy male. Riffling through the clothes he wore on that strong, hard body seemed unforgivably intimate, and she fumbled the door shut with a loud click that made her heart jolt with alarm.

Desperately listening in case someone came to check on the noise, she stood motionless.

Nothing.

She sucked air into starved lungs. Nell didn't take easily to deceit. Sneaking around and eavesdropping and telling lies went against her character. Another reason to leave Alloway Chase sooner rather than later. Much more chicanery and she'd be a wreck.

The next door revealed a bathing room of a luxury beyond anything she'd imagined when her world was confined to Mearsall. At last she found proof of sensual self-indulgence. The marquess presented a restrained façade to the world. Something at Nell's deepest level insisted that beneath that proper exterior lurked a man who appreciated pleasure.

The thought of James Fairbrother standing naked in this blue-tiled magnificence heated her blood. She couldn't help seeing him as he doused himself with water, stroked soap along his wet skin, lounged in the huge bath.

This time, although she closed the door carefully, panic

nipped more sharply. Her invasion of the marquess's rooms inflamed her senses in a way that appalled her.

One door remained.

Only her piercing need to run away made her proceed. If she failed at this hurdle, she was likely to fail altogether.

As she opened this last door, her hands shook so violently that her candle cast wild shadows over the walls. She felt like Bluebeard's bride breaking into the locked room. A discomfiting thought, as the nosy girl came to a nasty end in that tale. At least she did in the pragmatic version told around Mearsall's firesides.

The bedroom was so enormous that the candle's light didn't penetrate its far reaches. A fire burned in the grate, but the flames left most of the room in shadow. The room was circular with tall windows facing three directions. She must be in the castle's west tower. Quietly she closed the door behind her.

The huge four-poster bed sat on a dais, curtained in gold brocade. The ceiling was so high it dwarfed even this lofty structure. The covers were turned down, ready for the marquess's powerful body. Nell shivered with a dread that, she was ashamed to admit, included a dollop of forbidden excitement.

If she'd felt like she infringed the marquess's privacy elsewhere in these apartments, here where he slept, he could be standing at her elbow. A book lay open on the nightstand as if he'd just laid it down. A shirt draped across a chair. A black velvet dressing gown as soft as panther fur spread across the base of the bed, waiting for its owner to shrug it over his long body. She could picture him wearing it as he enjoyed a last brandy before sleep.

The image of Leath as his real, animal self, not the civilized man he presented to the world, was painfully vivid.

Here it was easy to envision him with a lover. Not a girl he tumbled to scratch an itch, but someone he wanted. Perhaps even…loved. Nell released a soft gasp of distress when she realized that the fantasy woman in Leath's arms bore her face.

Enough. She swallowed to control her queasiness. She didn't have long. And she couldn't waste it on nonsense.

Recalling Lady Mary's "ghost," she crossed to the windows to check that the curtains were closed. Then she set her candle on a small table and surveyed the room.

This vast, idiosyncratic chamber was full of interesting nooks and coffers. Fertile ground for her search. She leveled her shoulders and stepped toward a large studded chest near the hearth with the year 1676 picked out in heavy iron nails.

Then the unthinkable happened.

The door opened and his lordship strode in.

Nell caught her breath and held it as if somehow that made her invisible. Her queasiness changed to cramping horror.

Shock flared in his face then his gaze narrowed on her. He couldn't be nearly as appalled to see her as she was to see him.

"What the hell are you doing in here?" Thick black brows lowered over deep-set eyes. He was dressed informally. A loose white shirt and breeches with boots. He looked utterly terrifying.

Nell held her breath so long that it hurt when she exhaled. She felt dizzy with lack of air, stabbing dread, self-disgust.

Curse him, what could she say? What could she do? She faltered back, although there was no escape. Leath's formidable form blocked the only door. She should have thought of some excuse for being in his room. But what excuse could there be?

She dipped into a wobbly curtsy. "My lord."

His furious gaze didn't waver. "Just what are you up to, Miss Trim?"

"N-nothing, sir," she stammered. "I'm sorry for intruding. I'll leave you alone."

He didn't budge as she scuttled toward the door. Her knees trembled so badly that she feared she might collapse in a heap before she reached it. She darted past him, and for a brief, mad moment thought that she might make it.

Until he turned and slammed the heavy door in her face. "Not so fast, my inquisitive chit."

The impulse to haul at the handle died as it arose. She'd never win a physical battle against Leath. She panted, more with fright than exertion, and twisted to press her back against the door. "Let me out."

"Not yet," he said mildly, placing his palms flat on either side of her head. His calmness was more frightening than shouting. It hinted at the tight rein he held over his temper. He was so huge, this was like facing down a planet. An angry planet. Dear heaven, she was in such trouble.

"You're scaring me," she said, hoping to appeal to his softer side. He had one; he showed it to his mother. The problem was that if Dorothy's story was true—and surely it was—his benevolence didn't extend to women outside his class.

"You deserve to be scared," he said grimly.

Without touching her, his body hemmed her against the door. The evocative scent of his skin was rich in her nostrils. Something other than fear started to beat in her blood.

Hating herself, she met his uncompromising expression. "That's . . . that's not kind."

His eyes glittered. She knew he was no respecter of innocence. Even if he was, what was he to make of her invading his bedroom? Panic tasted rusty on her tongue and she licked dry lips.

His gaze dropped to the betraying movement. The same awareness that had extended between them their first night sizzled through the pause. "I'm not feeling kind."

She shivered. "Please..." she whispered. "Step back."

He loomed above her, impervious and unforgiving. "Not until you tell me what you're doing here."

"I..." Desperately she sought for some way to explain her presence. Nothing came to mind.

Black brows arched in cynical enquiry. "I what?"

"I can't think when you stand so close," she muttered crossly.

Despite the nasty edge to his soft laugh, the sound stroked along her skin. Every hair on her body stood to attention. This heady mixture of desire and alarm sent her into a complete spin.

"I don't want you to think. I want you to tell me the truth." He frowned. "Have you come to steal?"

She should be grateful for the accusation. It jolted her out of cowering like a mouse. She straightened and glared at him. "Of course not."

"Then what are you doing?"

She avoided his eyes. "I thought you were in the library."

"Catching Lady Mary." His acerbic response made her wince. His concentration on her burned like flame.

"I saw Wells bring you supper."

"What a busy little miss you are." It wasn't a compliment. "I already know you're the ghost."

Her eyes flashed up. "I wanted a book," she said desperately.

"One you can't find during the day?" His voice bit as he continued. "With dear Mr. Crane's advice on your choice."

If he was another man, she'd think he was jealous. But the great Marquess of Leath wouldn't care about a maid-servant's flirtations.

He went on before she could protest. "Surely you won't say that you're here for something to read."

She raised her chin. Knowing that she risked disaster, she said the only thing that came to mind. "I wanted to see where you sleep."

Surprise had him lurching back. "What the devil?"

She took advantage of the few extra inches of space to draw a breath, tangy with sandalwood. Turning red as a tomato would lend credence to her explanation. "Please don't make me admit this."

He watched her like a snake watched a rat. "Admit what?"

"Must I say? You put me to the blush." That at least was true.

"Yes, you must."

She pressed her damp palms to her skirts. How she'd love to punch him, but she had a horrible inkling that his jaw would be much harder than her fist. Dear heaven, help her to sound convincing. But not too convincing.

"Hasn't a servant ever been besotted with you, my lord?" To her surprise, her question emerged steadily.

"Not to my..." He spoke very deliberately. "Are you saying you have a penchant for me, Miss Trim?"

He didn't sound pleased. She should be relieved that he wasn't ripping her clothes off. After all, her confession could be taken as an invitation. Yet again it struck her that he was a remarkably restrained libertine.

She struggled to appear bashful instead of scared out of her wits. "It's embarrassing."

"I'm sure." He sounded skeptical, as well he might. "You've never seemed dazzled."

She turned her face away, staring at his hand spread against the door's rich mahogany. Like the rest of him, his hand was big and powerful and beautifully formed. Despite everything, she couldn't resist imagining that hand on her skin. His gold signet ring, visible symbol of his rank, gleamed evilly from his little finger. "I have my pride."

"Of course," he said drily.

She struggled to look humble and shy and innocent. All were true. Well, apart from the humble part. Her stepfather had frequently warned her that a mere sergeant major's daughter had no right to be so stiff-necked. "I'm aware of the gulf between us."

"And it breaks your heart."

If only she could squeeze out a convincing tear. "I can't help my feelings."

He didn't move closer. It just felt that way. "Do you really expect me to credit this balderdash?"

Her temper stirred. "You underestimate your effect on an impressionable girl."

He snorted disbelief. "More balderdash."

Damn him. A turbulent mix of desperation, anger, and reckless bravado gripped her. Frantic hands grabbed the front of his shirt. "I'll show you balderdash, my lord."

She stretched up until her lips crashed into his.

Chapter Seven

Leath stiffened—everywhere—under Miss Trim's unexpected assault. He had to give her credit. She'd dare the devil. He hadn't expected her to take this absurdity about her tendre for him to this length.

But then, he'd cornered her, hadn't he?

Her lips were soft and endearingly clumsy. She kissed like a young girl. This might be another ruse to disarm him, but he didn't think so. Even more unbelievable than her supposed infatuation, the glorious Miss Trim wasn't much good at kissing.

Which turned out to be a damned lucky thing. As it was, he was hard as an iron bar. If she demonstrated an ounce of skill, his sanity would dissolve completely.

Because he was still marginally sane, he caught her shoulders. For a moment, he reveled in her slender strength. Then with more difficulty than he wanted to admit, he pushed her away.

She panted as her lips slid free. Throughout the brief, urgent kiss, she'd kept her mouth closed.

"What—" She looked dazed, as if he'd painted her world with rainbows. Imagine if he'd kissed her back, taught her what to do.

Except that he refused to kiss women he didn't trust. And he most definitely didn't trust this one. Although the shine in her eyes, firelit amber, might almost convince him that she really was smitten.

She licked her lips again, slowly, as if tasting him. He bit back a groan and drew her closer, when good sense dictated that he throw her out on her delectable rump. Solving the puzzle of her presence was impossible when the wicked urge to have his way with her jammed his brain. He wasn't used to his head and his instincts being at odds. His head should be winning.

It wasn't.

"I give you points for trying," he said, the hint of savagery directed mostly at himself. Her flinch stabbed him with guilt, although heaven knew she'd asked for trouble.

"I'm sorry." Her slender throat moved as she swallowed. "If you tell your mother I kissed you, she'll let you dismiss me."

He was surprised that his mother had mentioned his attempts to send Miss Trim away. "If she knows you came to my room, that's enough," he snapped and felt guilty again when she flushed with humiliation.

"So you'll win."

More easily than he'd expected. He wondered why he wasn't happier. He should be dancing a jig, now that this conniving baggage had overreached herself. But his lips tingled from the pressure of hers. His head flooded with the lemon perfume of her soap, more familiar than it should be. Just the sound of her voice made him yearn.

He didn't believe that she wanted him. But by God, he

wanted her. Except she hadn't claimed to want him, had she? She'd claimed a silly schoolgirl infatuation.

It would serve her right if he showed her what risks she took. Tossed her onto his bed and flung himself on top of her.

Except...

Except in her face, he saw secrets and mysteries. But he also saw innocence. Whatever else she was, she wasn't experienced with men. That one awkward, incendiary kiss betrayed Miss Trim as a novice.

She played dangerous games.

He should send her away with orders to pack.

His hands tightened on her shoulders, holding her in place.

"Why don't you tell me to go?" she asked wonderingly. For once, she sounded like a bewildered young girl, not the woman whose actions tormented him with questions and whose presence banished his sleep.

"You want to kiss me?"

"No," she said quickly, then less certainly, "Yes."

She struggled to keep up the pretense of girlish adoration. Except that after she'd kissed him, he'd caught arousal stirring in her eyes.

"Which is it?"

She bit her lip and before he could stop himself, he bent to kiss her, to stop her torturing that luscious mouth. Her shocked gasp was a whisper of warm breath on his face.

His hands slid around her back, holding her as a lover holds a woman he intends to kiss. Thoroughly.

Knowing he'd pay, knowing this was absolutely the last thing he should do, he brushed his lips across Miss Trim's.

Nell still shook with reaction from her first kiss. The experience had left her confused and strangely frustrated.

She wasn't sure she'd enjoyed it, although it had been... interesting.

She hadn't expected the heat and intimacy and sheer physicality of placing her lips on a man's. His mouth had been firm and he hadn't responded. Not that she was sure what she wanted him to do.

For a long moment, Leath watched her with an unreadable expression. His hands dug into her shoulders and she feared that he was about to shove her out the door. She was bizarrely reluctant to go. She braced for a summary ejection from his room, then tomorrow a summary ejection from Alloway Chase.

His hold softened in a way she couldn't describe. She stared up at him, transfixed, afraid. No wonder poor silly Dorothy had fallen under his spell. He was the most compelling man she'd ever known.

Her skin tightened with anticipation. Slowly his lips skimmed across hers in a caress as different from her all-out assault as satin from iron.

The kiss lasted no more than a second, yet flooded her with such longing that her knees buckled. She leaned back against the door.

He still looked uncompromising. His features were all hard planes: strong bones, jutting nose, adamantine jaw.

Yet his lips... His lips had been softer than a feather.

She snatched a jagged breath and struggled to speak, but before she could, he gave her another of those sweet kisses. Did he linger a little this time? Taste her as delicately as he'd sample a fine claret?

Her breath caught as he raised his head and regarded her with familiar concentration. To steady herself, she hooked her hands around his neck. "That was..."

Lovely? Wrong? Frightening? Beguiling?

Heaven help her. Heaven condemn her. She'd started this. Now she'd opened the gates to destruction on a level she'd never contemplated.

One thumb trailed down the line of her jaw, leaving a tingling wake. His lips quirked in a faint smile that set her heart cartwheeling. The huskiness in his voice stroked across her nerves like silk. The clean, male scent of his skin surrounded her, too familiar in a man who should be a stranger. "You're not usually lost for words, Miss Trim."

She'd never been kissed before. She'd always imagined that whoever the lucky fellow was, he'd use her Christian name. Still, something about the way his lordship said "Miss Trim" made her shiver with excitement. And God forgive her, lately when she'd imagined kisses, the man kissing her had been Lord Leath.

Nell felt as if she toppled over a cliff. She should flee, forsake her quest for vengeance, forget that however unacceptable the attraction, she found this man so appealing. She should scuttle back to Mearsall and her dear, kind stepfather, and her dull existence, and be grateful that dullness promised safety.

"You shouldn't have done that," she said shakily.

"You kissed me first."

"Two wrongs don't make a right."

She wasn't surprised when he laughed. Even she thought that she sounded absurd.

"You seem new to the activity. I merely offered an alternative technique."

She thought she'd blushed before, but this critique set her cheeks on fire. "I don't go around kissing random men, my lord. I refuse to apologize for my inexperience."

"I'm glad." He caught her loosely by the waist. She was overwhelmingly conscious of those large hands holding her.

"For my inexperience?"

"That you made an exception to your rule."

"I suppose you're used to women throwing themselves at you," she mumbled, knowing she made a fool of herself. A man like Leath probably couldn't step outside without tripping over eager young ladies wanting to kiss him. Wanting more.

The idea of him doing more to her sent Nell's heart hurtling into her ribs.

He smiled. How she wished that he'd stop. That gentle curve of his beautifully cut lips set her pulse rocketing. "If only life was so exciting for a politically minded marquess."

She wasn't deceived. Even disregarding Dorothy's story, she couldn't see women ignoring his manifold attractions. He'd been angry when he'd discovered her in his room. She sensed no anger now. Just perpetual waiting.

She backed away and bumped hard into the door. "I must go."

His hands tightened. "You freely entered the lion's den, Miss Trim."

"Stop calling me Miss Trim," she said crossly, bracing her hands against his powerful chest. She told herself to push him away, but her disobedient fingers curved into hard muscle. He was so wonderfully warm. Beneath her right palm, his heart beat like a conqueror's drum.

The kiss had been intimate. Feeling the life pounding through him felt more so. What a mistake she'd made coming here. Even if she left immediately, she and the marquess would never be strangers again.

"Would you rather I called you Eleanor?" he asked silkily.

Her eyes widened. "Only my father called me Eleanor. Everyone calls me Nell."

"I rather like the idea of kissing Eleanor."

"I rather like the idea of going back to my room." She squeaked in horror. That sounded like a proposition. "Alone."

"So no curiosity?"

She saw by his expression that the shake of her head lacked conviction. "I'm sorry I invaded your apartments."

"I'm not."

Shocked, she stared at him. "You're not?"

"I have a lovely woman in my arms and no particular plans for the rest of the evening."

Her stomach lurched in dismay. Dear Lord, at last she saw the seducer. And as he'd so rightly said, she'd put herself squarely in his sights. She shoved his chest. It was like trying to move a monolith. "No."

"No?"

"*Droit de seigneur* went out of fashion with the farthingale."

"So you don't want to share my bed?"

"No." Although her blood beat hard and hot at the thought of having that big beautiful body as her plaything for the night.

"Yet here you are." The edge in his tone made her shiver.

"I...told you why."

"Yes, you're suffering a bad case of unrequited love."

She pushed at his chest again. "Not love. Just infatuation."

"Prove it."

Her wriggling stopped and she regarded him aghast. "I'm not a doxy." Bitterness seeped into her voice. "I don't even know how to kiss, as you so ungallantly pointed out."

His laugh this time held the characteristic grim note. Briefly when he'd kissed her, he'd looked like a gentler, younger, kinder man. Now the purpose in his expression made her quake with nerves. And unwilling excitement. She'd never stood so long in a man's embrace. Next to Leath, she felt small and feminine. Powerless too, which should terrify her. After all, he threatened ruin, and there was nobody to save her.

"You'll keep your chastity, although God knows you tempt fate."

"I thought you were in the library," she said stubbornly.

"No excuse."

"So let me go."

His smile wasn't reassuring. "Not until you've learned how to kiss a man."

She braced against him. "I think I'm better off not knowing."

"I'm appalled that a woman so lovely is untouched."

She narrowed her eyes. "Compliments won't make me stay."

"Perhaps not. But this might."

He captured her lips in a quick, commanding kiss. Odd how much he could convey without words.

"You...you flatter yourself, my lord."

"Do I? You're still here."

She gulped in air. She kept forgetting to breathe. Then when she did, Leath's musky essence intoxicated her, making coherent thought impossible.

Another inhalation. Only to realize that he no longer held her. His beautiful hands hung loose and open at his sides, although his rough breathing indicated disquiet.

She raised her hands from his chest, loathing how his warmth lingered on her palms, and reached behind her for the doorknob. "You'll stop me if I try to leave."

Nell had a horrible feeling that she sounded like she wanted him to keep her here.

"Try it and see."

Despite all the evil she knew of him, she had the strongest feeling that she could trust him with her life. Was she right? Or was she another stupid girl caught in a rake's net?

"Just a kiss?" she whispered, hardly believing that she wasn't already halfway back to her room. She wondered if he had any idea what potent effect his raw masculinity had on her frail willpower. "Can I trust you?"

The edge returned to his voice, although he didn't move. "You're the one who broke into my bedroom."

Completely unjustified guilt surged. He was a bad man and she'd been doing the work of the righteous. But she couldn't deny that she'd felt shabby breaching his inner sanctum. "One kiss and then I'll go."

"As you wish."

"You agree?" she asked in shock.

"It's time to move from negotiation to action, my dear Eleanor." To prove he meant it, he drew her into his arms.

Chapter Eight

M iss Trim's—Eleanor's—lips trembled against Leath's. Touching her was so sweet that he almost forgot that he didn't trust her. Not for a moment did he believe that she was smitten. On the other hand, he did, against all sense, believe that she'd never kissed a man before.

Where the devil had she been living? In a cave under a mountain? He always chose sophisticated, experienced lovers. But there was something breathtaking about setting his lips to Eleanor's and knowing he was the first.

This girl possessed no worldly skills to augment his pleasure. Which didn't mean there was no pleasure. There was far too much, damn it.

The proximity of his bed, the late hour, her tantalizing combination of shyness and eagerness. All conspired to erode his anger and suspicion, and remind him that she was beautiful and night after night he'd dreamed of touching her.

Gentleness won out as he tasted lips locked against him. A pang of inconvenient tenderness struck him as he recalled her kissing him as if battering him into submission. Now her resistance seeped away until she fit against him as though created to please him. He kissed the corners of her mouth, then nipped softly at her full bottom lip.

A muffled protest parted her lips.

It was enough.

The tip of his tongue invaded her mouth. Just that small incursion blasted him with enough heat to incinerate good intentions.

She jerked back, cinnamon eyes dark, troubled, heavy with desire. "That was . . . strange."

He smiled and cradled her head between his hands. "You'll come to like it."

"Are you sure?"

"I am." He beat back another wave of tenderness. When she stood willingly in his arms, trembling with the onslaught of new feelings and experiences, she undermined his every defense. Again he pressed his mouth to hers. His tongue traced the seam of her lips. "Open for me, Eleanor."

Her eyes were glazed. "I—"

Leath swooped, sliding his tongue into the hot depths and tasting her fully. He closed his eyes, the better to savor every nuance. She was sweeter than cherries or peaches or apricots. Like honey, but with a tart edge.

She made a sound in her throat. Denial or encouragement? Then her tongue fluttered against his, and this time, her sigh betrayed enjoyment. Her hands kneaded his loose shirt like a kitten sharpening its claws.

How long did he stand beside the fire kissing Miss Trim? He didn't know. Eventually, inevitably, kissing wasn't enough. His lips drifted across her face and down her neck. When he concentrated on a nerve at the junction of neck and shoulder, she cried out. Her fresh scent became richer, earthier.

He aroused her. God knew, she aroused him. His hand

shook when he raised it to the line of buttons descending from her demure collar. He fumbled at the fastenings—he, who hadn't fumbled with a woman's clothing since he'd left Cambridge.

Her face flushed with pleasure. Her eyes were closed and her glistening mouth parted as she awaited more kisses. She leaned into him as though her legs couldn't support her. He wasn't feeling too stable himself. His blood pounded hot and heavy, the need to touch her skin an insistent hum in his ears. Her breath emerged in ragged sighs and her strong, graceful hands curved around his shoulders.

The gray dress gaped. He felt like a traveler venturing into an unexplored land. How he'd fantasized about stripping away her nunlike clothing.

He bent to kiss her collarbone, lingered on the pulse fluttering at the base of her throat. Sliding one hand under her shift, he cupped her breast. The weight of her flesh in his palm crashed through him like a hurricane.

She gasped and stiffened. "This is wrong."

"Yes," he agreed. He might be a fool; he'd never been a liar.

"You promised...kissing only," she said unsteadily, although without withdrawing.

"Then let me kiss you again."

Her lips quivered with uncertainty until with a sigh, she succumbed to the heat. Her beaded nipple scraped his palm. When he flicked it with his thumb, she started and gasped into his mouth. She pressed forward, silently begging for more.

Her reaction excited him. Urgently he pushed her undergarments down to bare one breast to the firelight. Seeing that satiny white flesh crowned with deep pink made him shake with need. The sight was somehow more arousing because plain white linen covered her other breast. He felt as though he unwrapped the most wonderful present in history.

Unable to stop himself, he bent to take that pearled nipple into his mouth. She gave a soft cry and squeezed closer. He drew harder, curling his tongue. Then, when she panted and squirmed and dug her hands deep into his hair, he gently bit her. Another start of shock.

Dear God, she was so responsive. He couldn't remember a lover so attuned to pleasure.

Her swollen, parted lips beckoned him. He kissed her again, glorying in her quick, hot answer, even as he hoisted her high in his arms and carried her to the huge bed that he'd never shared with a woman.

When he came down over her, her legs parted to cradle him. He pressed into her mound, letting her feel his weight and size.

She wriggled and made a choked sound, but he was too far gone to pay attention. One unsteady hand stretched down to raise her skirts. He burned to touch her sex.

She made another strangled sound against his lips and caught his hand as it reached her thigh. Vaguely through raging tumult, he sensed that her body wasn't as loose and welcoming as it had been.

Wits dull with arousal, he raised his head. "Eleanor?"

His heart sank. She looked tense and afraid and unhappy. His hand stilled at her hip, although he couldn't bring himself to retreat.

"Stop," she said in a thick voice. "Please stop."

For a searing instant, he wanted to argue, persuade, seduce. She was so close to surrender. And he'd craved this joining from the first moment he'd seen her.

He grappled with the beast inside him. The beast fought back.

Gritting his teeth, he stared down at her and reminded himself that he was a man of honor.

"Of course." The concession nearly killed him.

She was right to protest. Heaven forgive him, he'd forgotten where he was. He'd forgotten every reason not to do this. Aside from his suspicions about her, she worked for him. A gentleman didn't harass the servants. From his earliest years, that tenet had been drilled into him.

Dear Lord, just imagine the scandal if London discovered that he'd retired to the country to lead a respectable life and immediately turned to swiving the maids. His political career would never recover. Even if, poised above Eleanor, his political career seemed sublimely unimportant compared to the throbbing weight in his balls.

Worse, he verged on becoming a liar. After promising to stop at kisses, he'd been close to taking her. And she was a virgin. Her uncertainty at every step she took toward ruin confirmed that.

He should be horsewhipped.

"Hell," he muttered and rolled away to sit on the edge of the bed. Burying his head in his hands, he sucked in shuddering breath after breath. He didn't dare glance at her. If he did, all good intentions would fly out the window and Miss Eleanor Trim would be a virgin no more.

And the Marquess of Leath would prove himself a cad of the first degree.

Prickling silences had become familiar. This particular silence drew blood. The fire crackled in the grate. Somewhere outside a fox barked on its nightly hunt.

"I'm sorry," she said dully from behind him after what felt like an hour, although reviving common sense insisted that it couldn't be nearly that long.

"You have nothing to be sorry for." He wished he sounded kinder, but he still struggled for control.

"I shouldn't have let you do that."

That made him turn. Her gaze was fixed on the gold and blue embroidery on the tester above the bed. She was back to looking like a marble carving. He felt a powerful nostalgia for the beautiful, rosy creature who had kissed him as if she'd die if she stopped.

She hadn't buttoned her bodice, although she'd tugged her shift over her breast. The thin linen did little to hide the voluptuous fullness or the pearled nipple. He squashed down a tide of lust as he recalled touching that perfect breast, kissing it. At his sides, his hands tightened into fists.

"Don't be a fool," he said more roughly than was justified. However right she'd been to stop him, desire swirled in his blood. He was honest enough to admit that if she hadn't spoken, he'd now be lying between her thighs discovering paradise.

Her lips tightened, but she didn't look at him. "That's the problem, I was a fool."

"It was foolish to wander into a man's room in the middle of the night," he said harshly.

He didn't think she had any more color to lose, but she turned even more ashen. "I've learned my lesson."

"I shouldn't have touched you."

"No." She paused, then spoke with searing bitterness. "I must go and pack my belongings."

"You shouldn't take the blame."

At last she turned her head in his direction. Shame clouded her amber eyes. "You're a marquess. I'm a nobody."

He winced, denial twisting his gut. "Please tell me you didn't feel compelled to kiss me because you work for me."

"No, kissing you was all my own stupidity," she said flatly.

He drew a relieved breath. "If it's any consolation, I've wanted to kiss you since that first night when you mowed me down like a runaway carriage."

He didn't know why he extended this torture of having her close without being able to touch her. He should send her away with a promise never to bother her again. Except that looking at her gave him such pleasure, however awkward this moment. His caresses had loosened the severe coiffure. Her chignon sagged onto her nape and curls of blond hair teased her forehead and cheeks in a damnably enchanting way.

When her gaze widened, the beauty of her eyes struck him anew. "Well, why didn't you?"

His laugh was dismissive. "I had no right."

He'd had no right to kiss her tonight either, even if she'd kissed him first. He returned his brooding gaze to the fire.

"You're the master here," she said listlessly.

"That's precisely why a gentleman doesn't pester the servants."

"Many do."

"And lose the right to call themselves gentlemen. It's unconscionable to take advantage of a woman who relies on my goodwill for her livelihood."

Silence descended again. Strangely, this time it felt considerably less charged. Eventually curiosity won out over self-loathing and he turned to her. Instead of the contempt or fear or anger that he expected, she looked baffled.

"What is it?"

"You're a strange man, my lord."

He frowned. "Because I've got some glimmer of a conscience?"

"Yes."

His lips lengthened with displeasure. "Nice that you have such a favorable opinion of me."

"Why should you care what a mere servant thinks?" She sat and began to button her dress. Her fingers were deft, but the pink in her cheeks indicated that his presence while she performed this intimate action disturbed her. She wasn't the only one disturbed.

He sighed with impatience. "You know, my lovely, it doesn't work. It didn't work when I first met you, and it's even less effective now."

He knew she wasn't trying to look seductive, but her sideways glance under those heavy lashes got him all hot and bothered again. "What on earth are you talking about?"

"Your pretense at humility. You're too remarkable, my beguiling Miss Trim, to fade into the wainscoting."

His praise didn't please her. "But I *am* a mere servant."

His laugh held genuine amusement. When he'd rolled off her, he'd felt like the lowest worm in creation, but this odd conversation restored his spirits. "You're not a mere anything, Eleanor."

Her eyes darkened in a way that did nothing to cool his simmering blood. "You shouldn't call me that."

"No, I shouldn't," he admitted ruefully, even as he wanted her to call him James. But that was a step too far, however ludicrous that seemed when he knew how she tasted and the precise raspberry shade of her nipples. "I've had my hand down your dress. Calling you Miss Trim seems a little silly."

Blushing, she shot him a resentful look. "I'd like you to forget that."

"For my peace of mind, it would be better if I did," he said wearily. Except he'd never forget it. That exquisite moment when he'd cupped her and heard her gasp with delight would haunt him forever.

"Can I go?" she asked.

"Can I stop you?"

"You did before."

Yes, when he'd been desperate to learn why she'd intruded

into his room. After that, he'd been desperate to kiss her. He wasn't a man familiar with desperation. Until the mysterious Eleanor Trim entered his life.

She was dangerous. And not just because he couldn't trust her as far as he could throw her. He still didn't know why she'd turned up tonight. She left him so befuddled, he hardly cared anymore. He sighed heavily. "Yes, you can go."

"Thank you, sir."

She abandoned him to a restless night. Damn it. Leath returned his attention to the fire, muffling the traitorous wish to be a different man, with different responsibilities. A free man without the weight of family expectations riding on his shoulders. A man who wasn't quite so nice about his honor.

He'd grab Miss Trim and kiss her into conceding. Then he'd make sure they both enjoyed a restless night. Twined together like ivy.

He'd expected her to rush away, but she left the bed slowly, almost reluctantly. Did she want to prolong his torment? If so, she succeeded mightily. He didn't trust himself to look at her. If he did, she wouldn't be going anywhere.

He heard her pad across to the door and he waited to hear the click as she left. When the silence extended, he braced himself to turn.

She stood across the room, rumpled, beautiful, alluring. Wide brown eyes studied him as if he presented an unanswerable question. He should find consolation in knowing that he wasn't alone in his confusion.

"My lord..." She rested her hand on the doorknob as if preparing for a quick escape. He couldn't blame her, given what had happened last time she'd tried to leave.

"My lord," she repeated softly, "I didn't kiss you because I work for you. I kissed you because...I've wondered, too."

What the devil?

"Eleanor?" Before he'd decided to stand, he was on his feet. He surged forward, although even now, he recognized that he couldn't tumble her and call himself a man of principle.

That miracle of a mouth, the mouth that tasted like heaven, curved into a wry smile. "Good night, sir."

She bobbed a brief curtsy, then fled before he caught her.

Chapter Nine

L eath's eyes were the color of a stormy sky.

Such a trivial fact for Nell to dwell upon, but easier than recalling how she'd teetered on the brink of disaster. When he'd risen above her on the bed, eyes of astonishing beauty had transfixed her. Not brown as she'd expected, but steel gray with a charcoal line around the irises, shadowed to mystery by sooty eyelashes. She was surprised she'd noticed so much with him lying between her legs, lifting her skirts.

Now the morning after tasted bitter, and she cringed at her unbridled behavior. Shame churned in her stomach as she approached the marchioness's rooms. Lord Leath had seduced Dorothy. How could Nell kiss the brute with such enthusiasm? How could she let him touch her in ways no man had touched her before?

Dorothy had entrusted her vengeance to an unworthy instrument.

But since fleeing Leath, doubts about his guilt had tortured Nell. He'd spoken of his principles before and she'd dismissed him as a hypocrite.

Then last night…

Leaning one hand against the wall, she gulped and faltered to a stop. She struggled to get her breath back against the dizzying recollection of those big strong arms wrapping around her.

Until that last squeak of self-preservation, when he'd been so appallingly close to taking her, she'd been mad for him. She'd loved everything he'd done. The kisses. The caresses. The murmured praise and encouragement. The heat. The intimacy.

What she knew about this man should disgust and terrify her. He'd bedded women all over England. He'd come close to bedding her. She shivered to remember that hard, insistent weight pressing between her thighs. Yet he'd stopped when she asked, and she couldn't mistake how he'd repented his loss of control.

When a woman lay at his mercy, what sort of rake let her escape unscathed? Nothing from last night fitted what she knew, except perhaps how the marquess attracted her like a magnet drew iron.

Was Dorothy mistaken about her seducer's identity? Why would she blame her fall on Lord Leath if he wasn't responsible?

And there was the inarguable fact that someone had seduced Dorothy.

Now what became of Nell's quest once the marquess proclaimed her a lightskirt? Could she convince the Duke of Sedgemoor of Leath's misdeeds with only Dorothy's last words as proof? Especially when Nell's own belief in his crimes wavered with every new day. She had a horrible feeling that Sedgemoor would dismiss her accusations as mere fancy.

Fate must decide.

She raised her chin and marched toward her ladyship's apartments, only to halt in the doorway on a betraying gasp when she saw Leath with his mother. For one searing moment, his gaze met hers. That sizzling contact transported her back to those torrid moments in his bed. Then he glanced away and continued discussing Lady Sophie's latest letter.

"Nell, you'll enjoy this. Sophie is redecorating the manor at Gadsden in the gothic style." The marchioness waved Nell toward her usual chair near the chaise longue. A chair beside the marquess's.

After last night, Nell couldn't bear to be so close to him. She retreated to the window seat. "How lovely, your ladyship."

The marchioness continued reading, but although Lady Sophie was an entertaining correspondent, Nell couldn't concentrate. She stared out to the dismal day. Rain pounded on the glass and wind lashed the trees against skies as gray as Leath's eyes. When his lordship terminated her employment, would she have to travel in this miserable weather? Would a carriage take her to the nearest coaching inn, or would he make her trudge through the storm?

"Nell?" the marchioness said.

"I'm sorry, your ladyship," she said quickly.

She hadn't heard a word of the letter, although she'd been aware of the marquess's rumbling responses. It was impossible not to remember that voice softening to black velvet. She was damned. Because however she despised her weakness, she couldn't bring herself to despise what he'd done to her. And deep, deep in her sinful soul, in a place that would never see the light of day, she regretted that he'd stopped.

More than confusion and self-hatred had kept her awake all night. There had been a humiliating dose of frustration too. Leath had readied her body for pleasure, then stopped before all those wonderful, unprecedented, astonishing feelings reached their unknown culmination.

"No matter." The marchioness smiled fondly. "I'll write to Sophie and make some suggestions before she goes on her headstrong way."

Guiltily Nell wondered if her ladyship would smile fondly after she knew about last night. Nell was amazed that Leath hadn't denounced her the moment she arrived, but after that one breathtaking glance, he hadn't paid her a scrap of notice.

"She's certainly headstrong," Leath said, and Nell noted the affection in his beautiful voice.

"Your sober ways clearly had little influence, James."

Such remarks only added to Nell's perplexity. The marchioness, who was no fool, seemed convinced that Leath was a pattern card of behavior. Nell was sick of struggling to fathom the man's character. He was a complete enigma.

An enigma who kissed like an angel.

"Not for want of trying," he said cheerfully.

"You must admit she's settled down since marrying Harry."

Leath's laugh was wry. "To my surprise."

"After a scandalous beginning, they've gone on very well."

"I'm not arguing, Mamma."

Nell stared at Leath. Could a man so attentive to his invalid mother treat his paramours with such indifference? Last night he could have thrown Nell down and taken her. Yet he'd been gentle, allowing for her fears. Was that just a rake's stratagem to ensure a willing partner?

"Nor are you agreeing," the marchioness said drily.

"I'll agree that my sister's rash marriage isn't the disaster I predicted."

"James, you're a devil," his mother said with a laugh. "Just admit that you were wrong."

Had he forgotten Nell's presence? She'd never heard him speak so frankly on family matters, although the dramatic events leading to his sister's marriage were no secret. The newspapers had been full of the elopement of pretty, rich Sophie Fairbrother with impecunious younger son Harry Thorne, the Duchess of Sedgemoor's dissolute brother.

Leath arched his marked black eyebrows, a smile hovering around his lips. Traitorous heat rippled through Nell. He looked dangerously attractive as he teased her ladyship. "My dear mother, I'm never wrong."

His mother laughed again and caught his hand. "Of course not, darling."

"I'll come and have luncheon with you, shall I?"

He raised his mother's hand to his lips and kissed it with a respect that set that forbidden corner of Nell's soul aching with longing. And bafflement. What was true? Dorothy's accusations? The man Nell came to know? The way she felt when she saw him?

She was only certain of one thing. Right now, the prospect of leaving the marchioness and, God forgive her, the marquess pummeled her heart with misery.

"That would be lovely." Pleasure rang in Lady Leath's voice.

He stood. "I'll see you later."

Nell braced for him to insist on dismissing the wanton Miss Trim. Surely he wouldn't leave his mother in a Jezebel's clutches. Her hands closed in her skirts and she stared at him so hard that he ought to burst into flame.

He nodded in her direction without looking at her. "Miss Trim."

Then he was gone.

Nell felt as if he left her dangling from a wire high above an abyss. What cruel game was he playing?

After two days, Nell was in such a state that she jumped at every sound. This was like waiting for an ax to fall. Yet still Leath didn't betray her to his mother.

This morning, she could bear it no longer. Once she'd settled the marchioness, Nell ventured downstairs. After his kisses, she'd lacked the nerve to seek him out. But if he meant to send her away, she had to know.

Her courage went for naught. His lordship had ridden to York with Mr. Crane and wouldn't be back until nightfall. So she had another day's respite, except that anticipating the blow was worse than facing her fate.

Once the household retired, apart from the footman assigned to let his lordship and the secretary in, Nell set up vigil at the top of the main staircase. She settled on a padded bench so old and dark with age that she imagined King Alfred must have sat on it.

It was still raining. October on the moors was bleak. Mearsall was only a few hundred miles south, but Kent seemed the work of a kinder, gentler Creator.

The hallway clock had struck eleven before Nell heard the great iron doorknocker. Curled up on the bench, she'd drifted into a doze. When she moved, she bit back a groan. She'd leaned against the wall at an awkward angle, and she was stiff from sitting still. And cold. She drew her cashmere shawl around her. It was finer than anything she'd ever owned, a gift from the marchioness. Yet again she muffled a pang of guilt at plotting trouble for the family. The marchioness was ridiculously generous. The difficulty was restraining the lady from showering her with luxuries.

The knocker sounded again before the footman pulled

back the bolts with a crash and grind of metal. Alloway Chase had been built to keep out medieval marauders.

"Good evening, my..." The footman's voice faded to nothing.

Nell tottered forward. The wind was so strong it whistled through the great hall and up the stairs to press her heavy woolen skirts against her legs. Below, John the footman reeled back.

"Help me, man," the marquess snapped, stumbling inside. "Don't stand there like a dead fish."

Her heart racing with fear, Nell descended a few steps before she realized that Leath wasn't hurt. Over one shoulder, he carried Mr. Crane.

"Yes, sir," John stammered, reaching forward. Mr. Crane's groan bounced off the stone walls.

"Not like that, you fool. Take his legs."

Nell rushed down. "My lord, what's happened?"

At her question, he looked up and she caught relief in his face. He was pale and streaked with mud. Water dripped off his greatcoat and he'd lost his hat. "Eleanor, you're here. Good. You can help. Crane's horse took fright at a stray dog and bolted."

Nell collected a lamp from a table and raised it high. "John, be careful. If he's hurt his back, you'll do more harm than good."

She spoke clearly and slowly and the young man immediately settled. The marquess's temper was understandable, but unlikely to get the best out of the nervous junior footman. Inevitably she was reminded of the night she'd met Leath. He'd been in a temper then too.

Thank goodness, the library wasn't far away. She carried the lamp ahead as Leath and John juggled the injured secretary. Despite their care, Mr. Crane moaned. He did, however, come back to himself enough to protest when they placed him on the sofa. "My lord, I'm not fit for indoors."

"Damn it, Paul, as if I care." Leath straightened the young man's limbs with brisk, gentle efficiency.

John stood back and stared helplessly at the injured man. Nell sighed. "John, light the fire. It's a cold night."

"Yes, miss," he said, although Nell had no real authority. Within moments, flames licked at the kindling.

"I'll wake Mr. Wells and have him send for the doctor." She took a spill and moved around the room lighting candles.

"No need. I sent a groom." Leath set a cushion behind Mr. Crane's head. "But it's a devil of a night. I don't envy him the ride there and back."

"Did Mr. Crane hit his head?"

"Yes." Leath brushed wet black hair back from his forehead.

"And lose consciousness?"

"Briefly."

"It's my arm," Crane said unsteadily. His face was drawn with pain and he clutched his right arm across his chest. "I think I've broken it."

"You took a hell of a tumble." When Leath helped him to sit, Nell saw that movement was agonizing. She jammed more cushions behind Mr. Crane to support him.

"Get blankets and pillows. And towels," she said to John, who still hovered. The young man snapped to attention and rushed out.

"I'd rather go to my room," Mr. Crane said faintly.

"Better not to move, old fellow. Miss Trim is right. You may have spinal injuries. God knows what damage I've done hauling you across the moors."

"It would have been easier to leave me there."

"No, the cold would have got you." Leath pressed a brandy glass to the secretary's lips. After a couple of sips, Mr. Crane choked. "But I curse myself for making you ride through that gale. We could easily have stayed in York."

Nell paused on her way to the kitchen and cast a searching glance at the marquess. His willingness to take the blame for this accident impressed her. Again, he defied her preconceptions. Could this be the man who had left Dorothy to bear his child in disgrace?

"You weren't to know the damned—dashed—nag would bolt." Mr. Crane cast Nell an apologetic look, polite even in his suffering. She liked Mr. Crane. When she'd imagined a husband, the man had been someone like the young secretary. Now, compared to the marquess, he seemed a nonentity.

Nell had developed a taste for the dark and dangerous since arriving at Alloway Chase. Heaven help her.

Alarmed at the admission, she headed for the kitchens. She poured warm water into a bowl, refilled the kettle, then set it to heat on the hob.

When she returned to the library, she heard Mr. Crane saying, "I don't want to cause any fuss."

"My good fellow—" Leath's impatience melted into a smile when he saw Nell. "Oh, bless you."

He stepped back to allow her to place the bowl on a table. He'd undressed down to shirtsleeves. Despite the fraught circumstances, she couldn't help inhaling his scent. Clean male and rain and horses. After their encounter in his bedroom, the scent was perilously familiar. And as heady as wine.

Nell struggled to concentrate on poor Mr. Crane as she knelt at his side. "I'll try not to hurt you."

The gallantry in Mr. Crane's smile touched her and he

bore her ministrations without complaining, although the lines bracketing his mouth indicated discomfort.

John returned, his arms piled high with bedding and towels that he placed at her side. Nell passed a towel to the marquess, who watched her with a level gaze that set her nerves prickling. "We need to get him out of his wet clothes."

"I tried to get his coat off, but it seemed cruel rather than helpful." He rubbed at his hair, although it no longer dripped water onto his wide shoulders.

"I'm all right, sir." Mr. Crane's strangled tone indicated that he lied.

"Perhaps we could cut off the coat," Nell suggested. She tried not to look at the marquess. He was dangerously approachable—and appealing—with his damp black hair ruffled and tumbling over his brow.

"Good idea," the marquess said. "John, will you fetch a knife from the kitchen?"

John scurried off. Nell turned her attention to drying Mr. Crane as best she could and tending his scrapes and bruises. The water in the bowl was soon cloudy with blood and dirt. She dropped the cloth into the water and started to rise, but to her astonishment, the marquess's elegant hand landed on her shoulder.

The contact shuddered through her. And strangely bolstered her strength. "I'll go. Your presence calms him."

Whether that was true or not, Mr. Crane breathed more easily.

"My lord, you shouldn't wait on me," the injured man objected.

"Stow it, Paul," Leath said.

"Thank you," Nell said quietly. "The kettle's on the hearth. The handle is likely to be hot, so you'll need a cloth to lift it. Or perhaps John can help."

The marquess sent her a mocking glance. "I'll have you know I can fend for myself."

She blushed, too conscious of that strong hand resting on her shoulder. She was glad she hadn't given him directions to the kitchens. She nearly had. But it was a stretch to imagine the magnificent Marquess of Leath in that workaday setting.

He lifted his hand, which offered her racing heart a reprieve, and collected the bowl. "Try and get some more brandy into him, Miss Trim."

When they were alone, Mr. Crane regarded her with rueful amusement that made her commend his courage. "His lordship is too kind."

"He values you." She rose to fill the brandy glass.

The liquor added a trace of color to his cheeks. She prayed that the broken arm was all that was wrong. He seemed cogent, but she needed to be sure. She set the glass on the table and collected a candle.

"Any other man would have left me on the moor and fetched help, instead of putting me on his own horse. The rain was coming down in sheets."

Nell wasn't sure what to say. The more she saw of James Fairbrother, the less she believed that he was Dorothy's treacherous lover.

She was passing a candle before Mr. Crane's eyes when the marquess returned bearing fresh water and a clean cloth. "I don't think he's done his head any lasting damage."

"You seem to know what you're doing." She heard the question in Leath's voice.

"I nursed my mother and my sister. And helped the village doctor when he needed an assistant. Apart from his arm, I doubt if Mr. Crane's seriously injured."

"That's a relief," her patient said as Leath placed the bowl on the table.

John came in and Nell bit back the urge to say "at last." Then she saw that he'd brought a large pair of scissors as well as a knife. "Well done, John."

Leath seized the scissors. "John, wait in the hall for the doctor."

"Very good, my lord." The young man bowed and left.

"I'll hold him." Leath passed her the scissors. "You cut."

"My lord..." Mr. Crane bleated.

Nell struggled not to jar her patient, but before she'd finished both she and Mr. Crane were sweating and shaking. After she'd splinted the broken arm, Nell felt ready to collapse. Mr. Crane was barely conscious and shivering under the blankets. Only Leath appeared in a good state as he stoked the fire to a roaring blaze. Nell admired his stamina. After all, he'd transported his secretary through a storm before assuming sickroom duties.

Mr. Crane looked tired, but more comfortable, by the time the doctor arrived. Nell stood wearily and collected the bowl, intending to fetch more hot water. And to save Mr. Crane's blushes when his breeches came off.

She was in the kitchen filling the kettle when some change in the air alerted her. She raised her head to see Leath in the doorway, studying her with a brooding expression.

Dear heaven, he was a gorgeous man. In his loose white shirt and with his hair untidy after the night's exertions, he made her heart turn over. Her hand began to shake and the kettle sloshed water over her dress. She hadn't been alone with the marquess since he'd kissed her. The memory was painfully vivid.

The memory. The shame. The confusion. The...desire.

He strode forward with his purposeful step and grabbed the kettle from her precarious grip. "Pass that over before you flood the place."

The brush of his hand made her wayward heart lurch with a dizzying mixture of fear and excitement. "I don't—"

"You're safe." He placed the kettle on the hob, giving her a chance to catch her breath. When they'd worked together to help Mr. Crane, they'd been a team. Now all the bristling, difficult awareness revived.

"I know." She wished that she didn't sound like she regretted the fact.

Chapter Ten

Leath leaned his hips against the draining board, studying Miss Trim. Nell. Eleanor.

She looked tired and jumpy. And beautiful. Her dress was damp and stained after helping Crane and a streak of dirt marked her lovely face. A strand of silvery blond hair escaped her daunting coiffure and dangled onto her breast. His hands curled against the cold stone bench behind him as he fought the urge to tug the pins away and see her hair tumbling around her like moonlight.

Two nights ago, she'd given him too much.

She hadn't given him enough.

"Thank you for your help."

"I told you—I've done a lot of nursing."

Lit to spellbinding shadow in the turned-down lamps, she stood on the flagstones. Her stance betrayed uncertainty and her eyes were suspicious. She was *always* suspicious. He was devilish tired of it.

He glanced down at his filthy boots. Selsby would haul him over the coals for the state of his clothes once he finally made it upstairs. "So you really are an orphan."

She stiffened, hostility replacing uncertainty. "Why would I lie?"

He fixed his gaze on her. "I don't know."

Pink tinged her cheeks and she avoided his eyes. Was that because she was a liar, or because she was a respectable woman alone with the man who had taken liberties? As always with Miss Trim, he wasn't sure of anything.

"My mother was ill for months before she passed away." She sent him a look which felt significant. He had no idea why. "And my sister Dorothy died in May."

"I'm sorry."

"So am I." She seemed to expect a stronger reaction. Again, he sensed that there were levels of meaning here that he missed.

"Your father was a soldier?"

"I'm surprised you remember that." She didn't sound pleased.

"Of course I remember." He recalled every encounter with this woman and every word she'd said. Perhaps because she was so damned elusive. There was nothing like mystery to whet a man's interest. "You intrigue me, Miss Trim."

To his surprise, she didn't take up the challenge. Instead she straightened with that innate pride so incongruous in a housemaid. "My father was a sergeant major in one of Rowland Hill's brigades. He was killed at Vimeiro in '08. I was only five, but my mother talked about him all the time until I'm not sure whether the memories are mine or hers."

"What was his name?"

"Robert."

So much loss in Eleanor's life. He'd wondered if she'd used the orphan story to gain his mother's sympathy, but looking at her now, he saw that whatever other lies she'd told, she hadn't lied about losing her parents. Compassion pierced him, softened his voice. "I'm sure he was a brave man."

"I believe he was. He was decorated and mentioned in dispatches."

The sorrow in her face made him long to draw her into his arms. Purely for comfort, he told himself. And didn't believe it.

She went on. "I've always been sad that his service record was lost. Along with his medals and his effects."

Leath stepped toward her. "That's a blasted shame."

"I've been thinking of him lately." Her attempt at a smile touched him in a place deeper than lust. He suddenly realized that cozy chats deep into the night were as dangerous as forbidden kisses. "Perhaps because . . . you call me Eleanor."

Leath knew he shouldn't touch her. If he touched her, her unusually confiding mood and the hunger that had tormented him since he'd kissed her would lure him to more. And she was a virtuous woman. While he was a gentleman. An affair would do neither of them credit.

It was a struggle to sound merely kind when his pulse pounded like a battalion of drums. "Have you contacted the War Office?"

She sighed. "My mother must have written a hundred letters, but at the time, the war was raging. They had more important things to think about."

"More important to them," Leath grunted. Sergeant Major Trim had given his life for his country. That deserved more respect than he'd received.

Behind him, the kettle boiled. Leath lifted it and poured water into a bowl. He expected Eleanor to smile to see him using a cloth to hold the handle, but she seemed lost in memories. It was as if she'd forgotten his presence. He should be grateful. There was safety in distance. But he couldn't help mourning the end of an interval when they'd spoken almost as...friends.

Hell, Eleanor Trim befuddled him more than anyone he'd ever met. He needed to talk to Dr. Angus about Crane. But still this woman held him as captive as if she'd cast a net over his head. He had a grim feeling that like a fish in the sea, he was well and truly hooked.

What in blazes was he going to do about it? He couldn't even blame Eleanor. She wasn't trying to captivate him. He retained a lurking suspicion that she didn't like him, however smitten she claimed to be, however hot her kisses.

"I wouldn't have managed nearly so well tonight without you." He hated how stilted he sounded. The awkwardness that abruptly descended reminded him that he'd been in the saddle most of the day and that hauling Crane through the rain hadn't been easy. He was cold and weary and, as he met Eleanor Trim's cool gaze, discouragingly lonely.

"I'm here to serve, my lord," she said neutrally.

Was she mocking him? He remembered all his reasons for avoiding this woman, not least her dashed slippery behavior. His eyes sharpened on her. "In fact," he said thoughtfully, "you were astonishingly quick to serve. You appeared out of nowhere."

She stared back as uncompromisingly as a young saint facing martyrdom. Except now that he'd kissed her, he'd learned that, with the right encouragement, she could sin gloriously. "I waited up to talk to you, my lord."

"What the devil have we been doing for the last twenty minutes?"

His sharp question made her frown. "I'd like to know your plans, given what happened the other night."

With a loud clank, he slammed the kettle back on the heat. A mixture of hope and disbelief set his heart banging against his ribs. He'd convinced himself that she was out of reach. Was he mistaken? "My plans? For bedding you?"

Her eyes widened with shock and she stepped back. Much further and she'd be in the corridor. "No, of course not."

"There's no 'of course' about it," he muttered, disappointment descending like a landslide. He wanted Eleanor Trim. At this moment, he wanted her more than he wanted his political career or his good reputation. For a brief, dazzling moment, he'd wondered if he might yet get her.

She licked her lips, setting his blood to flame. He needed to get out of this kitchen before he abandoned his honor. Her hands twined nervously at her waist, another characteristic gesture. "When are you going to dismiss me?"

He scowled, cranky with her, the world, himself. Heaven had created her to lie in his arms. Why did this world make that perfect outcome impossible? "What bloody rot is this?"

The tense line of her shoulders eased until she stood more naturally. How interesting that she was more comfortable with his bad temper than his questions. More than ever, he was convinced that she hid something.

"I can't bear this waiting, my lord. It's cruel. I know you want me gone. I heard you talking to your mother last week. When you caught me—"

"When I caught you red-handed in my bedroom," he said silkily, perversely beginning to enjoy himself. He'd had no idea that she'd been on such tenterhooks.

She nodded. "It's a good excuse to get rid of me."

"I have no intention of telling my mother that I kissed her companion. I told you that what happened was my fault."

"You also told me that gentlemen didn't chase the servants," she retorted.

"Miss Trim…" Although in his heart, he called her

Eleanor. "That night reflects badly on both of us. Perhaps we should close the door on it."

She regarded him uncertainly. "You don't want me to leave?"

Hell, no.

He bit back the quick reaction and spoke with as much avuncular reassurance as he could muster. By the look on her face, that wasn't much. "My mother is in better spirits these days."

"That's because you're home."

He frowned. "Not completely."

"That night you thought I was stealing."

A few days ago, he'd pushed for her banishment. Now he must have gone mad, because the thought of her departure made him want to punch the wall. "Nothing's missing."

"I could have been deciding what to take."

"Was that what you were doing?"

"No."

He waited, wondering if she'd confess her reasons for invading his apartments. But she remained silent. And watchful. Always watchful.

"I will discover your secrets, you know," he said evenly.

She started, then stood tall in the lamplight. "Your imagination runs away with you, my lord."

A faint smile curved his lips. "I don't think so." He collected the bowl and the cloth. "My instincts never fail, Miss Trim, and they scream that you're not what you seem."

"Then why keep me here?" she asked, puzzled rather than pert.

He shrugged and met her eyes, feeling as though he drowned in autumn gold. "Heaven knows, Eleanor, heaven knows."

Chapter Eleven

Nell slept late the next morning, a luxury for a servant. The doctor had pronounced Mr. Crane unhurt apart from his broken arm, but the hall clock had struck four before she'd settled the patient and cleaned up. The marquess had stayed to the last, which had surprised her. Something else that surprised her was Mr. Crane's unmistakable respect for his employer. During her previous encounter with the two together, Leath had snapped at Crane for wasting time with her.

The light outside her windows was bright. Yorkshire had such strange, violent, unpredictable weather. Howling tempest one minute, unreliable brilliance the next. It was so different from the green gentleness of her home. The landscape was as mercurial as the man who owned this barren wilderness. Except that the moors weren't barren. There were rich mines and valleys of good farmland. At first glance, the moors seemed all desolation and solitude. But when one looked more closely, there were hidden subtleties, secret treasures—an appeal more powerful for not being immediately visible.

Very like the Marquess of Leath.

After that odd, confiding conversation in the kitchen, his lordship had punctiliously kept his distance. One would imagine that he'd always called her Miss Trim and that he'd never kissed her.

She should be grateful. It would be too ironic if this quest to bring Dorothy's seducer to justice resulted in her own ruin. But stupidly, she missed that resonant voice saying her name as if she was the first and only Eleanor in the world.

Exhausted as she'd been, she'd taken forever to fall asleep. Now that she'd learned that her position was safe, she should feel reassured. But somehow she didn't. Instead, questions buzzed around her mind. As ever, with Leath, she had no answers. When she'd taken a risk mentioning Dorothy, she'd watched avidly for some hint of guilt. She'd seen nothing.

Then he'd drawn her into speaking about her father, something she always found painful. Nell had loved Robert Trim with a little girl's adoration, and through her mother's eyes, she'd learned to love him into maturity. Her mother had always mourned her first husband, fond as she was of scholarly William Simpson. It continued to anger Nell that some administrative bungle had deprived Frances Trim of those last tangible memories of Robert's life in Portugal.

When Nell hurried down to the marchioness's apartments, Leath was taking tea with his mother. The last time she'd seen his lordship, he'd been dirty and rumpled and worried for Mr. Crane. This morning, in a dark blue coat, buff breeches, and boots polished to a mirror shine, he looked ready for Mayfair. But the burning glance he cast her was familiar from last night. And as it had last night, the sight of him set her heart racing with excitement.

"Your ladyship, I'm so sorry. I overslept."

The marchioness waved her hand. "James told me about

your heroics. You needn't have rushed. Have you had breakfast?"

"No, my lady," Nell said, her conscience twitching at Lady Leath's concern. She'd imagined a closer relationship with the family would promote her cause. Instead it muddied her convictions. Perhaps she should leave, even without the diary. Every day, her loyalties became more tangled.

The marchioness gestured to a tray of cakes and sandwiches. "There's plenty here. Or I can ring for more."

"You're too kind." Nell meant it. She glanced at the marquess, expecting him to disapprove of this informality, but his faint smile lacked the usual reserve.

Overwhelmingly conscious of his intense gray gaze, she hesitantly chose some food and poured a cup of tea. The marquess's presence stole her appetite. Feeling awkward, she sat on the window seat, deliberately setting herself apart. "How is Mr. Crane?"

"In a sorry way, I'm afraid," Leath said. "Dr. Angus called again this morning and says it's a bad break, likely to take months to heal."

Poor Mr. Crane. He was distantly related to the Fairbrothers, but from a much less prosperous branch. His wages supported his sister and widowed mother in London. "How will his family manage?"

The marchioness laughed. "James, clearly Nell thinks you're a heartless tyrant."

Nell blushed. "My lady, I didn't—"

"Paul will continue to receive his salary," she said.

"After all, he was injured in my service." Leath's response was wry, rather than annoyed. Nell didn't trust this sudden amiability.

"Which leaves James without a secretary," her ladyship said.

Why on earth were they involving Nell in this discussion? "Perhaps your steward can help."

"Powter is far too busy. And he has an abominable hand." Leath studied her with an expression she couldn't read, although it made her shift uncomfortably.

"Nell writes beautifully. Her letters are works of art," the marchioness said. "She could help you, James."

Nell was so shocked that she fumbled the cup and spilled tea on her skirts. Nervously she slid the cup and saucer onto a small table and reached for a napkin to dab at the stain.

"Clearly she's overjoyed at the prospect." Leath's voice was as dry as sawdust.

"I'm not qualified," she said unsteadily.

"Don't be a goose, Nell," the marchioness said. "You're the most capable young woman I know. Is there anything you can't do?"

I can't resist your son. She set the creased napkin on the tea tray and told herself to stop acting like the goose her ladyship had called her. "I certainly don't feel up to filling Mr. Crane's shoes."

There, that came out almost sensibly.

The marchioness made an airy gesture. "It's only until James arranges another secretary from London. A couple of weeks at the most."

"What about my duties with you?" Under her lashes, Nell glanced at Leath. He looked particularly enigmatic. She wondered how he'd reacted when his mother had suggested this scheme.

"We'll try mornings with James and afternoons with me. We'll see how it works."

"His lordship may decide I'm completely inadequate."

He shot Nell a searing look. "Do you intend to ensure that's the case?"

She started with surprise, although it wasn't a bad strategy if she wanted to avoid him. "No, of course not."

"I'm collating a major report. It's essential I finish it," he said.

"It sounds complicated," Nell said doubtfully.

"So you won't help me?"

Oh, dear God, when he put it like that, how could she refuse? In truth, she was torn. The prospect of hours in the marquess's company terrified her. Already he'd undermined her defenses. She didn't need to see his brilliance in action. Because she had a sinking feeling that he was brilliant. His intelligence drew her almost as strongly as his big, strong body did.

On the other hand, this could be her opportunity. His secretary would have access to his papers. Perhaps the diary was amongst them.

"Good Lord, Miss Trim, I'm not asking you to do anything that you don't already do for my mother," he said impatiently. "There's no need for this soul-searching."

She leveled her shoulders and tried to convince herself that this wasn't a horrible mistake. "My lord, I'm willing to try. Thank you for your confidence."

Which raised another question. Why on earth did he want to work with her when he didn't trust her?

Leath soon recognized his blunder in taking Miss Trim as his secretary. But he needed help to finish these reports. And despite the thaw in their relations—a thaw that had turned into a tropical heatwave in his bedroom—he still didn't trust her. He wanted her under his eye until he learned her scheme.

He hadn't bargained on how disturbing her nearness would prove. After a week of struggling to pretend that Miss Trim was a female version of Crane, he was exhausted.

And making vilely small progress in his work. The moment she glided into his library, all thought of political economy scurried out the opposite window.

He couldn't even censure her for encouraging his distraction. She'd reverted to perfect servant mode. If she was infatuated with him, she did nothing to put herself forward. Instead, she was almost eerily self-effacing, speaking only when spoken to, willing to assist but not to make suggestions, fading into the background in her gray dresses.

Perhaps his kisses had killed her romantic interest. Perhaps she'd never had a romantic interest and she'd been in his room for some other purpose. For the life of him, he couldn't think what that could be. He found it impossible to see this self-possessed woman succumbing to curiosity and invading his room, however much she fancied him.

Even now, when she read out a list of figures that would bore any reasonable man into catatonia, he couldn't help recalling what they'd done in that wide bed upstairs. Her soft sighs when he'd kissed her. His hand curving around her breast. Worse, he couldn't help imagining what would have happened if she hadn't protested.

Leath stood staring out the window at the unseasonably fine day. He hoped the view would distract him from Miss Trim.

No chance.

Her docility should make things easier. But it ... didn't.

"My lord?" She clearly thought that low voice placed them on a purely professional footing. Instead it made him imagine her whispering naughty suggestions in his ear as he slid inside her. He burned to see her naked with that fairy hair drifting around her like a veil, offering glimpses of the white body beneath. Eve before original sin.

He turned. "I'd like to ride out to the drainage project in the west pastures."

From behind Crane's desk, she regarded him with that unreadable gaze that had driven him mad all week. "I'll finish that letter to your agent in Staffordshire."

"No, I want you to come with me," he said, and saw his own surprise at the suggestion he hadn't intended to make reflected in her face.

Then she once again became a cipher. "I don't ride, my lord."

She didn't want to accompany him. He couldn't blame her. She'd have to be dead not to feel the prickling sexual awareness.

"We can take the gig." He paused. "It's probably the last good weather. Don't you long to be out in the fresh air?"

Something wistful flashed in her eyes, but it vanished so quickly that he couldn't be sure. His voice deepened to persuasion, although they both knew that if he issued an order, she must obey. "Even my mother is sitting on the terrace. It's inhuman to stay cooped up."

At Miss Trim's reluctant smile, triumph surged. Lately she hadn't smiled at him, much as he resented noting the lack. Damn it, he should be glad that she played down the sizzle between them. But he'd reached a point where one more minute in this room would have him flinging her onto the couch and taking his pleasure.

"As you wish, my lord. I'll fetch my bonnet and shawl."

Cursing his susceptibility to this prim female, he rang to order the gig brought around. Perhaps a brisk moorland breeze would blow some sense into his thick head.

As he sat beside Miss Trim in the gig's confoundedly confined seat, Leath derided himself for a mutton-headed idiot. Every jolt bumped his hip against hers. On the drive from the house and bowling through the village outside the gates, that created a damned suggestive rhythm.

Bump. Release. Bump. Release.

He thought he'd go mad with it.

Worse came when they struck the rough track over the moors and the bumps became more violent. The contact of hip to hip lasted until he felt her heat through her serviceable merino dress, and her sweet, fresh scent filled his senses. He wished to Hades he could buy her some new clothes. Scarlet. Cut low. Clinging where gray wool suggested. What quirk of his nature made her puritanical costumes so provocative? Perhaps if she dressed to seduce, he'd lose this itch to tear every respectable thread away.

He pulled the gig to a stop at the crest of the hill that brooded over the western end of his estate. The horses needed to get their breath back.

So did he.

He tried to shift away, but the narrow seat stymied him. Illogically, her lack of response to his nearness chafed.

A ridiculous contraption of a bonnet hid her face, except for her chin and that lovely mouth. Her gloved hands lay clasped loosely in her lap. The wind that always blew here, even on the finest days, flirted with the fringe on the pretty paisley shawl that added unexpected color to her appearance.

"It's so beautiful here," she said softly.

He wanted to tell Miss Trim that *she* was beautiful. He resisted the urge and surveyed the miles of rough moorland with displeasure. "Really?"

"Don't you think so?" She turned and he found himself lost in cinnamon eyes. For once, they contained no suspicion. Just curiosity and interest.

With a frown, he returned to contemplating the inhospitable landscape. Gray. Stony. Unforgiving. Dangerous. "It's useless for anything except raising grouse."

"Do you enjoy shooting?"

He shrugged. "I'm not much of a hunting man."

"Unless you're chasing down members of the opposition." Her gaze was searching. "I always thought you loved the moors."

Uncanny that she read him so easily. Most people couldn't. "Of course I do, but I was brought up here."

"When I first arrived, I was terrified."

"The moors are terrifying. Bogs that will swallow a cow. Crevasses where you can fall and break a leg and nobody will ever find you. The weather crashes down cold and misty from a perfectly blue sky." Like today's, although instincts honed through a lifetime told him that the sunshine would hold, at least until tonight.

"Now I see magnificence. It's so big. Nothing petty or unworthy can survive under this sky."

Surprised, he stared at her. "I always feel free out here," he admitted, before he recalled that sharing confidences with Miss Trim was a bad idea.

"Do you miss it when you're in London?"

A month ago, he'd have laughed at the thought. Missing the wilds of Yorkshire when he was in the hurly-burly of power? Stagnating in this backwater instead of deciding his nation's destiny? Living quietly with his mother instead of exploring the amusements that the capital offered a bachelor with endless wealth and no domestic ties?

He surveyed this uncivilized landscape that had taught him so much when he'd been a restless boy. "Yes, I do."

"So why stay away?"

His smile was grim. "I can't become prime minister from an obscure hamlet thirty miles outside York."

"You can, however, lead a useful, satisfying life caring for your estates and your people."

"Miss Trim..." *Eleanor.* "This is a mere interlude while the world forgets the Fairbrother scandals."

"Lady Sophie's courtship had a respectable conclusion."

"How innocent that sounds when she set every tongue in London wagging. An heiress eloping with a disreputable member of a family known to be at odds with the Fairbrothers? It's the stuff of those sensational novels you read to my mother."

"At least Lady Sophie's happy."

"Oh, she's that. The worst is that Sophie's rebellion came hot on the heels of my uncle's exposure as a thief and murderer." He faced Miss Trim directly. Perhaps he mistook the situation, but he needed to clarify the issues between them. For her sake and his. "I can't risk further scandal."

She had such fine skin, fluctuating color betrayed her faintest emotion. "You needn't warn me off, my lord." Her response was curt. "I have no wish to become a rich man's plaything."

Bitterness tainted his laugh. "Then stay out of rich men's bedrooms."

"I learned my lesson." Her color flared hotter, making her eyes flash caramel fire. In her lap, her hands tightened around each other. "I know my place and I'm willing to keep to it. I hope you'll do the same."

"I'll do my best, Miss Trim," he said flatly and set the horses to a fast canter that precluded further discussion.

Chapter Twelve

Nell was reading one of the new books to Lady Leath when his lordship arrived the next afternoon. After the abrupt ending to yesterday's strangely intimate conversation, he'd reverted to Business Leath.

Business Leath had an impressive grasp of agricultural and industrial matters. Business Leath never fumbled to recall a name or date. Business Leath bit out his words with a crispness that made her want to salute the way some raw recruit had once saluted her soldier father.

Business Leath would never kiss his secretary.

This version of the multifaceted marquess might promise safety, but there must be something in the air. Every day safety became less appealing.

Until yesterday, she'd wondered if he even remembered kissing her. Now she realized that he too fought their attraction. She was ashamed at how difficult her struggle was. She'd told herself over and over that Leath was the man who had ruined Dorothy and only a self-destructive fool would consider yielding to him. But as the days passed, she had a horrible feeling that she might be just such a self-destructive fool.

She rose on legs that always went weak in his presence and curtsied. "Good afternoon, my lord."

The stern nod was pure Business Leath. "Miss Trim."

She should be glad. Business Leath posed no threat to her willpower. But she missed yesterday's closeness when he'd spoken of his home with such love that she'd made that stupid suggestion for him to stay. Fleetingly, she'd glimpsed this man's soul, and what she'd seen had intrigued and moved her.

"How are you feeling today, Mamma?" Leath kissed his mother's cheek with the fondness that always chipped at Nell's dislike. "It's another fine day. Perhaps we can sit in the gardens."

"That would be lovely, James," the marchioness said. "If you can spare the time. I know you're busy."

He shrugged as he took his usual seat. "If I lag behind, I have a very efficient secretary to help me." He sent Nell a mocking glance. "Please, Miss Trim, cease hovering."

His attention leveled on the chair she'd been using. Clearly he'd noted the way she retreated to the window seat half a room away when he visited his mother. His quick perception made her wary. He might appear focused on his own purposes, but a week as his secretary had taught her that those gray eyes missed nothing. Willing her heartbeat to slow, she sat where he indicated.

The marchioness smiled her delight. "I told you that Nell was just the woman to get you out of this mess."

"You were right." He paused. "But she falls short in one important skill."

Nell cast him a fulminating glance. She thought she'd done a fair job in a role that tested her. "My lord?"

He wasn't smiling, but the faint relaxation of his mouth indicated amusement. She'd never met a man who hid his reactions like this one. He must be a devil of a politician. She felt a twinge of sympathy for his opponents.

"The admirable Miss Trim doesn't ride."

Nell struggled to sound properly respectful. "A woman of modest means rarely has her own stables."

He sighed, and now she was certain that he teased. "I have stables."

The marchioness clapped her frail hands. "James, are you going to teach Nell to ride? What a wonderful idea. She'll love it."

"I appreciate your kindness, sir," Nell said, although appreciation was the last thing on her mind. Hoping that the marchioness wouldn't see, Nell narrowed her eyes on Leath. How on earth did this chime with yesterday's warning? "But this is unnecessary. As you pointed out, you're already busy."

Lady Leath regarded her with admiration. "My dear, I'm so glad that you don't let my son trample all over you. He can be overbearing."

"Mamma, for pity's sake," Leath protested.

"Well, you are," his mother said unrepentantly. "Poor Paul is a complete dogsbody."

"That's not true."

Nell hid a smile. "His lordship will be happy when his new secretary arrives."

At least that diverted the marchioness's attention from her companion. "James, what have you done about replacing Paul?"

Leath looked uncomfortable. Almost... furtive. "Matters are in hand."

Nell frowned in puzzlement. If he'd sent to London, or even York, for Mr. Crane's substitute, he must have written the letters himself. She certainly hadn't.

"Most mysterious," the marchioness said.

"Not at all," he said, and to Nell's annoyance, returned to the issue of riding lessons. "Until I get a new secretary, it's imperative that Miss Trim can sit on a horse."

"We managed with the gig yesterday," she said.

"We'll need to go cross country."

"Nell, James is right. Doesn't the idea of galloping over the moors thrill you, even just a little?" Regret that she usually fought gallantly to hide filled Lady Leath's voice. "I remember as a bride riding for hours beside James's father, discovering the estate. I've never felt so free."

Odd. Free was the word the marquess had chosen to describe his reaction to the moors too. "Horses are so big."

"Don't tell me you're frightened, Miss Trim," the marquess said. "I'm convinced that not even a herd of charging elephants could ruffle a hair on your head."

Little did he know that her attraction to one difficult marquess made her quake with terror.

He surveyed her down his long nose. "Or perhaps that's the devilish unbecoming way you pull it back."

It was her turn to protest. She raised a hand to where her hair strained from her forehead. "My lord!"

"He's right, my dear," the marchioness said. "I wish you'd let Nancy arrange it for you."

Nell hid a shudder. Nancy, Lady Leath's maid, was so jealous of Nell that she was more likely to tear out every hair on her head than create a becoming style. "It's not fitting."

"Nonsense," the marchioness said. "You and my son dwell too much on questions of rank."

"My mother is a revolutionary," the marquess said drily. "She'd happily march me off to the guillotine in the name of liberty, equality, and fraternity."

"Don't be silly, James. But sometimes you're ever so

stuffy." She sent Nell a disapproving glance. "And that stuffiness has rubbed off on you, my girl. I'm disappointed."

Reluctantly, Nell smiled. When she wanted her own way, the marchioness was more formidable than her formidable son. "I'll try riding."

"Excellent," the marchioness said.

Nell hadn't finished. "But if I show no aptitude, I ask that you both drop this subject."

"And if I need to visit some isolated corner of the estate?" Leath asked.

"If you're not home for supper, we'll arrange a search party."

To her surprise, he laughed properly. She'd never heard him express full-scale amusement before. The sound was wonderful. Liberated and joyous and rich. She found herself smiling at him.

Then she caught the marchioness's speculative expression and her smile faded to nothing. What on earth was she doing? Anyone would say she flirted with the marquess. And anyone would be right.

Already they spent too much time together. She told herself that she sought the diary, but it was days since she'd looked for it. Instead, she fell victim to Lord Leath's charm and intelligence. Now, heaven help her, she'd just agreed to riding lessons which she feared must involve physical contact. And she was too susceptible to the touch of those strong, elegant hands.

As Leath approached the stables the next day, the sun crept over the horizon. He wasn't surprised to see the woman who was his torment and his fascination waiting. Why the devil he did this, he couldn't say. In truth, he'd manage quite well without someone at his side in his estate's less accessible areas.

But when they'd shared the gig, he'd recognized Eleanor's longing as she'd gazed across the hills. She might repress her fiery spirit, but he knew its power. Her wildness called to him, just as the wild, magnificent landscape did.

"Miss Trim," he exclaimed, slamming to a standstill.

Strengthening light revealed one of those damned beguiling blushes. "Her ladyship lent it to me."

He told the reckless heart that always raced at the sight of her that Miss Trim in a scarlet riding habit was nothing extraordinary. "Those gray dresses are almost as much of an abomination as your hair."

The habit was old-fashioned. Of course it was. His mother hadn't been well enough to ride since Sophie's birth twenty years ago. But that didn't take anything away from the fetching ensemble.

"You're so rude." Self-consciously one leather-gloved hand touched the fiercely restrained hair. He winced to see it. She'd been extra severe this morning, as if to defy yesterday's criticism. A high-crowned beaver hat tied with a jaunty red scarf dangled from her other hand.

"You strike me as a woman who appreciates frankness," he said.

"Perhaps you should check whether I also appreciate a few kind lies," she snapped back.

Miss Trim had clearly started the day in a prickly mood. He must be completely insane to relish her peppery responses. He raised one hand and circled his finger, indicating for her to turn around.

She cast him a darkling look. "I may work for you, sir, but I'm an independent soul, not a doll."

"You and my dear mother are both rebels," he said wryly. "Indulge me."

Her sigh indicated impatience, but she cooperated with

a theatricality that made him want to laugh. His life was crammed with seriousness and purpose. Laughter wasn't a regular presence. Yet Miss Trim made him want to laugh— when he wasn't burning to haul her into his arms.

"Very becoming." In the beautifully tailored habit, she looked poised and elegant. She looked, he was shocked to see, like a woman of his own class.

How he'd love to banish every gray rag and adorn her in rich colors. Peacock blues. Emerald greens. Garnet reds. In his imagination, she dressed as the alluring woman she was.

Dear God, in his thoughts, he kitted Miss Trim out as his mistress. Heat shuddered through him at the forbidden idea. And somewhere, a terrible temptation stirred.

"Thank you," she said drily. "I don't need to learn to ride."

"You lost that argument yesterday."

Her lips firmed. "Only because you asked me in front of your mother."

This time he couldn't contain his amusement. "I've learned a few tricks from my years in politics."

She almost smiled. An almost smile from Miss Trim was more dazzling than the sun. "I'll have to be on my toes, I see."

She would indeed. Or she'd be on her back.

Luckily, he was saved from making that wish reality when a groom led out her pony. "Miss Trim, allow me to introduce one of nature's gentlemen, Snowflake."

At his name, the fat, white pony nodded his shaggy head. Miss Trim laughed. "I had nightmares about this. Snowflake isn't exactly what I imagined."

"I've decided to save the fire-breathing monster for tomorrow." Leath thanked the groom and took the reins. "Have you ever been on a horse?"

"No."

He regarded her searchingly. "You're not really fright-ened, are you?"

"No." She hesitated. "Maybe. Yes. A little."

"You're close to the ground on Snowflake."

"Easy for you to say."

He laughed again. "Do you need me to help you up?" Snowflake was too small for a woman of Eleanor's height, but Leath wanted her first ride to soothe her fears.

"I think I can manage."

Pity. His hands itched to circle that willowy waist.

Snowflake stood while Miss Trim settled gingerly on his back. Leath was surprised at her uncertainty. He'd believed her completely indomitable. This vulnerability was danger-ously appealing.

He passed her the reins and she grabbed them so hard that Snowflake whickered in protest. Knowing that contact was a mistake, Leath placed his hands over hers. "Gently."

"Sorry," she muttered and sat stiff as a board in the side-saddle as he checked her stirrup. She wore half boots, and when he twitched away the voluminous red skirts, a glimpse of white stocking crashed through him like a cannonball.

He stepped back. "How do you feel?"

She looked very unsure. "Like I'm sitting on a volcano that's about to erupt."

He snickered. "Old Snowflake is pushing twenty, Miss Trim. If he erupts, it will be into a mind-numbingly speedy stroll."

"That's scary enough."

"Courage. If you can face down a cranky marquess, this old pony is a doddle." He patted Snowflake, who looked half asleep—so much for Miss Trim's worries—and took the halter. "Are you ready?"

"No."

"You can't sit in the stable yard all morning."

"It's my first lesson."

"So start learning." Clicking his tongue to the somnolent horse, he moved forward.

"Oh, dear."

He glanced back. Miss Trim clutched the front of the saddle as though about to topple off. She looked utterly terrified.

"Deep breath."

"I think you should stop."

"I think you should let yourself fall into the rhythm of the horse."

"Please don't say 'fall.' "

He laughed again. Good God, at this rate, he'd be the life of the party once he got back to London. "Someone as graceful as you should have no trouble riding. Listen to your body."

Damn it, if she didn't want to hear "fall," he didn't want to hear "body." Teaching Miss Trim to ride was a risky enterprise. If only for her instructor.

Slowly he walked around the yard without looking back. He needed to get himself under control before he chanced another glimpse. When he finally did, he was pleased to see her sitting more naturally. "That's better."

"I still feel like I'm about to end up on the cobbles," she admitted, although she didn't look nearly so frozen.

"You'd have to jump. Snowflake's back is broader than most chairs."

"A horse armchair?"

He smiled, charmed, and wishing to Hades that he wasn't. "Precisely."

He led Snowflake around the yard again, then stood back to let Eleanor try on her own. As he'd expected, she quickly adapted to the horse's gait. A quick learner, Miss Trim. He knew that from working with her.

Inevitably, the idea of her being a quick learner here inclined his thoughts toward another kind of riding. With her mounted upon the Marquess of Leath rather than a fat, phlegmatic pony who hadn't accelerated past a trot in ten years. The sensual daydream of watching her undulate over his body occupied him to a point where he stopped watching.

"My lord?" She and Snowflake halted a few feet away.

"How was that?"

"I'm getting used to it."

"You'll come to like it."

"Perhaps." Although he was pleased to see her lean to pat Snowflake's white neck.

"Go around the yard again, if you please."

He smiled at her growing confidence. As for her riding something other than a horse? The wicked idea arose that where there was a will, there was a way. Surely one could avoid scandal, if one was careful. Perhaps he was too punctilious about protecting Miss Trim's virtue.

After all, she had a perfect right to say no to any offer.

Chapter Thirteen

"Sir Garth Burton to see you, my lord."

At Wells's announcement, Leath glanced up from the latest report from Derbyshire. Not that he concentrated with any purpose this morning. Miss Trim's presence—quiet, helpful, damnably tempting—at her desk made that impossible. The devil inside him kept whispering that if he invited her to his bed and she assented, the sin was hers.

"Garth Burton? Here?" he asked in surprise. Burton was among the few parliamentary colleagues whose support had never wavered, despite the scandals. But he lived in Wiltshire and Alloway Chase wasn't on the way to anywhere. This couldn't be a merely social call. What the devil was afoot? "Send him in."

Miss Trim had risen. "I'll leave you, sir."

A female secretary was unusual enough to cause comment, although unlike most of London's rattlepates, Burton knew how to keep his mouth shut. Still, perhaps it was best if his visitor didn't see her. But before he could respond,

Sir Garth was through the door, advancing with an enthusiastic lope and an extended hand.

"Leath, old fellow. It's been too long."

Leath returned the handshake with a warmth he didn't need to feign. "What are you doing in this neck of the woods? Yorkshire in October is an odd choice for a jaunt."

"Ah, thereby hangs a tale," Burton said, his eyes sparking with curiosity as they settled on Miss Trim.

"My secretary, Miss Eleanor Trim," Leath said drily. Eleanor dropped into a curtsy.

"Miss Trim," Burton said with a brief bow before shoving a satchel stuffed with papers at Leath. "Wellington sent me. The party's in chaos and if we're not careful the government will fall. He...*we* need your help."

"Mine?" Leath asked, wondering if the world had gone mad. At their last meeting, the prime minister had made him feel about as welcome as a cat at a mouse's birthday party. Without looking at Miss Trim, he knew that she watched him with an intensity that set the air crackling. He hoped like hell that Burton didn't notice.

"You're the only one with the imagination to save us from this blasted mess. Every attempt so far has only deepened the quarrel between the reformers and the voices of restraint."

"I'm recalled to London?" Leath asked, puzzled that he wasn't leaping about the room, cheering and ordering champagne. After all, this sojourn in the country was only ever meant as a temporary measure until the fuss over his uncle and Sophie blew over. His place was in Westminster steering the nation, not here mooning over his lovely secretary and counting the legs on his livestock.

A shadow crossed Burton's affable face. "No, not yet." He paused. "But I'm sure that your assistance will lead to reinstatement in the cabinet. Eventually."

Leath's smile was sardonic. Still, he wondered at the wave of relief sweeping through him that he needn't pack for an immediate return to the halls of power.

Sir Garth clearly mistook his silence for anger. "I'm sorry. I wish I had better news for you. You have no idea how we've missed you over the last weeks, especially with these damned rabble-rousers. Your good sense and deft touch would have nipped the trouble in the bud. If it was up to me, I'd be bundling you into a southbound coach right now."

"It's all right, Burton." And the strange truth was that it indeed was all right. "It's not your fault that I'm still persona non grata. Although I'm not sure what I can accomplish from this distance."

Burton looked almost as grateful to hear the composed response as Leath had felt when he'd realized that the man wasn't summoning him to the capital. "We need someone to find a solution that placates all involved."

"You've come a damned long way for a chat," Leath said tartly.

Burton laughed. "It's a devil of a problem. As you'll see when I give you the details."

The door opened and Wells directed the footmen to set up a meal. "My lord, I arranged a light repast as it's approaching noon and Sir Garth has been traveling. I hope that meets with your approval."

"It certainly meets with my approval, Wells," Burton said with the boyish grin that went a long way to hiding the sharp brain under his mop of ash-blond hair.

"Thank you, Wells," Leath said.

"I'll check on her ladyship, sir," Miss Trim said.

He stopped her with a wave of his hand. "No, I need you."

He had a sinking feeling that was no more than the truth. Perhaps he shouldn't be quite so glad that Burton's arrival didn't mean an immediate departure for London. Some distance from Miss Trim might remind him that he'd once been a sensible man.

To soften the command, he sent her a faint smile. "Please take notes." He turned to his colleague. "You'd better tell me everything. And don't waste time trying to place a positive gloss on it. I need to know just how much blood we have to mop up."

In the leafless woodland, early sun sparkled on the frosty grass as Nell guided her horse after Leath. She rode Adela, a sweet-natured chestnut mare who had replaced the stolid Snowflake as Nell became more proficient in the saddle. Ahead, his lordship sat astride a powerful black thoroughbred that looked ready to carry him to the gates of hell.

He'd been particularly quiet this morning. She assumed he brooded over his continuing exile from London. Yesterday's mail had detailed the successful results of his meeting with Sir Garth Burton last week. She wasn't surprised that Leath had rescued the government from disaster. But as she'd worked with the two men until after midnight, she'd found herself awash in admiration for Leath's tireless dedication and ability to follow a winding path to a solution that nobody had considered. Sir Garth had left the following morning, expressing frank disgust at a government that excluded a talent like Leath, whatever scandals darkened his name.

Leath must feel exactly the same. Her suggestion that he should stay in Yorkshire seemed even more inane than ever, now she'd seen him exercising his political skills at full stretch. Instead of using his remarkable qualities to guide the kingdom to greatness, he was stuck here teaching a servant how to ride at a sedate trot. If she was his lordship, she'd feel like punching something.

These morning rides had become a fixture. It seemed silly to look back and remember how old Snowflake had intimidated her. His lordship must have thought her a lily-livered creature.

He'd been a patient, kind, effective teacher. If the marquess had deliberately set out to prove he wasn't a villain, he couldn't have done a better job. She wasn't sure how Dorothy had come to accuse him, but Nell found it increasingly impossible to ignore the evidence of her eyes. And heart. She couldn't believe that the man who put up with her clumsiness as a beginner rider could so callously ruin a young girl. Somewhere someone had made a mistake. She didn't yet understand how, but she was convinced that in time she would.

No rapacious seducer would miss an opportunity to work his wiles. Yet while Leath had touched her a hundred times to set her right in the saddle, he'd never exceeded proprieties.

The shameful, inescapable truth was that she wished he had.

He drew his horse to a halt and turned to study her with a somber expression. She stopped Adela and spoke impulsively. "My lord, something's worrying you. Can I help?"

"Now there's a question." After a bristling silence, rarer over the last days, he spoke as though raising a matter of cosmic importance. "Yes, Miss Trim, you can. Whether you will or not is another issue."

Baffled, she watched him dismount with the powerful smoothness that invested all his movements. He crossed to help her from her horse. Today, for the first time, his hands lingered at her waist, and he only released her when she stepped away. Her skin tingled from his touch. When she bumped nervously into her horse, Adela whickered in protest and shifted.

Nell waited for Leath to retreat. Since he'd kissed her, he'd been careful not to frighten her. But he stood breathing unsteadily, staring at her as if wrestling with some massive dilemma. Her misgivings grew. He usually concealed his inner demons.

His great height and heavily muscled body trapped her against her horse. She was close enough to catch his masculine sandalwood scent, always evocative.

She stared into Leath's face and wondered with a mixture of trepidation and wicked excitement whether this turmoil meant he might kiss her. Something had stirred him up. His eyes glittered. His hands opened and closed at his sides.

"My lord?" Her chin tilted with reckless defiance. She ached for more kisses, whatever that said about her morals or her brains.

To her chagrin, he stepped away to gather the horses' reins. He led them to the edge of the clearing where they began to nose at the grass.

Turning back to Nell, he folded his arms across his impressive chest. "I have a proposition, Miss Trim."

Ah. She could guess what this was about. More disappointment soured her belly. Stupidly, briefly, she wished that he was a heartless seducer. At least a heartless seducer wouldn't leave her yearning. "You want me to continue as your secretary until Mr. Crane returns."

He looked surprised and a little put out. She couldn't imagine why when he'd given her the position because he thought she was clever. Even if now, with her heart only slowly resuming its rhythm, she didn't feel clever. She felt like just another silly girl in thrall to a man who would do her no good.

"Well, yes."

She perched on a convenient tree stump, resting her

hat on her lap. "You haven't done anything about finding a replacement, have you?"

"No." He approached her with that long stride that claimed ownership of the earth beneath his feet. Of course, here on the vast Alloway Chase estate, he did own the earth beneath his feet. A timely reminder of the vast gulf in status separating them.

"If her ladyship agrees, of course I'll help." She chanced a smile. "Especially after you've taken all this trouble to teach me to ride."

Without smiling, he stopped a few feet away. "You were a good pupil. And I enjoy our morning rides."

"So do I," she admitted. "There's no need to train someone else when it's only for another month or so. Mr. Crane tells me that the doctor is pleased with his progress."

Leath's brows lowered in the ferocious frown that had once terrified her. "You've seen him?"

"Of course."

Leath flicked his crop against one long muscular thigh. Snap. Snap. Snap. "In his rooms?"

She'd had some odd conversations with the marquess, but this one verged on the bizarre. "He's not supposed to wander around the house."

"I don't want you there."

She stiffened. "You imagine I make a habit of invading men's chambers to molest them?"

His jaw set at her reference to the night he'd kissed her. "I don't want you alone with Crane."

"Nothing untoward has happened." She resented her need to defend herself, although Leath was within his rights to doubt her intentions. "He's bored to distraction. I read aloud and write letters for him and try to ease his idle hours."

"If you're easing anyone's idle hours, choose me," he growled.

"You don't have any idle hours," she said, wondering at his reaction to her visits to Mr. Crane. The secretary had a small apartment on the second floor. She hadn't ventured beyond his sitting room. Looking at Leath, she decided that he wasn't likely to appreciate the distinction.

"Perhaps that should change." Leath stared at her meaningfully. Except that Nell had no idea what meaning he wanted to convey.

She tried to ignore how handsome he was. She'd always thought him striking, but these days, she saw so much character and intelligence, that he was the most remarkable man she'd ever met. She had a sinking feeling that any man she met after she left Alloway Chase would feel second-rate.

"Are you asking me to work longer hours so you can take more leisure time?"

His laugh held an acerbic note. "That's not what I'm asking. And while your innocence does you credit, it makes me feel like a satyr."

Oh, dear Lord in heaven…

Nell rose on watery legs and stumbled back. "This isn't about work, is it?"

"No."

"You're asking me…"

It was a novelty to see self-assured James Fairbrother look awkward. He shifted on his feet, then drew up to his impressive height and glared as if about to order her to write a complicated report. "I'm asking you to become my mistress, Miss Trim."

From the moment he'd mentioned her innocence, she'd guessed what was coming. Still the blunt words shocked her.

Her hat tumbled from nerveless fingers and she regarded him unblinkingly.

When she didn't respond, he ground his teeth. "You'd like to send me to the devil, I can see."

She swallowed to moisten a mouth dry with trepidation. "But you want to avoid scandal. It's why you're in Yorkshire."

He gripped his crop in front of him with both hands so hard that surely it must break. "I haven't reached my decision lightly."

"I can imagine." She whirled away and stared blindly into the trees. Nothing in the world felt stable anymore. This was like standing in the middle of an earthquake.

He went on more urgently. "I'll find you a house in a place where nobody knows us. Somewhere like Scarborough or Beverley. Somewhere within a few hours' ride so I can visit regularly."

"I'd leave Alloway Chase?"

Strangely she wasn't appalled at his offer, although she should be. After all, she'd been raised to keep herself chaste before marriage and she had Dorothy's sad example to deter any wayward impulses.

"Yes."

She turned. "I love it here."

His expression softened, but he still looked like he faced a firing squad. "There really would be a scandal if the world learned that I debauched my mother's companion in my mother's home."

"I...see," she said slowly. And she did. "So I'm to become a dirty little secret?"

He winced. "I've offended you."

Nervously she fiddled with a button. "Not as much as you should have," she confessed. When he stepped forward, she raised a hand to stop him. "You don't seem overjoyed at the idea of my ruin."

He looked troubled. "I'm not overjoyed."

"Oh," she said, stung.

He made an impatient sound deep in his throat and gestured with one large gloved hand. "I'm making a cursed muddle of this, aren't I?"

She linked her hands together at her waist to stop them trembling. "You're not…you're not displaying your usual aplomb."

He sighed and approached, this time ignoring her warning look. He untangled her right hand from her left and held it. "I've never asked a virtuous woman to sleep with me before."

Astonishment held her motionless, even as warmth radiated up her arm then down to her heart. "Never?"

His eyes lit with the wry humor that she found so appealing. "I won't lie and say I've never approached a woman, but they weren't virtuous."

"I'm sure."

However dangerous, she left her hand in his. They both wore gloves. The touch shouldn't be as powerful as it was, but her heart thudded like a drum. His clumsiness was endearing. So endearing that she couldn't quite summon a refusal.

His grip tightened. "You must know how much I want you."

She licked her lips and despite the dictates of common sense, couldn't help relishing his groan. "No, I don't think I do." She paused. "You know, this offer might be better couched with a few kisses."

His lips twisted with self-derision. "I don't want you making rash decisions."

"You think your kisses make me silly?"

His low laugh vibrated through her bones in a most disconcerting way. "Your kisses definitely make me silly."

Startled, she stared at him. "Really?"

"Really." He took her other hand. "You have no idea the trouble I've had concentrating on the irrelevancies from London. Who cares about the fate of the nation when I could be holding you in my arms?"

She'd had no idea. "My lord..."

"In the circumstances you should call me James."

Absurdly that unsettled her more than the invitation to his bed. "I don't think I could."

"You're a strange creature," he said softly and at last did what she'd wanted him to do since she'd left his bedroom. His lips skimmed hers with a sweetness that drizzled through her like honey.

She blinked up at him, dazed. "If you keep kissing me, I won't deny you."

To her regret, he released her. "You need to think about consequences."

She frowned. "If I think, I'll say no."

Desperation flashed in his silvery eyes. Wonder rushed through her. She'd never imagined that she could make the great marquess desperate. "You may never marry if you give yourself to me."

"There's nobody I want to marry."

He shook his head at her quick reply. "That doesn't mean that there won't be. I don't want you regretting your decision."

Feeling a sudden chill, she folded her arms. "If you keep talking, you'll convince me that this is the worst idea I've ever heard."

His lips quirked, although his amusement was sour. "It may well be."

"Then why suggest it?" she asked tartly.

"Because the thought of you torments my every hour. Because I must have you or go mad."

That was better. He spoke the words as prosaically as if he discussed a cattle sale, but his intense expression proved his sincerity. He gestured for her to return to her tree stump. "Sit down and hear me out. You need to know what you're getting into."

"Your bed, presumably," she retorted, before reminding herself that it wasn't wise to taunt him.

"I hope so," he said fervently and she covered her hot cheeks with her hands. It gradually dawned on her that this man could be her lover. If she became his mistress, she'd embark upon a life radically different from anything she'd planned. She hardly knew how she felt. If she was truly virtuous, she'd be furious.

She wasn't furious. She was…intrigued.

He stood a few feet away, watching her unwaveringly as she sat. "I'm a rich man and I'll treat you well. You'll want for nothing and any gifts are yours forever."

What he bought her might be hers forever. He however wouldn't be hers forever. He didn't need to say it. Even in the backwaters of Kent, people knew how such arrangements worked. She and Leath would stay together until he lost interest, then they would part.

Nell's rising bubble of excitement burst, leaving her flat and bitter. What was she doing, considering this? She was a girl from a respectable family, not a courtesan. Could she bear to give herself to a man, knowing that he'd cast her aside the moment he tired of her? A nobleman of Leath's standing might offer a woman of her humble background carte blanche. He'd never offer her marriage.

The question boiled down to whether she wanted the

marquess enough to abandon all hope of a conventional future. Because there was no chance on God's earth for a conventional future with Leath.

She was much like any woman. She might have waited to marry while Dorothy grew up, but she wanted a husband and children and a home of her own. Security. *Love...*

For reasons that she refused to examine, the admission that she wanted love jammed a lump the size of Canterbury Cathedral in her throat. She'd been blessed with love. Her father, her mother, her stepfather, her half-sister. Although only her stepfather remained this side of heaven.

If she became Leath's mistress, she'd have to cut herself off from William Simpson. He'd never forgive her fall. It had been bad enough witnessing his grief and humiliation over Dorothy.

She couldn't do this. No matter how she yearned.

Still Leath explained the business of being a mistress. Would her choice be different if he'd been unprincipled enough to kiss her into a melting puddle of surrender?

"I'll put the house in your name. And buy you a carriage and horses. You'll have a fashionable wardrobe." He paused. "I forbid any gray."

Nell was too troubled to respond to his teasing. Who knew it was so hard to turn away from the primrose path? But of course, standing squarely on this particular primrose path was a handsome man who made her blood sing.

When she didn't speak, he went on. "And an extravagant allowance."

She needed to say something. The longer he spoke, the more he'd think that she favored his proposition. Strangely, the possibility of facing Dorothy's fate hadn't entered into her thinking. Now it did. "What about children?"

His gray eyes were shadowed and he began to snap the

crop against his thigh again. "I'll make generous provision for offspring, but don't mistake me, life is tough for bastards. Even someone as highly placed as the Duke of Sedgemoor suffers because of questions about his legitimacy."

Her eyes sharpened. "Do you have any offspring?"

"No." His smile was rueful. "I've always been chary of scandal. The irony is that having worked so hard to keep my good reputation, my uncle and sister went ahead and tainted the family name. I may as well have played the libertine."

Once she'd have thought that he lied. Once she'd believed him a debaucher of the vilest sort. No longer. Still she was astonished to hear herself speak the truth. "My half-sister Dorothy died in childbirth after her seducer deserted her."

She'd reached a point where she knew he wouldn't recognize Dorothy's name or fate. Instead his gaze darkened with compassion. Her heart, which insisted she ignore her head's dictates, squashed into a messy little lump of goo. He dropped his whip and kneeled beside her, wrapping her in his arms. "Eleanor, I'm so sorry."

He'd touched her more often than he should. He'd held her in desire. But this felt different, as though he cocooned her in a blanket to keep her safe. Since her mother's death, nobody had held her purely for comfort. In her family, she was the strong one.

For one forbidden moment, she leaned into Leath. He was warm and smelled like heaven. If heaven smelled like horses and sandalwood. Only as she relinquished the burdens of duty and vengeance and virtue did she realize how tired she was.

Right now if Leath offered to keep her in his arms forever, she'd say yes. Just for the privilege of nestling her head in this wonderful hollow between his neck and his shoulder that seemed created for her.

She allowed herself a few seconds of blessed ease before straightening. The temptation to stay was too overwhelming.

He withdrew and leveled a searching gaze upon her. "You haven't answered me." His voice lowered to the deep velvety tones that lured her even when she wasn't in his arms. "My lovely Eleanor, will you share my bed? I promise you pleasure and respect and comfort." He paused. "And joy and friendship."

She gave a choked laugh and realized that her eyes were wet. She was such a mess, she hadn't realized that she was crying. "I'm not sure whether I should be honored or whether I should slap your face."

"You can slap me all you want if you say yes."

She needed to escape his drugging nearness. She shifted and he, perceptive as always, let her go.

"That's a powerful incentive to consent."

He stood and stepped away. The hunger in his eyes made her wish that she could give another answer. Or that she wasn't used to thinking ahead and making plans and counting consequences.

"You're not going to agree, are you?" He bent to retrieve his crop.

For one blazing minute, she wondered whether she could throw her bonnet over a windmill. The marquess didn't offer everything, but he offered a lot. She didn't care about the worldly rewards, although she appreciated that he wanted to look after her. She did care about the friendship and the joy. And the pleasure. Even in her inexperience, her body heated at the idea of lying beneath him.

She scooped up her hat and stood. This riding habit was the most beautiful dress she'd ever worn, but it was borrowed. It was made for a lady, and she was a pretender.

She needed to remember that she was a temporary

visitor to this world. All this fraternizing with the aristocracy turned her a little insane. Nell Trim belonged at the shabby schoolhouse in Mearsall.

The dose of reality should bolster her will. But these days, her will was sadly weak. Perhaps she'd feel stronger once she no longer looked at this magnificent man and imagined him her lover.

She raised her chin. "Thank you for asking. Thank you for being so frank." She saw that he already knew what she'd say. "Despite the appeal—and the offer is appealing—I can't accept."

She waited for him to argue. Or worse, because she knew she couldn't resist, convince her through kisses. He might claim that he spent his time buried in political work, but when he touched her, she recognized a man who knew what he was doing. He must guess how powerfully he drew her and what little he needed to do to persuade her into his bed.

"Very well." He turned and caught the horses. "We should return to the house. I want to check the geologist's report for the Derbyshire property."

Amazed, Nell waited as he led her horse across. "That's all?"

His smile was bleak. "I offered. You declined. We'll say no more."

Hardly believing that he'd taken his rejection so calmly, she let him toss her up into the saddle. No lingering at her waist now. He was all business.

When she sat on Adela, his smile became more natural. He gathered her reins and curled her fingers around them. "I won't make life difficult because you refused, Miss Trim."

Miss Trim, she noticed, not Eleanor. Her heart ached at the change, although Miss Trim was much more likely to hold out against his attractions.

"That's very...forbearing," she said unsteadily.

He mounted his black stallion and turned back the way they'd come. The chestnut followed purely through her own devices. Nell wasn't capable of putting two thoughts together.

"I'll survive my disappointment."

Nell wasn't sure she could. Wicked, wicked girl she was. But as she trailed behind the handsome lord on his devil horse, she couldn't help wondering if perhaps, despite every prudent reason for denying him, she'd made a terrible mistake.

Chapter Fourteen

It turned out that Leath was a man of his word—of course he was; Nell already knew that. He became all business and made no further reference to houses in Scarborough or banishing her gray dresses. The only change in her routine was an end to their morning rides.

Nell told herself that only a wanton creature would mind that he so coolly accepted her refusal.

Clearly she was a wanton creature.

While her denial left Leath unaffected, she couldn't stop thinking about becoming his mistress. She had a hundred good reasons for saying no. Good reasons wilted to nothing compared to her attraction to the marquess.

She'd relinquished her suspicions about Leath and he'd stopped watching her as if expecting her to steal the silver. Thank goodness he never mentioned her supposed infatuation. Although with every day, that desperate confession shifted from self-serving lie to discomfiting reality.

Never before had she been obsessed with a man. Nell had always been too busy mothering Dorothy and caring for her stepfather to indulge in romantic nonsense. Now romantic nonsense gained an unbreakable hold. Leath's company produced a queasy mixture of exhilaration and embarrassment. Instead of a responsible woman of twenty-five, Nell felt like a silly, overemotional adolescent.

She should be grateful that Leath didn't sulk, but the giddy girl inside her resented his distance. Distance that made her cry into her pillow each night and struggle against the urge to rail at him each day. And every hour brought Mr. Crane's return closer. Soon Nell would only see the marquess when he visited his mother.

Far safer for her wayward heart if she returned to Kent. She hadn't come to Yorkshire to pursue a lifelong career as a domestic servant. She'd arrived on a quest that had taken so many turns since that she hardly remembered where she'd started.

She stayed.

Because she couldn't bear to leave.

Nell was adding some figures three weeks after Leath's curiously prosaic invitation to ruin when he strode in from his morning gallop. Despite a return to inhospitable weather, he'd taken to long rides each dawn on the devil horse. Today the wind howled against the windows, and the fire blazing in the hearth did little to dispel the chill.

Or perhaps Nell's coldness came from within.

She supposed for a punishing rider like his lordship, dawdling along with a beginner must count as the height of boredom. It said much for his good manners that she'd never felt his impatience.

"Good morning, my lord," she said dutifully, rising and curtsying.

"Good morning, Miss Trim," he said as if he'd never

touched her and kissed her and asked her to become his lover. Without facing her directly, he glanced across the papers and packets littering his desk. "Ah, the mail is in. Capital."

She was foolish to mourn his lack of attention, but still regret stabbed her. As he lifted a large package, she glumly returned to work. He never let her touch his correspondence until he'd sorted it. "One for me, I think."

It was all for him, she wanted to point out. Sexual frustration and lack of sleep turned her mood acidic, not that he deigned to notice. Last night, she'd lain awake into the small hours, wondering whether to leave. Or sneak out of her room and run down the miles of corridor to Leath's apartments.

Only his scant recent interest in her had kept her chastely tucked up in her lonely bed. Wretched. Longing. Confused.

She bent her head, trying to ignore the marquess as he settled behind his large desk. Eventually, she stopped fighting and glanced up.

The cold gray light shone starkly on him, highlighting his thick black hair, damp from his rainy ride, and the aristocratic, commanding features. If only James Fairbrother wasn't so handsome. But she'd long ago realized that more than his looks attracted her. She admired his intellect and humor, and the deep streak of kindness beneath his occasionally forbidding exterior. Working with Leath had taught her more about the world than she'd ever imagined in quiet little Mearsall, despite her stepfather's scholarly interests. Until she'd met the marquess, she'd had no idea of the complexities of the nation or the personalities behind the power.

She frowned at his lordship's air of suppressed excitement. "Good news, sir?" she asked, before remembering that she'd do better to keep her mouth shut.

"Yes." He gave her his first proper smile since their conversation in the clearing. "Come here, Miss Trim."

He never called her Eleanor now. Nor had he renewed his invitation to call him James. Of course not. They were back to master and servant.

Obediently she rose and stepped in front of his desk. "Yes, my lord?"

"Please sit down."

Worried, she drew a chair forward and sat. Had she done something wrong?

"This is for you," he said with the secret smile that always heated her blood.

She needed to catch her breath before she took the packet contained inside the first one. She frowned. "What is it?"

"See." His lordship leaned back in his chair. The smile now flirted with his eyes. Whatever this was, it gave him pleasure.

Puzzled, disturbed—the marquess in a fine mood was perilously appealing—she inspected the packet. It was heavy and marked with official seals. The wrapping was ragged and stained and looked like it had been through a war.

She squinted to decipher the faded writing. Astonishment flooded her. She raised her eyes to find Leath observing her with a tenderness that sliced through her heart. When he was distant, she could barely resist him. When he treated her as though he cared for her happiness, she was sunk.

Except that he didn't have to tell her that he'd gone to considerable trouble to place this particular object in her hands. And he'd done it because he cared.

"It's my father's war record," she forced out in a choked voice.

"It is."

"You found it. After all this time." She gulped to dislodge the emotion damming her throat. Her hands crushed the brown paper. "How?"

He shrugged. "I pulled a few strings, asked the right questions, spoke sternly to a few dullards who were unacceptably slow to respond."

She knew enough about the War Office's labyrinthine processes to recognize his modesty. He must have pursued this issue to the ends of the earth. "Where . . . where did they find everything?"

"In some dusty corner of Whitehall, misfiled with old military ordinances."

She blinked, telling herself she wouldn't cry. "You don't know how much this means to me."

"I can guess." Regret clouded his steel-gray eyes. "I'm sorry that it arrives too late to be any use to your mother."

"Perhaps she should have enlisted the help of the marvelous Marquess of Leath," Nell said, attempting lightness, but sincerity thickened her voice. Because what he'd done *was* marvelous. The most marvelous thing that anyone had ever done for her. Probably the most marvelous thing that anyone would ever do for her.

Her praise made him uncomfortable. "It was nothing, Miss Trim."

It was everything. "Thank you."

He smiled. "Won't you open it? I gather from my contacts that your father has a proud record."

"Yes." She placed the packet on her lap, smoothing where she'd crinkled it in her excess of gratitude.

He stood and moved around the desk. "Ah. You'd like a moment's privacy."

She did. She had an awful feeling that if the marquess stayed, she'd fling herself into his arms. "I'll go to my room."

"No need." He bowed as though she was his equal and left.

Clumsily Nell opened the package and spilled the contents onto the desk. Official-looking documents listing her father's deployments. A tangle of glinting medals, proving her mother's stories of Robert Trim's heroism. And, most precious of all, a bundle of her mother's letters. The sight of that elegant, slanting writing made her heart clench with love and grief.

She should wait to read them. She was supposed to be working, and the marquess had been considerate enough to grant her this time alone. But she couldn't resist opening the top letter. She'd look at one, then pack everything away to examine at leisure.

"Miss Trim!"

Blearily she looked up from the last letter, written after her father's death but before her mother learned of his fate. Nell had been the first to break the seal. The love and trust in her mother's words had split her heart. Like the other letters that her father had clearly read and re-read, it was full of daily details of Mearsall life, including fond descriptions of young Nell. It was like having her mother whispering in her ear.

"My lord..." She struggled to rise, clutching the poignant letter. "I'm sorry I've taken so long."

"For God's sake, there's no need to apologize," he said gruffly.

"I should have waited." She set the letter on the desk with the others, and wiped her eyes. She'd told herself not to cry, and she'd been crying like a drain for the last hour.

"No," he said.

"I'm ready to work now," she said faintly, fumbling in her pocket for a handkerchief. "After you did this wonderful thing, I mustn't inconvenience you."

"Damn it—" He bit off whatever he'd meant to say and seized her in his arms. "I hate to see you cry."

"I'll stop," she said, eyes overflowing.

"Miss Trim…" His grip tightened and he drew her against his chest. Immediate warmth and security surrounded her.

"I shouldn't give in to my feelings," she mumbled into the white front of his shirt.

He settled her more firmly. "Don't be a goose."

His rough affection was her undoing and she started to sob in earnest. She'd always recognized the tragedy that her parents had loved each other so deeply and had lost each other too soon. But those brave letters revived her sorrow with the added sharpness that now, as a woman, she knew the pain of loss in a way that her childhood self hadn't.

She had no idea how long she cried, but eventually the edge of her reaction blunted. She realized that she rested against Leath on the couch near the fire. She sucked in a shuddering breath and sat up, or at least tried to.

"I'm sorry," she muttered, too embarrassed to look at him.

"Dear Lord, Eleanor, you break my heart," he growled and drew her close once more.

Hearing him call her Eleanor devastated what little composure she'd gathered. But this time as she wept, he was more than a purely comforting presence. This time, she was aware of his clean masculine smell, the broad, powerful chest beneath her cheek, and the strong arms holding her.

When she realized that her hands ran up and down his back in a way that had little to do with solace, she stiffened and drew away. This time he released her. She slid back to establish some space between them.

He watched her with an unreadable expression before his mouth quirked with characteristic humor. "Should I risk telling you that the War Office is sending his belongings? They should be here within the week."

Nell wiped her eyes again and gave a choked laugh. "You'd be a brave man to chance that, my lord." And caught a flash of disappointment at her use of the formal address.

Shock shuddered through her. She'd been so wrong. So very, very wrong. Leath's desire hadn't died. He hadn't forgotten kissing her or asking her to be his mistress.

Thrilled, uncertain, she met the hunger blazing in his eyes.

"Don't think it," he said flatly.

"I don't—"

"Yes, you do." His expression hardened. "You owe me nothing. I started the process of finding your father's medals long before I asked you to become my lover."

Before she could remind herself that touching him was dangerous, she took his hand. "I'm sorry. And so grateful."

He frowned and she waited for him to retreat, but he turned his hand over and laced their fingers together. This contact of skin on skin grounded her in a way that nothing else had in these last weeks. "I don't want your gratitude."

She bit her lip, wanting to tell him that she'd be his mistress, seeing only ruin and heartbreak ahead if she did.

With a muttered expletive, he released her. "Don't look at me like that, my girl, as if you've no idea what I'm talking about." He stood and stalked toward the window, keeping his back to her. "You know exactly what I want from you, and bloody gratitude has absolutely nothing to do with it."

Tonbridge, Kent, November

Greengrass slammed into his room at the King's Head and in disgust flung the day's pitiful pickings onto the deal table beneath the window. The coins' clatter was nowhere near as satisfying as it had been in Taunton.

He was running out of fresh territories. No matter how desperate they were, the women he'd threatened six months ago lacked ready money for a second round of blackmail. The buzz of recent sexual satisfaction warmed his blood—they still had something to offer—but cash proved harder to get.

He tugged the diary from his coat—he wasn't fool enough to leave it lying around—and tossed it on top of his takings. Perhaps the time had come to catch the fat pigeon he'd been holding in store. The proud and noble Marquess of Leath would surely pay good brass to keep this family scandal under wraps.

Greengrass had waited to pluck this particular bird because it would only come to his hand once. Now the prospect of this final haul off the diary, and a rich one at that, made his fleshy lips spread in a gloating smile.

Chapter Fifteen

Leath rode toward the river with Miss Trim trailing behind on her chestnut. They were on their way to one of the most isolated farms on his domain. The afternoon was gray and stormy, befitting his cantankerous humor. It was sheer hell wanting a woman who didn't want you.

Except he'd lay money that Eleanor did want him. He'd glimpsed enough longing looks when she thought he didn't notice to realize that he wasn't the only one suffering a bad case of frustration.

He understood why she'd said no. She wasn't a woman to give herself lightly. He'd been a cad to ask her. Her refusal, while a blow, had been expected. Eleanor Trim deserved better than to become some rich man's toy. Even if this particular rich man felt like his yen for his mother's companion was the most serious issue in a life dedicated to serious issues.

Long hours near Miss Trim without touching her counted as torture. But despite the excruciating deprivation, he wasn't looking forward to Crane's return.

Poor Crane. At this rate, Leath would push him off another horse just to enjoy Miss Trim's company for an extra month or two.

So low had the Marquess of Leath fallen.

He hadn't fallen quite as low as he might. Every night, he lay restless in his huge bed and imagined slamming into the library the next morning and sweeping Eleanor into his arms and kissing her until she couldn't spell the word "no."

Then the sun would rise and he'd remember that while he wanted Miss Trim, he also liked and respected her. Once, the threat of scandal would have deterred him. Now inconvenient fondness held him back from testing his rusty seductive wiles. So instead of snatching what he wanted, he would set out on another headlong gallop across the moors, hoping against hope that fresh air and speed would make him feel better.

An utterly futile endeavor.

The depth of empathy he felt for Miss Trim was more terrifying than his rapacious desire. After all, he was a man and she was a beautiful girl. He'd be unnatural not to want her. But he only had to recall his reaction when she'd sobbed over her father's war records to know that more happened here than a physical itch. That day, he'd wanted to hold her forever and give her everything she wanted. The overwhelming drive to protect her had left him reeling.

That overwhelming drive was more dangerous than desire. Even when desire flung him to the brink of madness.

At the riverbank, he reined in his horse and turned back to Miss Trim. She looked tired and downcast. The troublesome sexual awareness between them played on her nerves too.

"Be careful. The bank is chancy and the river is swollen after the rain."

"Yes, sir," she responded in a subdued voice.

She'd been quiet since she'd cried in his arms. Perhaps his

confession that he wanted more than gratitude had frightened her. He really should send her away. Neither of them could find peace while they were together.

But the thought of losing Nell made him want to howl denial. Seeing her was agonizing. Not seeing her would be worse. His London cronies always said Lord Leath reserved his passion for politics. How they'd laugh to see him now.

A shout from beyond the river bend pierced his brooding. This part of the moors was miles from the nearest habitation, usually home to only birds and the wind.

Despite the mucky ground, he spurred his horse into a gallop. Behind him, he heard Nell urge her mare to follow.

Two boys stood on the bank calling to another boy who was flailing in the river. Leath immediately recognized them. The Murray children, at that troublesome age where they were convinced of their immortality. The lad in the water was Will Murray, ten years old and as full of mischief as a monkey.

"Hold my horse." Leath leaped from the saddle and rushed forward, flinging away his constricting coat. He didn't bother to check whether Miss Trim obeyed. He trusted that she would.

Will went under as he was swept downstream. "Help!" he shouted, surfacing. "Help me!"

"Don't you dare set foot in this river," Leath snapped to Will's brothers.

When he dived into the flood, the cold turned every muscle rigid. Leath was a strong swimmer, but the water's power appalled him. Ahead, Will sank again. It felt like hours before the boy bobbed up.

Leath fought the current to stay in place. He couldn't make headway against it, but as luck had it, the flow pushed the boy toward him.

He grabbed for the lad, but missed. Next time, he caught the young ruffian. His hand curled hard around the linen collar and he wrenched the boy into his body. Will was so terrified that he fought Leath's hold.

"Stop it." Leath struggled for a tone of effortless command. Icy water splashed his face and he found himself propelled along, helpless as a twig.

Will's glazed eyes met his and Leath saw that the boy was so panicked, he didn't realize that help had arrived. Leath's grip tightened as he struggled to stay afloat. "Listen to me, Will Murray. Neither of us is going to drown today so you'd better damn well do what I say."

This time, despite the roar of the water, Leath's authority registered. Reason seeped into the boy's gaze. "My lord!"

"Lie still and let me take you in to shore."

"Yes, my lord," he gasped.

Leath caught Will under the chin and swam crosswise toward the bank. When in London, he regularly rode out to Hampstead Heath to swim and now he was grateful that he had. Even with Will's cooperation, progress was tough. The river's force was lethal. Using the current to power his sidestroke, he struggled to keep their heads above water.

Eventually the flood washed them into a quieter loop. Leath stumbled to his feet to receive a joyful welcome from Will's brothers and Miss Trim, who waded in and slid her shoulder under his arm. With her support, he staggered toward the bank. Behind him, the boys lugged Will to dry land.

The whole incident was over in minutes, but Leath felt as if he'd gone ten rounds in the boxing ring. The water was littered with debris and he could swear that a forest of logs had slammed him. He sucked in painful gusts of air and tightened his hold around Nell's shoulders.

"I'm too heavy," he grunted. Talking tested his strength.

"Nonsense. Can you get up the bank?"

"Yes," he said, not sure he could. But with her help, he managed to crawl onto the grass. Gasping, he collapsed.

"Are you all right?" She rested her hand on his heaving shoulder as he battled to fill his lungs. Even in his extremity, that touch seared through the wet shirt.

"Yes," he said, wanting to say more but unable to summon breath.

"Stay there."

"You're so . . . high-handed," he managed to force out.

Her grip on his shoulder firmed in encouragement. "If you can be rude, you'll live, my lord."

Choking on a broken laugh, he lay like a stranded fish while she approached the boys. Will seemed in better case than his rescuer. At least he had the strength to sit up, although he was pale and shivering.

Miss Trim spoke to the brothers before she helped Will toward Adela. She'd had the sense to lead the horses to where he and Will had washed ashore.

Leath struggled to his knees. He wasn't sure if he could stand, confound it. He was bruised from the pummeling, but at least breathing no longer hurt. The problem was that as pain faded, chill struck deeper. On dry land, it might be late autumn. In the Alloway River, it was Arctic winter.

"Give him my coat." He was appalled at how hoarse he sounded.

"You'll be cold," she said.

Every second, strength returned. "I'll get by."

She looked dubious, then when she saw how Will shivered, she nodded. Most people jumped at Leath's slightest word, but not Eleanor Trim. "Once Will's safely home, my lord, I'll return for you."

He'd recovered enough to notice the way she regarded him. His hard-won breath jammed in his lungs. He'd never seen that expression before. Her large eyes glowed and a flush brightened her cheeks. Perhaps the biting wind whipped up her color. But the smile flirting with her lips made his heart, only just settling, kick up and race as it had raced when he'd fought the river.

Eleanor turned away before he identified what lay in her eyes. She helped Will into Leath's coat which she'd tied to his saddle. The boy looked so woebegone in the voluminous black folds that Leath hid a smile. Hopefully today's fright taught young Master Will a lesson about recklessness, although given what he knew of the lad, he had his doubts.

Using a fallen branch as a mounting block, Nell scrambled into her saddle. She reached down to help Will up behind her.

Battling to hide how much effort it took to move, Leath crossed to the heavily laden mount and caught the bridle. "I'll meet you at the Murray farm."

"Shouldn't you go home and find some dry clothes?"

Presumptuous wench. His lips twitched. "I want to make sure Will suffers no ill effects from his dip."

He passed the reins to her and inadvertently or deliberately her hand brushed his as she took them. Bizarre that he was freezing, yet that subtle touch blasted him with heat.

She stared hard at him, her eyes conveying some message that he couldn't read. "My lord?"

"What is it?"

The smile flirting with her lips broadened into something glorious. "The answer is yes."

Chapter Sixteen

Surely Will, plastered to her back as she galloped toward the Murray farm, must hear her heart pounding. Despite the marquess's coat, the boy was wet and cold, yet Nell felt like a huge fire burned inside her. A fire bright enough to light her whole life.

Watching Leath unhesitatingly risk his life in a raging river to save a lad with more spirit than sense, she'd recognized all her havering as the victory of fear over desire.

Nobody would ever compare to James Fairbrother. Despite Dorothy's example, despite her stepfather's moral strictures, despite her own sense of self-preservation, she couldn't relinquish the chance to know this extraordinary man in every way possible. Eleanor Trim was about to become a marquess's mistress. And she couldn't summon a shred of regret. Instead, that fluttery, new sensation under her ribs felt like happiness.

She'd meant to wait, to tell Leath her decision when they were alone, but she'd looked into his exhausted, austere, beautiful face and found herself unable to hold back.

As she'd expected from a man so perceptive, one word was enough. She'd seen the flare of joy in his eyes and her heart had leaped like a salmon up a river.

Somewhere she'd fallen in love with his lordship. Perhaps when he'd been so kind to his mother. Perhaps with his kisses. Even if Nell hadn't already loved him, she'd be halfway there after he found her father's effects.

So much had made no sense, until she'd watched Leath dive into the flood and realized that if he died, she didn't want to live.

If Leath were a simple, ordinary man, she'd marry him, bear his children, build a long and fulfilled life together. But he was no simple, ordinary man. If she surrendered to this complex, gifted creature, she couldn't expect a conventional happy ending.

Even if Leath loved her—and while she knew he liked her and wanted her, she had no idea if he felt more—the world would frown upon any marriage between a marquess and a sergeant major's daughter. A mésalliance would destroy Leath's lifelong political ambitions. Even if he was willing to make such a sacrifice, now that she'd seen his flashing brilliance in full flight when Sir Garth visited, she couldn't accept it. She couldn't make him less than he was. That would degrade her love to mere selfishness. If lowly Eleanor Trim wanted the Marquess of Leath in her bed, it must be without the church's blessing.

A thunder of hooves signaled Leath's approach. In his soggy clothes, he must be turning to ice, but the fiery look he sent her blazed right through her.

Mrs. Murray reacted to her son's ordeal with the calm common sense that Nell expected, although her thanks to Leath were sincere and extensive. While Nell appreciated that the woman needed to express her gratitude, staying for tea was almost unbearable. Nell had spent weeks hankering to kiss his lordship. Now, any postponement irked. Leath appeared his usual unflappable self, until Nell caught a sizzling glance aimed in her direction and realized that he too chafed at the delay.

Still, Nell couldn't gripe at Leath drying out before the roaring fire in the Murrays' front room. She didn't want him perishing of pneumonia before she'd had her wicked way.

It felt like hours before she and Leath galloped across the moors again. Mrs. Murray's feather-light scones congealed into hard stones in Nell's stomach now that finally she was alone with the marquess. When she'd given him her consent, she'd brimmed with courage. Now she was as nervous as a cat on a stove.

They careered into the grove where he'd asked her to be his mistress. He hauled his horse to a rearing stop and vaulted to the leaf-covered ground. In two long strides, he crossed the space between them. Before Nell could snatch a breath, he caught her around the waist and swung her down.

She glimpsed glittering need in his eyes before his mouth took hers in a kiss of such urgency that her knees folded beneath her and she collapsed against Adela. The mare snorted and backed away.

Heat flooded Nell, tightened her nipples, puddled between her legs, trapped the breath in her lungs. On a muffled gasp, she grabbed Leath's powerful shoulders to stay upright. And to touch him. How she'd longed to touch him.

Ruthlessly, his tongue parted her lips and slid inside to stroke hers. If he'd kissed her like this in his bedroom, she'd have fled in terror. Now she arched closer. He was hard against her belly. Once that too would have terrified her, but not now that she'd surrendered to desire.

Ravenously he claimed her mouth, setting her aflame. She moved her tongue against his, relishing the hot rasp.

Too soon he raised his head and stared down at her as if he saw nothing else in the world. "You meant it?"

She licked swollen lips. He was more delicious than wine. She nodded and struggled for words. That kiss had smashed every thought but the need to be close to him. "Of course."

His laugh was close to a groan and he leaned in until his forehead bumped hers and they shared each breath. The intimacy was as powerful as his rapacious kiss. "I couldn't trust myself to look at you and still keep my hands off. Do you have any idea what torture you've put me through?"

A wry smile tilted her lips. "I might have an inkling."

Her hands curled into his shoulders, then drifted down his powerful chest, feeling the heat beneath the wrinkled shirt. It gradually dawned on her that she could touch him when she liked. The thought was arousing.

He kissed her again. This time, she did more than cling in bewildered delight. Feverishly she explored him, feeling the hard muscles, the thunderous beat of his heart. Such a valiant heart. She wrenched her lips from his and pressed a kiss to his chest.

He angled her face up until their eyes met. "I want you so much, Eleanor."

How she loved the way he said Eleanor.

His gaze sharpened. "What is it?"

"You're the only one who calls me Eleanor." She couldn't help smiling. She should lament her ruin, but she'd never felt so free.

"You'll always be Eleanor to me." He looked younger, happier, than she'd ever seen him. "Although calling you Miss Trim always gives me a delicious frisson. I've dreamed of debauching the prim Miss Trim."

"Oh," she said, and he laughed.

"Well may you look smug."

"Of course I'm smug. I've caught myself a wonderful man." She cradled his face between her hands, reveling in the fact that she could, and pressed her lips to his beak of a nose. "Rather terrifying, I'll admit, but definitely a handsome fellow. And the only man I've ever kissed."

He drew her closer for a thorough kiss that had her knees imitating string again. "When you say things like that, I feel like a beast for everything I want to do to you."

"Now?"

She saw him consider having her, here in this lovely, lonely clearing. She also saw the moment good sense won. "You deserve better."

"I want you so much, I hardly care," she confessed, knowing she made herself dangerously defenseless, but unable to stop. Every time he kissed her, love melted her very bones.

"Eleanor, you humble me."

She blushed. "Would you rather I played games? I'm not experienced enough to know what I should do. Should I pretend reluctance?"

Another cracked laugh. "Dear God, you'll drive me mad. No, don't play games. You're all that's fine and true. I feel like I see into your soul."

When she recalled her lies, she suffered a momentary twinge. But none of that mattered now. What mattered was that the man she loved wanted her and she wanted him.

He kissed her again. "I thought I had no chance. You sounded so certain when you refused."

"If you'd kissed me like that, I wouldn't have had a hope."

A shadow crossed his features. "You should marry a good, respectable man and look forward to a gaggle of children and a home of your own."

As she stared into eyes the color of pewter, the high tide of her euphoria ebbed. "If this is the only way I can have you, I can bear it."

Regret darkened his expression before he pressed his lips to hers. The wildness retreated, but his tenderness turned her heart to syrup. With no reluctance, she abandoned that mythical good man and accepted that her fate was forever entwined with the Marquess of Leath's.

When he withdrew, they were both shaking. She found it immensely moving that she, unimportant Nell Trim, made this superb man tremble. A muffled sound of disappointment escaped her as he stepped back. "Why did you stop?"

This time his groan held no amusement at all. "You take me to the edge, my darling. And this isn't the place. Or the time." He glanced up at the turbulent sky.

She hadn't noticed that the weather closed in. "When?"

He caught her hand and raised it to his lips. "Would you come to me tonight?"

Consent rose to her lips, but wouldn't emerge. She'd been a housemaid mere weeks, but it had shocked her how intimately the staff observed the family's habits. "If I come to your bed at Alloway Chase, everyone will know."

"Yes."

"I don't want the other servants to call me a slut."

The word hung between them, harsh, ugly, and sadly true. "I'll never think of you like that."

She searched his face, wanting reassurance. "Your mother deserves my respect. I can't do it."

"I want you so much."

Something in his tone made her frown. "You're testing me."

Self-derision edged his smile. "I suppose I am. This morning, I struggled to resign myself to never having you.

Now all my dreams come true. You can't blame a man for questioning such a miracle."

She smiled back. Something about his vulnerability made her heart squeeze in a painful ecstasy of love. She swallowed and struggled to make sensible decisions. "You don't want a scandal."

How odd to think that before she came to Alloway Chase, deceit had been completely foreign to her. Since then, every day she'd told lie after lie, and now she signed up for a lifetime of subterfuge.

"Right now, I don't care."

"But you will," she said flatly. She stiffened her spine and told herself to be brave. If she wanted the marquess, she must pay the price.

"So I must resign myself to more lonely nights?" The question was wry, but she heard his frustration.

"Oh, Leath…"

He hauled her up for another ardent kiss. But she'd reached a point where kisses no longer satisfied. Even in her inexperience, she knew that for both of them, only consummation could allay their raging desire. Still, she gave herself up to him with a fierceness that left them both panting.

One powerful hand curled around her buttock. The other cupped her face. The mixture of overt demand and sweet care threatened her resolve and she muffled a sob. "I thought once I said yes, this would be easy."

The strengthening wind whipped her damp skirts around her legs. The storm around her paled in comparison to the storm in her soul.

"Nothing worthwhile is easy," he said with a hint of grimness.

"I won't change my mind," she said firmly.

Such relief flooded his face that for the first time, she

realized quite how much he wanted her. Her gloominess about the future retreated.

"Thank God," he breathed and kissed her quickly, withdrawing before passion ignited. His features were tight with control, hinting at the restraint he exercised here where he could lift her skirts in seconds.

She moved closer and rested against him. His arms encircled her, surrounding her with his familiar scent, tinged with lingering traces of river water. "I have to trust you not to expose us to the world's censure."

His embrace tightened. "I'll do my best, Eleanor. With sleepless nights ahead, I'll have plenty of thinking time."

"I'd rather be lying beside you."

"Believe me, I'll do my best to find a quick solution."

A fat drop of rain hit her head. She looked up and another landed on her cheek. The wind tore the last leaves from the trees around them.

"It's been a watery day." She struggled to make their separation bearable. After this, seeing him without touching him would be torture.

He laughed softly. "It's been a marvelous day. I look forward to an even more marvelous day."

"Don't make me wait long," she said softly, as freezing rain swirled around them.

"I curse that we must wait at all," he said with a hint of savagery that carried into his kiss.

Chapter Seventeen

Lowering clouds brought early dusk to the isolated cottage tucked into Derbyshire's Peaks. For two days, Nell had waited here. Leath had promised to arrive today, but the evening drew in without him. A dizzying mixture of longing and nerves kept her at the parlor window overlooking the graveled drive. A drive that remained empty, despite all her dedicated watching.

The day after Nell had agreed to become his mistress, Leath left Alloway Chase for a week, ostensibly to visit another estate. While away, he'd sent her a letter bristling with daunting practicalities, softened only by a "yours, James" at the end. Sentimental fool she was, she'd slept ever since with that letter under her pillow. She'd hoped that tonight she'd have more than his words to keep her warm.

Disconsolately she turned away from the rain outside.

He'd come. She knew he would. But the delay was excruciating. Nearly two weeks ago, she'd vowed herself to a man in a rush of passion, and all she had to show for it was a few kisses.

She dropped onto the brocade couch before the roaring fire. Derbyshire seemed even colder than Yorkshire. There was snow on the surrounding hills and when she'd ventured out to explore the garden, she lasted minutes before hurrying inside to the warmth.

She'd left the marchioness's employment with a story about caring for an ill aunt. Since then, she'd crossed another wilderness and settled into this exquisite bower.

Nell appreciated Leath's discretion in his choice of love nest. This thatched house with its snug parlor and cozy bedroom upstairs under the eaves held a touch of the fairy tale. The larder was stocked with all manner of delicacies, enough to last the week. Leath had arranged every luxury except servants. She was desperately glad that she wouldn't have to face knowing eyes.

She hadn't yet heard his lordship's long-term plans. Somewhere she'd need to accustom herself to life as a fallen woman. She and her lover couldn't hide in this sanctuary forever, making do for themselves.

How she wished Leath would come. Avoiding grim reality became more onerous every moment. A woman who gave everything up for love shouldn't sit alone on a cold night, contemplating the lonely years ahead.

Sighing, Nell rose and lit the candles. She wandered into the kitchen to pour a glass of wine. The wind whipped the trees outside so violently that she found it in herself to be glad that Leath wasn't on the road.

Sipping the rich claret, she stared out the kitchen window. Then she trudged back to the parlor. She wasn't hungry, but it was too early for bed.

"Eleanor?"

She raised her head and stared at the towering figure dripping onto the flagstones in the hallway. "My lord?"

The shock of seeing him when she'd reconciled herself to another night alone was too much. To her utter mortification, tears flooded her eyes.

"Oh, my darling." Flinging away his greatcoat and dropping his bags, he rushed forward and caught her wine before she spilled it. Curling one arm around her waist, he slid the glass onto a table before enveloping her in his heat, his power, his sheer presence.

"I'm sorry," she muttered, struggling not to weep into his chest. The scents of leather, sandalwood, and Leath flooded her senses. "You gave me such a surprise."

His embrace tightened. "I didn't mean to be so late. The damned horse went lame outside Matlock and the weather's been horrid."

"You should have waited until tomorrow." The battle against tears wasn't going well.

"And spend another day without you? I'd rather cut off my arm." He swung her around until he collapsed onto the chaise with her lying against him. "Eleanor, Eleanor, don't cry. I thought you'd be happy to see me."

"I am," she wailed into his shirtfront. "You'll think you've taken on a complete lunatic."

His laugh held a fondness that went a long way to soothing her distress. "It's the wait. It's enough to drive the sanest person—among whom, dear Miss Trim, I count you—mad."

"You won't believe this, but I rarely cry."

"Did you think I wasn't coming?"

She burrowed more deeply against him. "I trust you."

"I'm glad." A note in his beautiful voice had her lifting her head.

"I truly am happy to see you," she said, not sure whether he'd believe her. With a shaking hand, she brushed her tears away.

"I know you are," he said with a twitch of his lips. He caught her face between his hands and studied her as if she were the most precious thing in the world. "And I'm over-joyed to see you. It's been a long ten days."

"Oh, yes," she said fervently. She sniffed and a choked giggle escaped. "I must look a fright."

"You do rather," he said with a smile. "A delightful fright."

"What a welcome I've given you."

Briefly he pressed his lips to hers. "Thank you for waiting."

Nell had a bleak premonition that his mistress would devote many hours to waiting. She shoved the thought to the back of her mind where all her other misgivings lurked.

James Fairbrother was a good man. Nell knew that to her bones. The rules of their world made it impossible for them to be together without shame and secrecy. So she must accept shame and secrecy. Other women lived with that. She could learn to. Dear Lord, let her learn to.

Right now, the man she loved was inches away, whereas the future seemed so distant. "After ten days, is that the best you can do, my lord?"

His lips curved. He wasn't a man who smiled easily, except with her. The thought melted her last doubts. "I feel rather awkward kissing a woman who addresses me so formally."

"Perhaps you need more practice."

"Do you mock me, Miss Trim?"

"It would do you no harm." She'd seen how people respected and admired him. He seemed poignantly short of people who treated him as an equal. Even Sir Garth Burton's attitude had verged on hero worship.

His expression turned serious. "Please, Eleanor, call me James."

She rose on her knees and pressed provocative little

kisses across the cool, damp skin of his face. His striking features had lured her since that first alarming encounter outside his library. She could stare at him for days and only become more fascinated.

A glance of her lips across the wide forehead concealing his miracle of a mind. Another to where his pulse beat at his temples. A row of kisses along his hairline, tasting rain. Three deliberate kisses down that intimidating nose.

"I'm sure…James…wouldn't leave me…stuck on a… precipice of…uncertainty for nearly…a fortnight," she said between kisses.

More kisses along hard, slanted cheekbones and along his jaw. His skin was rough with stubble. This tangible proof of his masculinity thrilled her.

"Eleanor—" He caught her waist between his big, powerful hands.

"Only wicked Lord Leath would…leave me so long," she said, her voice muffled against his neck. He smelled so wonderful. Fresh air. Horses. Male musk as his desire stirred.

"If wicked Lord Leath tells you that he left Alloway Chase before dawn to reach you, would you relent, sweet Miss Trim?"

She nipped him sharply, then drew back. "Truly?"

"Truly." He tipped her back onto the chaise and loomed over her. "I won't have scandal darkening your name. If I left too soon after you, questions would be asked. My mother is no fool."

Troubled, Nell met his silvery eyes, seeing evidence of his arduous day in the weariness under his excitement. Because he was excited. Even before she'd kissed him, she'd known he was in a lather to have her. "Did she say anything?"

"No. When I told her I had business in the south, she merely…*looked*."

Nell raised her chin with false bravado, as the thought of the marchioness knowing what they did made her cringe. "I'll get used to this."

Tenderness lengthened his mouth, softer and fuller than the mouth of the man who ran Alloway Chase. Just as his gaze was softer as it rested upon her. Whatever this recklessness cost her, she knew that the James Fairbrother she held now was hers and hers alone.

This time when he kissed her, he lingered, sucking on her lower lip until she parted for a luxuriant exploration. Every bone in Nell's body melted. "That was lovely," she sighed.

"You're lovely."

"If you've been traveling all day, you'll be hungry. Shall I find you something to eat?"

His eyes focused on her and she squirmed at the heat in those silvery depths. "I don't want food. I want you." He laughed at her nervous squeak. "Have I shocked you?"

She shook her head. "No."

His smile broadened. He stood, extending his hand. "I will before I'm done. Will you come with me, Eleanor?"

Feeling like her heart expanded to the size of a mountain, she rose on her elbows. It was silly to be uncertain. After all, they weren't in this cottage to play piquet. But she suddenly felt very small and defenseless. She swallowed to dislodge the lump in her throat.

"Yes," she wavered and took his hand. His touch restored faltering courage and she met his eyes with something approaching confidence.

He kissed her. She awaited passion, but there was only more of that aching tenderness. Sweeping her up into his arms, he sipped from her lips as if he couldn't get enough of her.

"Leath!" she gasped, clinging to his neck. "You can't carry me upstairs."

His laugh rang with triumphant happiness. "Right now, I think I could carry you to London."

She tugged the wet black hair at his nape. "I don't want to go quite that far."

"In that case, Miss Trim, let me take you above and ravish you."

She loved the way he said "Eleanor." She loved the way he said "Miss Trim." Dear God, she was in such a bad way, she just loved him.

"I've wanted you to do this ever since you first kissed me," she admitted shyly, leaning her cheek against his chest as he mounted the narrow staircase.

"Ah, that powerful infatuation." She heard the smile in his voice, although she was too bashful to meet his eyes. While she wasn't a timid woman, she'd never before had a handsome man carrying her away for his pleasure. "I've wanted to do this ever since that first night in my library."

She couldn't resist glancing up. "Surely you believe that I'm smitten."

It seemed safe to admit that much. Something told her that he wouldn't welcome hearing of the depth and power of her love. His conscience already pricked him. If he knew the extent of her emotional vulnerability, she had a horrible feeling that he might send her away.

He shouldered his way into the bedroom where she'd lain alone, missing him, the last two nights. Earlier she'd drawn the curtains and lit the fire. In the flickering flames, the four-poster bed loomed like a challenge.

He kissed her and she strained after him, seeking more heat. When he kissed her, she couldn't think. Now, she desperately didn't want to think.

"I'm rather smitten myself," he admitted. "You have magic, Miss Trim."

Juggling her in his arms, he flung back the covers before gently setting her down. She sank into the bed and stared up at the man who would soon possess her. In his gray eyes, she caught an echo of her troubled thoughts. They'd battled their better selves to reach this point.

She rose against the pillows. "Whatever happens, I'll never regret this."

"I pray not." He stroked her cheek as he sat beside her. "I've dreamed of seeing your hair loose. May I take it down?"

Although her presence gave him permission to do much more than unpin her hair, she inched forward. "Yes."

She knew he'd had lovers. She knew that she wouldn't be the last woman he enticed to his bed. He wasn't a rake, but he was an attractive man in his prime who led an active life. Whatever her heart might wish, she didn't even believe that she meant anything special to him. She invited complete devastation if she placed a romantic gloss on this affair.

Every sensible reminder faded to naught when she saw the care and need in his face. Any illusion that he entered this liaison lightly vanished. He looked as though tonight his world changed forever.

With breathtaking slowness, he drew the first pin from her hair and the significance of the action made her want to weep again.

She sat motionless as he slid another pin free, then another. One heavy blond tress tumbled over her shoulder. She closed her eyes to hide her tumult. This unbinding of her hair, hair that she'd never let down for a man, marked her transition from virginal Nell Trim to Eleanor, captive of sensuality.

More would come. He'd undress her. She'd see his nakedness. His body would slide into hers. Yet this moment seemed the beginning of true intimacy.

By the time her hair flowed around her, Leath breathed in gusts. His hands touched her delicately, as if the slightest fumble might shatter her.

Then nothing.

Slowly, reluctantly, she opened her eyes. Leath stared at her as though she was a star fallen from heaven to light his way.

"It's glorious." Her heart expanded at the awe in his voice. "You're glorious."

He caught her hair up against her cheeks so it slipped like silk against her skin. "Kiss me, Eleanor. Kiss me before I die of wanting you."

Chapter Eighteen

The woman with brilliant amber eyes kneeling on the bed was a breathtaking stranger. A magical curtain rippled around her. Soft as mist. Shining as the moon. Hints of subtle gold like shadows on silver. Leath looked at Eleanor's unbound hair and thought of clouds and lace and filigree.

The abundance transformed her pure beauty to fierce magnificence. For so long, he'd yearned to see her like this. She was no longer self-contained Miss Trim, who had tantalized him for weeks. Instead she was a creature of fire and ice. She was the perfect mixture of allure and restraint. His desire mounted higher. And triumph, however unworthy, rose too.

Tonight this luscious creature would lie in his arms. He had the privilege of teaching her joy. Feeling that he touched something outside the realm of earth, he buried his hands in the silky hair, glorying in its texture. Then holding her face up, he pressed his lips to hers.

She trembled, reminding him that for all her lush beauty, she was new to this. His conscience howled, but the satiny slide of her hair in his hands and her warm scent made him deaf to principle.

All his life he'd tried to do the right thing. Mostly he'd succeeded. But when it came to Eleanor Trim, he tumbled headlong into sin. And smiled as he faced damnation.

He kneeled before her and kissed her long and luxuriously. She tasted like the promise of spring, even as winter settled its icy grip around them.

When she was sighing and kissing him back eagerly, he released the top button of her gray dress. The moment when the linen collar parted to reveal her throat thundered through him like victory. Still kissing her, he rested the tips of his fingers on the intriguing notch in the center of her collarbone, feeling her pulse kick and flutter.

He leaned closer and released another button. Then another as he nipped at her bottom lip, drawing a whimper of pleasure from her. Her excitement made his heart leap.

Leath stroked the sweet skin he'd uncovered. When he'd touched her like this before, he'd been too carried away with the encounter's unexpectedness. Tonight he intended to take his time. Not just because she was a virgin. He'd wanted this woman for so long, he meant to engrave each incandescent detail on his mind. Even when he was a very old man, he'd relive the softness of her skin, her ragged breathing, her scent.

Another button. This was like undressing a nun. A nun whose mouth blazed passion and whose hair flowed in silvery temptation.

Six buttons. Six small victories. He slipped one hand under her gaping bodice and cupped her breast. He was gentle, leashing his hunger. She made another choked sound against his mouth. When his thumb flicked her nipple, she squirmed, squeezing closer.

She might hide her sensuality under plain dresses and

severe hair, but he'd known from the first that her soul was flame. Now when she delivered herself to his caresses with an abandon that made his heart somersault, he realized that every fantasy fell short of warm, living reality.

"Eleanor, Eleanor, Eleanor," he murmured, setting a rain of kisses to the corners of her lips, across her cheeks, down her neck. Every inch was glorious. He found a place at the curve of her shoulder where the scrape of his teeth had her crying out.

"Yes," he hissed. "Yes, my darling, don't hide what you feel."

Eleanor released a choked laugh, even as she quaked under another nip to her neck. "You make me wild."

Her voice cracked. She didn't sound like his efficient secretary or the woman who had dared him with her eyes even when pretending humility. He beat back his triumphalist mood and managed to speak softly, although determination infused every word. "I want to make you wild."

The wonder was that he'd just started. He teased her nipple with more purpose, rolling, pinching, stroking, making her pant.

Until on a harsh cry, she shuddered, her hands gouging his shoulders.

Dear God in heaven. She'd come with just his touch on her breast. She'd go up like fireworks before they were done.

Humbled, he drew back to see her. She looked flushed and startled. And voluptuous. Her mouth was red and full. Slowly she opened her eyes until he drowned in topaz, radiant with lingering pleasure. And the seeds of knowledge. A reminder to take his time, get everything right. They had days—and nights—ahead.

An uncertain smile teased her lips. "That was..."

He smiled back. Nobody in his life made him smile like

Eleanor did. If she left, his life would become a prison. "Surprising?"

Her smile widened and her eyelids lowered in a carnal expression that had him fighting the urge to push her onto her back now. "Well, that too."

He slid his hand from her breast, delighting in the way her hair tangled about his wrist as if every part of her strove to cling to him. "I need to see you."

"I hope you'll return the favor."

Shocked, he stared at her. "Really?"

She nodded. "I'm sure you're quite magnificent."

Heat seared his cheekbones. "I'm a horridly big bugger."

Her laugh held a sultry note and he recalled that he'd never intimidated Miss Trim.

"I love how overwhelmed I feel in your arms." She licked her lips and he bit back a groan. That mannerism had provoked him for months. "The effect would be even more powerful if you took your shirt off."

"As you wish, my lady." He felt no awkwardness addressing her as a woman of his class. Outside in the workaday world, a gulf as wide as the Atlantic separated them. Here, in this quiet room, they met face to face as equals, united in desire.

His hands shook as he shrugged off coat, neckcloth, waistcoat, and finally his shirt.

"Oh."

Did that tiny squeak indicate disappointment? The attention she fixed on his chest made him squirm. He was built like a prize fighter—in London, he regularly sparred at the fashionable boxing saloons. His size daunted most men. To Eleanor, he must seem a hulking ox.

Thick black hair covered his chest, proof of his animal nature. Dismay twisted his gut. Perhaps this first time, he should take her in darkness. True, he'd miss the wonder of seeing her, and he'd spent so many lonely nights imagining her naked. But someone so large and blatantly male must terrify a girl who had never known a man.

Dear God, wait until she saw his cock. If his chest made her nervous, she'd run screaming once she caught sight of it. He wasn't a monster. He knew he was in proportion. But his proportions were notably generous. He'd managed previous encounters without injuring his partners, but Eleanor was a virgin. Perhaps he should ask her to close her eyes when he removed his breeches.

Still, she didn't speak.

"I warned you," he said gruffly when the silence became unbearable.

"Yes, you did," she murmured, licking her lips again. Damn, he wished she'd stop doing that. It did awful things to his heart rate.

"I won't crush you."

At last she raised her eyes and delighted astonishment shuddered through him. "I don't mind if you do."

"Eleanor..." he said helplessly, seizing her shoulders.

Her expression dazzled him. "Do you have any idea what the sight of you does to me?"

"You're not afraid?" he asked shakily, fingers curling into her shoulders.

Her laugh cracked. "Of course I'm afraid. I've never done this before. But I'm also...excited."

"Oh, my darling." Moved by her honesty, he kissed her with all the gratitude in his heart. Gratitude that she was here. Gratitude that she wanted him.

Through the kiss, he felt her tentative touch on his chest. One glancing connection before she snatched her hand away. His skin tightened. The next time, she lingered. Her other hand dared a quick caress. He groaned encouragement against her lips. She leaned in with more purpose.

Her lips left his to follow the path of her hands. The hot innocence of her kisses made him burn. Everywhere she touched, she branded him hers.

"Hell."

She stopped kissing his nipples. "Don't you like this?"

He tried to smile, but he'd wager it was a grimace. "Too much."

"Good." She scraped her teeth over his nipple and he stifled another oath. "A man's body is so...interesting."

In a fury of impatience, he tugged the demure dress over her head, leaving her in her plain white shift and corset. He wasn't sure why, but her practical clothing made his heart constrict with emotion.

"You have no idea how these puritanical frocks have taunted me." He flung the dress across the room. "I felt like a lecher every time I looked at you done out like a damned pilgrim, and all I wanted was to rip the rags from your back and toss you onto the desk."

A gurgle of amusement escaped. "You'd have given Mr. Wells a fit."

"Bugger Wells. With the slightest encouragement, I'd have jumped on you there and then."

Against the unadorned linen, her skin was rich and creamy. Unable to resist tasting her, he nibbled a line down one shoulder. She tasted fresh and delicious. She smelled of warm woman and lemon soap. In his younger days, he'd pursued a courtesan or two. None of their jasmine or rose came near to stirring him the way Eleanor Trim's clean scent did.

"You seemed so controlled."

When he lifted his head, he met that level gaze that

always made his breath catch. "You don't know how close you came to being ravished against the bookcases."

He fumbled with her corset. His fervor made him all thumbs.

Another delightful gurgle. "I wish I'd known."

"I thought you must have. Everything you did was so precisely calculated to send me into a frenzy."

"Surely not," she said, although he saw her satisfaction as she gradually accepted her power over him. "And you've known that I'm…I'm helpless against you since the night I came to your room."

Leath gave up on the laces and ripped the corset in two. She gasped and raised her hands to her breasts, outlined against the chemise. Pink nipples pressed against the linen. The sight made him mad to see the rest of her. But her swift modesty reminded him what was at stake. He kissed her again, relishing her unfettered response. His hands tangled in her extravagant hair.

"Shall I help with your boots, my lord?" she whispered.

"Good God." He sat back. He'd been so focused on arousing her that he'd forgotten that he'd come up here sweaty and tired from a day in the saddle. "You'll think I'm a lout."

"Hardly." She smiled as she rose from the bed. In her shift and petticoat, she looked like a virgin sacrifice. His conscience pinched, but he gave it the cut direct.

"Are you wearing drawers?" he asked, astonished how raw he sounded.

He loved her blushes. "Yes."

"Take them off."

Leath expected protest. She'd been an unruly servant. He couldn't imagine as a mistress she'd be much different.

That devilish alluring smile curved her ripe lips. Slowly and teasingly, she hitched up her petticoat, revealing pretty ankles. With a few deft movements that put his efforts with her corset to shame, white cotton slipped to her feet.

As she kicked her drawers away, he gulped with admiration and growing arousal. He'd been right about the fire in her soul.

Still smiling like a siren, she kneeled before him. His heart gave another great thump. He couldn't resist picturing what she might do from that position. On her knees with her hair in disarray, she was every man's fantasy. Except that he didn't deceive himself about her strength. If she bent to his will, it was because she wanted to.

He slid to the edge of the bed and extended one long leg. He relished the delicious jiggle of her breasts when she tugged at his muddy boot.

Once the boots were gone, he drew her up between his thighs to kiss her. He couldn't get enough of that succulent plum of a mouth. Her taste would haunt him forever.

He untied her petticoat and tugged the frail shift over her head, tumbling her hair into wild ripples. Her hair was so thick that it concealed her from his starving gaze. The urge to see her body pounded like a huge hammer, but her eyes arrested his attention. She appeared uncertain and awkward, no longer the self-confident hussy who had kicked her drawers to perdition.

Gently, gently…

Carefully, he stood and drew her to her feet. "Let me look at you."

Eleanor blushed a delightful pink and her gaze fluttered from his. She was an enchanting mixture of the brazen and the shy. Even as he hungered to take her, he savored this delicate surrender.

"I've never stood naked before a man," she muttered.

He wanted to tell her that if he had his way, no other man

would enjoy the privilege. Until with stabbing regret, he recalled that he could have no permanent call on a mistress's loyalties.

He beat back the thought before it contaminated his happiness. Because despite his qualms, he was happy. Happier than he could ever recall in his dutiful, busy, useful existence.

All because he wanted a beautiful girl who wanted him too.

Such a simple solution to life's mysteries. Perhaps he should propose it at the next sitting of parliament as the answer to the nation's woes. That would make the opposition sit up and pay attention, by God.

He wanted to say something clever to disperse this choking cloud of emotion. But yet again simplicity won over false bravado. "You're so beautiful." ·

She must have heard his reverence because she looked him square in the eyes. He watched uncertainty melt into trust. And something he didn't want to name. Because if he did, he'd have to name the same thing in himself.

"So are you."

Her openness charmed him. Hell, everything about her charmed him. Particularly her nakedness. To ease the solemn atmosphere, he smiled and caught her hand. "I'm blessed. A gorgeous girl with bad eyesight."

Eleanor laughed, as he'd intended. And as he'd yearned to do since he'd first seen her, he took stock of her loveliness.

Any attempt to make light of what happened was doomed. Words jumbled in his throat. He'd dreamed for so long of this moment. Now she stood bare and willing before him. Tinged gold in flickering firelight.

Tenderly, Leath slid a wing of hair aside, revealing her breast. He feasted his eyes on her. On the white skin. The sinuous lines of breast and hip. The long, lissome legs. The flat belly with its neat navel and soft nest of curls below. Curls darker than her moonlight hair.

She exceeded his fantasies—and in his fantasies, she'd been exquisite.

Raising his eyes, he saw that she watched him with that deep seriousness that was so innate to her. He tried to smile reassurance, but he was too moved to succeed. What emerged wasn't what he wanted to say at all.

"Are you sure, Eleanor?"

Chapter Nineteen

N ell trembled with nerves and anticipation. The urge
to wrench the sheet from the bed and huddle into it
was almost irresistible. She only kept still because if she
betrayed her abject terror, his lordship would surely decide
against fulfilling his nefarious plans.

While she was frightened, she also wanted. Desire tri-
umphed over trepidation. Just.

She shifted from one foot to the other. Her grip on Leath's
hand tightened and she swallowed to moisten a mouth arid
with fear. "I'm sure."

"You don't sound it." His expression warmed with the
tender smile that always made her feel like she stood in sun-
light, but nothing hid his edginess. His jaw was sharp and
a muscle in his lean cheek jerked in an erratic dance that
echoed the bump and skip of her heart.

She struggled to inject a wry note into her voice, but
all she achieved was breathless uncertainty. "I'm standing
here without a stitch of clothing, my lord. The die has been
cast."

His smile faded. "I'll know you're sure when you call me James."

She stepped into the shelter of his body. This was like standing beneath a huge oak tree. He was like oak, true and strong and deeply rooted where he'd grown.

"I know this is wrong." Nell's voice was scratchy as though she hadn't used it in a long time. And so low that he bent his dark head to hear her. "It goes against everything I was taught." She confessed the miserable truth. "When my sister fell victim to a wicked seducer, despite how sorry I was for her, I thought she'd been a fool."

He winced. "Yet here you are in a wicked seducer's arms."

She summoned a smile. "I wish the wicked seducer was holding me closer."

"I never want you to think this was a mistake."

She had a nasty inkling that she might. Not now. Not tonight. Not while they were together. But when he made his brilliant society match and resumed a public life that left no place for an illicit arrangement with his housemaid? Then, oh, yes, then, she'd wonder about her choice.

She raised her chin, battling to ignore the fact that she was as naked as the day she was born. How on earth had she ever believed that this man ruined Dorothy? Right now, his principles struck her as a complete nuisance.

"I'll regret denying what I feel tonight." Impatience sharpened her voice. "Leath, I'm standing here, begging you to touch me. How much more must I do to convince you that if you don't take me to bed, I'll spend the rest of my life sorry that I missed this chance?" She frowned and wondered if perhaps she'd mistaken his reluctance. What if chivalry wasn't at the root of it? "Unless you've changed your mind."

His lips twisted in self-mockery. "You know how much I want you. I can't hide it."

Her gaze shifted to the front of his breeches. A gasp of awe—and, she had to admit, apprehension—escaped her.

Bitterness tinged his laugh. "I'm a selfish lover, Eleanor. Once I have you, I won't easily let you go."

She shivered, this time with anticipation. "I like the sound of that."

Dear heaven, if she let him stew on his scruples, she'd be as virgin tomorrow as she was now. What a sad outcome that would be. She drew his rich scent into her lungs and told herself to be brave. She'd been brave coming to Alloway Chase. She could be brave in pursuit of pleasure. Still her legs were wobblier than jelly as she linked her arms around his neck, feeling the silky tickle of his hair against her fingers. "Kiss me."

He tensed with surprise. His lordship was used to taking the initiative.

She'd been painfully conscious of her nakedness, but with her skin sliding against his, the promise of the night to come charged through her like runaway horses.

He swallowed a groan and placed his hands around her waist. Hunger lit his eyes to silver. "Eleanor—"

"Kiss me." Deliberately she pressed her hips forward until she met that impressive bulge in his breeches. Despite her instinctive hiss of shock, her heart swooped like a swallow learning to fly.

Another deep breath. More heady scent.

Courage, Nell.

"I want you." Her voice was steadier than it had been all night. "I'm not afraid."

She saw the moment he abandoned every consideration except desire. His hunger incinerated her fear to ash, making her declaration true as it hadn't been when she'd spoken. His grip firmed. His chest brushed her breasts as he inhaled.

"My beautiful girl…" he whispered and took her lips in a kiss unlike any before. Perhaps because this kiss wasn't an end in itself, but a doorway to more.

With unconcealed sexual intent, he nipped sharply at her lip. She shifted and moaned as heat pooled between her legs. Curiosity throbbed inside her. The curiosity to know the man she loved as her lover. Her craving built for ultimate connection.

Every inch of her hummed with need. Pleasure sang through her veins—pleasure tinted with frustration. She growled low in her throat as his hands drifted over her body. The devil merely laughed and nibbled at her neck as if savoring her impatience. He brought her to the brink then held her over the void in an agony of suspense.

"Leath…" she forced out. "I'm ready."

"Not nearly, sweetheart."

His rough tone offered some compensation. If this seduction threatened to shatter her, at least she wasn't alone. She bit his chest, making him jump. "Stop tormenting me."

"Enjoy the journey."

"I want to arrive," she protested, biting more fiercely.

"Little cat," he muttered, burying his hand in her hair and pulling her head back until she met his blazing eyes. "If you bite me again, I'll bite back."

"I'd like that," she gasped, even while in the far reaches of her mind she wondered where calm, sensible Nell Trim had gone.

"So would I." He nipped her shoulder through cascading hair. She shivered under his teeth, even though he wasn't nearly as ferocious as she'd been.

"I told you I want you," she said helplessly, running her

hands over his chest and digging her nails into his skin. At this rate, he'd be a bloody mess. Right now, she gloried in marking his body. If only she knew how to mark his heart.

"Not enough." He sounded almost angry.

So did she. "You're so smug."

Leath grabbed her dancing hands and kissed her fists. "If I'm not careful, I'll rip you to shreds."

If she'd been in her right mind, that would make her take to her heels. In her het-up state, his warning tugged at her as inexorably as the moon tugged at the sea.

"Please..." she sobbed, rubbing against him. She loved the hair on his body, fascinatingly different from hers, coarser, warmer, so male.

"Stop trying to flay me and be patient." He kissed her again and this time his hands trailed down her back, making her wriggle.

"More," she insisted.

He laughed breathlessly and cupped his hands beneath her bottom. When he hoisted her high, the angle of his kiss transformed to flashing pleasure. Instinctively she twined her legs around him, pressing her heels into his buttocks.

This new position placed the hot, needy part of her fiendishly close to that alluring hardness. His breeches became a major irritation. With a long moan, she slid against him and felt a spark of sensation, akin to those dazzling, astonishing reactions that had roared through her when he'd played with her breasts.

Intrigued, she tried it again and basked in his fractured groan. "Stop it, you witch."

"I like it," she said breathlessly. "Don't you?"

"Of course I do," he muttered, burying his face in the curve of her shoulder. Without following her down, he swung her onto the bed.

"My lord?"

He stared at her sprawled across the sheets. His expression made her dig her fingers into the cool linen.

"Leath?" She bit her lip and the frenzy inside her expanded, changed to something she'd never felt before, despite knowing that she loved this man with every breath in her body.

"You're remarkable," he whispered, as if he spoke in a church and not in a bedroom where he claimed a new mistress.

Her heart slammed to a stop, then hurtled off again. He'd looked at her with desire before. He'd looked at her with affection. What she read in his face now went deeper. He looked at her as if he'd never beheld anything so perfect, as though she lit his world the way he lit hers.

The feverish desperation, as much fear that her nerve might fail as desire, drowned in this new feeling. A feeling that would sustain her whole life, whatever happened after tonight.

The stark honesty on his face was devastating. She closed her eyes. The words "I love you" hovered too close to slipping out.

When the mattress sagged, she opened her eyes to see that at last he'd stripped off his breeches. But before she could discover the mysteries of his body, he slid between her legs, supporting himself on his elbows as he rose.

Leath surrounded her. The arms that caged her were heavy with muscle. His shoulders and chest filled her view. She raised her knees to frame his hips and brushed the black hair back from his broad forehead. "Show me," she whispered.

He turned his head to touch a kiss to the racing pulse at her wrist. When he took the beaded peak of one breast between his lips, she cried out at the pleasure, then again when he stroked between her thighs, finding a place that radiated wild sensation.

As he slid one long finger into her, she felt a subtle stretching. She started, then again when he brushed his thumb against that extraordinary place. She was slick and hot. He didn't seem to mind.

By the time he stroked her deeply with two fingers, she was quivering and panting. The world began to whirl and she dug her fingers into his impressive biceps to keep her balance. What he did pleased her, but it also pushed her toward some end that ranged beyond reach.

He settled more firmly between her thighs. She stared up at his face, knowing that the moment had come. He looked uncompromising poised above her, his weight on his hands. She'd have been afraid, except in his eyes, she saw breathtaking tenderness.

She stroked his jaw, feeling the prickle of beard. His expression softened. Carefully he pushed her knees higher, opening her. He brushed against her and she whimpered with surprise. He was so hot and hard, and even without seeing him, she recognized his size.

Leath kissed her sweetly. "Trust me, Eleanor."

She arched upward. "I want this."

"Dear Lord, so do I," he said with brief humor, and she choked back a laugh even as he shifted forward.

She felt a probing pressure, then a slow stretching. Not painful, but uncomfortable. The sheer strangeness turned her rigid.

"Don't fight me, Eleanor," he said unsteadily.

In the firelight, she saw what it cost him to proceed so gradually. The skin on his face looked too tight for the strong bones beneath, and his lips thinned and lengthened over his straight white teeth as he struggled for control.

He edged further and she tried not to resist. This possession didn't hurt, but it felt alien. With one hand, he caught her under the hips and angled her up. The pressure changed, but still felt awkward. She bit back another whimper and sank her teeth into her lower lip.

He kissed her. She lay so stiffly that it took her a few moments to respond. When she softened into the play of his mouth, something inside her softened too. He made a low sound of approval and inched forward.

"Are you all right?" he asked gruffly, raising his head. He looked different. His eyelids were heavier and his pupils were so large that his eyes turned black.

She ran shaking hands over his shoulders and down his back, feeling the force of his restraint. His skin was damp and his breath emerged in jagged bursts. "Yes," she said, although she wasn't sure.

There was still no pain, but nor was there much pleasure, if she discounted the kiss. After his incendiary caresses, this wasn't what she'd expected. With every touch, she'd begged for more. But this intimacy made her feel hemmed in and invaded.

His sandalwood scent flooded her senses. Sharper and stronger than his everyday self. Smoky with arousal. The part of him inside her was as hard as oak and just as unforgiving. She squirmed to settle him more comfortably, but it didn't help.

Gasping, he rested his hot face against her shoulder. "This will improve."

That stirred strangled laughter. "I hope so."

"Relax."

"Easy for you to say." Before he could respond to her remark, she turned her head to kiss his temple. "I trust you."

"Right now I'm not sure I deserve that," he said grimly.

Her fingers clutched his shoulders. His muscles tensed and his hips retreated. Then on a guttural groan, he advanced and something inside her tore.

She cried out and dug her nails into his back. Squeezing her eyes shut, she told herself she could endure this. She loved him, she could endure this.

He stopped moving. For a long time, she didn't even feel him breathe.

What he'd done had hurt. She'd known it would, but the pain stunned her. Tears trickled from under her eyelids.

When he moved, she braced for more pain, but the worst had passed. She still felt stretched beyond the bounds of nature and pinioned to the bed. Opening her eyes, she found Leath watching her with a devastated expression. He looked like he'd suffered worse than she had.

She reached up to smooth the frown drawing his brows together. "I survived."

"I hurt you."

"A little. But it's bearable."

While she would lie to comfort him, it was true. She didn't feel nearly so uncomfortable. She'd never been this close to anyone. She shifted to settle his weight, and thought that there might even be some pleasure.

"Let me make it better than bearable."

Nell wasn't certain if she wanted to continue. Surely now that he'd taken her, it was over. But she saw in his eyes that hurting her had hurt him. She struggled to smile. "Go ahead."

The joining had eased to fullness. Leath didn't appear so stricken, thank goodness. After he'd taken her maidenhead, he'd looked ready to slit his throat.

Very carefully he retreated. To her surprise, those same muscles that had clenched on his fingers tightened. He withdrew almost to the point of leaving her body and she took her first full breath in what felt like hours.

"So we're lovers," she said softly. Now that he no longer squeezed inside her, she almost felt good. Surely like most things, she'd get better at this, the more she did it.

Leath's radiant smile warned her. "Not nearly, my lovely Eleanor."

Before she could question his triumph—because that was what it looked like—he flexed his hips and slid inside. Apart from a faint twinge, he didn't hurt her this time.

"Oh." She released a huff of amazement.

"You'll see," he said, pausing before withdrawing.

A thousand sensitive nerves felt the smooth pull. And they all trilled with pleasure. This time, her "oh" conveyed delight.

Her deathly grip on his back loosened and she stroked him, enjoying the ripple of muscles under her hands. "Do that again," she demanded.

He leaned forward and kissed her, hard and thoroughly. She sucked his tongue into her mouth, filling her senses with his taste. He lingered at the peak of his thrust so that she felt doubly possessed.

Leath stared down, eyes alight. "Better?"

"Oh, yes," she admitted on a hiss.

Nell arched as he joined her and unbelievably the pleasure swelled. He filled every inch, but now she relished the experience. She felt claimed from the top of her head to the tip of her toes.

He changed the angle and a sky full of fireworks exploded inside her. This was even better than when he'd used his fingers. This was like flying, or galloping on the fastest horse.

Better than that.

Much better than that. Much, much better than that.

"How lovely," she murmured as he repeated the action. Every time he moved, he found some new way to please her.

Sensation spiraled upward. Up and up with every stroke of his big, wonderful body. She was gasping, reaching, straining after something. Something beyond her knowledge.

Still he moved, inexorable as the ocean, powerful as the roll of the earth.

She rose and rose. Then he tilted her hips, plunged deep and her tension shattered into a million glittering stars. As the shining flood swept her away, she cried out his name.

Chapter Twenty

At last she'd called him James.

The satisfaction of hearing his name on Eleanor's lips almost outweighed the satisfaction of feeling her clench around him in ecstasy. Well, perhaps not.

And none too soon. For hours, Leath had been on a tight rein, knowing that what he did tonight set the tone for their affair. Yet still he'd hurt her.

Then everything, praise heaven, had come right.

Quivering with reaction, she stretched beneath him. He kissed her with all the reverence in his heart. She was beautiful. Magnificent. A woman in a million. He didn't deserve her, but by God, he meant to cherish her. While breath remained in his body, nobody would harm her.

He closed his eyes and at last sought his own pleasure. The measured, deliberate thrusts became choppier. Still, he didn't let go. He remained desperately aware of her innocence.

She closed her eyes and her breath emerged in uneven gasps. Her hands linked loosely around his neck. Through the building storm, he saw that she looked utterly exhausted.

It had been a long night. And he was about to close it with a climax like none before. The surge of power began at his toes, flooded up through his legs then concentrated in his balls. The pressure was everywhere. His head. His lungs. His gut. His cock.

His muscles tightened to shredding. His heart hurled itself into his ribs. He sucked in a breath, then released it on a long, shuddering groan as his seed spurted into her.

He jerked once, twice. Then again.

The pounding rush extended beyond his experience. Whatever magic this woman possessed, he wanted more of it. This was a night of miracles.

She cried out with pleasure as every bone in his body dissolved to water. He hardly had energy to breathe. The urge to collapse upon her was overwhelming, but at the last minute, he rolled aside, taking her with him. The arms he lashed around her were heavier than stone.

"James..." she murmured sleepily, pressing her head to his galloping heart. "Dear James."

The sound of his name blasted through him like cannon fire. The glow remained from those blazing moments when he'd spilled into her. He felt extraordinarily weary. As though he'd climbed the highest mountain or dived to the depths of the sea.

"Are you all right?" He couldn't forget how tight she'd been, how tight she was now.

He spread his hands across the damp skin of her back and brushed his cheek against her ruffled hair. Her scent surrounded him, redolent with fulfillment.

She pressed closer. "I'm...wonderful," she said, sounding awed.

"You are indeed wonderful." He'd been awestruck himself, and he had a deal more experience than the virtuous

Miss Trim. Except as he'd slid into her slender body, he'd felt untouched and renewed. Only with Eleanor could he call this an act of love.

Because he did love her.

Damn him for a numskull. He'd loved her for weeks, but he'd been too thickheaded to see it.

Joy flooded him. He'd never imagined falling in love. He had nothing against the idea, but he'd grown up without intimate friends and he'd never before felt a deep connection with a woman. He had colleagues, he had mentors, he had acolytes. The occasional lover. But nobody who addressed his soul as its equal.

From the first, Eleanor Trim had done that. Only she had seen him for the man he was.

She shifted, murmuring lazy satisfaction into his chest, and their bodies separated. He felt brief regret, then remembered that this was merely the beginning. They'd stay in this cottage a week and make plans. He couldn't ignore the demands of his real life, but somewhere he'd find room for Eleanor.

The inescapable fact was that lying here, holding her, listening to the rain patter against the windows—the storm had calmed even as lightning had flashed in this room—this moment felt more real than anything before. His so-called real life was unimportant compared to his need to keep this woman. She was as essential to him as air.

He already saw that there would be repercussions. He was accounted a brave man, but apprehension at what he'd started here pricked cold and sharp at his contentment.

Leath told himself that powerful sex turned his mind to mush. Tomorrow, his brain would return to its ruthless, ambitious, logical ways. No man made a lifetime commitment to a paramour. He owed his family a brilliant aristocratic wedding and political success at the highest level. A temporary mistress couldn't upset plans made in his cradle.

A temporary mistress…

Eleanor snuggled closer. The way she drifted off in his embrace moved him in ways he couldn't explain. He shifted to settle her more comfortably and drew the covers to keep her warm.

He'd never slept with a woman. It would never have occurred to him to linger cuddling the experienced ladies who had shared their favors. Yet while Eleanor's nearness stirred his hunger—he had an almighty hunger to appease—he didn't wake her. Not just because only a brute would use her again so soon.

The fire died down. He probably should do something about stoking it, but he was too contented to budge. Through the shadows, he watched Eleanor's beautiful face. She was so lovely. The sight of her made his heart dip in delight. It always had. He should have long ago realized that he was in love.

He closed his eyes, yet something clawed at him, rattled his peace. As he stared into the night, he realized that it was a single word.

Temporary.

Nell stirred to warmth and a glow of happiness. Strong arms encircled her. Musky scent teased her senses. She rested her head on a man's bare chest and his heart thudded beneath her ear. She nestled closer to that reassuring sound.

It was early. Pale light edged the curtains, but the sun was yet to rise. The room was dark. The fire had died long ago.

"Good morning," a deep voice murmured above her head.

She stretched against James, loving the hot slide of his skin. So far, life as a fallen woman was full of splendid surprises. She hadn't expected the pleasure she'd found last night, especially after the awkward beginning. She hadn't expected to feel so blissful waking in the marquess's arms.

"Good morning, my lord," she whispered back.

"I was James last night," he said softly.

"James." She said the word slowly, relishing the mellifluous hiss.

She kissed his chest, the hair tickling her nose. Luxuriously she rubbed her foot along his leg, feeling the rasp of hair there too.

"If you keep doing that, there will be consequences," he said on a rumble of amusement.

"How terrifying," she said drily. He started the day interested, she discovered.

She gasped when he tipped her onto her back and rose above her. "You're an impudent baggage."

Breathlessly, she laughed, running her hands over his broad shoulders. "I don't think you should call me names."

"I do." He glanced a kiss across her nose. "Sweetheart."

She shivered at the playful contact. The last traces of sleep ebbed.

Another kiss between her eyebrows. "Darling."

A squeak of pleasure escaped. She liked him to tease her. She liked it even better when he kissed her at the same time.

"Dearest." Two kisses this time, one on each fluttering eyelid. "Sweeting."

She tilted her chin in silent invitation. This game was diverting, of course it was. But her lips tingled for the taste of his.

"Beautiful girl." A kiss on her ear and a subtle puff of breath that made her toes curl.

She caught his arms in eager hands. "You won your point, my lord."

"My lord again?" He nibbled a line from her jaw up to her

ear and nipped at her earlobe. Another shivery ripple had her squirming into the sheets.

"Perhaps I want to call you names too."

He bit her earlobe again, then tugged with his teeth. She caught her breath. Who knew that something as humble as her ear offered such pleasure?

"Call me James, Eleanor."

"Will you kiss me if I do?"

"I won't if you don't."

Her eyes narrowed. Last night, she'd learned many things about James Fairbrother, Marquess of Leath. One was that she wielded more power over him than she'd credited.

She tried to read his expression, but the darkness defeated her. Instead, she sought other clues. His jagged breathing. The heat of his skin.

"You want me," she whispered, walking her fingers across the taut line of his shoulders and delighting in the way his skin tightened under the caress. She bumped her hips up to confirm his readiness. "You can't hide it."

He groaned and scraped his teeth down her neck. His beard chafed her delightfully. "No, damn you, I can't."

"That makes me happy." She tugged at his hair and he grunted as he kissed a particularly sensitive spot on her neck.

"I'd like to make you happy."

"Then you know what to do."

"Witch." He raised his head. "You'll still be sore."

She shifted, lifting her knees. Her thighs brushed his hips and she tilted into his pulsing virility. Pulsing virility that would soon be inside her if she had her way.

A wriggle to test for pain. She experienced a few twinges, but nothing to compare to her need. Even if he hurt her, the profound union when he joined his body to hers outweighed all discomfort. "Perhaps if we're careful."

He dropped his head and took her mouth in a tender kiss. Her lips parted on a sigh.

Even through the dim light, she felt his heated gaze. "I love that you're not coy. From the first, I wanted your honesty."

"I thought you wanted my surrender," she said, only half joking.

He smiled, his teeth a flash of white in the darkness. "That too." He kissed her again, running his tongue along the seam of her lips until she opened. "I'm merely human."

"Show me how human, James." She stretched up to prolong the kiss, using her tongue.

He lowered over her. His kiss spoke of stirring passion, but tenderness lingered like a star through mist. "With pleasure." He paused. "But, Eleanor, if you want me to stop, I will."

"Oh, my dear." She curved her hand around his strong neck. Her tone wasn't teasing. Instead she sounded like she choked on the love flooding her. He made her feel as fragile as lace and as strong as steel. She swallowed, moved to tears. Now was no time to yield to emotion. She'd entered this arrangement knowing that a mistress was neither permanent nor essential in a man's life. Yet every moment strengthened the bond between them.

If she started to believe in forever, she asked for a world of anguish.

She didn't know if he heard the betraying wobble in the endearment. She suspected he did because his kiss was sweet.

She caught his shoulders and angled forward in blatant invitation. He stroked her, there where she wanted him so badly. She shuddered and a whimper of enjoyment escaped. Before consenting to be his mistress, she'd come to terms with loving him. Now every touch left her shaking with desire.

Last night, he'd built her arousal slowly, but this morning he seemed, like her, impatient. His thumb brushed that place that shot thrills along her veins, then he shifted and hot thickness pressed into her.

She prepared for pain. But he slid into her smoothly and her body welcomed him the way the earth welcomed the sunrise. She gasped with wonder.

He shuddered into stillness. "Am I hurting you?"

She arched, changing the angle in the most delicious way. Another sigh of pleasure.

"Eleanor?" His voice cracked with strain. "Answer me."

She tugged him down for a hungry kiss. His hips flexed as he pushed deeper.

In the early light, she caught his faint smile as he raised his head. "I'm taking that as permission to continue."

She luxuriated in the long, slow glide of his body. How had she lived without this? But of course, she'd waited for the right man. As Leath circled his hips, setting off a fresh cascade of sensations, she knew he was the lover that she'd dreamed of all her life.

"Yes," she managed to say before closing her eyes on a moan as he thrust more purposefully, so deep that surely he must touch her womb. A declaration of love surged, but he shifted, withdrawing with a voluptuous languor that banished everything but pleasure from her mind.

He moved again and again with a primeval rhythm. Last night, she'd scaled the ladder to heaven. But this powerful possession of her body—a possession that extended to her heart too—proved that a thousand roads led to paradise.

Her hands trailed up and down his back, feeling his muscles tense then relax with every thrust. Ruthlessly, he tipped her, changing the angle again. Fresh heat seared her. She moaned when he kissed her tight nipples.

This time she dared to explore further. He plunged hard as her hands fluttered over the small of his back, then discovered two intriguing dimples on either side of his backbone. She'd always known he was a well-built man, but his naked form was pure power. She felt surrounded, conquered, devoured. She felt strong and fulfilled.

She ventured lower to caress firm buttocks. He jerked and bit out a curse when she scraped her fingernails across his flesh. The air was heavy with the scent of their mating.

He nipped her neck, making her shudder. The feeling that rose each time he entered her body surged. But he went still before she reached her climax.

"Not . . . yet," he gasped against her damp skin.

"I want this." She was barely aware of what she said. She plowed her fingers into his buttocks, compelling him to move. "I want you."

"Keep wanting me." He retreated and advanced.

She bowed up in response. His face filled her vision. Stark with arousal, flushed, mouth stretched over his teeth.

She hovered so close. So tantalizingly close. Again he stopped before she toppled over the edge. "You're torturing me."

His grunt might indicate frustration or amusement or both. "I want to show you what we can create together."

The light now was bright enough to reveal every strained line on his face. Deep brackets framed his mouth. She hooked her legs across his back, linking her ankles.

"Let go," she crooned, running her hands over his shoulders. "Let go."

"Eleanor, you destroy me," he gasped.

He jerked forward, claiming her, and this time as she rose, the wave was too great to stop. On a cry she broke through to the summit, then the whole world crashed around her in a rain of fire. The pleasure dashed her against the sky then back to earth then back to the sky.

Through the blinding tempest, she heard his guttural groan. Her body clenched anew against the surge of liquid heat and her fierce response drowned everything except joy.

And the fact that she'd love him until she died.

Chapter Twenty-One

Nell woke in Leath's—James's—embrace. Briefly, she basked in voluptuous memories of the night. When she wriggled free, he made a sleepy complaint, but didn't wake. The morning was brisk, and she rubbed her arms as she studied her lover.

The light revealed signs of tiredness, but he looked more at ease than he had at Alloway Chase. Only last night had she realized that the sexual pull between them had worn at him as it had worn at her. She had a feeling that if she woke him, he'd assuage that sexual pull again. But the weariness in his face—and knowing that she'd have his attention later—led her to kiss his bristly cheek, then collect her clothes from the floor. She blushed to remember how they'd got there, although surely a woman who had passed such a wanton night had no right to blush.

She washed and dressed in the small room adjoining the bedroom, wincing as muscles she'd never used before protested. Not that she minded. She felt as though the world was painted bright gold.

The world in fact was dark gray. Rain struck the windows with a force that made Nell grateful to be inside with the man she loved. A faint smile curved her lips as she wondered whether he'd take her back to bed this morning. She hoped so. Last night had hinted at oceans of sensuality waiting to be discovered.

She wandered downstairs to the kitchen, setting up breakfast and making tea. After missing dinner, James would be hungry. Then she tidied the parlor and set the fire. The housewifery was second nature. She'd run her stepfather's house since her mother's death. But she'd never worked for the comfort of a man who shared her bed.

Braving the weather, she retrieved a few bedraggled late roses from the bushes around the door. Upstairs all remained quiet.

Nell turned her attention to the entry hall, where James had flung his greatcoat and luggage before he'd carried her away to heaven. Usually he was the most orderly of men. She smiled to think that he'd arrived in such a fever he hadn't even stopped to hang his coat to dry.

For a lost moment, she hugged the damp greatcoat. This morning her progress was woefully slow. She kept stopping to recall the night: a daring caress; a tender kiss; wild sensations sizzling through her. The thought of James Fairbrother left her staring into space for minutes at a time. If she wasn't careful, she'd turn horribly dreamy. She'd never been in love before. The emotion's all-encompassing power astonished her.

Sighing at herself, she hung James's hat and coat beside her cape on the hooks near the door, then turned to his bags. He'd brought only a leather valise and a satchel of papers. The satchel was familiar from their first encounter in his library. In the days when she was convinced that the

Marquess of Leath was evil personified. How far she'd traveled since.

After lugging the bags into the parlor, she set the valise near the stairs. When he woke, he'd want his shaving gear and a clean shirt. She rubbed her face with one hand. He'd chafed her last night. And, she blushed to note, not just on the face.

She lifted the satchel onto the mahogany desk in the corner. The bag was heavier than expected and not fastened properly. When she slung it up, the contents cascaded across the priceless Turkey rug.

She smiled to think that even here, he brought work. Then she glimpsed her name on some legal document.

Curious, she gathered the papers and bore them to the couch. A quick glance at the document revealed that it set out Eleanor Charlotte Trim's agreement to become James Fairbrother's mistress. She didn't read it from beginning to end—it was dauntingly thick—but the man so thorough in political and estate matters had been equally thorough when it came to her ruin. There were provisions for allowances and gifts. And children.

When she reached the paragraphs mentioning progeny, her hand curved over her belly. She wasn't overjoyed about bearing the marquess's bastard, but she accepted that pregnancy was likely. Perhaps a baby already grew inside her. The thought of a child never free to claim its father shaved a few layers off her contentment. Perhaps she should wake James and make him remind her why she'd taken this reckless step.

Sighing, she set away the contract. James had drawn it up for her protection, but she couldn't like it. The dry language left her cringing. She felt like something the marquess had purchased.

A pile of letters bound with cord lay beneath the contract. Nell had no right to pry into James's correspondence so she bundled everything up.

Until a word caught her eye. A word that turned her blood to ice.

Baby.

Knowing she committed an unforgiveable breach of privacy, she snatched up the sheet of cheap paper. The hand was unformed, as though the woman writing it had little or no education. It was dated a week ago and signed "Your dearest Celie."

Bile stinging her throat, she read the pathetic lines addressed to the great marquess, pleading for money to support the little girl they'd made together. Fumbling, she knocked aside that letter and read the next. The same, except signed Mary and dated a fortnight ago. This child was a boy.

It couldn't be true. It couldn't.

Nell's mind insisted she stop, pretend that she'd never seen those pathetic words. But a force stronger than self-protection gripped her.

She read each letter more quickly, until she barely glanced at the last one. Another name. Another girl who could barely write. Another baby. Another desperate plea sent within the last month.

Numbly she stared down at the papers littering the sofa and the floor.

Leath had seduced all these women after he'd abandoned Dorothy, and there had been multitudes before Dorothy if Nell believed in the diary of debauchery.

She believed.

One letter had slipped behind a cushion. She straightened it and started to read.

This one was different. Someone called Hector Green-grass wanted Leath to pay him ten thousand guineas in return for a certain document. The short note, written in a vilely knowing tone that made her skin crawl, invited the marquess to arrange a meeting via a tavern in Newbury. It mentioned no names, but she immediately knew that he was talking about the diary of Leath's sexual exploits. The lecherous marquess had fallen into a blackmailer's clutches.

Nell closed her eyes and struggled to calm her pitching stomach.

Dorothy hadn't lied. Even down to the diary.

On a muffled cry, Nell lurched to her feet and rushed outside, leaving the door banging in the wind. She retched into the flowerbed, bringing up watery tea and not much else.

Feeling woozy, she stumbled upright, clinging to the cottage's whitewashed wall. Her legs trembled near collapse. Behind her eyes, the sad, begging, incriminating letters marched, one after the other. Each representing an innocent girl who had fallen foul of a rake's lies. Each representing a life destroyed.

She vomited again, although nothing was left inside her. Still she heaved until her stomach hurt. But nowhere near as badly as her heart.

Eventually she stood, head swimming. With an unsteady hand, she wiped cold rain from her face. More than anything, she wanted to scrub every inch of her skin. But she couldn't risk returning upstairs. Not when that brute lay in wait.

Disgust threatened to crush her into the mud. But this wasn't time for self-hatred. She'd have years to regret her stupidity and weakness.

Now she needed to escape. The scale of Lord Leath's

evil staggered her. She couldn't comprehend that the man she thought she'd known turned out so rotten. Turned out to be the man she'd originally believed him. He'd used her. Worse, she had an agonizing premonition that after her blistering anger cooled, she'd discover that he'd broken her heart too.

But she wasn't defeated. Finally she had proof of his sins. And, she thought, straightening, she was in Derbyshire. She'd always intended to enlist the Duke of Sedgemoor's influence to bring down the wicked marquess. His Grace's family seat, Fentonwyck, was mere hours away.

Leath's preparations for their affair had included delivery of a sweet little bay mare for Nell. She almost smiled. Before she was done, he'd be sorry he'd taught her to ride.

She must go. Before he woke. Before she saw him and recalled his filthy hands all over her. Worse, how she'd begged him to touch her.

Her stomach revolted again, but she placed a quelling hand over it. She might want to curl up somewhere dark and lonely and hide for the rest of her life. But she'd promised her beloved half-sister vengeance, and by God, she meant to get it.

Lifting her chin and squeezing her betrayed love into a tiny rancid ball deep in her soul, she rushed into the house and collected the letters. All the time, she strained to hear any sound from upstairs.

If Leath knew her plans, heaven knew what he'd do to her. Once she'd thought he was the last man to resort to violence. But then, she'd also convinced herself that he wasn't Dorothy's seducer. Nell's instincts when it came to the marquess were tragically flawed.

She flung her cloak around her and ran, slipping and sliding through the rain, to the stables. In her heart, one prayer echoed over and over: that she'd never see the Marquess of Leath's lying, handsome face again as long as she lived.

Leath stirred to what sounded like a horse galloping away. But surely that couldn't be. He'd chosen this cottage for its seclusion—and for the rugged beauty of the countryside. It must just be the wind rattling the windows.

He yawned and stretched luxuriously. He couldn't remember the last time he'd slept this late. He had no idea of the time, but the light outside, even with the rain, indicated a morning well advanced. He'd stayed awake most of the night, dwelling on transcendent pleasure, the woman who lay so confidingly beside him, and the paths his life had taken. And might yet take.

Through the long, quiet hours, Eleanor's presence had filled him with gratitude. What had happened extended beyond the physical realm. Their union changed everything. He wasn't a fool. He knew this bond was rare and precious. He knew that to prove himself worthy of this gift, he must overturn all his old certainties.

When he'd stirred in the early hours and found her so sleepily sensual, he couldn't stop himself. She'd taken him into her body and he'd felt like he'd found home. In a way he didn't understand, she turned the world to light. But he understood too well that if she took the light away, he'd languish in eternal darkness.

Now he was hard and ready for Eleanor who, by the feel of the sheets, had left the bed hours ago. He shivered. Odd to be so cold and so hot at once. And he was hungry. Unprecedented sexual satisfaction gave a man a big appetite. For food and for the woman he wanted.

He rose against the pillows. Where was Eleanor? The

cottage was eerily quiet. He was a little disappointed that she hadn't wakened him with a kiss—and with what came afterward. When he found her, he'd seduce her back to bed. After breakfast. Smiling at his plans, he scratched his chest and rolled out of bed.

To save her modesty, he tugged on his breeches. He let his shirt hang loose around his hips. He should wash. He should definitely shave—which meant retrieving his luggage from where he'd abandoned it in his elation at seeing Eleanor.

He pounded down the stairs to the neat parlor. But it was empty. Clearly Nell had been about. The room was tidy and he was almost sure that the roses on the windowsill hadn't been there last night. A fire blazed in the grate, making the room deliciously warm.

Where the devil was she? The weather was vile, too vile for a ramble across the hills. Frowning, more curious than worried, he searched for his mistress. He didn't need long. The house was little more than a cottage.

Leath grabbed his greatcoat, now neatly hung beside the door, and noticed with relief that her cape wasn't there. She must be in the stables.

His increasingly frenetic hunt through the outbuildings turned up no Eleanor Trim. And no sign of the Arab mare he'd bought her. He burst into the windswept yard between the stables and the house, flummoxed. The weather had deteriorated, yet she'd gone riding. Why?

He recalled those pounding hoofbeats. Not the wind after all.

What on earth was her game? The house was stocked with all they needed. And this wasn't a day for a pleasure jaunt.

Had he mistaken everything last night? Had he frightened

her into running away? Dear God, don't let him have hurt her. He'd tried his best to be gentle.

Sick with worry, he trudged back to the house, huddling into his coat against the driving rain. He hoped to Hades that wherever Eleanor was, she was warm and dry and safe. He tried to reassure himself that she'd merely wanted some fresh air. But he couldn't quash the certainty that something was vitally wrong.

He let himself back into the house and searched more thoroughly for some clue to her whereabouts. This time, he noticed his satchel on the sofa.

He frowned and crossed to empty it onto the upholstery. The contract slid out. Had that scared her away? Everything there was for her benefit—and the benefit of any children they produced. But after a night of passion, perhaps she balked at hard practicalities. He grimly recalled her reaction to his last attempt to discuss provisions for her welfare.

Eleanor Trim hadn't easily consented to be his mistress and only powerful desire—and he hoped, something stronger—lured her to his bed. Perhaps seeing herself as a kept woman in black and white had chased her off.

Except she was braver than that. And if the agreement didn't meet her approval, the woman who had stood up to him so often was perfectly capable of expressing her displeasure.

Leath supposed that he should be annoyed that she riffled through his private papers but right now, he was too desperate to learn where she'd gone—and more important, why—that he hardly cared. He'd lifted the satchel to slip the contract inside before he noted the absence of the other papers he'd carried ever since they'd started arriving at Alloway Chase in appalling numbers.

No, no, no. If she'd found those heartbreaking letters, what the hell had she thought?

He'd been worried since he'd come downstairs. Now horror shrank his belly to the size of a walnut. He checked each pocket in the satchel. The letters from the women the Marquess of Leath had betrayed were missing.

At last he knew exactly why Eleanor had left.

Chapter Twenty-Two

As he galloped through rain and wind back to Alloway Chase, Leath had plenty of time to condemn his recklessness in taking the satchel to Derbyshire and his even greater recklessness in leaving it unattended. Although what else could he do but keep those letters with him? If they fell into the wrong hands, the scandal would put every other scandal dogging his family into the shade.

He should have stowed the satchel somewhere safe when he'd reached the cottage. But he'd wanted Eleanor for so long and so desperately that when he'd seen her, he could think of nothing else.

Too late for regrets. What he had to do now was find her and explain.

Wet, angry, worried sick, lonely, he slammed into the great hall well past dark. Even after one night in her arms, Eleanor's absence carved a rift inside him. He'd hoped against hope that he might catch up with her on his way. No such luck.

He flung his dripping greatcoat at John and asked with a snap, "Is Miss Trim here?"

The footman looked startled. "No, my lord. Miss Trim has returned to her family. A relative's illness, I understand."

The story they'd concocted when planning their affair. Except one night surely didn't constitute an affair, damn it.

If only Nell had waited to confront him.

He sighed. Today "if only" had been a constant refrain.

Might his mother know where Eleanor had gone? They'd always chattered away like a pair of magpies. In the days when he hadn't trusted the helpful Miss Trim, that swift intimacy had troubled him.

Did he still trust Eleanor? Those letters could do enormous damage to the Fairbrother name and destroy his political career. Something in him insisted that the woman who had surrendered her virginity with such breathtaking sweetness wouldn't betray his secrets.

So why had she taken the letters? He hoped he'd soon have the chance to ask her.

It was too late to disturb his mother. But if the marchioness had some clue to where Eleanor went to ground, he needed to talk to her.

He mounted the elaborate marble and gilt staircase two steps at a time and strode toward his mother's rooms. A sharp knock at the door summoned Nancy, his mother's maid.

"My lord," the woman stammered, curtsying. He'd caught her at her mending. In one hand, she held a lacy fichu with a torn border. "Her ladyship has retired."

To assuage her insomnia, his mother usually took a book to bed. She'd told him that since Miss Trim's reading recommendations, she'd started to enjoy the hours before sleep. "Can you see if she's awake, Nancy?"

He stepped into the sitting room and watched Nancy light a couple of candles before disappearing into the bedchamber. Impatiently he prowled to the window, staring into the stormy night. Was Eleanor out in this weather? He prayed wherever she was, she was safe.

"My lord?"

"Yes?" He whirled around and his face must have betrayed his frustration. Nancy, who had known him since he was a boy, retreated swiftly.

"Her ladyship will see you."

Leath struggled for a shred of civility. Yet every hour without Eleanor pushed him closer to exploding. "Thank you."

He entered the shadowy vastness of his mother's bedroom. She was propped against the pillows, wearing a cream lace peignoir and a cap over her fair hair.

He hadn't been in here in years. His mother guarded her privacy, although he knew that she suffered excruciating pains in her legs when it was cold and wet as it was tonight.

"James," she said in concern, taking off her spectacles and extending her hands in his direction. "What's the matter?"

He caught her hands and kissed her cheek. "Mamma, I'm sorry to barge in, wet as a herring and covered in all my dirt."

"Has something happened?"

Damn it, he should have taken a few minutes to wash and change before intruding on his mother and frightening her. "Yes." He frowned. "No."

She patted the mattress beside her. "You don't sound very sure."

He sighed and slumped onto the bed, retaining her hands. It had been such a bugger of a day, he appreciated the loving connection. "I need to find Miss Trim."

"Nell? You know she left last week."

"Do you know where she went?"

"Home to her family, she said. Her aunt is ill." A frown lined the fine-drawn face that retained traces of youthful beauty. "It's odd. I thought she was an orphan."

"One can be an orphan and have aunts," Leath said, trying not to squirm. His mother had always guessed when his younger self was up to no good. Not that he'd been much trouble. Family expectations had weighed too heavily. "You must miss her."

His mother didn't smile. "Of course I do." She paused. "But nonetheless I'm glad she's gone."

Shocked, he tugged free. For the first time since Eleanor's disappearance, her whereabouts weren't paramount in his mind. "What the devil?"

His mother tapped his cheek in fond reprimand. "James, my life may be restricted, but I'm not blind."

He stiffened, even as dismay knotted his gut. It seemed he was no better at keeping secrets from his mother than he'd been as a lad. Still, he tried to cover his tracks. "I liked Miss Trim."

His mother finally smiled. "Not at first."

"I was worried at how quickly she gained your confidence."

"James, I'll say it again—I'm not blind. Nell made an unlikely housemaid, but her heart was true. I believe because her heart was true, she left."

Leath had a sinking feeling that was the case. She'd seen those incriminating letters and decided she'd tossed her chastity away on a rake. But he wouldn't give her up without a fight. Once he bloody well found her. "You think the aunt is a lie."

"I think that Nell recognized what was happening between you and made the only choice she could."

James hid a wince. "I—"

His mother raised a hand. "Don't bother prevaricating. The air all but sizzled."

"She didn't encourage me," he said uncomfortably.

"No, but that didn't mean she was unaffected." Regret

tinged his mother's voice. "I'm not so old that I can't remember temptation. I blame myself for flinging you together. By the time I'd realized what trouble I'd caused trying to get you to acknowledge Nell's qualities, it was too late."

"I'm a man of principle." What a liar he was.

"Yes, I thank God that you are. If you were like your uncle, I'd despair for the title. But sometimes attraction is too strong, even for a man of principle. You've never chased the servants before, James."

"I didn't chase her," he said uncomfortably, feeling like he'd been caught stealing bonbons from the larder.

"No." Her voice hardened. "Because you understand that the only role Nell can occupy in your life is as your mistress."

"Mamma, a man doesn't discuss such—"

She made a dismissive noise. "Don't treat me like a fool. Eleanor Trim is no man's temporary bedmate."

"You're right." All last night, he'd lain awake, holding the precious woman who had given herself with such wholehearted joy, suffering similar qualms.

"And you can't marry her."

With a low growl, he surged to his feet and strode across to the window. He rattled the curtains aside to reveal the storm. What was the point of lying? His mother had apparently known for weeks that he had a yen for Eleanor. "She's the most exceptional woman I know. She should have the world at her feet."

"I agree."

Surprised, he turned away from the depressing weather. "I don't understand."

His mother's body might have failed her, but her spirit remained strong. The stare she leveled on Leath cut to the soul. "She's not for you, James."

He gritted his teeth and spoke the words that had beat

in his head like a drum since last night. "She's intelligent, beautiful, perceptive, generous, conscientious. In everything but her humble birth, she makes the perfect marchioness."

His mother, always pale, turned ashen and recoiled against the pillows as if he'd threatened to strike her. "Oh, James, I'm so sorry." Compassion weighted her voice. "You're in love with her. I should have realized."

He wanted to deny it. But how could he? He loved Eleanor and in making that love a shameful secret, he'd done her a heinous wrong. "Surely that, most of all, qualifies her to be my wife."

His mother no longer looked like Boadicea ready to mow down a Roman legion. Instead her gaze was agonizingly sad. "Yes, it does. But as you said, her birth makes your marriage unthinkable."

"You always lecture me on equality," he said resentfully.

"Darling, she's a wonderful girl. But she and I both see what you refuse to recognize. The Marquess of Leath can't marry his housemaid and expect society to shrug its shoulders. You'd lose all the respect you've earned as a future leader of the nation. And a woman as proud as Nell would rankle at the world's disdain."

Did he want to marry Eleanor? She deserved a more honorable role than mistress. He'd always known that. That left two alternatives—make an honest woman of her or part from her forever. The second option condemned him to a barren wasteland. "There's no legal impediment."

His mother sighed with impatience. "We both know society's rules. Marrying the girl who cleans out your fireplaces, however worthy she is, would turn you into a pariah."

"Perhaps it would be worth it," he muttered, facing the window again to avoid his mother's disapproval. Wondering where Eleanor was, he caught the gold brocade curtain in one hand. He was no closer to knowing. When he'd asked his mother about his beloved's whereabouts, he hadn't expected an inquisition. He'd been naïve in the extreme.

"James, I beg of you, don't sacrifice your ambitions because you've lost your head over a pair of pretty brown eyes."

Numbly he stared into the night. "It's more than that, Mamma, and you know it."

Another sigh. "Yes, I do," she said reluctantly. "You aren't a shallow man."

"All of this is moot. I don't know where she is."

"And you want me to help you find her?"

He turned and bit out an appalled curse. His mother stood unsteadily, clinging to one of the carved posts rising from the baseboard. She hadn't stood without assistance in years. His conscience, already twitching over Eleanor, howled. Her expression warned him against helping her.

He'd driven his mother to this. For a man who prided himself on his scruples, he'd made a sodding mess of things.

"I fear for Miss Trim's safety." That at least was true.

His mother frowned. "She's safer away from you, wherever she is."

"So you won't help me?" This was the closest he'd come to a serious quarrel with his mother since adolescence.

"I won't let you sacrifice everything you've worked for."

Angry words rushed to his lips, but when he saw her face, he bit them back. "Please tell me."

His mother straightened against the bedpost. The burning light in her eyes made mockery of physical frailty. "Even if I knew where Nell is—and I don't—I wouldn't tell you. She's left for your sake as well as her own. This ridiculous infatuation hasn't overturned her mind the way it's overturned yours."

"I intend to find her."

His mother's hand tightened around the column until the

knuckles shone white. "And if you find her, what will you do? Crush all my hopes? All your father's hopes?"

He flinched. "I just want to make sure she's safe."

His mother's face crumpled and tears glittered in her eyes. Despite her constant pain, his mother never cried. "Stop lying to me—and stop lying to yourself. No man who marries his housemaid will become prime minister. You'll be a laughingstock. And for what? A girl who can never play her role as the Marchioness of Leath with any conviction? Surely you're not so far gone in madness that you think that a fair bargain."

Was he? He didn't know. What he did know was that he felt like the lowest worm in creation for distressing his mother. He crossed the room and put his arm around her waist to stop her falling.

"I'm sorry I've made you unhappy."

She was unyielding in his arms, although she couldn't hide her relief once he'd returned her to bed. "But you're not sorry about this destructive path you take." His mother's hand closed convulsively on his arm. Her voice vibrated with urgency. "I beg you to reconsider."

He straightened. "I won't do anything rash."

All his life, she'd worked toward her son achieving the political greatness that fate had denied his father. If it became public knowledge that Eleanor was Leath's mistress, the world would snicker. But if one of the nation's greatest noblemen married his housemaid, an almighty scandal would ensue, one that would echo down the generations.

His mother was right. The kindest thing Leath could do for Eleanor was to let her go, let her find a good, respectable man who would love her and give her the life she deserved. Except that she was no longer a virgin. Guilt cut deeper every time Leath thought how he'd wronged her. Guilt that came with a wicked serve of pleasure as he recalled her body opening to his.

His mother was right about something else—Leath loved Eleanor and given his steadfastness, the affliction was likely to be permanent.

"James, you'll break my heart," his mother whispered. She looked deathly tired now that the brief vitality fueled by temper faded.

"Forgive me, Mamma," he said softly, kissing her forehead and stroking back the strands of graying blond hair that escaped her cap.

Her expression didn't lighten. They both knew that an appeal for forgiveness wasn't capitulation.

Chapter Twenty-Three

Nell finally reached the end of the meandering drive leading up to Fentonwyck. This huge baroque palace was the family seat of His Grace, the Duke of Sedgemoor. The man the papers described as Leath's implacable enemy. The man she prayed would expose the marquess's crimes to public scrutiny.

She was shivering and soaking wet and her feet had turned into blocks of ice hours before she'd passed through the neat village clustering around the estate's elaborate wrought-iron gates. Her mare had started limping a good ten miles ago and now trudged at her side, head lowered in misery. After Nell's night with Leath, riding had felt like the worst torture—until she'd tried hiking through the storm.

"Not far now, darling," she whispered to the horse, although the wind whipped her words away.

On Nell's other side, the taciturn gatekeeper who braved the weather to accompany her stumped along, holding his lamp high. He wore oilskins and carried an umbrella. He'd offered one to her, but it provided little protection.

Still, she appreciated his kindness. He'd suggested she wait in the gatehouse while he fetched the duke, but Nell couldn't bear any delay. She itched to lay her evidence before Sedgemoor at the earliest opportunity. She prayed that the letters had survived the journey. They were packed in straw and sealed in a saddlebag.

"There be the house," the gatekeeper said, the first words he'd spoken in what felt like hours. "His Grace be entertaining."

Nell gulped, stopping abruptly at the sight of the long façade. Even through the rain, Fentonwyck's magnificence was visible. A symmetrical row of windows, nearly all lit despite the late hour. A curved double staircase rising to a balustraded terrace.

When she'd found those damning letters, she'd thought only as far as escaping Leath and fleeing to his enemy. Now that she stood outside this enormous house, feeling friendless and bedraggled, she quailed from facing a pack of supercilious aristocrats.

"I don't—" she began.

But the gatekeeper slogged on through the rain and didn't hear. Nell mustered her fading strength and followed him. Her mare—she hadn't even had a chance to ask Leath what the animal's name was—sensed that shelter was near because she moved more readily when Nell tugged the reins. The beast had been a gallant companion and Nell had suffered more than one pang over forcing the fine-bred horse to struggle on through exhaustion.

To her relief, the man took Nell around the back into a yard surrounded by outbuildings. Everything dissolved into movement and noise so that more quickly than she'd ever imagined, she found herself wrapped in a towel and dripping onto the tiles in a small office near the kitchens. Somehow through all the activity, she'd remembered to grab the saddlebag. Her numb fingers had trouble holding it. There was a fire in the hearth, but the heat returning to her skin was more painful than restorative.

Vaguely through her daze, she heard the door behind her open. "Miss Trim, you needed to see me urgently?"

Unsteady with cold and dread, she slowly turned. She'd never seen the Duke of Sedgemoor, although sketches of him often appeared in the papers. She couldn't mistake that the tall, serious man regarding her with a mixture of interest and wariness was familiar with command. Leath conveyed the same air, although physically he was more heavily muscled.

"Your Grace," she whispered, dipping into an awkward curtsy.

His hand caught her elbow as she struggled to rise. "Dear girl…"

"You'll curse me for interrupting your evening," she said, although that was hardly the most important thing she had to say. Tiredness and heartbreak made her stupid.

His grip was firm and strangely comforting. "That doesn't matter. Rest now and we'll speak tomorrow."

She heard kindness, then reminded herself that she'd believed Leath was kind. These powerful men defied her instincts. "No, I must do this now."

Shivering, she thrust the wet saddlebag forward. The room started to recede in an alarming way and she had a superstitious terror that if she failed at this last challenge, she'd fail altogether. "You must destroy the Marquess of Leath."

The duke's eyebrows arched in astonishment and he stepped back without taking the letters. "James Fairbrother?"

Bone-deep bitterness emerged through her exhaustion. "Is there another?"

"My dear Miss Trim…"

"He's ruined hundreds of innocent girls, including my sister Dorothy. I want…"

She paused. Even through her desperation, she understood that one did not tell a nobleman of Sedgemoor's standing what one wanted and expect him to leap to obey. She licked her lips and tried to straighten, but shudders racked her. She clutched the towel more closely, but it was as sodden as her dress and offered no warmth. She edged toward the fire, hoping to bolster her strength. Her head pounded and she had difficulty grabbing a full breath. Still, she made herself go on.

"I'm here to beg Your Grace to take action against this man."

Nell wasn't sure what she'd expected from the duke, but it wasn't a cool and assessing inspection that made her feel beneath contempt. "Miss Trim, you can't go around making wild accusations," he said, the chill contrasting with his former kindness.

She raised her chin. She could do this. For Dorothy, who had deserved so much better. For all Leath's victims. She didn't count herself in that number. She'd invited her downfall. Unlike those other girls, she'd known what he was, yet she'd fallen as readily as a ripe plum from a tree.

"I have proof." She battled to straighten her arm as again she held out the saddlebag. "You'll see."

He took the bag, mainly to save her from dropping it, she thought. "I'm sure there's some mistake."

Even through the storm in her head, a storm as violent as the one outside, a grim premonition arose that she'd made a mistake. This handsome, dark-haired man didn't behave like someone who finally had his foe in his sights.

"No," she croaked. "No mistake."

"His lordship's reputation—"

"Is a sham like his lordship," she snapped, before reminding herself that she acted like a yahoo and that if she wasn't careful, the duke would throw her out on her ear. If he did, where could she go to obtain vengeance? The marquess would squash any lesser man who came against him the way his boot squashed a bug.

The duke placed the bag on the floor and took her arm again. "You're not well."

"That doesn't matter," she said in a rush, knowing that her legs wouldn't support her much longer. "All that matters is that you stop him."

"We'll talk when you're feeling more yourself."

The duke's voice echoed eerily. She'd felt so frozen when she came inside. Now the fire in the grate crawled along her skin like biting ants.

She dug her fingers into his sleeve. "Please," she tried to whisper. Darkness edged her vision. "Please…"

The floor rose up to strike her.

In too much turmoil to sleep, Leath retreated to his library. He bitterly regretted quarreling with his mother. All his life, he'd been protective of her frail health. But making his peace with his mother meant sundering his connection with Eleanor. And he wasn't willing to do that.

He threw himself into the leather chair behind his desk and watched John light the candles and set the fire. When he was alone, he glanced around this extravagant room that he'd always loved, and at last recognized that Alloway Chase was indeed haunted. Not by poor Lady Mary reputed to walk the battlements on windy nights, although God knew the night was windy enough to wake a hundred specters.

No, the ghost who haunted him was the woman he loved.

"Goddamn it," he growled, slamming his hands on the leather blotter and upsetting a pile of mail.

He rose and gathered the letters, idly flicking through them. Reports from his various estates. Invitations he had no intention of accepting. Correspondence from his dwindling number of political allies. A letter from Berkshire that must report on the search for that blackmailing bastard Hector Greengrass.

Leath's heart crashed to a stop and he ripped one particular letter from the rest. Hands shaking, he tore it open and moved closer to the fire to read it.

It was from the inquiry agent he'd engaged to check Miss Trim's background. She'd arrived bearing impressive references from a Lady Bascombe of Willow House in Sussex. The agent had written several times saying that he was yet to locate the manor.

Urgently, Leath scanned the few lines. Far too few lines to convey much information, he quickly realized. Sykes had covered Sussex from top to bottom and side to side and he could categorically state that Willow House did not exist. Lady Bascombe was equally fictitious.

Feeling sick, Leath lowered the letter.

The knowledge that Eleanor had deceived him from the start made him crush the note into a ball. Yet while he was bewildered and angry, he wasn't surprised. He'd always known that she wasn't what she claimed. As his mother had said, Eleanor was a most unlikely housemaid. She hadn't even tried to hide that she'd been educated beyond the level of most servants or that her proud spirit was unaccustomed to bowing to authority.

The problem now was that if Eleanor had fabricated her history, he had no idea where to look for her. Was her name even Eleanor Trim?

Then he recalled her father's war records. Whatever else was false, everything she'd told him about Sergeant Major Trim was true.

Her father had been a Kentish man. With sudden determination, Leath returned to the desk and wrote instructions to Sykes to continue the hunt in Kent. Now he sought Eleanor Trim, daughter of Sergeant Major Robert Trim, late of Wellington's Army in Portugal. Leath included all the information he had, including the timing of her mother and her half-sister's deaths, and prayed that it was enough.

Chapter Twenty-Four

Nell stirred from sleep and blindly slid her hand across the bed, seeking James. When she encountered empty space, she remembered everything and opened her eyes with a sharp cry.

"Miss Trim, pray be calm." A lovely dark-haired woman leaned over her with a concerned expression. "You're safe here at Fentonwyck."

Behind the woman, the room was vast and decorated with paintings that Nell recognized as masterpieces. She struggled to sit, wincing as her body reminded her that yesterday she'd traveled miles.

Had it been yesterday?

"What happened?"

The stranger was round with child and wearing a beautiful loose gown in green velvet. Her black eyes were bright with amusement and interest. "Last night you appeared out of a thunderstorm, spouting extravagant denunciations against Lord Leath, then you fainted into my husband's arms. It was a performance worthy of the Theatre Royal."

Nell felt as though she'd been battered by rocks, but she still managed to blush. This beautiful creature must be the Duchess of Sedgemoor. "Your Grace, I'm sorry to disrupt your household."

Her Grace laughed. "Your arrival brightened up a party that became odiously dull. Please don't apologize."

Nell felt increasingly awkward. This room was fit for a queen, not a mud-spattered nobody. "I've put you to great inconvenience."

"Rubbish. We have plenty of space and a regiment of servants standing idle." She rose and crossed to the window where she flung the curtains wide with a rattle that made Nell flinch. Nor did the bright light help her pounding head.

It was late morning, over twenty-four hours since she'd discovered proof of Leath's offenses. What had he done when he found her missing? He must know that Nell's possession of the letters meant exposure. He'd be furious, and desperate to silence her before she sparked a scandal.

She should be terrified. But it was difficult to be frightened cocooned in this feminine bower, with a duchess inquiring after her comfort. Leath couldn't hurt her here.

She was such a fool—despite everything she knew, she found it hard to see his lordship hurting her at all.

The thought of Leath stabbed like a knife and made her want to curl up and howl out her agony. She cringed to remember that betraying moment when she'd reached for him. How was it that after one night, she couldn't imagine waking up without him beside her?

"I planned to see His Grace then leave."

"You're in no fit state to go anywhere." The duchess sent Nell an assessing look. "And I hardly think Sedgemoor will accept the documents you produced without asking about your dealings with Lord Leath."

Curse these blushes. If she wasn't careful, the duchess might guess just what her *dealings* with Leath had involved. "You've seen the letters?"

"Of course," the duchess said coolly, crossing to a gilt and marble table where a tea tray waited.

After nigh drowning in yesterday's rain, it seemed absurd to be so thirsty. Nell fought to leave the bed, weary muscles resisting the activity. Only then did she realize that she wore an embroidered white lawn nightdress that would cost a housemaid more than a year's wages.

The duchess turned from pouring tea to catch Nell's attempts to stand. "What on earth are you doing?"

"It's not fitting for you to wait upon me, Your Grace."

"Nonsense." Calmly she finished preparing the tea. "Lie down. I'm surprised you're awake at all. You looked ready to give up the ghost. But the doctor said that with rest, you'll be fine."

"The doctor..." Nell fell back. Whatever her mind demanded about leaving this room, her legs weren't ready to take her.

"Yes." Her Grace glided across the pale blue floral carpet that matched the ceiling's plasterwork and extended a cup and saucer. "He came last night."

Automatically Nell took the tea, although her hand shook so badly that she feared spilling it over the exquisite bedding. "I've put you to so much trouble. This wasn't what I intended."

The duchess waved a graceful hand and slid a brocade-covered chair closer. "I've told you no apologies are necessary."

Why was this woman so needlessly kind to a stranger? "I must dress and see His Grace."

The heavily pregnant duchess sat with endearing clumsiness. She leveled an unwavering stare upon Nell. "Once you've regained your strength."

Before Nell could argue, a knock heralded the arrival of a striking blond woman carrying another tray. "I intercepted the maid outside. I can't contain my curiosity any longer. Who is your mysterious invalid, Pen?"

The duchess smiled and Nell caught her breath at the woman's beauty. In the newspapers, she'd seen sketches of the Duchess of Sedgemoor. Scandal had shadowed the union from the start, even before the duke and duchess became embroiled in Sophie Fairbrother's elopement. "Come in, Genevieve. I'm surprised Sidonie isn't here too."

"She's in the stables with Jonas, admiring your guest's mare." The newcomer's ice-blue eyes sharpened on Nell with unconcealed interest as she deposited the tray on a table. "Jonas says that Leath bought that bay at Tattersall's last week. He particularly remembers because he went up against the marquess for her and lost."

Nell felt as if her cheeks must catch fire. "I'm sure he's mistaken."

"Jonas has a memory like a steel trap for horseflesh." The blond woman paused. "Actually Jonas just has a memory like a steel trap."

With every moment, Nell felt more out of place. The gatekeeper had mentioned the house party, but only now in the presence of these elegant women who were clearly good friends did she realize how she'd intruded.

To Nell's astonishment, the duchess took her hand. "Miss Trim, please ignore Lady Harmsworth. She has an inquiring mind."

The blonde laughed. "You mean I'm incurably nosy, Pen."

Her Grace sent her friend a quelling glance before turning back to Nell. "You needn't tell us anything you don't want to."

"I'd…I'd like to see His Grace as soon as possible," Nell

said tremulously, wondering why she didn't open her mouth and denounce Leath.

"Have your breakfast," the duchess said in a soothing voice.

The thought of eating under Lady Harmsworth's inquisitive gaze made her stomach revolt. The papers had been full of stories about the famous scholar who last year had married the ton's darling, Sir Richard Harmsworth. An inquiring mind, indeed. And one Nell, in her weakened state, was in no shape to defend herself against. "Thank you, but I'm not hungry."

"Of course you are. We'll leave you in peace."

"But—" Lady Harmsworth protested.

The duchess stood. "Miss Trim has barely caught her breath since her ordeal."

Resisting Her Grace was like trying to fight a cloud of feathers. Despite Nell's demurrals, the duchess and Lady Harmsworth soon had her tucked up in bed with the tray on her knees and fresh tea on the nightstand.

At last they gave her the blessed relief of privacy. Nell took her first unconstricted breath since she'd awoken to this astonishing treatment. She told herself that if she persisted, justice would prevail. But as she contemplated the delicacies before her, all she felt was lonely and betrayed.

A soft knock disturbed Leath's troubled doze. He shifted and wondered why his head wasn't on its usual soft pillow, but resting on something much more unforgiving. He needed a few dazed seconds to understand that he'd fallen into oblivion at his desk. As if in disapproval, the hall clock struck ten.

Self-disgust thundered through him. How could he sleep when Eleanor was in trouble? Sitting up, he rubbed heavy eyes. He ached, and there was a crick in his neck.

Wells entered with a letter on a silver salver. "My lord, forgive my intrusion, but this just arrived from the Duke of Sedgemoor and the messenger insists it's urgent."

Sedgemoor? Why the devil was Camden Rothermere writing to him? They'd met occasionally since Sophie and Harry Thorne's wedding in May. Relations had improved, thanks, Leath admitted, to the new duchess, a woman remarkably ready to forgive. But the duke and he would never be friends.

"Thank you, Wells." Leath picked up the letter. If Sedgemoor expected immediate attention, he could rot in hell. Leath had more important matters to worry about than some trivial request from His Grace. Two footmen entered the room to set breakfast on a side table as he stared in a funk at the letter in his hand.

Leath started when Wells passed him a cup of coffee. "I took the liberty of arranging a meal, my lord."

"Bless you." He was still half asleep, tormented by images of Eleanor alone and unprotected. Damned fool of a woman. Why hadn't she waited, instead of taking to her heels?

The fog in his head cleared as he sipped his coffee. The footmen finished fiddling and left. Knowing he wasted his time, and worse, incited unwelcome curiosity, he glanced at his butler. "Has there been word of Miss Trim overnight?"

Wells's demeanor remained impassive. "No, my lord."

Leath sacrificed his pride, and was surprised that it hardly hurt at all. "Do you know where she's gone?"

Wells stared into the distance. "She said she returned to her family."

"Was she likely to confide in anyone below stairs?"

"No, sir."

Leath gritted his teeth. "Is that the best you can do?"

Wells focused on Leath and betrayed a hint of the man

beneath the servant. His voice became less clipped. "Miss Trim became her ladyship's companion not long after starting here. She didn't have time to develop close ties with any member of staff, my lord."

The coffee made him feel almost human. "And she wasn't like the other housemaids, was she?"

Astonishingly, Wells's mouth twitched. "If she hadn't arrived with such good references and if we hadn't been short-staffed, I doubt I'd have taken her on. As it was, I assumed that she'd quickly prove unsuitable."

Well, that answered one question that had always bothered him. Wells was too sharp to miss that Eleanor Trim wasn't the usual servant. "So she wasn't liked?"

Wells looked shocked. "My lord, you misunderstand. Of course there was some jealousy at her quick promotion, but Miss Trim never put on airs and anyone with sense could see that she was good for her ladyship. I would say that she was very well liked indeed. We were all sorry to hear that because of family illness, she had to leave."

"So where should I start looking for her?"

Wells refilled Leath's cup. "Her last place was in Sussex. The mistress there, a Lady Bascombe, described her in superlatives."

And that had been a pack of lies from beginning to end, Leath now knew. "I'd appreciate it if you keep an ear open for any mention of Miss Trim's destination."

"Have you asked Mr. Crane? He and Miss Trim were friendly."

Leath's shoulders tensed the way they did before a boxing bout, even as he knew he couldn't clout Wells. The man was at least twenty years older than he was and apart from that, he'd faithfully served the Fairbrothers all his life. "What do you mean by that?"

"Exactly what I said, sir. Miss Trim helped Mr. Crane when he was incapacitated."

Leath told himself to back down. If anyone knew that Eleanor had been chaste, he did. At this rate, the servants' hall would buzz with gossip that his lordship had gone completely dotty over a housemaid.

The servants' hall, unfortunately, would have it right.

"Her dealings with Crane were completely innocent," Leath snapped.

"Yes, my lord. I implied nothing else." Wells watched him steadily and Leath cringed at the lack of surprise in his eyes. For all his attempts to conceal his interest in his mother's companion, apparently everybody at Alloway Chase had noticed it.

"I'm sorry, Wells. I'm worried about her."

The butler bowed. "I shall make discreet inquiries."

"Thank you."

Once Wells left, Leath realized that he hadn't opened Sedgemoor's message. Sighing, he broke the seal. Then, picking up his half-empty coffee cup, he read the few scrawled words. And slammed down his cup so hard that coffee splattered across the desk.

Chapter Twenty-Five

Not until afternoon could Nell escape the duchess's benevolent tyranny and arrange an appointment with the duke. Physically she felt stronger, although the wound in her heart over Leath's treachery seeped perpetual poison.

A footman escorted her across a gleaming parquet floor to a closed door. Nell squared her shoulders, but she feared that she'd left her courage in the cottage in the Peaks. She smoothed her skirts, unaccustomed to the feel of the rich fabric. Apparently her dress was still drying. This gorgeous dark blue gown belonged to Lady Hillbrook, who was close to her size. The duchess was long and lean like an elegant greyhound. Lady Harmsworth was built like a valkyrie.

Lady Hillbrook, another beautiful brunette although less inclined than the duchess to insist on her own way, had provided a couple of dresses more extravagant than anything Nell had ever owned. Although she reflected sourly that Leath's mistress would wear clothes like this. She vaguely remembered a dress allowance in that prosaic contract. Probably she should be flattered that he'd had it drawn up.

If those pathetic letters were any indication, he hadn't taken such trouble with the other women he'd duped.

The thought of those letters and what she owed Dorothy steadied wavering courage.

The door opened and she stepped into a spacious library, more leather and mahogany than Leath's extravaganza in marble and gold, but just as impressive. She gulped back traitorous weakness, as memories of hours working with the marquess overcame her. Hours when she'd deceived herself that she served a man of principle. She'd fallen in love with that man, but he was a chimera. Her love had been fatally misplaced, but the effort to crush it hurt. Dear God, it hurt.

She blinked back tears and realized that this encounter would be even more daunting than expected. The room overflowed with tall, well-dressed men. She blinked again and raised her chin. She'd risked so much for this moment. She couldn't falter. Even if, despite everything, some shameful element deep in her soul recoiled from Leath's destruction.

Nell told herself that she felt guilty about the marchioness. But the truth was that her foolish, faithful heart hadn't relinquished its love. And the futile hope that she was mistaken. That those letters were meant for some other Marquess of Leath. That she'd misunderstood Dorothy's dying words.

"Miss Trim, how are you feeling?" The duke abandoned his companions and approached with a ground-eating stride that reminded her painfully of Leath's prowl.

Stop it, Nell. You're only torturing yourself. Avenge Dorothy, then go away and establish a life.

Except that even now, she couldn't imagine a life without the vile, duplicitous Lord Leath. She really was a hopeless case.

"Your Grace." She dipped into a curtsy, hopefully more graceful than last night's stumble.

He took her arm with a firm gentleness that reminded her of the duchess and drew her toward a seat near the fire. The crowd dwindled to a handsome blond man and a brawny figure with horrific scars marking his saturnine face. Both took chairs near her while the duke stood before the hearth.

A rough-coated brindle hound rose in front of the fire and wandered lazily across to Nell. For a moment, intelligent dark eyes inspected her, then he settled on the floor at her side with a doggy groan.

"Don't mind Sirius," the fair man said.

"I've ordered tea. Would you like some?" Sedgemoor clearly sought to put her at ease. But her eyes immediately fastened on the papers near his elbow on the mantelpiece. Familiar papers. Papers condemning the Marquess of Leath.

"No, thank you," she said faintly, grateful to be sitting. She had a horrible feeling that if she tried to stand, her legs might crumple beneath her. Her hand dropped to fondle the dog's soft ears. At least one creature in this room seemed to be on her side.

As if understanding her nervousness, the blond man sent her an encouraging smile. Thanks to the newspapers, she knew who these men were. The Adonis was Sir Richard Harmsworth, arbiter of fashion. The scowling beast was Jonas Merrick, Viscount Hillbrook, reputedly the richest man in Europe. All this masculine power in one room made her feel short of air. She gulped against faintness.

"Miss Trim, I hope you don't mind that I've invited Lord Hillbrook and Sir Richard to hear what you have to say," Sedgemoor said.

The two men bowed in her direction as Sedgemoor

performed the introductions. She straightened and told herself for Dorothy's sake, she could do this. She'd failed her sister in her last months. She wouldn't fail her now.

Nell steadied her voice, although she was sure they heard the betraying huskiness. "The more people who know about Lord Leath's offenses, the better. The whole point of bringing you the letters, Your Grace, is for you to make their contents public."

There. She was committed. She ignored her heart's anguished entreaties to give Leath the benefit of the doubt. She had no doubts.

"Before I take this further, I need to know a little more. Whether the letters are genuine, for example."

Surprised, Nell stared at him. All through yesterday's purgatorial journey, she'd played this scene out in her mind. She'd imagined that she'd show the duke the letters, he'd gratefully accept this chance to crush his enemy, then he'd take control of the marquess's comeuppance. Stupidly, it had never occurred to her that His Grace might doubt the letters' authenticity.

"We're not questioning your honesty, Miss Trim," Sir Richard said. "But it's possible that someone is using you to harm Leath, some political enemy perhaps."

She stifled a bitter laugh. "The letters are real. I took them from his lordship's personal luggage yesterday morning." She paused. "And I have my own reasons for wanting to bring Lord Leath to his knees."

Hillbrook and Sir Richard shared a speaking look, and she clenched her fists in her lap, trepidation retreating behind rage. Finding those letters had reawakened her anger and grief over Dorothy's death. That anger now gave her impetus to continue.

In a low voice and with a firmness that surprised her, Nell

set out the tale of Dorothy's ruin and her decision to seek justice for her half-sister. She spoke about her weeks at Alloway Chase and her thwarted attempts to find proof of the marquess's debauchery. The only part of the story she didn't share was her idiocy in falling victim to the libertine. She made no attempt to hide her deceptions and failures, apart from her heart's failure to recognize a liar.

By the time she'd finished, the short twilight had deepened into night. His Grace had lit the candles, but the room was shadowy and the atmosphere felt increasingly conspiratorial.

She was grateful that the men had listened without interruption. If she'd needed to stop and defend her statements, she'd have lost all confidence. "When I found the letters, I came here, seeking a champion."

"But why come to me?" Sedgemoor asked. "Had we met?"

"No, Your Grace. The newspapers said that you and Lord Leath were at outs. I hoped you'd have a vested interest in helping."

Sir Richard frowned. "If what Miss Trim says is true, the man is a rabid dog."

Hillbrook too looked troubled. "If it's true. I must say I haven't seen anything to indicate villainy at this level."

"The letters prove it." Nell struggled not to sound desperate. "If you don't believe me, track down the women who wrote them. And there's the added proof of the letter blackmailing his lordship for return of the diary."

"Ah, the diary," Sedgemoor said thoughtfully, steepling his fingers and tapping them on his chin. He now sat in the circle with the rest of them. "Lord Leath doesn't strike me as a man partial to melodrama. And surely he's too clever to leave such condemnatory evidence."

"It clearly exists." After hearing her story, how could they doubt that Leath must be stopped? "Dorothy saw it and this Greengrass man claims to have it."

"Cam and I have experience of Greengrass," Sir Richard said. "I wouldn't trust him as far as I can throw him. And given he's a big brute, that's not far at all."

"Although I hear you bested him in three punches," the duke said, surprising Nell. She'd immediately labeled the elegant fellow as decorative rather than useful.

Sir Richard looked uncomfortable. "Genevieve told you about that, did she?"

"She told Pen." ·

"That's the same as telling you." Sir Richard glanced across at Nell. He was the least imperious of the three men. His blue eyes were kind and when he smiled, she felt like he meant it.

Lord Hillbrook seemed to reserve judgment, but when he examined her, his cold black eyes pierced to her soul. Pray God he didn't see the roiling confusion there or the humiliating truth that Leath's dupes included Eleanor Trim.

His Grace was harder to read. She picked up no hostility, but her revelations hadn't roused his enthusiasm.

Sir Richard slouched picturesquely in his chair. He was the handsomest man she'd ever seen. It was difficult to imagine him married to the terrifyingly clever Genevieve. "My apologies. We speak in riddles, Miss Trim. This isn't our first encounter with Hector Greengrass. He worked for Leath's uncle, Neville Fairbrother, whose outrages would make your hair curl."

"Clearly Lord Leath comes from a rotten tree," she said grimly, still struggling against feelings of disloyalty toward her deceitful lover. "The family connection must be how Greengrass got the diary."

"The evidence against Leath seems damning," Hillbrook

said slowly. "But I still find it a stretch to believe that he's responsible. For a start, I can't see how his parliamentary work left him time to pursue women up and down the country. The fellow must never sleep to be so busy in the government and still fit in all this wenching."

Nell studied the three men and saw that her story, while it had undoubtedly moved them, hadn't convinced them of Leath's guilt. She surged to her feet, disgust and outrage twisting like snakes in her belly. Her sudden movement startled Sirius from his doze and he jumped up, bristling.

She should have realized that when push came to shove, justice wouldn't outweigh the aristocratic bond. These men were reluctant to expose Leath as a blight on the country, because they were linked through birth and prestige. A black mark against the marquess constituted a black mark against all noblemen.

She wouldn't let them close ranks. "If you won't help me, I'll go elsewhere," she said adamantly. "The press will be interested, I'm sure."

All three rose when she did. Part of their gentleman's code. Like protecting their own. The duke spoke in a soothing tone. "My dear Miss Trim, let's not be hasty."

She frowned. "We need to be hasty. Lord Leath has done enough damage."

Nell couldn't interpret the look that the duke sent the other two men. "We know you believe that. But before we take action, we need to be sure the facts are straight. If we attack Leath publicly, only to find that we're on shaky ground with our accusations, he'll sue us for libel then continue with impunity."

"We need to be certain of our footing," Hillbrook said. "Although I understand your impatience."

"Especially after weeks in the cad's company," Sir Richard said.

She searched his face, but found no ulterior meaning to his comment. "I owed it to my sister."

The heat in her cheeks flared as she remembered what she'd done with wicked Lord Leath during those weeks. Thank God these men weren't mind readers. Although when she saw Lord Hillbrook's eyes narrow, she feared that perhaps he might be.

No, that was her guilty conscience speaking. She'd been misled and mistaken. Now she aimed in the right direction. She'd avenge Dorothy. She'd make sure Leath despoiled no more innocent girls. And if she died trying, she'd mend the jagged chasm in her soul.

"With investigation, it's possible that we'll find more evidence," Hillbrook said.

She sighed. "I hoped that my part was done and I could leave everything to you."

Sedgemoor smiled. His air of self-containment and competence provided the perfect foil for Leath's energy and cleverness. "Miss Trim, we only ask you to stay while we dig a little deeper."

"You can contact me in Mearsall," she said desperately. She was frantic to return to her old life, to prove that she was the same person she'd been, to forget tall, gray-eyed lords who lied.

"A few days," His Grace said. "These allegations are so grave, we'll have to back them to the final word."

Unwillingly she nodded, although disappointment tasted bitter. She didn't want to play the crusader. She wanted to find somewhere to hide away and come to terms with her sins. And her broken heart.

To Nell's dismay, her warm welcome at Fentonwyck continued. She'd assumed that after that interview with His Grace and his cronies, she'd remain in her room awaiting developments. Or in view of her status as lowborn interloper, the duchess would shift her to the servants' quarters. Even if upon arrival, the Rothermeres had mistaken her for some wayward gentlewoman—her clothes were cheap, but her horse definitely wasn't—when she'd told her story, she'd been frank about her humble background.

But instead of exiling her to the attics while these powerful men decided whether to support her, the duchess invited her to dinner. It meant an odd number at the table, but Nell quickly realized that these six remarkable people didn't stand on ceremony. Nell also recognized the strong bonds of friendship between them. Most painful of all, she'd be blind not to see the love uniting each pair.

Under Lady Hillbrook's teasing, terrifying Jonas Merrick became almost human and his eyes shone with adoration when he looked at his wife. The Harmsworths seemed mismatched, until Nell saw them together and noticed how Sir Richard's elegant manners offset his wife's eccentric brilliance. Sedgemoor was clearly head over heels in love with his beautiful, pregnant duchess. And his duchess basked in the glow.

Nell's love for Leath was so new and now so hedged with poisonous vines and sharp thorns, she could hardly bear the company of all these blissful couples. And there was the added bite that, even if Leath had been the man she'd thought, the world would never allow her to claim him openly. As his mistress, she'd always hover on the fringes of his life. Once he tired of her, she wouldn't even have that much.

As customary in great houses, the ladies left the gentlemen to their port. Nell tried to claim tiredness. If she intercepted one more loving glance, she'd scream. But the duchess insisted that she stay downstairs for tea. Knowing that she owed these people a debt of gratitude—not to mention that she wanted them to join the campaign against Leath—Nell remained.

To her surprise, she found the conversation well within her compass. Her stepfather had followed the news and her weeks at Alloway Chase had sharpened her political awareness. After some hesitation, more about invading the intimacy between these friends than feeling out of her depth, she joined in.

"Miss Trim, I'd love you to visit me in London," Lady Harmsworth said warmly from her place on the sofa, after they found they agreed on the faults of the latest Scott novel, *The Fair Maid of Perth*. The lovely blonde stuck a few desultory stitches into the embroidery on her lap. "We could do the rounds of the booksellers."

Nell, whose troubles had briefly receded, blushed. She sat near the fire, a place of honor that the duchess had insisted she take. "Lady Harmsworth, you're too generous, but I'm returning to my stepfather's house."

"You're from Kent, my husband says. Kent to London isn't far."

"A lowly sergeant major's daughter belongs in a different world, my lady," Nell said.

She'd grown up unthinkingly accepting the gulf dividing the classes. Since falling in love with Leath, it struck her that a rigidly stratified society brought untold trouble. If Leath wasn't a great lord, would his lechery meet with such success? A poor man had neither time nor money to tour the country debauching local virgins. A poor man couldn't dazzle a clutch of country bumpkins with his London glamor. And a rich man had more chance of weaseling out of the consequences of bad behavior.

Perhaps she became a quiet revolutionary.

Thoughtfully Lady Harmsworth surveyed her. "You imagine that I'm a bloodless aristocrat like Pen and Sidonie?"

Lady Hillbrook sent her a fondly impatient glance from the facing sofa. "Doing it too brown, Genevieve. My father wasn't much further up the social scale than yours."

The duchess laughed from beside Lady Hillbrook and Nell experienced a pang of unworthy envy. This lovely woman lived with a man she adored in an exquisite house, and the child they expected would be loved and secure. Any child Nell had with Leath—and the possibility of pregnancy remained, despite her rage—would be branded a bastard. His lordship's cold-blooded contract ensured that their offspring wouldn't be thrown penniless upon the world, but she flinched from tarring her children with illegitimacy.

"I'll hold up the flag for the useless aristocracy." The duchess raised her hand. "I'm not ashamed of where I've come from."

Nell's resentment melted away. It did her no good, after all. And she liked the duchess. She liked all these women. If the world was a different place, she could even imagine friendships forming. The ladies were clever and funny and they'd all been far too generous to a woman who descended upon them bringing the threat of chaos. The battle to destroy Leath would be neither clean nor quick. The marquess would fight to his last breath. Even when she'd thought him a good man, she'd recognized his tenacity.

"I'm a mere vicar's daughter, Miss Trim," Lady Harmsworth said. "I'm used to getting my hands dirty."

The duchess snorted in a very un-duchesslike fashion. "Hold to that story, Genevieve, and we'll all imagine you grubbing on your bony knees in the dry, stony soil to dig up a shriveled turnip for each night's supper."

"Wearing filthy rags and clogs," Lady Hillbrook added.

The duchess shivered theatrically. "While the cold, cold wind whips around you."

Nell couldn't help laughing. The idea of elegant Lady Harmsworth anywhere but in a room such as this was so incongruous. But then, she'd learned to fit in with extravagant surroundings too, hadn't she?

"You sound as if you're having a fine time." Sedgemoor stood in the doorway, surveying them with an indulgent eye. "Perhaps we should have abandoned our port earlier. Richard bored us with some damned dull nonsense about the latest colors in waistcoats. Nearly went to sleep over my glass, it was so tedious."

"Trying to help you cut a dash, old man." Sir Richard sauntered past his friend and took his place on the sofa beside his wife. "Seems a pity for the incumbent of one of the nation's greatest titles to dress like a damned Quaker."

"Better a Quaker than a blasted harlequin," the duke retorted, although it was clear that neither man took this argument seriously.

"Children," Lord Hillbrook said repressively, prowling across the room to stand behind his wife. He rested his hand on the bare shoulder revealed by her daringly scooped décolletage.

Nell realized that she stared at the Hillbrooks and glanced away with a blush. She wasn't used to these open displays of affection. She barely conquered another nasty pang of jealousy.

She didn't want Lord Leath to touch her with casual confidence. She didn't want to warm to the brush of his fingers against her neck, just as Lady Hillbrook clearly warmed to her husband's touch. James Fairbrother was the lowest worm who ever lived. If she could, she'd crush him under her heel.

She stared into her cooling tea and told herself that one day she might even believe she meant that.

"Speaking of harlequins," Sir Richard said, leaning against his wife's arm with more disconcerting physical intimacy, "are you embroidering a bulldog wearing a rainbow, my love?"

Lady Harmsworth raised her eyebrows with a haughtiness contradicted by the sparkle in her eyes. "You're such a humorist, darling. Anyone can see that it's an Arab bazaar at sunset."

"Mmm," her husband said, obviously unconvinced. "Looks like a pug losing his lunch to me. But I've never claimed much grasp of arty nonsense. That's all up to Pen and Cam."

"This cushion is perfect for your library," Lady Harmsworth said sweetly. "It matches my set of Grecian ruins. You so admired those."

"Dear Lord save us," Sir Richard muttered quite audibly.

The duke remained standing. "Miss Trim, may I have a word?"

Her unexpected enjoyment of the interplay between the Harmsworths evaporated, leaving behind a tangle of nerves. "Your Grace?"

Lady Hillbrook rose to rescue the delicate teacup from her insecure hold. "Cam doesn't bite," she whispered. "And if he does, I'll come and beat him off with a fire iron."

The idea of Sidonie Merrick taking a club to the lofty Duke of Sedgemoor almost made her smile. "Thank you." Nell stood on legs made of water, despite Lady Hillbrook's encouragement.

Approaching the duke, she passed Lady Harmsworth. Sir Richard wasn't far wrong. The supposed Arabian scene did indeed look like a bilious puppy.

"There's something in your story that I need to clear up." His Grace took her arm and drew her along a corridor. "It shouldn't take long."

As he ushered her into the library, the air slammed from Nell's lungs. If Sedgemoor hadn't held her arm, she'd have fallen as ignominiously as she had upon arrival at Fentonwyck. Everything in the room tunneled to one point.

"You!"

Before her stood Lord Leath.

Chapter Twenty-Six

When she whitened, Leath instinctively stepped forward. Then the loathing on her face made him falter. "Eleanor?"

She remained trembling in Sedgemoor's grip and Leath forced himself not to strike the man's hand away. Eleanor looked about to collapse, and he ached to take her in his arms and tell her everything was all right.

But of course, everything wasn't all right. Everything was in an infernal coil. Unless Leath could get her to listen with an open mind, he couldn't see how to resolve the mess.

He'd arrived in time to wash and change his shirt, and meet Sedgemoor here in the library. In increasing horror, he'd listened as the duke had revealed the truth about Eleanor Trim—at last. He grieved for her poor tragic half-sister, and for Eleanor's sorrow and anger. However misguided she'd been.

But where did this confounded tangle leave them?

Eleanor's eyes burned like coals in her ashen face as she shook free of the duke and stumbled back. Did she mean to run?

"Wait!" Leath didn't care what that desperate plea revealed to this man who had never been his friend. "Eleanor, please stay."

She bumped into the closed door behind her, eyes wide with fear. Did she really think he'd offer her physical harm? Leath's gut knotted with anguished denial.

Her agitated gaze found Sedgemoor. "What have you done?"

The duke maintained his famous sangfroid, although Leath didn't mistake the watchful expression in those icy green eyes. A watchful expression that changed to compassion when he looked at Eleanor. "Last night, I sent a message to Alloway Chase telling Leath that you were here and why. Miss Trim, I know this seems like a betrayal, but you've made serious allegations against his lordship. He deserves a chance to defend himself."

"I don't want to see him." Looking like a trapped animal, she screwed her hands into her skirts. However furious Leath was with her—and he was ready to wring her neck for her unjust suspicions—he hated her distress.

"I'm prepared to stay while you two talk," Sedgemoor said evenly.

Leath regarded him with virulent dislike. "I pose no threat to Miss Trim."

"So you say." Eleanor's voice vibrated with a repugnance that made his heart clench into a cold fist.

"Miss Trim, I believe that's true. His lordship's first words when he arrived inquired after your well-being."

She looked unimpressed at Sedgemoor's defense. "He wants the privilege of silencing me himself."

Leath was equally unimpressed. Sedgemoor had no right to probe a man's feelings, damn it. "I'd like to speak to Miss Trim alone."

She turned as pale as milk and cast Sedgemoor another frantic glance. "Don't go."

"Go." That tone always sent Leath's political enemies scurrying.

Still he was surprised when Sedgemoor nodded. "I'll set a footman in the hallway."

"It's not enough."

"Damn it, Eleanor." Leath's temper flared, despite his determination to stay calm. "You've survived in my company since September. The odds are good that you'll still be breathing tomorrow morning."

She recoiled. "You didn't know I was working against you then."

Sedgemoor studied them. Leath hoped for the sake of the duke's health that he wasn't hiding a smile. "Miss Trim, I'd wager my fortune that you're safe."

Before she could protest, he left the room, shutting the door firmly. A leaden silence crashed down.

"I don't have to stay," Eleanor said mulishly and whirled around to tug at the doorknob.

"Eleanor," he said quietly.

At the sound of her name, she stilled. Her shoulders rose and fell as she inhaled. Slowly she turned. Over the last few minutes, he'd seen her terror and hatred. Now she regarded him like a stranger.

His soul revolted at that idea. They'd shared a bed. He believed that Eleanor Trim was the other half of his soul. God grant him the eloquence to convince her to give him another chance.

"I don't care if you hurt me," she said coldly.

His temper, barely controlled, fueled by worry and sleeplessness, sparked anew. "Hells bells, do you really think I would?"

Her face remained a beautiful mask. Since she'd deserted him, he'd hungered for the sight of her. But her stony expression made him want to break something. "I don't know anything about you."

"Yes, you do," he barked before his tone lowered to acid derision. "And surely you credit me with the intelligence not to murder you with a house full of witnesses."

"You're angry enough." Contempt dripped from her words. "And desperate enough. I mean to bring you down, my lord."

She'd already brought him down, did she but know it. Mere weeks in Eleanor Trim's company and his life was bedlam. "I still won't hurt you."

She tilted her chin. "That would sound more convincing if you weren't trampling me."

Shocked, he realized that in his rage, he crowded her. She pressed against the door to avoid contact with his vile self. The urge to grab her and kiss her until she forgot this nonsense surged, but he beat it back. He glanced down at his fisted hands. No wonder Eleanor was frightened.

While she seemed certain that nothing between them had been true, he remained sure of her. He'd always been sure of her obstinacy. A disconcerting quality in a housemaid. In a woman who set herself up as his enemy, it was dangerous. He stared into her eyes, eyes that had once been full of sweet passion, and saw fear and anger and courage.

The courage reminded him why she was worth every effort. Why he'd allow her more leeway than anyone else. He stepped back, uncurled his fingers, and spread his hands. "I'm sorry."

She frowned as though his apology made no sense. He bit back another snarl as he realized that she hadn't expected him to act like a civilized man, but like the cur she believed him. So far, he wasn't doing much to refute that opinion.

Sighing he gestured for her to move into the room. "Please sit down. We need to talk."

She didn't budge. "No, we don't."

If his life wasn't spinning completely out of control, he'd smile at that stalwart response. He pointed toward the chairs near the fire. "Please."

Eventually she pushed away from the door and edged across to the hearth. With a pang, he noticed what a wide berth she gave him. He noticed something else. "Where did you get that dress?"

"It's Lady Hillbrook's." The exasperated glance she shot him as she perched on a chair was a painful reminder of their former ease with each other. "My clothes are still at the cottage."

"Whose fault is that?" he snapped, following with deliberate slowness so that she wouldn't feel pursued. Although he stalked her now as carefully as a starving tiger stalked a stray goat.

"Yours." She sat rigidly and folded her hands in her lap.

The dark blue dress brought out the satiny whiteness of her skin and the pale splendor of her hair, caught up in a more elaborate style than usual. She looked like a great lady. How he wished that his mother could see her. He wasn't entirely delighted with her finery. When Miss Trim had flitted about his house in her puritanical dresses, he'd lived under the happy illusion that he alone had noted her beauty. She'd been his private treasure. Anyone seeing her now would be rightly dazzled.

There was a chair close to hers. Now that the shock of seeing her passed, he was able to consider strategy. With a completely assumed nonchalance, he took the seat on the opposite side of the fire. "You lied to me. There's no Lady Bascombe. No Willow House."

She frowned as if struggling to remember. "I needed references to work for you."

"So you wrote them yourself?"

The frown deepened. The accusation of dishonesty troubled her. "I hated lying to your mother."

She didn't say that she'd hated lying to him. He had so far to go before she'd give him a chance. For a man who spent his life coaxing people in directions they didn't want to take, he was depressingly unsure whether he'd win her over. "She doesn't know you did."

"She will."

Yes, bugger it. If Eleanor's plot succeeded and those infernal letters became public, his mother would indeed know that she'd fostered a traitor. "Sedgemoor told me everything. I know why you joined my household. You wanted proof of my crimes."

"I found it," she muttered, looking down at hands clasped so tightly in her lap that the knuckles shone white.

He ignored that. "Finally I understand so many things. Not least your night wanderings and why I found you in my bedroom."

She'd been worryingly pale, but now pink colored her cheeks. "I nearly died when you came in."

Bitterness edged his tone. "I'm sure."

Eleanor cast him a searching glance. "I thought that you'd be furious."

"You also thought that you'd be far away and safe from retribution," he said in that same grim voice. "Under bloody Sedgemoor's protection."

Her eyes widened. "Not in...that way."

He almost smiled. "No, not in that way. Sedgemoor's notoriously devoted to his wife."

"I'd heard you were enemies. I thought he'd welcome the chance to destroy you."

Leath arched his eyebrows, beating back barely contained

outrage. How could she range herself against him like this? "When you're basing a fiendish plot on gossip, you should make sure it's up to date, my dear."

She glared. "Don't call me that."

For all her composure, she was no closer to relenting. His voice lowered, although he could barely hide his hurt disbelief. "You came to my house, convinced I'd defiled women up and down the country. You inveigled yourself into my mother's life, my life, under false pretenses."

A hunted expression entered her eyes. "Given your sins, deceit is justified."

"What about your kisses? Were they justified?"

She flinched so violently that her back slammed into the chair. "You can't—"

"Can't what?" He couldn't restrain his anguish. "Can't remind you that two nights ago, you lay in my arms?"

She raised a shaking hand to cover her face. He wondered if she hid from her seducer or from the truth inside herself. "Don't."

"Why did you give yourself to me?"

She lowered her hand to reveal eyes dull with misery. "Because I'm foolish and weak, and I convinced myself that you weren't the man I knew you to be."

"Or perhaps you discovered that you were mistaken about me in the beginning."

She winced. "Those letters show the truth. You behave as if I've wronged you, when your misdeeds reach to the sky."

"I'm sorry about your sister."

"You should be sorry," she retorted, cutting as a whip. "You killed her."

He rose, fruitlessly wishing he could ease her grief. "No wonder you hated me."

She stumbled to her feet and glared at him. "Don't pretend this is news to you. Dorothy's in your diary, the one that man Greengrass has. I know you were in Kent when she was ruined."

"I—" He stopped. "Good Lord, so I was that summer. I was at a strategy meeting at Penshurst."

Triumph lit her eyes as though she'd landed the winning blow. "You used my sister, then abandoned her to disgrace. When she told you she carried your child, you mocked her with foul details of the other women you'd despoiled."

He felt sick. "Does that sound like something I'd do?"

She stood trembling behind the chair, hands digging into the leather back. "I don't know you well enough to say."

"Yes, you do." His attention remained unwavering. "So you think that having ruined your half-sister, I ruined you too?"

He couldn't mistake her shame. "Of course."

Like an acid tide, rancor rose. "Well, at least I didn't boast of prior conquests."

"I found the letters before you could," she said stubbornly.

He wanted to seize those slender shoulders and shake sense into her. He wanted to fold her in his arms and soothe away her wretchedness. "Ah, the letters."

"They prove Dorothy's accusations." Her tone sliced like razors. "They prove I'm your dupe."

Impatiently he sighed and ran his hand through his hair. "They prove someone using my name ruined your sister and those other women."

Her eyes flashed. "I can't blame you for trying to play me for an idiot. After all, even knowing what I did, I fell into your bed."

He cast her an annoyed glance. "Doesn't that strike you as significant?"

Her hands clenched against the leather. "Don't taunt me."

He stepped closer. "Eleanor, my uncle seduced those women under my name. I've been trying to compensate his victims. I had those letters because I was afraid that they'd fall into the wrong hands and be misinterpreted." He sighed again. "And that's just what happened."

She snarled and backed away. "A likely story. Far more believable that my half-sister accused her betrayer as she died. There's only one name in those letters, my lord. One man receiving blackmail demands."

Defeat's cold breath chilled his neck. She sounded so immovable. "Eleanor…"

She made a slashing gesture with one hand. "I told you not to call me that."

He loved her strength so much, even when she turned it against him. "What shall I call you? My darling, my sweetheart, my lover?"

"Your victim," she bit out, but she poised quivering a few feet away and he knew she listened.

"I could swear that everything you believe is false, but it's only words," he said slowly. He drew himself to his full height and faced her the way he'd face a hanging. "Remember everything you know about me. Remember what we shared. Remember, damn it, that I haven't looked at another woman since I met you. Then tell me I'm the philanderer you describe."

Something that looked like fear crossed her face and she faltered back. "You're such a liar."

Feeling like he set his heart out for her to stamp upon, he remained where he was. "I've never lied to you." He paused. "While you've lied from the beginning."

Her color had long since faded. She looked as pale as the wraith his superstitious servants had once thought her. "I won't listen. You twist everything."

He willed her to relent. "Yet even believing what you did, you shared my bed."

"Because I'm a fool."

"Because in your heart you know I didn't seduce your sister."

"I need to follow my head, not my heart."

Recognizing this as his last chance, he spread his hands in appeal. He had no confidence that he'd prevail. "Think, Eleanor, think. Think of everything you know about me, and tell me that I could commit these crimes. Tell me that you could give yourself to such a man."

She regarded him with glassy eyes, myriad expressions flickering across her face. Some he could read. Rage and disgust, certainly. Shame. Guilt. Determination.

Despairingly he reached out, then realized that his touch was the last thing she wanted. In a low voice, he made one last plea. "Trust me, beloved."

Chapter Twenty-Seven

Helplessly Nell stared into Leath's face. He shredded her heart into bloody gobbets. He looked so hurt. He looked so sincere. He looked as if her merest word could devastate him. Yet how could a humble creature like Eleanor Trim hold such power over this great lord?

She'd imagined when she found those letters that he'd never again be a danger to her. But her love, she discovered, was tenacious. And stupid.

Her love insisted that he hadn't lied. Her love urged her to fling herself into his arms and beg him to forgive her for doubting him.

That same stupid, immovable love made her ache to assuage his exhaustion and unhappiness. If he'd been home to receive Sedgemoor's message, he must have ridden all those miles from the cottage to Alloway Chase the same day she'd left. Then he must have turned around and headed for Fentonwyck. The timing made no sense otherwise. Was he so eager to see her? Or eager to stop her revealing what she knew?

Everything, everything had two conflicting sides. Nell felt ripped apart. Either the marquess was the good man she'd once thought. Or his transgressions condemned him to the lowest circle of hell.

Right now, looking into his strained features, she could almost believe him. Except that the man who had seduced those women must have been a convincing liar.

His story was plausible. Lord Neville Fairbrother had irrefutably been a villain. Was the nephew another rotten apple from the same tree? After tumbling headlong in love with Leath, she knew his ability to charm the most virtuous woman.

"Eleanor?" Her name in that resonant baritone contained every beautiful note in the world.

Nell squared her shoulders against a shiver of awareness and tilted her chin, battling to look defiant, when every atom wanted to stop fighting. How she wished he'd never come to Fentonwyck. Hating Leath from a distance was so much easier.

"I can't..." She tried to sound strong and dismissive, but her voice emerged as a whisper. "I can't decide now."

"Yes, you can," he said implacably, jaw hardening.

"Don't bully me," she snapped, welcoming anger. If Leath continued to stare at her with such yearning, she'd burst into tears. And that weakness would invite every other weakness home to roost, including the one that would make her forgive him, whatever he'd done.

Confusion left her dizzy. She shook her head and stumbled toward the door. She could no longer bear to be in the same room as Leath. Wanting him. Loathing him. Verging on trusting him. Not trusting her instincts. This was like wrestling with an enemy in a mirror.

"I can't let you go." His desperation scraped across her skin.

"I must," she said brokenly.

As she passed, he caught her arm. "Do you believe me?"

"Release me." She meant to demand, but instead she begged. It was so unfair that even now, his touch made her blood churn with desire.

"Do you believe me?" he repeated in an urgent voice that vibrated through her.

He looked pushed to the edge of endurance. Two days ago, before she'd found the letters, she'd have followed her heart. But those letters hadn't only destroyed her certainty in him, but also her certainty in herself. How could she be sure that desire didn't fool her into seeing honesty and need—and something that looked like love, God save her—in his silvery eyes? How could she be sure of anything, now that the Marquess of Leath proved false?

"I don't know."

"Yes, you do."

She jerked without breaking away. "Stop saying that. My sister died speaking your name."

"But without my child in her belly," he said harshly.

"How can I believe you?"

She saw his expression change to anger and purpose—and flaring passion. A snarl bared straight white teeth. "Perhaps this will convince you."

Fear engulfed her like a rush of icy water and she parted her lips to call for Sedgemoor's footman. But before she could make a sound—at least so she told herself as she hung from his grip—Leath's mouth crashed into hers.

The kiss was all about dominance. She felt none of the heartbreaking tenderness, familiar from the cottage. She should be glad. That tenderness had been a lie.

Although even now, she had difficulty believing that.

She kept her lips closed as his physical reality enveloped

her. Heat and musk, overlaid with horses and sandalwood. With a muffled groan that vibrated on her lips, he wrenched her closer until she sprawled against him, too aware of every muscled inch.

She tried to force a gap between them, but against his implacable hold, she had no hope. The last time she'd been in his arms, they'd shared a joy that she refused to recall, because events since had tainted it so fatally. The last time she'd been in his arms, he hadn't needed to fight to keep her. She'd been avid to stay—and she still couldn't forgive herself.

He raised his head and stared down impatiently. "Kiss me, Eleanor."

"Your kisses are lies," she hissed, straining uselessly in his embrace. She'd always known how strong he was, but only now, when he used that strength against her, did she realize how gentle he'd been.

Her fear—and wicked excitement—sparked higher when his eyes narrowed in rage. "Then let me lie some more, my dear."

She was mortified how easily he restrained her with one arm. He caught her chin and tilted her face. His grip was hard without bruising. She resented that he retained such control when his nearness ate at her willpower like rust at metal. "You're contemptible," she spat.

The smile curving his lips was wolfish. He knew how she struggled against giving in. "Let me prove it."

Nell's panic mounted to titanic heights. Not panic that he'd hurt her. Despite her silly fidgets earlier, he wouldn't crush her rebellion with violence. No, he'd crush her with pleasure. And with the aid of the enemy inside Nell, the woman greedy for his touch.

Ruthlessly he kissed her. "Open for me, damn you," he muttered.

She flattened her hands on his chest and tried to shove him away. This was like trying to move a mountain with a spoon. A warm, breathing mountain. A mountain that smelled like the promise of heaven.

He nibbled at her lips until she trembled. Still she wouldn't relent. Even when she was so giddy with need that if he released her, she'd fall.

"Let me go."

At her hoarse plea, he took advantage to slide his tongue between her lips. The satiny invasion shuddered through her and made her hands curl into his coat until she held him instead of pushing him away. He kissed her until she clung without any show of reluctance. If his touch could vanquish her like this, could he be the evil man she believed him? Could he deceive her so profoundly?

After their night together, he knew what stirred her. In her daze, she didn't recognize the purpose in his touch until her bodice sagged. Vaguely she was grateful that he'd unhooked her dress instead of ripping it away. Even through rocketing arousal, she knew that beneath this calculated seduction, he was angry. If she had any pride, that anger should freeze her responses. Instead it whipped her to a frenzy.

"You're a...swine," she managed to hiss, then spoiled any show of defiance by turning her head until her lips met his.

"You don't know the half of it," he sniped back, sounding like he hated her.

She couldn't even pretend that her shiver wasn't anticipation. He'd always had this power. Only now did he exercise it with no regard for her inexperience. And the brazen, unprincipled woman who had never stopped wanting him, no matter what he'd done, reveled in every caress.

Those strong, capable hands, hands that had once touched

her so carefully, wrenched at her clothes. He groaned deep in his throat as her breasts bobbed free. Before she thought to cover herself, he bent to suck her nipples. To her humiliation, they ached for his touch.

His hands spread across her back, curving her into him to offer better access. She muffled cries of delight as he scraped his teeth over one crest and set her on an exquisite edge.

As a bite intensified the pounding pulse between her legs, she cradled his silky head to her. She moaned, and the sound spoke surrender. At last she admitted that she wanted this. She was as damned as he was. God help her if he truly was the villain of her accusations.

He hauled up her skirts. Staggering, she parted her legs to let him touch her where she yearned. He shuddered and muffled a curse as his hand curled around her mound. She gasped into his shoulder when he invaded her with one long finger, stroking to build a response that already threatened oblivion.

Still no tenderness. He touched her hard, lifting her quickly toward climax.

Then when she was on the brink, ready to tumble over into rapture, he pulled free. She'd so lost contact with reality that this seemed spiteful, rather than a merciful escape. With another moan, she pressed forward, digging her fingernails into his fine cambric shirt. Somewhere in this profane encounter, he'd ripped away his coat.

Still he didn't resume that glorious torture. Instead he caught her by the shoulders. Slowly she opened eyes that she'd kept closed against shame and confusion.

His expression was composed and watchful. She'd almost believe that she suffered this lust alone. If he wasn't hard against her quaking belly. If his eyes didn't glitter with primitive hunger.

"What is it?" Her voice sounded raw, as though she'd already screamed her fulfillment to the roof.

"Do I have your consent?" he asked hoarsely.

"Don't talk." Past all caution, she cupped him.

He groaned and ground into her palm. For a heady moment, she thought she'd won, then his grip firmed on her shoulders. "Is it yes, Eleanor?"

She scowled, her skin itching for his touch, a heavy, yearning weight in her belly. A braver woman would own her desire. Cowardice won out. "I have no choice."

His eyes narrowed. "Yes, you do."

Was he a monster or was he everything she'd always wanted? Her heart insisted that she couldn't love him so much if he was truly evil.

"Devil take you, Leath," she grated. "Do what you must."

"Only if you agree." His jaw was iron with determination. She knew him well enough to recognize that when he looked like that, she had no hope of prevailing.

Still, she could try. Very deliberately, she stroked his length. Even through his breeches, she felt his pulsing heat. She meant to claim some power in this battle—because for all the passion, it was a battle. She underestimated her reaction to the audacious ploy. Before she'd completed the leisurely caress, her knees threatened to buckle beneath her.

He caught her hand before she could repeat the action. "One small word, Eleanor."

On a sob, she released the breath she'd held and sagged into him. She hooked her free hand around his neck and the softness of his hair against her fingers was her final undoing.

He didn't feel like a monster. He felt like the man she loved. Her sigh was laden with tears. "Yes."

Chapter Twenty-Eight

Relief punched the air from Leath's lungs. Roughly he tore at the strings of her drawers until they sagged about her ankles. Eleanor stepped free as she fumbled clumsily with his breeches. He wasn't in much better case as he brushed her hands away and unfastened the front fall.

A downward glance tinged her cheeks with pink, a reminder that she remained in so many ways an innocent. The tenderness that he experienced only with her surged, but he beat it back. Be damned if he'd be gentle. If she was so determined to believe him a heartless seducer, he'd seduce her heartlessly. Her suspicions made him want to howl with pain and rage.

The memory of the doubt in her eyes, eyes that had held such wonder the last time they'd been together, made him ruthless. He hitched her up, cupping her bare bottom in his palms. She gasped with surprise.

The gaze that met his was feverish with excitement. She clutched at his shoulders and laced her legs around his waist. "Leath?"

Last time, she'd called him James. It hadn't missed his attention that she'd used his title all night. James would coax her to arousal, awaken her gently but thoroughly, make magic. Leath was a barbarian. Leath cared only for his own pleasure.

"Hold on tight," he snapped, anger flaring as he recalled her accusations.

He turned, feeling the delightful tumble of her weight, and pressed her against the wall. He waited for her eyes to darken with fear, as they had when she'd tried to run. Instead he caught another unearthly blast of excitement and she wriggled down, almost taking him.

No, my lady, I'm in charge here.

He rubbed against her until she moaned with frustration and tore at his hair. How he'd love to keep torturing her. Except torturing her, he tortured himself.

"Damn you, Eleanor." He thrust powerfully.

She was tight, so tight, but sleek as oiled satin. When he was sheathed to the hilt, she clung, crushed between the wall and his body. Every breath pushed her breasts against his chest. He held still, claiming her without words. Then remorseless, he moved in and out, forcing rhythmic gasps from her. Those husky little sounds punctuating his ferocious possession made him crazy.

Soon, far too soon if she hated him as she declared, the ripples began. On another guttural curse, he tightened his hips and pushed so deep that she lifted against the wall. Then he kissed her to muffle her cries of completion as he pumped into her. In an ecstasy of release, he flooded her.

As he slumped, she kissed him back just as ardently. Her arms tightened with a trace of what his needy heart read as care.

Triumph rang out. Then he looked down into her shocked

face, saw her great eyes bruised with anguish, and a trace of blood on her reddened lips where he'd kissed her too hard.

Acrid shame at his wild abandon clenched his gut.

Roughly he pushed free, breaking the connection. He held her waist until she found her feet. He stepped back, wanting to appear controlled, but he couldn't steady his hands as he fastened his breeches.

She watched without speaking, leaning against the wall and panting. He couldn't read the expression in her eyes. They were dazed with sexual satisfaction, but the line of her voluptuous mouth hinted at tears.

Of course she wanted to cry. He'd treated her like a doxy. Right now, he couldn't see that he was much improvement on his despicable uncle.

Her pale hair tumbled about her shoulders. She looked untouchable when she put it up, but when it fell about her shoulders in a silvery shawl, she always looked like a wanton. She made no attempt to cover her sweet white breasts with their proud raspberry crests. Renewed shame stabbed Leath as he noticed a bruise on one pale slope.

He couldn't help recalling her at their first meeting. He'd turned her from that pure, beautiful creature into this temptress. And God forgive him, she was even more beautiful now. No matter how he chastised himself, he couldn't help wanting her still. He'd want her until the day he died.

Every time he looked at her, he saw more to aggravate his guilt. A red mark on her neck revealed where he'd bitten her. He wanted to ask if she was all right. But he quailed from inquiring after her well-being when he'd destroyed it.

He straightened without shifting his gaze. "No apology can redress my behavior." Because his emotions swam too close to the surface, his voice emerged hard and clipped as if he was still angry with her. When all his disgust was leveled at himself. "I never touched your sister, but you have every right to hate me for what I just did. I treated you appallingly, despite my respect for you. Do whatever you must. I won't bother you again."

"What about the scandal?" Her brows drew together. "Don't you care if I make the letters public?"

Her voice was thready. Her throat moved when she swallowed, as if even those few words tested her. A pox on his damned impetuosity. Until he'd met Eleanor Trim, he'd had no idea that a beast lurked inside him. He supposed until he'd met Eleanor Trim, nothing had been important enough to awaken his inner savage.

"Right now I don't give a tinker's damn about the letters." He reminded himself that however heartsick he felt, he had responsibilities. "If...if there are consequences from what we just did, let me know."

Good God, she had him stuttering. How low she'd brought him.

Her eyes widened and she swallowed again. Abhorring him as she did, the prospect of bearing his child must be anathema. But it was too late to take back what they'd done.

Too late. Too late. Too late altogether.

He cursed himself for taking all the sweetness they'd shared and turning it into this nightmare of lust and anger. Unable to bear looking at her when everything between them had foundered, he faced the door. "Good-bye, Eleanor. And God bless you."

"Don't I get to say anything?" she asked unsteadily.

Wearily he turned back. "I know you loathe me. You don't need to go into details."

Her chin tilted upward. "Stop telling me what to do."

"Very well, I'll listen." He planted himself with grim stoicism. "I owe you that much."

She studied him, expression enigmatic. To his relief, she tugged her bodice over her breasts. Her disarray inevitably made him want to tumble her again, despite the weight of self-hatred. Leath had always despised men at the mercy of their baser urges. What a smug prig he'd been.

He noticed her faint stumble as she stepped away from the wall. Another pang of guilt. Another twinge of satisfaction to remember pounding into her as if the world ended any minute.

When she left him, his world would end.

Unexpectedly she approached. After that unceremonious mating, he thought that she'd want to get as far away as she could. "When you touch me, you drive everything else from my mind."

What the hell? Astonished, he stared at Eleanor and the confession tumbled from his lips, although surely she already knew the truth. "You drive me mad too."

His shock rose when for the first time tonight, her mouth curved in a faint smile. "That's good."

"It is." Then he realized what she'd said and frowned. "Is it?"

Bewildered, he watched her step even closer. Soon, she'd be near enough to touch. Whatever his good intentions, if she ventured within reach, he'd haul her into his arms. And then he'd prove himself a brute indeed.

She bit her lip and her eyes fluttered down with the first sign of shyness. She'd been too busy hating him to be shy. "I hope so."

He was accounted a brave man, noted for his dash in the boxing ring, and with a pistol and blade. But her next step forward drove him into retreat. "What do you want?"

For a long moment, the stark question lay between them, as tangible and deadly as a sword.

She licked her lips again and he bit back a groan. After that mighty release when he'd filled her with every drop of his anguish, he shouldn't be ready for a woman for at least a week. But as he caught a drift of rich female scent, he wanted to kiss her until she yielded again.

"God help me, Leath," she said in a low voice that lifted every hair on his body. "God help me, but despite everything that's happened between us, I want you."

He didn't move.

Uncertainty darkened her eyes to brandy. "Don't you care?"

In frustration, he ran his hand through his hair. "Of course I bloody care. But you don't trust me. You accuse me of unspeakable things."

She stared him down. "If that was true, could I feel as I do in your arms?"

"Are you saying you trust me?"

Her hands twisted together at her waist. Her voice emerged as a whisper. "I'm saying that for both our sakes, I hope my heart is leading me right. I hope that you're not the man who destroyed my sister, but the man I've pledged myself to, body and soul. Heaven save us both if I'm wrong."

Shocked disbelief held him paralyzed, before he swept her up into a kiss that made a mockery of regret.

This time, Leath's touch was different. The hunger remained, but his kiss lured instead of commanded. Nell quivered with anticipation as he tumbled her down onto the leather couch.

His hands lit fires everywhere they touched. After losing herself so spectacularly in his arms—against the wall, no less—she was sure no scrap of energy remained for pleasure. It turned out that she had much more than a scrap. By the time he tugged her dress over her head and unlaced her corset to kiss the peaks of her breasts, she moaned and moved restlessly. His teeth scored one hard nipple, shooting jagged lightning through her. She bit back a cry.

He settled between her legs and she bent her knees, arching to bring him closer to where she wanted him. Again. Forever. She pushed his shirt up his back and let her fingers play across flexing muscles as he feverishly kissed her shoulders. She sucked in his delicious scent, redolent with arousal. Her stomach clenched with forbidden excitement.

"Take your shirt off," she muttered in a voice that she didn't recognize. This time, she could demand too.

He reared up and carelessly hauled his shirt over his head, flinging it away. He came down over her, bearing his weight on his arms. Nell made a deep sound of enjoyment as her rapacious hands explored him.

That broad, naked chest with its silky black hair set her heart cartwheeling. He was breathtakingly strong. The memory of how he'd held her so effortlessly against the wall made her shiver with pleasure. To punish him for that turbulent union, she curled her nails over his nipples.

"Witch..." he grunted, shuddering. It was the first word he'd spoken since carrying her to the couch. It sounded like an endearment.

As her hands tore at his breeches, she nipped and licked her way across his chest. He reached to help her and she released a drawn-out hiss when her hand closed around hard flesh, satin over a steely core. He felt so potent and vital.

Fascinated, she looked down. His nakedness remained a mystery. She'd been too overwhelmed on their first night and tonight's tempestuous mating had given her no chance for leisurely exploration.

She tightened her grip, making him jolt. He groaned and

angled forward in encouragement. Tentatively she slid her hand toward the nest of black hair at the base of his belly.

"Beloved Lord in heaven," he groaned. A muscle danced in his cheek and his lips tightened.

"Should I stop?" she asked uncertainly, gently squeezing him. Holding him here, where he was most a man, teased her appetite.

"No," he said, his voice raw. He rolled over until she rose above him. He caught her hand, firming her grip and shifting her fist up and down in a compelling rhythm.

"Like this?" To her delighted astonishment, he grew even heavier.

"Yes," he said on a long exhalation. He still looked tormented, but she came to realize that strain didn't necessarily mean displeasure.

Soon Leath was breathing roughly. He seized her hand, but tempered his impatience with a sweet kiss across her knuckles. She sighed, then sighed again when he kissed her lips with more sweetness. He shifted until they sat facing each other.

Blindly she wriggled closer, bracing her hands on his chest. Hardly knowing what she did, delirious with desire, she squirmed on his thigh. Keening whimpers escaped her and her nails marked his skin.

Leath grabbed her hips and lifted her. "Take me," he grated out. "For God's sake, take me."

Uncertainty pierced her fog of need. "Is it possible?"

His short laugh cracked and his hands dug into her hips. "Try."

He drew her close for another kiss, biting gently on her lower lip. The mixture of pain and pleasure turned her liquid and she shifted downward. To her shock, he slid into her with exquisite smoothness.

"Oh."

He nipped her neck at the place that always sent her wild. She felt another surge and took him completely.

Unsure, excited, a little frightened, Nell gripped his shoulders. His jaw seemed chiseled from granite. His long, expressive mouth parted. Under heavy lids fringed with thick eyelashes, his eyes were black with arousal.

She knew enough to read his expression as profound satisfaction. And when she instinctively wriggled to settle his thickness, he closed his eyes and exhaled in shuddering pleasure.

Her hand curled into his shoulders as she clenched, provoking another long exhalation. "Shall I move?"

"Ride me as you will," he bit out. His Adam's apple bobbed as he struggled for restraint.

He wasn't a man who relinquished the upper hand easily. He wasn't a man who relinquished the upper hand at all, if he could help it. Yet here she was, naked except for her chemise and stockings, holding him deep inside. If that explosive encounter against the wall had proven anything, it was his physical superiority. Yet he gave her the initiative.

A slow, pleased smile curved her lips and this time she deliberately tightened around him. To the music of his groans, she adjusted her position.

Experimentally she rose. She loved the glide of his body. She loved to control the pace and depth. His hands flexed on her hips and she waited for him to take charge. But he didn't. She poised above him, their bodies only just joined, then descended hard. Immediately he filled her.

Nell couldn't credit how different this felt. She'd like to do this again. And again.

She swiveled her hips. Through her chemise, his hands

framed her waist. Their joining seemed more decadent because neither was naked. Every time she moved, his breeches slid against her thighs.

Her breasts bounced wantonly. He caught one peak between his lips and drew until she cried out. She broke the contact as she sank, eager to feel him inside her.

His breath emerged in humid gasps and a fine sheen of sweat covered his torso. Every time she took him, her muscles clamped, demanding his surrender. Such heady knowledge that she'd brought him to this edge. Except that she too verged on climax.

She wasn't there yet. Not...quite.

This time when she took him, he tilted forward to nibble an incendiary path up her neck. When he reached her mouth, his tongue stabbed into her the way his body did. She sucked hard, loving the taste of his desperation.

Kissing her as if he starved, he stroked that secret place between her legs. She launched into flight, crushing her face into the hot curve of his shoulder to stifle her guttural cry as she split into a thousand incandescent shards.

Through her rapture, she felt him push upward. Heat flooded her. As her body milked him, he flowed endlessly. For time without measure, she floated in a golden orb where she only knew delight and the warmth of Leath's arms.

After an eon of glory, she drifted back to earth as softly as a feather on a gentle breeze. Nell opened her eyes to find him tipping her back against the couch. After he'd taken her against the wall, she'd read so many conflicting emotions in his eyes. Sexual repletion. Anger. Regret. Now she saw joy. The dark gray shone like the lake at Alloway Chase at dawn.

As she stared up at this man who watched her as if she was the greatest miracle in creation, she believed in him completely. No heartless seducer could make her feel so precious. It was beyond any deceiver's art.

She swallowed, preparing to confess that she no longer doubted him. But he spoke before she mustered a word.

"Marry me, Eleanor."

Chapter Twenty-Nine

Leath felt Eleanor stiffen beneath him, then frantic hands shoved him away. She toppled off to crouch with a hunted expression before the fire. She looked like she hated him again. Which hurt even more, given that seconds ago she'd been staring dreamily into his eyes as if she never wanted to leave him.

He sat up, running a hand through his hair. "I take it that's a no."

She scowled as if he'd suggested some perverse liberty. "You're feeling guilty because you've ruined me."

"For God's sake, Eleanor, that's not why I proposed."

"I'm sure it isn't." Her tone indicated the opposite. She looked magnificent on the red and blue rug with her breasts catching the fire's glow. The flames lent her hair a hundred different colors.

When she noticed the way his gaze lingered on her chest, she clumsily tugged her chemise into place. He couldn't help regretting her modesty, although having her half naked did nothing for his concentration.

She looked around, flustered. "What on earth are we thinking, staying in here so long? Everyone will know just what we've been up to."

"That's not why I proposed," he repeated grimly, ignoring her sudden concern for propriety. If his behavior shocked the Sedgemoors and their friends, too bad. "But I have ruined you. Earlier tonight, I treated you like a tart I picked up off the streets, instead of a woman I esteem."

The resistance ebbed from her expression. To his surprise, she laid her hand on his knee. "You were angry and you set out to teach me a lesson. But we both know that's not how it turned out in the end."

"I lost control." His gut cramped to think what little reverence he'd shown her against that bedamned wall. Worse, he'd be a liar if he said he hadn't enjoyed it.

"I love that I make you lose control," she whispered, staring at him with shining eyes. "And I never felt like you didn't care. Either time."

His lips twisted. "I care too much." A confession of love hovered, but her dismayed reaction to his proposal silenced him. Right now, he felt infernally vulnerable. He didn't like it, but he didn't know what to do about it.

"I felt your care in your hands and your kisses. That's why I believe you didn't ruin Dorothy."

He sighed, although her declaration of trust settled warm and sure around his aching heart. "I probably should have told you about my uncle."

"Why? You owed me nothing."

"Perhaps not at first. Once you became my mistress, you had a right to know about the shadows in my life. I'm so ashamed that a man who shares my blood wreaked such harm."

"Harm which I blamed on you." Remorse thickened her

voice and her hand clenched on his knee. "I have more to feel guilty about than you. I lied from the start."

Wondering if she'd reject his touch, he laid his hand over hers. To his surprise, she laced her fingers through his. After their raw passion, that simple, affectionate gesture shouldn't cut so deeply. But it did. Perhaps because there had been times tonight when he'd thought she'd hate him forever.

"You weren't to know that my uncle had assumed my identity."

She looked troubled. "Is that it? Months of deceit and you dismiss it by saying I meant well?"

Leath shrugged. "I forgive you."

He hardly cared that she'd lied. If not for her quest, they wouldn't have met. While she'd caused him an ocean of heartache, and was likely to cause him an ocean more, the idea of never knowing her chilled his blood. Eleanor had enriched his life beyond his wildest hopes. Even if she abandoned him now, she'd leave a better man than the one she'd encountered outside his library that windy September night.

Her softening gaze pierced his heart. "You're remarkable, Leath."

His grip tightened. "You called me James at the cottage."

"James," she murmured, and the soft music of his name on her lips dissolved all lingering resentment. "Despite everything I knew about you, I couldn't ignore the evidence before me. You're a good man."

"Thank you." He raised their joined hands and kissed her knuckles. "Then when you found those letters, you were afraid you'd been duped."

"Like Dorothy," she murmured, rising on her knees and cupping his jaw with a tender gesture that made him wonder if she returned his love at least a little. "And I wasn't my usual sensible self that morning in the cottage. I still hadn't reconciled myself to becoming a fallen woman."

"What about now?"

"Now I can't help cringing to think that everyone will guess exactly what we've been doing in this library."

"I'm a big reader."

Despite her reluctant laugh, a blush heated her cheeks. "What you did to me was so exciting. I'd like you to do it again."

"I promise, my love." He didn't choose the endearment lightly. "When we're married."

He wasn't surprised that she tugged free and shifted beyond reach. "The Marquess of Leath can't marry his housemaid."

That was exactly what his mother had said. And again his whole being rejected the statement. "Why?"

She regarded him impatiently. "You know why."

"Tell me."

She rose and prowled around the room, her knee-length chemise revealing shapely calves and ankles. "Cinderella is a nice story, but in the real world, great noblemen don't marry girls like me."

"Like what?"

"Girls of no pedigree. Girls who work for their living." She ducked behind the couch. "Girls society will despise."

"Sedgemoor doesn't despise you," he said neutrally. "What the devil are you doing?"

She rose, struggling to fasten the gown that had given him pause when he'd first seen it. "Getting dressed."

For a few seconds, he observed her futile wriggling. "Come here."

"Thank you." She stepped around the couch and presented her back.

He stood. "Lift your hair."

With a grace that jammed the breath in his throat, she raised the glorious tumble of silver. He stared transfixed at the elegant line of her neck and shoulders. Sweet heaven, she was lovely everywhere. He kissed her nape. She shivered and released a little exhalation of pleasure.

He smiled as he made short work of the dress's fastenings. The primitive who came to the fore with Eleanor wanted her half naked. Hell, completely naked. But they were in another man's house and while they'd been left alone, that happy state mightn't continue.

She returned to the argument. "The duke and his friends were kind."

He sat. "So?"

"So I'm a fleeting visitor. I'm not a permanent fixture."

"I wouldn't be too sure."

She turned in a swirl of dark blue silk. "You're talking nonsense. I can't marry you."

He surveyed her, hands clasped loosely between his spread thighs. "Does that mean you don't want to?"

"I don't want you to do something that you'll regret," she snapped.

That didn't answer his question. Interesting. "Why should I regret it?" he asked, still in that even tone.

"Because I'm a peasant and you're a great lord," she almost snarled, stepping away as if distance could silence him.

He smiled. "You're a natural aristocrat, Eleanor. My mother recognized it. That's why she made you her companion."

Eleanor didn't look pleased. Given rotten apples like his uncle, she mightn't aspire to join the aristocracy. "Your mother would be appalled to think you contemplated marriage with a poor sergeant major's daughter. She's plotting a brilliant political alliance with a powerful family."

Leath fell back on an uncontroversial answer. "She likes you."

"As a servant, not as a daughter-in-law." Her eyes narrowed. "What about your career? If you marry me, your dreams of influence are finished. You've hated the recent scandals that exiled you to Yorkshire. Imagine the scandal if you marry the girl who scrubs your floors."

He glimpsed searing regret beneath her anger. He surged to his feet. "The girl who advised my mother on her reading, who's the best secretary I've ever had, who's at home in a ducal residence, who's charmed everyone on my estate. The girl I want in my bed."

"I will be in your bed. For as long as you want me."

He made a slashing gesture. "You deserve more." His voice deepened into urgency. "You're not made to be my light of love. You're made to be my partner, mother of my children, mistress of my house."

She took another uncertain step back and he caught her arm to save her getting too close to the fire. She was trembling. He hadn't realized that. She sounded so calm.

He expected her to pull away, but she remained unmoving. "I can't have all that and have you."

His heart slammed to a stop, then began to race. The declaration blared through him like a fanfare. Staring into her wide golden eyes, he wondered if this admission meant that she loved him. "You can have me if we marry."

"Not without destroying everything you want," she said in a dull tone, breaking free.

"I've learned over the last weeks that I can live quite happily away from the corridors of power," he said mildly.

"In the short term. In the long term, you'll repent sacrificing your hopes because you feel guilty about seducing a virtuous woman." Her caustic laugh startled him. "What a fool I was to think you a rake. I couldn't be further from the truth."

He glared at her. "You make that sound like an insult."

Her sigh was weary. "I want you to see reality, my lord."

She used the formal address deliberately, to emphasize the gulf between them. Resentment roughened his tone. "And what of the reality of my child growing in your womb? Do you see yourself bringing up a clutch of bastards? Where will your pride be then?"

He'd hit a nerve. "I gave up on pride when I became your mistress."

It was his turn to laugh. "Rubbish. You're the most stiff-necked woman I know. You'd make the Queen of the Amazons look humble."

He caught another glimpse of the vulnerability that she struggled to hide. "Why are you doing this? You're a clever man. You know marriage is impossible. You knew that when you asked me to be your mistress."

"I've had time to think."

Her lips turned down. "You've had time to feel responsible for my ruin."

Leath stalked toward the decanter on the sideboard. He could do with a drink. He passed Eleanor a glass, firelight striking ruby lights from the claret.

"This cruel world we live in is particularly cruel to bastards," he said evenly. "If you don't believe me, ask Sedgemoor, Hillbrook, and Sir Richard. All suffered because of the circumstances of their birth."

She frowned. "They seem happy."

"They've been lucky enough to find the right women." He spoke from the depths of his heart. "As have I."

She stepped back so abruptly that she spilled wine over her hand. "You devil."

He seized the glass before she ruined the lovely gown. "Careful."

She stared at him uncompromisingly. "My lord," she said austerely, "you've done me the great honor of asking me to be your wife. I regret that I must decline."

His hand clenched on the two glasses. "Eleanor."

She regarded him, did she but know it, as haughtily as a princess. "You have my answer, Lord Leath."

No sweet whisper of James now. "I won't leave it at that."

"I wish you would."

"I want you for my marchioness, Eleanor." He placed the untouched wine on a side table. "And I'm a stubborn man."

She sighed. "You say I deserve better than a place as your mistress? Well, you deserve better than to let a passing affair dictate the course of your life."

"You're not a passing affair," he retorted, stung.

The sadness in her smile made him want to shout denial to the rafters. "Yes, I am. Because when you make your grand, politically advantageous marriage, as I sincerely hope you do, our affair will be over."

"What bloody drivel is this?"

"It's not drivel," she snapped.

He seized her arms. "Shall I try and convince you to accept me?"

Anger flared in her face. And reluctant excitement. "You imagine you can seduce me into saying yes?"

"We'd both enjoy it if I tried," he suggested, although already she shook her head.

"You won't taint what we share with ulterior motives."

He wasn't so sure of his scruples. "I'll ask you to marry me again, Eleanor."

"I'll say no again, my lord." She stepped away. "You'll waste your time."

"It's my time," he said calmly. He could afford to be patient. She might change her mind. After all, she'd said no when he'd asked her to be his mistress, hadn't she?

Yes, he could wait. He had a strong suspicion that once she found herself with child, she'd be less adamant. Even if his yearning soul wanted her to marry him because she couldn't live without him, not because she faced the bleak reality of bearing his bastard.

She looked tired. And beautiful. Tonight had been so crammed with turmoil that he was a beast to expect her to pledge herself just for the asking. Short hours ago, she'd loathed him. At least now he saw grounds for hope. She'd never said that she didn't want to marry him. She was worried about his well-being. He needed to convince her that their marriage was the best way to promote his happiness.

He smiled and extended one hand. "Let's not part on a quarrel, my darling."

After a hesitation that made his heart falter, she curled her fingers around his. That touch made him feel that he stood where he was meant to be. Such power she had.

"Don't ask again, please," she said in a low voice. Her eyes were dark with misery.

He drew her unresisting into his arms until she rested on his chest. "Not tonight, at least."

Nell closed her bedroom door and slumped against it in utter exhaustion. She felt like she'd been through a battle. Yet her fight with James had only started. He wouldn't give up this lunatic idea to marry her. Even as he'd given her a reprieve, she'd read his intractable expression.

She shut her eyes and prayed for strength to deny him, however much she yearned to become his wife. If she hadn't lived at Alloway Chase and seen his dedication to the political life, perhaps she'd relent. If she hadn't known his mother and heard about his beloved father's shattered dreams, perhaps she'd relent. But Nell knew that if she cost James everything he'd worked for, he might forgive her, but she'd never forgive herself.

She bit back a sob. How odd to think that today, she'd been so set on his destruction, yet now for his sake, she sacrificed her dearest hopes.

"Miss Trim, are you all right?"

Shocked, Nell opened her eyes and peered through the shadows. The fire was lit and a candle flickered on the nightstand. In a dark corner, Lady Hillbrook was curled up on a chair.

"Your ladyship . . ." Nell stammered, sick with embarrassment. After what she and James had done in the library, she could imagine what she looked like.

"I'm sorry for startling you." Sidonie Merrick stood and approached. "Pen wanted to check on you. I talked her into letting me wait instead. She needs her rest."

"You're both too considerate," Nell said, cheeks aflame. She retreated against the door, although there was nowhere to hide, and her tumbled hair and disheveled clothing must betray her.

"Lord Leath didn't hurt you?" Lady Hillbrook asked in consternation.

Nell shook her head. "No. I was mistaken, it turned out. He's innocent of wrongdoing. His uncle used his name when he seduced my half-sister."

It seemed bizarre to boil the whole tempestuous drama down to three short sentences. Although of course so much remained in the balance. How her affair with James proceeded. Greengrass's blackmail. James's political future.

"I'm not surprised. Neville Fairbrother was a vile

creature." She gestured toward a side table. "Would you like some brandy? You look...shaken."

Nell flinched. She knew she looked more than shaken. Still, it was easier to cooperate than resist. She collapsed onto a chair. After all that ardor and emotion downstairs, her legs felt rubbery.

"Thank you," she whispered as the lovely brunette pressed a glass into her hand. She sipped, coughing on the taste.

"Drink it all." Lady Hillbrook placed a slender hand on Nell's shoulder. "I know I'm a stranger, but I understand something of your feelings. Jonas and I traveled a rocky road to happiness too."

"Your ladyship..." A hundred lies claiming the slightest acquaintance with James rose, but as she met Lady Hillbrook's perceptive gaze, they died unspoken.

"You don't have to say anything, Miss Trim," she said softly. "But if you'd like someone to talk to, I promise that I won't leap to judge you by the world's narrow standards."

"You...you don't know what I've done," she muttered, avoiding the other woman's scrutiny.

Lady Hillbrook's soft laugh as she took the glass surprised Nell. "We all do silly things when we're in love, Miss Trim."

When she'd discovered Lady Hillbrook waiting, Nell thought she couldn't feel more mortified. Now having her deepest heart put on view made her want to sink into the floor. Tears flooded her eyes. "Please..."

"We knew the minute we saw your horse that you meant something special to Lord Leath."

Despite everything, Nell choked on a laugh. "My horse? That's mad."

"Perhaps. Were we wrong?"

"His lordship..." What could she say? His lordship was reckless with his future? His lordship made her sigh with helpless love? His lordship would break her heart before he was done? Any impulse to amusement, however bleak, died.

Squeezing her shoulder, Lady Hillbrook bent to kiss her cheek. "You want to be alone. And you think I'm prying." The sincerity in her voice appeased Nell's stirring resentment. "I know how it feels to believe that you bear the world's troubles all alone."

"There's...there's nothing to be done," Nell said, before realizing how that broken little admission confirmed Lady Hillbrook's suspicions.

"There's always something to be done."

"Not in this case," Nell muttered, digging her hands into her skirts.

Lady Hillbrook's smile was compassionate. "Be brave and follow your heart, Miss Trim."

"My heart is no reliable guide," Nell forced out, desperately wishing the woman would go. Her pride became more threadbare by the minute.

"Sometimes it's the only guide that matters." Lady Hillbrook stepped away. "But of course, you wish me to the devil."

Nell summoned a smile. She hoped it looked more genuine than it felt. "I wouldn't be so rude."

Lady Hillbrook laughed softly. "You know, Miss Trim, you'll do. You really will. And don't let anyone tell you differently."

Nell frowned, not sure whether this was a compliment or not. "You're..."

"Not making any sense, I can see. I shouldn't torment you. I just wanted to tell you that you're not alone, although I imagine you feel like it in this house full of strangers."

"That was kind," she said.

Lady Hillbrook sent her a shrewd glance. "It would be kinder to leave you in peace."

"Thank you," Nell said in relief. When she'd come upstairs, she'd dreaded that her brazen antics in the library might arouse disdain and disgust. This undeserved offer of friendship was harder to accept.

Lady Hillbrook turned toward the door. "Good night, Miss Trim."

"Good night, your ladyship," she whispered, before Lady Hillbrook granted her the privacy for a good, long cry.

Chapter Thirty

I t's time we found a solution to the Greengrass problem."
Hillbrook settled into a chair in Sedgemoor's library and
brought the delicate coffee cup to his lips. "He's clearly up to
his old tricks."

Sedgemoor had called this meeting of Leath, Hillbrook,
and Harmsworth after breakfast. Leath understood Eleanor's
pique at being excluded. But she'd done enough, however
misguided, in this quest to end his dead uncle's baleful influence. The task was men's business now, not least because
the others had experience with that dangerous thug Hector
Greengrass.

He'd cut off his hands before he put Eleanor in danger.

How he'd hated letting her go last night, especially when
they'd only just found each other again. But he retained
enough discretion to know that he couldn't share her bed.
Not without shaming her.

"I had men scouring the kingdom for the bugger after that
swine Fairbrother shot himself..." Sedgemoor cast Leath
an apologetic glance from his seat near the hearth. "Sorry,

old man. I know he was your uncle, but he was rotten to the core."

"Don't apologize for insulting the blackguard," Leath said, standing near the window. The view outside was wet and gray and uniformly gloomy. "I wish he'd been drowned at birth."

"It's easy enough to disappear under a different name." Harmsworth lounged against the mantel, looking like an illustration from a fashion periodical. His surprisingly disreputable-looking hound lay a few feet away. Leath had always dismissed the baronet as Sedgemoor's brainless satellite. But noting the firm jaw and intelligent eyes, now he wasn't so sure. "Greengrass took a leaf from his master's book. I gather your uncle stole your name to despoil virgins up and down the country."

"Apparently," Leath said drily.

"And among these women was Miss Trim's sister," Sedgemoor added. "Damned bad business, that."

"Half-sister. Which is why Miss Trim used her real name at Alloway Chase."

"That's one enterprising female."

"She has no shortage of courage." Leath kept his tone noncommittal, although he suspected that all these men— and their wives—guessed that he and Miss Trim were more than former enemies, now reluctant allies. The fact that he and Eleanor had been left alone last night spoke volumes for what these sophisticated, clever people assumed about his relations with his housemaid.

He wondered what they'd say if they knew he'd proposed to that housemaid. And that the housemaid had had the temerity to say no.

"Greengrass is skulking somewhere in Berkshire. At least the address where I'm to take the money is in Maidenhead. The first letter came from Newbury."

The mail at Alloway Chase had included a letter from Greengrass responding to Leath's agreement to buy the diary. The ruffian had changed his point of contact. Clearly he was cunning and wary. He needed to be to escape justice so long.

As Hillbrook leaned back in his chair, a sardonic smile creased his scarred face. "I credit the fellow's sense of humor in choosing his location."

"None of this is a matter for jest, Jonas," Sedgemoor growled. "You saw those letters. Neville Fairbrother used those women and abandoned them to starvation and disgrace. I wish I'd shot the cur myself instead of leaving him to take the easy way out."

"I only got the blackmail demand a week ago," Leath said. "My agents have tried to locate him, with the hope that the law could take him unawares. They haven't had any luck, despite setting up a watch on the Newbury inn."

"One wonders what Greengrass has been living on since he fled Little Derrick," Harmsworth said thoughtfully. "That was over a year ago. It's odd that he's waited so long to squeeze you over the diary."

Hillbrook agreed. "He wouldn't hesitate before tightening the screws on a victim."

"Perhaps after Lord Neville's fall, he was nervous about tangling with the aristocracy," Sedgemoor suggested.

Harmsworth frowned. "I can't see Greengrass nervous at the Last Judgment. After failing so ignominiously in Little Derrick, he'd be set on causing mayhem."

"He and Fairbrother went damned close to finishing you and Genevieve." Anger resonated in Sedgemoor's usually calm voice. "We all have scores to settle, not just Leath."

"We know where he wants to collect the money," Leath said. "He must be holed up near there. Especially as he's demanded payment within the week."

"Leath, you don't mean to do what the bugger wants?" Harmsworth asked.

He bared his teeth at the man he'd once considered his enemy. "No. I mean to get that bloody diary and destroy it—and in the process destroy Greengrass, too."

"Bravo," Hillbrook said drily. "I'm in the mood for a jaunt into the Home Counties."

"In this frigid weather, anything south of here sounds good," Sedgemoor said.

"Hear, hear." Harmsworth raised his cup in an ironic toast.

Leath frowned at this circle of influential men. "I don't understand."

"Very simple, my dear Leath," Sedgemoor said with that superior air that had always irritated him, particularly over the last year when relations between the Fairbrothers and the Rothermeres had been colder than today's temperature.

Strangely Leath wasn't as irritated as he used to be. Love must have softened his heart. Or his head.

"Yes, very simple," Hillbrook repeated. Another superior bugger. Any room Jonas Merrick entered always seemed too small for his dominant presence. But again, Leath's usual urge to punch that ruined face was absent. "We all owe Greengrass a reckoning and if we can achieve that while getting you out of a fix, we're delighted to assist."

Leath stared across to the fire. "I can handle this, although I appreciate your support."

Sedgemoor laughed and to his surprise, rose to clap him on the shoulder as if they were friends rather than men forced into superficial politeness by a runaway wedding. "Don't be so damned prickly. Why should you have all the fun?"

Shocked, oddly moved, Leath glanced around the room. The others regarded him steadily, without hostility or equivocation.

"You still should have damn well warned me before making my uncle's crimes public," he said, although the words lacked the rage that had prompted him to work against Sedgemoor and his cohorts.

Sedgemoor extended his hand. "Let bygones be bygones."

Six months ago, if anyone had said that he'd accept Camden Rothermere's friendship, he'd have laughed. Six months ago, he and the duke had come to blows over Sophie's elopement.

Yet now, he found himself smiling and taking Sedgemoor's hand. "A new beginning, Your Grace."

Gripping his hand with impressive strength, Sedgemoor surveyed him down that long ducal nose. "Well said."

Leath cleared his throat as Sedgemoor released him. All his life he'd been in essence a lone wolf. Now it seemed he had a woman he loved. And an offer of friendship. A series of friendships, he realized, noticing that Hillbrook and Harmsworth observed him with an approval he couldn't imagine he deserved.

"So that's set." Hillbrook rose and offered his hand too. In a daze, Leath accepted it. He hardly knew this man. For most of Jonas Merrick's life, his supposed bastardy had excluded him from society. "We're off to Berkshire to crush an adder."

Harmsworth rose to shake Leath's hand too. He smiled with the easy charm that Leath had formerly dismissed as weakness. "Welcome to the gang. We'll do the blood brother ceremony before lunch."

"We'll be on our way to Berkshire before then," Sedgemoor said.

Leath found himself laughing. "I'm embarrassingly eager to shout, 'All for one and one for all.' "

"Now to tell our wives that we're adventuring without them," Hillbrook said wryly. "I'd rather face Greengrass."

Sedgemoor smiled. "Pen will welcome some company."

"I'm sure Sidonie will stay—once I've convinced her that I can survive without her pistol guarding my back."

"Genevieve is giving a lecture to the Royal Society next week. She'll want to return to London." Harmsworth had married a famous bluestocking. The thought of such a mismatch had given Leath many a nasty laugh in the last year. Now he wondered if the Harmsworth marriage was the disaster he'd predicted.

"She can travel with us," Sedgemoor said.

"We'll get all the way to Mayfair before we convince her that we can succeed without her pistol too," Harmsworth said with a mocking melancholy that didn't hide his fondness for his wife.

"She has her own score to settle with the devil," Hillbrook said on a sober note. "You can't blame her for wanting to see the end."

"I can't blame her," Harmsworth said. "But I'll be damned before I let her get within ten feet of that rabid cur."

"Sedgemoor, would I push this new amity if I asked you to shelter Miss Trim until everything's cleared up?" Once, the idea of asking a favor from the arrogant duke would have stuck in Leath's craw.

"Of course. Pen will like that."

"Thank you." Eleanor wouldn't appreciate being left behind. If he knew his Miss Trim, she'd want to be in at this drama's climax.

Chapter Thirty-One

Nell dug her heels into the newly named Ginger's sides as she caught sight of the horsemen and coach from the top of the hill. The gallant mare, who had given so much on the way to Fentonwyck, broke into a run.

Whatever else Nell thought of James right now—and a few choice adjectives had crossed her mind since she'd read the note that he'd left her as a good-bye—she admired his taste in horseflesh. Ginger was a marvel.

Lord Hillbrook rode a huge black horse at the rear of the cavalcade. At Nell's approach, he drew the snorting beast to a halt. James was ahead with Sedgemoor. She assumed Sir Richard was inside the coach with his wife, and that the handsome gray hack tied to the vehicle was his.

"Miss Trim," his lordship said, sweeping his hat off and bowing from his superior height.

"My lord," she said grimly. She felt nervous around Jonas Merrick with his scarred face and watchful eyes.

"You must have ridden like the devil."

His expression livid, James cantered back past the coach. "What in Hades are you doing here, Eleanor?"

He was so angry he forgot to call her Miss Trim. She didn't care. She was angry herself. "This is my quest."

"No longer."

"That's not your decision."

She watched his jaw work as he controlled his temper. She knew he wanted to insist that it was his decision. If she'd agreed to marry him, he might have a point. Right now, he didn't. He knew it. And he didn't like it.

"You don't ride well enough to keep up," he said.

"Is that the best you can do?" she asked coldly. With a faint smile, Sedgemoor observed them from a distance.

James's lips flattened in impatience. "Go back, Eleanor. This is no place for you."

"It's exactly the place for me."

The coachman had drawn the vehicle to a stop. Sir Richard stepped out, dressed for making social calls in Mayfair. "Miss Trim, you decided to join us?"

"Only briefly," James bit out. "She's returning to Fenton-wyck."

"No, she's not," Nell responded coolly.

Lady Harmsworth's head appeared from the window and she waved. "Miss Trim!"

James cast Nell a disgusted look. "I could take you."

She smiled with false sweetness that he should read as a warning. "Tied to your saddle?"

His jaw became harder than granite. "If necessary."

"And once you get me there, how will you make me stay? Leash me in the stable like a dog?"

He grumbled low in his throat. She glanced at Lord Hill-brook, who stared fixedly across the wild country rising on either side of the lonely road. She suspected that he was trying not to laugh. She returned her attention to the man she loved— and right now wanted to push onto his well-bred backside.

"Don't be ridiculous," he muttered.

"It's a long way back, Leath," Sir Richard pointed out. He didn't hide his amusement nearly as well as Hillbrook did.

"I can catch you up," he said.

"And I can follow again," Nell said. "I don't even need to follow. I read the blackmail letter. I know you're going to Berkshire."

"It will be dangerous." He nudged his horse closer, his words for her ears alone. "I can't bear to think of anything happening to you."

She recognized this tactic. He appealed to her feelings for him. Because of course he knew that she cared, even if he didn't know that she loved him beyond all measure. "I can look after myself."

"Brave and foolish words, my love," he whispered. "For my sake, go back to Fentonwyck. I promise we'll bring everything to a satisfactory conclusion."

"I'm sure you will."

He looked marginally easier. "So you'll listen to reason?"

"So I'll see you in action." Her tone turned flinty. "You're wasting time, my lord."

"Devil take obstinate women." His horse shifted as he shortened the reins.

She smiled. "I hope you'll take note of this moment."

He narrowed his eyes. He knew that she referred to her unsuitability as a bride. "You can stay in London with Lady Harmsworth," he snapped. "If she won't have you—and who can blame her?—you'll stay at Leath House. Locked in the cellars, if need be."

Nell shot him an unimpressed glance. "We'll see."

"Come into the carriage with me, Miss Trim," Lady Harmsworth called. "We never finished our discussion on *Mansfield Park*."

"With pleasure, your ladyship." Nell's smile held a mere hint of triumph, whatever victorious fanfares rang out in her heart.

James dismounted and stalked across to lift her from Ginger's back. "If you think I'm not angry that such an inexperienced rider as you galloped hell for leather across this wilderness, you're much mistaken."

She regarded him under lowered eyebrows as he set her on her feet with a decided bump. "You're not my keeper, my lord."

"If you sign the contract in my luggage, I will indeed be your keeper."

She refused to blush, despite his attempt to discomfit her with a reminder of her surrender—something the long day in the saddle had made painfully apparent. "A mistress has more freedom than a wife, my lord. A mistress may leave as she pleases."

"Damn you," he muttered, although his hands were gentle at her waist. "You're not going anywhere."

"You're mistaken, my lord. I'm going to Berkshire."

To her surprise he laughed. It was a weary laugh, but she knew she'd won when he caught her hand and squeezed it briefly. "You'll make my life a nightmare."

Her smile widened. "Undoubtedly."

Knowing he watched, she exaggerated the sway of her hips as she strolled toward the carriage. There was something heady in owning her power over him. If he tried to keep her in London with Lady Harmsworth, she'd fight again, but for now she had her way. And the memory of his touch to fortify her.

The cavalcade started up, except Sir Richard now rode, claiming he'd only be an intruder inside the carriage. Nell approved of Sir Richard. Behind his lazy smile, he was kind and perceptive, and he adored his wife.

Last night, Nell had cried herself to sleep. But she'd woken this morning determined to take charge of her life. She'd be Lord Leath's mistress. If there were children, she'd love them so much that they wouldn't care about their illegitimacy. And when time came for James to marry, she'd leave him with her head high and the knowledge that, whatever the world's opinion of her, love had guided her actions.

"You're looking very intense," Lady Harmsworth said from the seat opposite. She had a book open on her lap and Sirius snoozed at her feet.

"I'm thinking about meeting Greengrass," Nell said, which should have been true. Despite facing down James, Nell didn't underestimate the danger.

Lady Harmsworth settled against the leather upholstery and surveyed her with a piercing intelligence that reminded her uncomfortably of Lord Hillbrook. "Greengrass is seriously outmatched with our four knights in shining armor on his trail. I have no doubt that right will prevail."

"Lady Harmsworth, you misunderstand," Nell said unsteadily.

Her lips firmed with amused impatience. "You think I'm unforgivably nosy."

Nell did, but she couldn't say so. She braced herself against the coach's sway and looked out the window. "You've all been so kind." That was true too. "But until last night, I blamed Lord Leath for my half-sister's death."

Sympathy shadowed Lady Harmsworth's vivid face and she reached for Nell's hand. "Neville Fairbrother has so much to answer for. I gather that you've accepted Leath's innocence. You were arguing like old friends just now."

"You always knew he was innocent," Nell said, flushing with mortification. She'd lain awake last night, cursing her recklessness in Sedgemoor's library. Anyone could have come in. She was almost more discomfited that nobody had. It hinted that her affair with James was no secret. "All of you did, from the moment I produced the letters."

Lady Harmsworth straightened, releasing Nell's hand. "Leath has a reputation as a man of principle. The wretch who ran around England ruining innocent girls sounded more like the uncle than the nephew." Her eyes conveyed loathing. "But of course, I have personal experience to rely on."

Something in Lady Harmsworth's face indicated that she'd endured horrors at Lord Neville's hands. After a shocked moment, Nell returned her attention to the bleak winter landscape. She'd only met this woman a few days ago. Too short a time for these intimate revelations.

"I've apologized to his lordship for misjudging him." Then she wished she hadn't spoken. An apology implied a relationship more equal than marquess to housemaid. To distract her ladyship—although she had a grim feeling that nothing distracted Genevieve Harmsworth when she pursued answers—she spoke quickly. "I misunderstood so much. I believed that his lordship and the duke were sworn enemies."

"There were a few sour notes. Leath's political ambitions hit a wall once his uncle's crimes became public, and he blamed my husband and Sedgemoor for that. Things got even more fraught when Harry and Sophie ran away. Of course, the press exaggerated the feud."

"Those stories made me bring the letters to His Grace."

"Thank goodness you did."

"Thank goodness I did." To think that Nell could have gone to the newspapers. To think that she could have destroyed James's political career completely and forever.

To think that if she agreed to marry him, she'd achieve that anyway.

"I hardly know Lord Leath," Lady Harmsworth said in a neutral voice. "But I have a feeling that won't remain the case. I see signs of growing rapport with the others."

A relieved breath escaped Nell. Perhaps her ladyship didn't intend to interrogate her about the marquess. She was glad to see the seeds of friendship between James and these dynamic men. She'd long ago recognized his isolation.

When Nell didn't speak—anything she said would reveal unsuitable familiarity with James's private life—Lady Harmsworth continued thoughtfully. "Which means, I imagine, that we'll see more of the marquess."

Nell remained silent, but she raised an unsteady hand to the leather strap by the window. The weather outside was bitterly cold with a wind that would slice through steel, and she was too inexperienced a rider to enjoy long hours in the saddle. Nonetheless she wished she'd stayed on Ginger and never stepped inside this spider's web disguised as a luxurious conveyance.

Lady Harmsworth sighed. "You're a sphinx, Miss Trim."

"I enjoyed *Mansfield Park*," she said with an edge of desperation.

To her surprise, Lady Harmsworth laughed. "Well, I didn't. There, that's covered our literary discussion." She regarded Nell searchingly. "It's not easy loving an exceptional man. I speak from experience. As would Sidonie and Pen, if you asked them. Although you're far too discreet to do such a thing, I know. You really will make the perfect politician's wife."

Nell made a distressed sound. "You're speaking cruel nonsense."

"You think I torment you for my entertainment," Lady Harmsworth said with a regret that even to Nell's hostile ears sounded sincere. "I'm sorry, Miss Trim." She paused.

"Blast, I can't have a good coze with a woman I call Miss Trim. Can't I call you Eleanor?"

Nell regarded her stormily. "That isn't appropriate, your ladyship." She placed an ironic emphasis on the formal address.

Lady Harmsworth smiled. "Don't tell me you're a snob."

"Not at all," Nell said coldly. How could she have liked this woman?

"I told you, I'm a humble vicar's daughter."

"You're a famous scholar," Nell snapped, tired of Lady Harmsworth downplaying her status purely to winkle out her secrets.

"I wasn't when I met Richard. And a female scholar doesn't meet general approval, believe me. Most people consider our match completely laughable. I'm such a bluestocking and he's society's beau ideal."

"He has lovely manners," Nell said.

To Nell's surprise, Lady Harmsworth laughed. "I deserve that." She spoke more softly. "I'm going about this completely ham-fisted. Richard would be ashamed of me. I just want you to know that you're not the first woman to fall in love with a man she believes is impossibly out of reach. If you need advice or help or a shoulder to cry on, I'm offering my friendship."

Nell, who thought her cheeks couldn't get any hotter, met Lady Harmsworth's eyes. What could she say? Admitting that she was Leath's mistress would put her further beyond the pale than working as a housemaid.

She managed a smile, slightly wobbly, and spoke with a genuine warmth that she didn't have to work to summon, to her surprise. "Please, I'd be honored if you called me Nell."

Chapter Thirty-Two

He's there." Leath stepped into the hired coach on a side street. Inside, Sedgemoor, Hillbrook, and Harmsworth were ready for action. At least he'd convinced Eleanor to wait at Maidenhead's best inn. She'd reluctantly cooperated when he'd pointed out that fears for her safety would distract him from the confrontation.

He went on. "Or at least the driver says that a heavily built bald bruiser is sitting at a table between the two doors. If it's not Greengrass, it's someone who wants more than one exit available."

"Ugly as sin," Harmsworth said.

"Sounds like our man," Leath said.

"At last the weasel has emerged from cover," Hillbrook said with grim satisfaction. "You'd think he'd be more cautious about collecting his blood money than to meet you face to face."

Leath's smile was equally grim. "In the note arranging this rendezvous, I told him that I got the diary before I handed over the money, or we had no deal."

"He didn't threaten to publish?" Sedgemoor asked.

"I told him to go ahead. It was my terms or nothing."

"That was rash," Harmsworth said.

Leath shrugged. "Not really. If he publishes, I won't pay him to keep quiet. And however scandalous the diary, I doubt any newspaper can amass ten thousand guineas."

"I still take my hat off to you, Leath," Sedgemoor said. "You're a cool devil."

"After this last year, I'm becoming inured to scandal," he replied drily.

"Gad, you're well behind the rest of us," Harmsworth drawled. "We three drank scandal with our mother's milk."

Leath laughed, then returned to the business at hand. "So you'll cover the doors?"

"Yes," Sedgemoor said. "We three and the coachman should be plenty."

"Don't budge until I've got the diary and you see me leave the inn. Any trouble inside could injure innocent bystanders. Once he's outside, we nab the sod wherever and however we can."

Hillbrook glanced at the others. "Good luck, gentlemen. I've wanted to take Greengrass down since last year."

Sedgemoor and Harmsworth looked ready for murder. Leath wasn't surprised. Now that he knew the full details of his uncle's crimes against them, crimes committed with Greengrass's aid, he finally admitted that any grudge he'd carried against these men was unjustified.

He left the shabby coach and strode toward the Laughing Bullock. A good ten paces behind, the coachman Brown followed, armed and ready.

Leath pushed his way into a taproom buzzing with afternoon trade. He'd deliberately dressed down in breeches and a plain buff coat, but speculative stares indicated that he still didn't blend in.

He looked over the sea of heads and quickly located a man fitting Greengrass's description. Despite the crush, the fellow sat alone at a table for four. Clearly the other patrons recognized the wisdom of giving this hulking thug a wide berth.

Greengrass glanced up, as if sensing Leath's eyes on him. Ugly as sin indeed. The piglike eyes narrowed with gloating pleasure and he made an exaggerated gesture of welcome toward one of the empty chairs. His other hand hoisted a tankard of beer.

"Your lordship, how kind of you to come." The rough voice had an Essex accent.

Leath stared down his nose. "I realize you want to savor your triumph, Greengrass. But let's get this over with."

Greengrass's fleshy lips stretched in a nasty smile. "Lord Neville always said that you think your shit doesn't stink."

"Charming."

"Sit down and take your medicine, my boy."

Leath raised his eyebrows in contempt and sat with a nonchalance designed to tell Greengrass that he didn't have the upper hand. The man's eyes lit as they leveled on Leath's satchel. "Is that it?"

"Yes. Let's end this."

"Not here. If anyone gets wind of what's in that bag, we'll have a bloody riot on our hands."

"I don't trust you away from witnesses," Leath said coldly.

"We'll not go far, just the alley behind the inn." He licked his lips in anticipation. "But give us a look first."

"First show me the diary."

"Don't you trust me?"

"Call me a cynic."

With a slowness that grated, Greengrass reached into his surprisingly smart dark green coat and produced a leatherbound book. "Here it be."

Heart racing, Leath took the pestilential journal. He'd never doubted that the diary was real. Greengrass had sent a few pages of filth when he opened negotiations. And it was just the sort of touch his uncle would give his villainy, keeping a detailed record as if his victims formed part of his collections.

Greengrass snatched it away. "Uh-uh. Show me the color of your gold."

Carefully, Leath cracked open the satchel to give Greengrass a glimpse of the handful of ten pound notes that rested on top of piles of cut newsprint.

"Paper?" Greengrass spat in disgust.

"Use your head, man. I can't lift that amount in coin."

"Paper money can be traced."

Leath laughed drily and lied. "Once I've got the diary, you can disappear with my blessing. Do you think I want you and your flapping gums before a judge?"

Greengrass took a swig from his tankard, then banged it down on the noisome table. One beefy hand splayed over the book. "That makes sense. Although don't imagine I'll keep quiet if you gyp me."

"Prove that's the diary," Leath snapped.

"You're mighty pushy for a bloke whose reputation hangs by a thread."

Coldly Leath regarded Greengrass. "Right now I'm two minutes from consigning you to hell and your threats with you."

Greengrass grinned, unconvinced. "Brave words. You're here and you've got my brass. I'd say you'd do pretty much anything to protect your high and mighty family name."

"Show me the diary," Leath bit out.

After a pause to demonstrate his power, Greengrass opened the journal and, holding it, slid it toward Leath. The light in the inn was terrible, Leath suspected to stop patrons inspecting their purchases too closely. But he recognized his uncle's incongruously beautiful copperplate and caught some words he wouldn't use in polite society.

Greengrass snapped the book shut and tugged it back. "Satisfied?"

He'd kept Greengrass talking as long as he could to give the others time to take their places. Brown the coachman stood at the bar to back him up. "Yes."

"Then let's go." Greengrass drained his mug and rose, tucking the diary into his coat.

Hell's bells, Harmsworth and co were right about him being a huge bugger. Greengrass's hairless head brushed the blackened beams on the stained ceiling. Leath dwarfed most men, but he felt like a molehill beside a mountain.

Greengrass gave a mocking wave toward a door that Leath hadn't noticed. As they stepped into a dark corridor, he slid his hand into his pocket and curled his fingers around a pistol. He hoped like hell that the others found this exit. He hoped like hell that the strapping coachman saw that he and Greengrass used neither of the identified doors. Brown's orders were to report any deviation from the plan to Sedgemoor.

Still, Leath was armed with two guns and he had a knife in his boot. If Greengrass played up, he was prepared.

Greengrass pushed a small door and crouched to go through. Leath bent to follow and found himself in a choke hold as he emerged.

"Give me the bloody money."

Leath raised his pistol. "There's no need for this." With Greengrass's arm squeezing his windpipe, the words emerged as a croak. "A clean exchange, then we go our separate ways."

"You're too easy, my fine lordship," the man grunted into his ear, ignoring the gun. "Lord Neville called you the proudest cove in England. Proud coves don't bend so polite to blackmail. There's some trick."

Leath wrenched Greengrass's arm from his throat. He gulped air into his aching lungs and aimed the gun. "I want the diary."

Greengrass sneered. "You're not a man to kill in cold blood."

"Perhaps not, but I'd maim without blinking," he snapped, sidling to bring the end of the alley into view. It was ominously empty. How the hell had they missed this exit? Last night, he and the others had thoroughly checked the inn. He'd have laid money that they'd counted every door and window.

"Just testing your mettle, my lord." Greengrass reached for the diary.

Behind Leath, running feet thudded in the corridor. Greengrass's hand stilled.

Good God, no. Not now.

Clearly the Almighty wasn't listening. The coachman burst through the door. "My lord!"

Greengrass stiffened and swore. "You bastard."

Faster than lightning, he punched Leath in the head. Pain exploded behind his eyes and he staggered into the rough brick wall. Brown grabbed him before he fell, but he was in no mood to thank the fool.

When Leath's vision cleared, Greengrass aimed a pistol at Brown. Leath might be furious with the dolt, but he didn't want him dead.

"Give me my money, you slimy sod."

"Hoy!" Leath bellowed to alert the men watching the inn. Surely they weren't far away.

The street remained empty.

"I'll bring him down, my lord."

"Don't move, you idiot," he snarled to the coachman. "He'll shoot you."

Greengrass's laugh was low. "That I will, if you don't hand over that bag."

Damn, in this restricted space, he couldn't get a clear shot at Greengrass without risking hitting Brown. "Give me the diary."

"Oh, no, my hearty. You cheated. That means no prize."

"The inn is surrounded. You'll never get away," the coachman said.

"Shut up, blockhead," Leath snarled.

Greengrass's eyes narrowed until they were pinpricks in his massive face. He hauled Brown closer, making the man a shield. "You don't play fair, your lordship. Now hand over my money and I'll be off."

"What about the diary?"

Greengrass smiled, clearly convinced that he retained the advantage. "The price has gone up another ten thousand. And I'll thank you to be a bit straighter in your dealings, my fine fellow."

"Leath!"

At last. The shout from the end of the alley came from Harmsworth.

Greengrass turned, hatred contorting his face. "What the hell is that bugger doing here?"

"Give up, Greengrass," Leath said, voice still hoarse. "There's nowhere to go."

Greengrass cocked the pistol. "I'm not done yet."

"My lord, watch out!" The coachman twisted and launched himself at Greengrass.

"Be careful, man!" Leath shouted to Brown as Harmsworth sprinted toward them.

There was a shot and a scream, then Brown reeled against the wall, one hand lifting to a patch of bright red on his shirt. "Blimey."

Leath surged forward and clipped Greengrass hard on the chin. The man staggered back, then snatched for the loaded pistol. After a short, vicious struggle, the gun fired, missing Greengrass and striking chips off the brickwork.

Greengrass slammed forward and grabbed the satchel. Leath struggled to hold it and draw his knife at the same time. Then he realized that Greengrass's hands were too occupied to protect the diary. Leath ripped at the green coat for the book. He shouted in triumph as he dragged it free.

"No, you bloody don't," the man grunted.

"Yes, I bloody do," Leath responded, dodging another punch. "Harmsworth!"

Sir Richard, thank God, was nowhere near as stupid as Sedgemoor's coachman. Despite Leath's clumsy toss, Harmsworth caught the book. "Good throw, old man."

"Leath! Harmsworth!"

Leath couldn't see past Greengrass, but he heard Sedgemoor's shout. "Here!"

"You really did play me false, you lying swine," Greengrass said, grabbing Leath's shoulder in a bruising grip and swiveling him around so fast that his head swam. "So much for being a man of honor."

"You're a rat in a trap," he grunted, splaying his hands against the bricks to keep himself upright.

"Not bloody likely," the man growled and with a violent push, shoved Leath into the wall. When his head met the bricks, everything went black.

A shot exploded as he opened his eyes. Greengrass's elephantine form disappeared inside the inn. Sedgemoor rushed in pursuit. Leath told himself to follow, but the command came from far, far away.

"Leath?"

Blearily he saw Hillbrook's concerned face above him.

He'd collapsed onto the filthy cobbles. He raised a hand to his throbbing skull and struggled to think. Someone groaned beside him. "How is Brown?"

"He'll live." Hillbrook glanced at the coachman. "Looks like the bullet missed his vitals. Not that I'm any expert."

"Damn fool deserves to suffer," Leath grumbled, gradually remembering the disastrous sequence of events.

Another groan pricked Leath's conscience, although he'd wanted to shoot the man himself when he'd burst in so disastrously. A murmur of voices indicated that Harmsworth offered Brown assistance.

"Greengrass got the money," he said unsteadily, leaning against the wall.

"It's only fifty pounds."

"Says the richest man in Europe." Leath struggled to stand, but Hillbrook settled a hand on his shoulder.

"Stay there until you can see straight. You got the diary."

"Did I?"

Hillbrook smiled grimly and pointed to Harmsworth. "Look."

Careful how he turned his head, Leath saw the volume in Sir Richard's hand. Despite pain and anger, a tendril of satisfaction unfurled. "I did, didn't I?"

Hillbrook's smile broadened. "Good work."

"Sod got away," Sedgemoor announced from Leath's right. "There's a cellar with a passage through to the river."

"Must be why he chose this place," Harmsworth said. "I've made the mistake before of underestimating the brute."

"It doesn't matter." Leath's voice sounded thick in his ears. "Without the diary, he's got no leverage."

Hillbrook helped him up. "Come on; let's get you back to Miss Trim."

Leath staggered and cursed his clumsiness. Gratefully he

accepted Hillbrook's shoulder under his arm. "She won't be impressed that I let the blackguard scarper."

Sedgemoor took the other arm. "She won't care when her wounded hero returns."

For some reason, Leath found that description enormously funny and he laughed. At least until his stomach lurched in protest. Wounded hero indeed.

"I still think you should see a doctor." Eleanor rose from her chair across the dinner table.

They were in Leath's private parlor at the Royal Swan, Maidenhead's best inn. Earlier, all five had enjoyed a meal to celebrate the diary's retrieval. Leath's head pounded, but he'd done his best with a single glass of champagne. The other men had made up for his abstention, raising glasses in increasingly lunatic toasts.

Eleanor had been reserved, but it was impossible to remain shy in Richard Harmsworth's presence, and she'd soon joined the festivities. Leath had smiled to see her so easy in the high-bred company. More ammunition for his campaign to marry her. He merely bided his time before asking again. He suspected she guessed that. After she'd recovered from the shock of seeing his injuries, her manner had turned wary.

He appreciated the welcome the three men gave her. Even more, he appreciated that each had since found an excuse to leave the parlor.

Now Eleanor approached him, beautiful eyes dark with concern. It was a cold night and she looked so warm and inviting. In her neat gray dress, she seemed more his Miss Trim than the gorgeous creature in silk at Fentonwyck. He'd wanted that woman to the point of madness, but there was something familiar and delightful about this Eleanor.

Gently she ran her hand over the back of his head. Even such a delicate touch had him hiding a wince. She brushed her lips across his thick dark hair, so lightly that he barely felt it. Except that his lonely heart yearned for her care like a man dying of thirst yearned for a river.

Still gently, she caught his jaw in one slender hand and tilted his face. She rested her other hand on his shoulder as she scrutinized him with a detailed attention that made his bones melt with longing. She pressed another butterfly kiss to the bruise on his cheekbone. "You quite terrify me, James; you're so scarred and bruised."

He smiled. This was the first time she'd called him James all night. He raised his hand and pressed her palm against his jaw. "Who needs a doctor when I have Miss Trim? Will you stay tonight?"

For the sake of her reputation, he'd engaged a separate room for her, although he'd ensured it was across the corridor from his. A man lived in hope, after all.

She stared into his eyes and briefly he thought she might agree, before she shook her head. "No."

He tried to find comfort in her audible regret. "Are you sure?"

Amusement lit her eyes to gold. "Stop tempting me."

She kissed his mouth. Her scent surrounded him. Fresh. Lemony. Eleanor. He parted his lips to set the kiss on fire, but she withdrew. "Your head must hurt like the devil."

"Another part hurts worse," he complained.

She snickered. "You'll live."

"Cruel beauty."

She turned and laid her hand on the diary. "So this is the book that caused all the trouble."

His smile faded. "No, my toad of an uncle caused the trouble."

"Have you read it?"

"No." He struggled to hide his disgust at what little he'd seen. Pages of his uncle's banal and profane prose, all expressing relentless contempt for his lovers. Leath had been sickened and depressed. "Do you want to check what he said about your sister?"

Sadness dulled her eyes. "No. She paid the price for her recklessness. She was an innocent led astray. I don't need to know more. What are you going to do with the diary?"

"I'd like to burn it so that it does no more harm." He stared at the book. "But it's the only record we have of my uncle's sins. I'll have to track down these women and make sure they're all right. Only the bravest and most desperate have written to me, I suspect."

Eleanor studied him, eyes glowing in the flickering light. "You're a good man, James."

The compliment warmed him, especially given her past suspicions. "I'm glad you think so."

"I worry that Greengrass is still out there," she said with a shiver. "By now he'll know that the satchel was packed with newspaper."

"He'll go to ground somewhere close. We'll find him." Leath sat back and opened his arms. "Come here."

She didn't shift. "I told you I can't stay tonight."

"I know," he said drily. "But that doesn't mean you have to stand so far away."

Her lips flattened with a fond exasperation that made his poor heart stutter. So desperate he was for any sign that she felt more than mere desire. "It's all of two feet."

"Too far."

"And you've been in a fight. You're covered in bruises."

"You can take off my clothes and check if you like."

"James."

"Please?"

She sighed. He waited for her to stick to her guns and walk away, but she crossed the minimal distance between them and curled up on his lap.

She was right. He was covered in bruises. With Eleanor in his arms, he didn't give a damn. His hold tightened as she rested her head on his shoulder with a trust that he couldn't take for granted. Not when only days ago, she'd hated him.

"I was terrified when you went to meet that man." Her soft confession vibrated with emotion.

He kissed her forehead. She'd tied her hair in a loose knot. His fingers itched to unpin it, but he restrained himself. He didn't need more torture. "You hid it well."

"Did I?"

He laughed shortly. "No."

She nestled closer. "I held my breath until you came back."

"Kiss me," he whispered.

She framed his head between her hands. The light in her eyes made him imagine that she loved him. She drew him down until their lips met. The contact lasted long enough to turn his blood to honey.

She nipped his lower lip and placed glancing kisses along his jaw. This time when she stopped, he growled deep in his throat. Her teasing provoked him. He hadn't been alone with Eleanor since that explosive evening in Sedgemoor's library. On their journey south, they'd stayed in Northampton, then spent another night at Rothermere House, Sedgemoor's luxurious pile in Grosvenor Square.

Leath settled her to allow better access to her mouth. Her hand traced a searing path up his chest, although the atmosphere remained sweet rather than sultry.

"Kiss me properly," he murmured.

A frown creased her brow. "Are you up to it?"

He laughed and bumped her with his hips. He expected her to wriggle away, but she shifted closer. "You're tormenting me."

"A little. To pay you back for frightening me." She paused. "To pay you back for getting hurt."

Sweetness flared to heat and he groaned. "Eleanor…"

He didn't hold back when he kissed her. By the time he raised his head, she strained against him. Her dress was unbuttoned and his hand curled around her breast.

"You're dangerous," she muttered, shoving aside his shirt and kissing his chest where his longing heart beat to the sound of her name.

He kissed the satiny white flesh above the pert pink nipple. "Stay with me tonight. Nobody need know."

"Yes, they will," she retorted, even as she arched nearer.

Unable to ignore the encouragement, his lips closed on the peak of her breast. She cried out and her fingers tightened on his shoulders.

"We could make love now," he said unsteadily. "Then you could return to your room and nobody will be the wiser."

"I hate the idea of people sniggering about…us." She stared at him, troubled. "I'm not a very convenient mistress, am I?"

He spoke the words that he'd promised himself he wouldn't say until this mess with Greengrass was resolved. The words that would blast all this lovely, warm intimacy to hell.

"You'd make a highly convenient wife."

Chapter Thirty-Three

"Not this again." Nell scrambled away. She put her hands on her hips and stared James down.

Unfortunately, his lordship was as dogged as she was. His chin jutted belligerently. "Eleanor, will you marry me?"

"No." She whirled away, missing the luxuriant rustle of Lady Hillbrook's gown. The narrow skirts of her gray dress didn't lend her temper the same grandeur. A sign of how dangerously easy it would be to tumble into the fantasy that she belonged in James's world. That his clever, rich, aristocratic friends would accept her. That she made a fit consort for this outstanding man.

"Is that all you have to say?"

When she turned, she saw he'd risen. He rested one hand on the back of the chair where for a few blissful moments she'd leaned into him as if he was her rock in a turbulent world.

He remained her rock in a turbulent world. But she could never claim him publicly. Not without damaging him. She stiffened her spine and prepared to crush her dearest dreams to dust. "If you marry me, you'll never be prime minister."

"I don't give a rat's arse about being prime minister. I'd rather have you."

His language shocked her and she faltered back before remembering that she must appear strong. "You *can* have me—as a mistress."

"I want more."

"There is no more. Desire must be enough." She turned toward a mirror to fix her hair. The face in the glass was rosy with kisses, but the eyes were frightened.

She saw him reflected behind her. In his bruised face, his smile expressed endless affection. "We have more than desire and you know it."

Her wayward heart lurched with love. When he smiled like that, he was nigh irresistible. "Stop it," she snapped, turning on him.

He was still smiling. How she wished he wouldn't. "Stop desiring you? Never."

His gaze conducted a leisurely exploration of her body. Without touching her, he set every inch tingling. Slow heat shimmered inside her, turned her blood thick and sluggish. Her stomach quivered with longing. She shifted to relieve the heaviness between her legs.

He read her reaction. His smile broadened, became wolfish. She blushed to think what ran through his mind.

"Desire is no basis for marriage." Her sharpness targeted her own susceptibility rather than James.

"It's a start," he said patiently.

"You're just worried that as your mistress, I'll be all reluctance and propriety."

Amusement lit his eyes. "Tonight doesn't bode well."

She dared to step toward him. "I need a little time to accept my place in your bed."

They stood face to face like adversaries. She was torn

between running away and clinging to him like the ivy clung to the ancient walls of Alloway Chase. When he took her hand, she jumped as if burned.

"I don't argue with your place in my bed." His thumb stroked her palm, stirring her restlessness.

"You can't forsake the plans of a lifetime."

James drew her to an oak settle, black with age, near the fire. He sat beside her, keeping her hand. "I've changed since I met you."

Despite being so overwrought, a wry smile curved her lips. "These days you're not always convinced that you're right."

"Ouch," he said amiably, laying his arm along the back of the long seat. They must look like two sweethearts, instead of a nobleman and the lowborn woman he'd lured into an illicit affair. "I'm right about making you my wife."

"No, you're not."

"And of course, you never think you're right," he said drily, toying with tendrils of hair escaping her knot. "Don't you want to know how I've changed?"

"I don't think so." She stared fixedly into the fire.

"Coward."

"Definitely."

He tugged gently at her hair until she faced him. "When my political allies told me to avoid London until the family name smelled a little sweeter, I thought I'd been banished to the lowest circle of hell. I've always enjoyed the hurly-burly of power. Now I had nothing to look forward to except cattle and crops and early nights."

She didn't interrupt. She was no fool. There was a "but" in this tale.

His voice lowered until the baritone stroked her skin like warm silk. "Instead I discovered a woman who lodged herself in my soul and wouldn't shift, no matter how often I reminded myself that I never bother the servants."

She couldn't help smiling. "You bothered this particular servant quite a lot."

He didn't smile back. "And while I'd been a diligent landlord, my estates always came second to my political hopes." He paused. "Then I found that living at Alloway Chase, managing my lands, arguing with that intriguing woman, proved a thousand times more fulfilling than anything I'd known before."

"You've only been home a few months," she said acidly. It was so difficult to shore up her defenses when he said everything she hungered to hear.

He frowned. "I'm not a changeable man."

"Which is why I know that your political ambitions aren't dead. Chin up, James. You won't be in the cold forever. You're too exceptional."

He stretched out his legs and contemplated the toes of his boots. "That's kind of you to say so."

She made a dismissive gesture. "It's the truth."

"These weeks at Alloway Chase have given me so much." He shifted from fiddling with her hair to massaging her nape. Pleasure rippled through her.

"I'm glad," she said jerkily. When he touched her, thinking became an effort.

"And one of the greatest gifts, apart from you, is coming to understand that I've devoted my life to fulfilling my father's dreams, not my own."

Dismayed, she tugged free of his drugging caresses. "That's not true."

He sighed. "I'm thirty-two years old and asking you to marry me is the first decision I've ever made without outside influence."

She wanted to tell him that if this was an example of his independent thinking, he needed to go back to taking advice. But she wasn't so mean, not when she read the harrowing sincerity in his silvery eyes.

"I know you believe what you say," she said slowly.

He frowned. "I want you to believe it too."

"Well, I don't. If I marry you, I'll make you a laughing-stock." She slid away from him. "And desire doesn't last."

"How do you know?"

Nell laughed without humor. "Ask those girls in your uncle's diary."

"You can't compare what I feel for you to my uncle's self-ish lust."

She knew she did James an injustice. And that she hurt him. Then she reminded herself that their marriage would hurt him much worse than a refusal now. Still, her voice softened. "I'm sorry, James. Whatever you say, I can't believe that there's anything more behind this proposal than desire, guilt over ruining me, and a passing fancy for the rural idyll."

Temper darkened his face and he surged to his feet, glaring at her. Once she'd have cringed. He was large and power-ful, and his rage charged the air.

Perhaps she'd changed too. Calmly she stood and met his brilliant gray eyes.

"What about love, Eleanor? Where does that count in your dismissive list?"

That one little word "love" made her stagger back. "Love?"

He loomed over her like a mighty cliff. "I love you."

The declaration sounded like a curse. If he'd made a heartfelt vow, perhaps she'd doubt him, but his militant tone convinced her. Still she tried to deny it. "No."

He grabbed her arms. "Yes, Eleanor. A resounding yes."

"But I'm your housemaid," she protested weakly.

"Shut up." He kissed her with boundless tenderness.

She wrenched away. "Stop."

He caught her shoulders and stared down at her with an urgency that made her want to scream. "Eleanor, I love you and I want to marry you. Will you be my wife?"

Her mind flooded with what would happen if she confessed her love and consented. Happiness now. An acknowledged place in his bed. Legitimate offspring. James at her side for the rest of her life.

Then other, bleaker thoughts. Men and women who once respected him sneering at the mention of his name. James seeing unworthy candidates rising to the office that should have been his. James bored and unhappy with his choice, but, because he was a good man, struggling to hide it day after day.

Nell couldn't do that to him. She couldn't do that to herself.

His declaration of love fed her starving heart, but she couldn't harm him. If she married him, she'd undoubtedly harm him. She squared her shoulders and forced out the most difficult words she'd ever spoken. "No, my lord, I won't."

The agony of denying him multiplied a hundredfold as she read his reaction. Surprise—he'd thought to persuade her this time. Acrid disappointment. Anguish.

His hands clenched on her shoulders. "I love you, Eleanor."

"Stop saying that," she said harshly, breaking free and trying not to cry. His declaration should be a crowning moment. Instead, it threatened to crush her.

"I believe I can make you love me."

She loathed the bewildered pain in his voice. "You can't make someone love you."

"I won't stop asking."

Dear God, could this get worse? "You must."

"No."

He pushed her too far. "Then I can't be your mistress."

He staggered as if she'd hit him. "What?"

"I don't want to leave you." She was surprised to sound so sure. "But your demands are impossible."

His ironic gesture sliced at her heart. "My apologies."

She watched him withdraw, attempt to protect himself, struggle to salvage some pride. She understood pride. She might be a poor soldier's daughter, but her spirit was unbending. It was yet another thing she and James had in common.

He couldn't hide the blow she'd struck to his soul, no matter how he tried. Witnessing his wretchedness came close to smashing her determination. The words "I love you, James," rose to her lips, but she savagely bit them back and tasted blood as she sank her teeth into her lower lip. If she admitted her love, he'd win. She knew enough of his tenacity to understand that.

And in that victory, he'd lose everything he'd lived for.

"I'm sorry I've hurt you." She knew how inadequate that sounded.

"I'll survive," he said grimly.

She bit her lip again, but that pain couldn't compare to the pain in her heart. "I hope you'll forgive me."

From under lowered dark brows, James regarded her like an enemy. "You've escaped pretty scot-free so far for your sins. After all, you lied from the beginning, you thought absolutely the worst of me despite all the evidence, and you offered me up to a man you thought plotted my destruction."

She raised her chin, wishing she was angry. Anger would be easier than this sorrow. "You're not upset about any of that."

"I'll make you marry me." He caught her and swooped to press his lips to hers in a passionate kiss that continued the argument without words. To her distress, her body, already primed, melted into liquid arousal.

"Stop," she choked out. "For pity's sake, stop."

For a long moment, she wondered if he heard. And if he heard, whether he'd heed her.

James released a despairing groan and slumped against her so heavily that she swayed. "I can't do this."

The black misery in his voice knotted her stomach. With a muffled sob, she curled her arms around him and let this strong, marvelous man rest in her embrace.

His ragged breathing slowly calmed and the desperate clutch of his hands on her hips gradually eased. Finally he shifted away and regarded her with lifeless gray eyes. "I'm sorry, Eleanor."

"No, I'm sorry," she whispered, glancing toward the blazing hearth because she couldn't bear his scrutiny. She loathed herself for what she did to him. If she stayed here, she'd end up in his bed. Feeling as she did now, weak, needy, eager to soothe his pain, she'd surrender. And that small surrender would lead inexorably to the larger surrender of consenting to marry him.

With one shaking hand, she made a curtailed gesture. She retreated toward the door. "I must go."

"Eleanor…"

She turned away. If she cried, he'd use it against her. "Please, leave me be for tonight." She gulped for air, as if she hadn't taken a breath in hours. "Please."

Without waiting for his answer, she turned the handle

and stumbled into the empty corridor. She leaned against the wall, struggling to dam her tears.

James returned her love, and she could hardly endure it.

The clock downstairs struck one. The inn was quiet. Maidenhead's best hostelry didn't encourage carousing.

On wobbly legs, she straightened. She couldn't return to her room. If James pursued her, that's where he'd look. Right now, one more touch could prove her downfall.

The inn had a small garden that she'd discovered this afternoon while awaiting news of the ambush. Perhaps fresh air and solitude would offer a new perspective, and she'd stop wanting to crumple into a sobbing heap because she'd hurt a good man.

Greengrass huddled into the shadows in the Royal Swan's garden. It was a perishing cold night and he clutched his thick coat around him, although a man of his bulk was insulated against the chill.

Who would have thought that Lord Leath turned out as slippery as his late-lamented uncle? Now Greengrass had lost the diary that had provided such a steady income. He was richer by a miserly fifty quid and piles of useless paper. Someone would pay for this unfortunate situation. Every penny he was owed.

It would be safer to retreat to his cottage in Lampton Wyck, but after that scuffle in the alley, he was angry. He'd easily tracked Leath and those other hoity-toity sods to the Royal Swan. Where else would men with such sense of their own entitlement stay?

Since escaping through the tunnels, he'd watched the inn. It would be easier to track his prey from inside, but even he wasn't that cocky. Still he'd learned a lot about Leath and his cronies. Including the fact that they traveled with a woman.

He'd tipped a maidservant a penny to tell him about the rich gentlemen and their doxy. The whore had her own room and dressed like a nun. That didn't gull Greengrass. A woman alone with a pack of men was at best, mistress to one, at worst, a strumpet brought to amuse the lot. After working for Lord Neville, Greengrass knew the peccadillos of the so-called upper classes.

The chit was his obvious target. Leath might cheat a poor man, but he'd balk at abandoning a female to a villain's mercy.

Greengrass had paid the obliging maid another sixpence to smuggle him up the servants' staircase. He'd glimpsed the slut as she went to dinner with her keepers. A looker. Rich men had the brass to pay for beauty. And that air of innocence never came cheap.

Aye, he could see why a self-satisfied ass like Leath wanted to tumble this wench.

Greengrass's problem was getting his hands on her. If she slept alone, he could break into the inn and abduct her. But odds were that at least one lucky bloke shared her bed.

He'd asked the maid to keep an eye on the doxy. That hadn't cost him anything but a quick tup against the stable wall. The girl was a plain thing with a wall eye and no acquaintance with soap and water, but Greengrass wasn't fussy. As he emptied himself inside her, he'd found himself thinking about the pretty blond piece instead of the sturdy maid with her heavy thighs and grasping hands. The Fairbrother men might be a rum lot, but by God, they had excellent taste in trollops.

As if Satan himself eavesdropped on his thoughts, the door from the inn silently opened—no squeaky hinges at the Royal Swan—and a slender figure slipped into the walled garden. Unable to believe his luck, Greengrass remained hidden as the girl wandered into the moonlight. Pale hair. A dress he wouldn't keep for a dish clout. Graceful.

A slow, triumphant smile spread across his face and he gave a low hum of anticipation.

Chapter Thirty-Four

The cold made Nell shiver, but she couldn't go inside and face James again. Not until she felt strong enough to resist him. Wiping roughly at her tears, she stepped onto the moonlit grass.

Could she follow her ultimatum through? How could she stay if he persisted in this ludicrous quest to marry her? She recoiled from more than just the prospect of conflict. She knew herself well enough to recognize that somewhere, someday, he'd find the words to persuade her. And she couldn't do that to him.

A rustle in the shrubbery interrupted her frantic thoughts. She retreated a step, then exhaled with relief when a lithe black shape darted through the shadows. Tonight the Royal Swan's cat was on the prowl.

The cat stopped to study her with unblinking eyes. Nell leaned down and made encouraging sounds, rubbing her fingers together. The animal flicked its tail in disdain and disappeared into the bushes.

Nell straightened with a sigh. She was feeling so low that even a stray feline's rejection stung.

Another rustle. The cat must have company on its midnight revels. This garden would offer good hunting. Like everything at the Royal Swan, it was well kept, but filled with hidden bowers.

A cloud passed over the moon and the fairyland garden turned dark. Nell wrapped her arms around herself.

A twig cracked to her left. Her nerves pricked. That didn't sound like a cat. With a quicker step, she turned toward the inn.

A huge hand covered her face, while a brutal arm clamped across her stomach and slammed her backward into a massive body. "Not so fast, lass."

She struggled, but her screams emerged only as muffled squeaks. She kicked hard at the man's shins.

"Stop that, you little bitch." The low, menacing voice with its flat accent was unfamiliar. He jammed his arm against her so hard that she retched. Pain stopped her wriggling.

"That's better. Do what I say or I'll shoot. Do you understand?"

Her nostrils flared as she struggled for air.

"Understand?" he barked.

She nodded.

"Do you know who I am?" The very quietness of his voice iced her skin with terror.

She nodded again. The minute he'd grabbed her, she'd guessed that this must be Hector Greengrass.

"Clever puss, aren't you?" He paused. "And I know who you are. Lord Leath's fun."

Horror tightened her throat. If he knew her connection with James, her chances of escape were nil.

She stared at the inn, praying that someone was awake

and looking outside. In the moonlight, she and Greengrass must be visible. But the windows remained dark. A high brick wall surrounded the garden, hiding it from the street. Even if anyone was out and about in the town at this hour.

"He'll have to pay me twenty thousand to get you back in his bed. But first you'll warm mine."

Her instinctive jerk of revulsion made him laugh. "About time you got a real man between your legs."

She gagged against his hand. She could smell his lust, that and stale sweat and tobacco. Nor did she mistake the ominous weight pressing into her lower back. She made herself stand still. Her squirming clearly excited him.

Oh, James, help me. Please, please, help me.

Only as she made the silent plea did she realize that she prayed to the man she loved rather than the Almighty. Hoping that blasphemy hadn't doomed her, she sent a plea to heaven too.

The Lord helped those who helped themselves. She bit the hand covering her mouth until she tasted blood.

"Bloody hell," Greengrass spat without, damn him, loosening his grip. He crushed her midriff until she near suffocated and kneed her in the back. Despite her vow not to cry, hot tears of agony pricked her eyes.

"No more of that, flower." Greengrass hauled her around to face the gate. "If you're too much trouble, I'll wring that pretty neck faster than you can say King George. Do you understand?"

She nodded, too scared to muster further defiance. There must be something she could do, but with his heavy body wrapped around her, she felt powerless and thickheaded.

"Good."

Abruptly Greengrass released her. She lurched away, but before she could take advantage of the moment, something cold pressed into her temple. "No games now. I'd hate to spoil that pretty face."

Nell gulped, more frightened than she'd ever been in her life. "You..." She stopped to lick her lips, her mouth was so dry with dread. "You're wasting your time. Lord Leath doesn't care about a doxy."

Greengrass's low chuckle made the hair rise on the back of her neck. "He's a gallant fool. He won't leave a woman with me. He knows what I'll do to her."

Bile soured her mouth. She knew too. "Twenty thousand pounds is a fortune. Nobody will pay that."

"He will. And I have a feeling that you're more of a bargaining chip than you say. Start walking. Slowly now, and no tricks."

She should be relieved that he no longer held her. But the chill iron of the gun proved she was as helpless as ever.

Nell straightened and moved, only to stumble on a dip in the path. Nearly ripping her arm out of its socket, Greengrass wrenched her upright. "Careful."

She took another step before he dragged her to a staggering stop. "What was that?"

Nell's heart pounded so loudly in her ears that she'd heard nothing. The faint, unlikely hope that James had arrived crumbled to ash when the cat reappeared, a mouse struggling in her jaws. Nell knew just how that mouse felt.

"Move." Greengrass released her arm and shoved her between the shoulders. With grim resolution, she obeyed.

Trees shadowed the wooden gate, making that corner of the garden as dark as a coalmine. Nell shivered with dread as she entered the tunnel of vegetation, although common sense insisted that Greengrass wouldn't rape her so close to the inn.

"Open the gate," Greengrass snapped.

She pushed without result. "It's locked."

"There's a bolt. Find it and pull it back."

She dreaded leaving the garden. Out in the street, she had a superstitious fear that she'd be beyond rescue.

Greengrass jabbed the gun at her head. "Let's get out of here."

"I'd rather you stayed right where you are." The deep voice emerged from the impenetrable blackness further along the wall.

James?

Nell stiffened in shock. Then strangling fear rose anew. Now the man she loved was at risk too.

"Well, bugger me dead," Greengrass said. "Don't try anything smart, your lordship. I've got a gun pointed at your whore's head."

"And I've got a pistol leveled at your kidneys," James said.

"One flick of my finger and she's dead."

"James, I'm so sorry." Nell squinted to see him, but the gloom defeated her. Every time she shifted, the pistol barrel chafed her temple. The sensation wasn't pleasant.

"Has he hurt you?" James asked.

"No."

"Thank God." She heard his overwhelming relief. She hoped Greengrass didn't. It gave him too much power.

"Well, this is an interesting bind." Greengrass's tone was mocking.

"Grounds for negotiation at least," James said with equivalent mockery. "Return to the clearing. And don't try anything."

Nell held her breath. Would Greengrass resist the order as she knew he wanted to?

After a pause, Greengrass grabbed her arm and spun her around. "Walk, flower."

When they emerged from the shrubbery, the moon shone clear. Nell chanced a peek at the men behind her. Greengrass looked stolid and menacing. A quick turn of her head, although every instinct screamed to stand still with the gun so close, revealed James behind Greengrass.

"Let the girl go," James said.

Greengrass laughed softly and jerked Nell back against him. "Why should I do that when she's my only counter on the board, now you and those bastards gypped me?"

"We can wait here until dawn when I'll undoubtedly have reinforcements," James said calmly. "You can't imagine that you've got a chance in hell of getting away."

"The whore dies in any case. If I'm cornered, why keep her alive?"

"Release her and I'll let you free." Nell couldn't see James's face, but she knew what that offer cost him.

Greengrass chuckled. "The minute you've got her, I'm dead as a haddock."

"I won't risk her life in a scuffle."

"James, don't trust him," Nell begged. She heard seething hatred in Greengrass's voice and guessed that he'd sacrifice his safety to kill his enemy. "He wants you dead."

"I do indeed." His grip on her arm tightened until pins and needles pricked her fingers.

"Be brave, Eleanor," James said. "I won't let anything happen to you. Ever."

"Rash words, laddie," Greengrass scoffed.

"I promise that I'll see this lady safe, even if it means rattling the gates of heaven."

James declaration rang with certainty and valor. But God help her, she heard more. Anyone listening would know immediately that he loved her.

Her heart slammed against her ribs. Upstairs when he'd

declared his love, she'd believed him—up to a point. Now when they both faced such danger, she couldn't mistake that love invested every word he spoke to her.

She'd been such a blind fool. How could she hesitate to become his wife? How could she weigh worldly considerations against their chance to live as one, to have children, to grow old together?

Nell desperately wanted to believe James when he vowed to save her, but at this moment, she couldn't imagine that they'd both escape. Dear Lord above, she didn't want to die. Most of all she didn't want to die without telling James that she loved him.

She sucked in a deep breath and leveled her shoulders. A preternatural calm descended. She shut Greengrass's loathsome presence from her mind. She shut everything out, except the endless universe of love she heard in James's voice.

"I love you, James," she said, surprised at how firmly the words emerged. "No matter what happens, I will always love you."

"Eleanor?" He sounded shocked.

"Believe it, my love," she said.

"I love you too." Such simple words, but each heartfelt syllable reinforced her courage.

"How touching," Greengrass said sarcastically.

Nell was immune to his jeers. Her heart felt clean, and finally her brain started to function. There must be some way she could help James and give them both a chance to seize the bright future that until now had seemed out of reach.

She'd wanted a weapon. What a ninny she was. God had given her two good hands, hadn't he? And Greengrass currently held only one of her arms, leaving the other free to do some damage and hopefully create a diversion.

Without taking time to count consequences, she stretched up and back to dig her fingers into Greengrass's eye.

"Bloody hell!" He lurched and his hand clenched painfully on her arm. Gritting her teeth against surging revulsion, she clawed deeper.

Fleetingly, the pistol slipped away from her head. Knowing it might be the last thing she ever did, Nell collapsed as a dead weight against his legs, screaming for help.

"You little bitch!" Like the sound of doom, she heard the click of the safety lock just above her, far too close to her ear. Automatically she curled up as small as she could.

Through James's despairing "Eleanor!" the pistol blasted. The world turned black.

Chapter Thirty-Five

Sick with horror, Leath watched Nell slump to the ground. Without making a conscious decision, he jammed his pistol behind Greengrass's ear and pulled the trigger. The hulking brute grunted, staggered forward past Eleanor's body, and fell with a thud.

His enemy was dead. Apart from the cessation of immediate danger, Leath couldn't give a damn. He flung the pistol into the darkness and fell to his knees beside Eleanor.

"My darling..." he choked out, hauling her into his arms. Her proud, astounding declaration of love echoed in his heart.

Her head flopped back, tilting her pale, perfect face to the moon. When they'd first met, he'd thought of flawless white marble. Now that memory turned his blood to ice.

Desperate for any sign of life, his shaking hand brushed untidy tendrils of hair back from her bloody forehead. Her eyes remained closed, thick lashes shadowing her cheekbones.

"Don't die. Don't die," he whispered, clutching her to his chest as if his warmth could revive her. His hands were sticky with her blood. His gut knotted in denial. Why in blazes had she done that crazed thing? Why had she risked her life?

Except that he knew. She'd trusted him to use the moment. How ironic that so often he'd begged her to trust him, and right now, he wished to the depths of hell that she hadn't.

"Eleanor, darling, for God's sake, don't leave me." He plastered her to his body, rocking back and forth. "Don't ever leave me. How can I go on without you?"

The agony of losing her shuddered through him. How could fate give him this magnificent creature, then snatch her away? By God, he wouldn't let her die. He'd defy heaven and hell to keep her.

He bent his head to feel her breath on his skin. He didn't trust his hearing. His ears still rang from the gunshot. Or perhaps he was deaf to everything except his pounding need to know she was alive.

"What the devil's all this?"

"Greengrass shot her." He didn't look up at Sedgemoor's arrival. "I think she's dead."

Eleanor's frozen features cut Leath like a saber. In the moonlight, the blood matting her hair was black as pitch.

Sedgemoor glanced toward Greengrass's unmoving bulk, then bent to take her dangling wrist between his fingers. Leath's grip tightened as the bristling silence lengthened.

Sedgemoor sent him a quick, reassuring smile. "There's a pulse."

Leath regarded him in disbelief. The prospect of her death was so crushing that he hardly dared hope. She felt so ominously still. "You're sure?"

"I think so. Let's get her inside, out of this cold." He paused. "And if you don't loosen your grip, you'll smother her, no matter what damage the bullet did."

"What's happened?" Harmsworth ran across the grass

with Hillbrook striding behind, carrying a lamp. "I heard a scream and two gunshots."

"It seems Greengrass shot Miss Trim. Then Leath must have shot him. The bugger's over there."

"Is Miss Trim all right?" Hillbrook asked, briefly glancing toward Greengrass's body.

"We dearly hope so," Sedgemoor said grimly, reaching for Eleanor. "Check and make sure the bastard really is dead."

"She's mine," Leath snapped, hands tightening on her slender, gallant shoulders. He was vaguely aware of Hillbrook bending over Greengrass's body.

Despite the moon and the lamp and the gradually waking inn, impenetrable darkness crushed him. He'd wondered once what would happen if Eleanor took the light away with her. Now he knew, and the pain was beyond bearing. He lowered his head over her motionless body and whispered a prayer for her survival that emerged from the depths of his soul. And knew that it wasn't nearly enough.

Cradling Eleanor as though the merest bump might break her in two, he struggled to his feet and strode toward the inn's open door.

Carrying her, he marched past Sedgemoor, Hillbrook, and Harmsworth. The men stood silently as if holding a vigil, then followed him. He hardly noticed. All that mattered was the still form in his arms.

"My lords, I heard gunfire," the landlord said as Leath shouldered past him and a noisy crowd of servants and guests.

"Get a doctor," he bit out, heading for a small parlor off the hallway.

"And the magistrate," Hillbrook said behind him. He and Sedgemoor followed Leath.

"But what on earth has happened?" the man asked in bewilderment.

"My dear sir, let me tell you." Harmsworth stayed behind and had the sense to close the parlor door on the curious onlookers.

Leath found it in him to be thankful that Harmsworth handled everything. Hillbrook ranged before the entrance, in case Harmsworth's explanations failed to appease the crowd.

Very carefully, Leath laid Eleanor on the padded settle before the hearth. Sedgemoor lit the lamps until the room blazed. The light only fed Leath's anguish as he saw her clearly for the first time since the shooting. Her head was a mess of blood and red streaked her wan cheeks. She remained terrifyingly still. Damn it, he saw no sign that she breathed.

He stroked back her tangled hair. "Eleanor, darling, come back to me," he murmured, taking her hand. "Come back."

Vaguely he was aware of Sedgemoor stoking the fire to life. He couldn't feel the heat. If his beloved died, he'd never feel warm again.

He tried but failed to find a pulse. Had Sedgemoor lied? Was she dead after all? It was more than he could endure. Her absence crashed down on him, suffocating as an avalanche.

Cold, cold forever. No Eleanor now or in the future. That was damnation indeed.

In an excess of grief, he collapsed onto the seat and held her in his arms, resting her head on his shoulder so that he could see her face. The blood staining her pale hair was an abomination. He curled over her, praying more desperately than he'd ever prayed in his life.

"Don't die, my darling," he said, over and over, an idiot plea to a woman who had moved too far away to hear. "Don't die. I won't let you."

"Courage, Leath," Sedgemoor said, placing a hand on his

shoulder. The encouragement couldn't melt the ice encasing Leath. "She'll pull through."

After a knock, Hillbrook opened the door. Leath heard a murmur of voices, but didn't glance away from Eleanor's ethereal features. She already looked as though she belonged to the next world, not this one. He wanted to bellow his fury and sorrow to the sky.

"This is Dr. Manion, Leath," Harmsworth said gently. "As luck would have it, he's staying in the inn."

"Please let me see my patient." The doctor pushed forward and set his bag on the floor.

Leath's arms firmed around Eleanor. "Help her. I beg of you, help her."

"She was shot?" The man with a strong Dublin accent leaned down.

"Yes."

"Please shift out of the way, my lord, to permit an examination."

Leath didn't budge. His deepest impulse was never to let her go. Illogically, he remained convinced that his touch could keep her alive.

Sedgemoor's grip on his shoulder tightened. "Come on, old man. Let Dr. Manion do his work."

Hazily he glanced at the other men. Anything outside the reality of Eleanor lying unresponsive in his arms held no significance.

"Lord Leath?" The doctor's voice was calm.

"She can't die," Leath said stupidly. "You can't let her die."

The doctor maneuvered around Leath to lift Eleanor's wrist. For a yawning chasm of a moment, he paused. "Her pulse is strong."

Uncomprehendingly Leath stared at the doctor. Then,

gloriously, he felt faint movement in the body pressed to his chest. Against his heart, Eleanor made a muffled protest.

"Eleanor?" he choked out.

"My lord, I must insist you stand aside," the doctor said. Eleanor's lashes fluttered almost imperceptibly.

"Sweetheart? Say something, for God's sake." When her lips parted on a breath, he felt like an ax struck him. He'd been so convinced that Greengrass had killed her. "Darling?"

Her eyelids moved. He sucked in his first unfettered breath since he'd watched her fall in that nightmare moment outside. He couldn't doubt that she was alive. But still he needed to hear her speak.

Heavy eyelids hesitantly lifted over dazed amber eyes. "James?"

"Thank God," Sedgemoor murmured.

A frown crossed her face. "My head hurts."

"Oh, my love," Leath said in a cracked voice and kissed her with all the reverence and gratitude in his heart. Gently, softly. Her response was a ghost of her usual ardor, but it barreled through him like a tidal wave. He'd thought that she'd never kiss him again.

"You're...you're crying," she whispered jerkily. She raised an unsteady hand to his cheek. "Why are you crying?"

"I thought I'd lost you," he confessed.

Unbelievably, amusement quirked her lips. "Don't be silly. You'll never lose me. I love you."

With that declaration of feelings too new for him to accept as his due, she closed her eyes. "No, don't go. Eleanor!"

He fought as Sedgemoor and Hillbrook dragged him out of the way. "I can't leave her."

"Give the man room," Hillbrook said impatiently, gripping one arm.

"I need hot water," Dr. Manion said without turning.

"I'll arrange it," Sedgemoor said and disappeared out the door.

Panting, Leath kept his attention on Eleanor. Her skin was ashen, but in some imperceptible way, she now seemed unmistakably alive.

"Doctor?" he asked. Hillbrook must have realized that reason prevailed and released him.

"Give me time," the man grunted.

Sedgemoor returned with one maid bearing a bowl of steaming water and a second with a pile of towels. Finally the landlord appeared, carrying a tray with a brandy bottle and some glasses.

"Capital," Hillbrook said. "We all need a drink. Where's Richard?"

"Dealing with the magistrate. The fellow's not happy about a dead body at Maidenhead's best inn," Sedgemoor said. "But the famous charm is working its magic. The man's agreed to wait to hear exactly what happened, especially as Richard's giving him chapter and verse on Greengrass's crimes. By the time he's finished, the town will probably present Leath with a medal for ridding the world of a menace."

Leath paid little heed to the conversation. What did he care about magistrates when Eleanor's life hung in the balance? He itched to hold her, whatever logic said about the doctor needing space.

Dr. Manion stood at her side, cleaning her head wound. How in Hades could she live when there was so much blood?

"My lord?" The landlord offered Leath a brimming glass of brandy.

He stared back dully.

"Take it, Leath, you need it," Hillbrook said.

He grabbed the glass and swallowed the liquor in one hit. "Should she have lost consciousness again?"

The doctor didn't look up. "Patience, my lord."

Leath slammed his glass on a table and rushed forward. He needed to touch her, to reassure himself that she breathed. This close, he could see that the water in the dish was ominously red. "Don't hurt her."

"I'll do my best," the man said flatly.

"If you save her, I'll give you a thousand pounds." Leath loomed over the doctor's shoulder. He would cut off his right arm in return for one word from Eleanor. Hell, he'd cut off his head if it meant that she smiled again.

The doctor's lips tightened. "I can only do what my skills allow—and what God's mercy permits, sir. Pray stand further off. You block the light."

"Ten thousand pounds."

"You can offer the crown jewels or sixpence, my lord," the man said shortly. "I said I'd do my best and that's what I'll do."

"Don't pester Dr. Manion," Sedgemoor said, and threw Leath into a nearby chair. "Tell us what happened outside."

"I don't—" He sucked in a shuddering breath and looked at these two men who against all expectations, he now counted as friends. "You're trying to distract me."

"He's trying to stop you from strangling Dr. Manion," Hillbrook said with a grim smile. "Your fussing won't help Miss Trim."

Leath straightened. "She won't die," he said calmly.

Instead of deriding his lunatic statement, Hillbrook responded evenly, "Of course she won't. But in the meantime, satisfy our curiosity."

"Yes, old man," Sedgemoor said, handing him another brandy. "I want to know how all our plotting to leave you alone with your lady love resulted in this disaster. How the deuce did you both end up outside?"

"Eleanor took to her heels when I asked her to marry me."

He waited for disapproval, but Sedgemoor's hand settled on his shoulder again. Despite the dread in his heart, he appreciated the support. "If you asked me to marry you, I'd run off too."

He didn't smile. "Greengrass must have been lurking in the garden. By the time I found her, he'd decided to hold her to ransom at gunpoint."

"Did he, by God?" Hillbrook said.

"Eleanor fought back and he shot her."

"At least you killed the bugger," Sedgemoor said.

"Yes." Leath didn't give a rat's arse about Greengrass when his love lay so silently. The doctor seemed to know what he was doing, at least. He was gentle with Eleanor and his ministrations appeared confident and efficient.

"Drink up," Hillbrook said.

Leath stared hard at Eleanor. "She's been out so long. It can't be right."

As if she'd heard, Eleanor flinched and whimpered. To Leath, this moment when her eyes cracked open felt like watching his first sunrise.

"James?" she asked feebly.

"I'm here, darling." He shoved his glass aside and crossed the room.

"James?" Her hand rose in a shaky attempt to find him. "Where are you? What happened?"

Ignoring the doctor's frown, he laced his fingers through hers. "Greengrass shot you."

"The swine." This time when she looked, he knew that she saw him. "I hope . . . I hope you shot him back."

The response was so like his darling that a choked laugh escaped. "I did indeed."

"Good." She closed her eyes. For a moment, he thought

she'd drifted off again, but her hand tightened weakly around his.

"Don't talk."

She ignored his command. She definitely returned to life. "Did you hear me say I love you? I do, you know."

The tightness in his throat made speaking difficult. "Yes, you told me before you took that damned stupid risk in attacking Greengrass." A damned stupid risk that yet might finish her.

A faint smile hovered around Eleanor's colorless lips. "I knew you'd beat him."

His grip firmed, as he dared destiny to steal her away. "If you leave me, I'll never forgive you."

The smile strengthened. "Don't be a dunderhead, James. I told you, you won't lose me."

The doctor's face was austere. "I'm Dr. Manion, young lady, and I'm here to tell you that you've had a lucky escape. The bullet scraped your skull without any lasting damage that I can see. But head wounds can be unpredictable so I'm advising only cautious optimism."

Leath stared speechless at the doctor. When he'd carried Eleanor inside, he'd been so sure that she wouldn't make it.

"I'm not going to die, Doctor."

Her certainty made Leath want to kiss her. "You're damned right about that."

"My lord, I really would proceed better if you all left me in peace," Dr. Manion said sternly. "I'll send for you if there's any change."

"James..." She drew a breath. Even this short exchange tested her strength. "James, please do as the doctor says."

Hillbrook stood beside him. "Best to cooperate, old man. I've got the steadiest set of nerves in England and even I'd shiver in my shoes if you glared at me the way you're glaring at Dr. Manion."

Only with the greatest reluctance did Leath agree to go. He lifted Eleanor's bloodstained hand to his lips for a kiss of heartfelt gratitude. "I'll be right outside. I love you."

She regarded him with such trust that his heart turned over in his chest. "That's all I need to know."

Her voice faded. Her eyelids drooped and the hand in his went limp.

"Doctor?" Leath turned to Manion in panic.

"She's asleep."

Sedgemoor ushered him away. Leath was in such a daze of anxiety and hope that he barely noticed. The last he saw of Eleanor as the door closed was her lying heartbreakingly quiet under the doctor's ministrations.

Chapter Thirty-Six

Nell stirred and carefully opened her eyes. Her skull thumped as though devils played football inside it and the light streaming through the windows made her wince.

Immediately she remembered everything. When she gingerly turned her head, she wasn't surprised to see James slouched asleep in a chair beside her bed. He looked utterly exhausted. Dark hollows surrounded his eyes, deep lines ran between his nose and his mouth, and his usual morning stubble threatened to become a fully grown beard. His bruises faded to a mixture of blue and yellow and gave him an uncharacteristically disreputable air.

He looked like he'd been to the gates of hell and back. She'd promised him that she wouldn't die, but she could see that he hadn't believed her. A faint sound of distress escaped her.

He jerked and sat up, rubbing his eyes, then leaned forward to seize her hand where it lay above the covers. "Eleanor, darling, are you awake at last?"

"I think so," she said croakily. She felt like sandpaper lined her throat.

Relief flooded his face. He kissed her hand, then turned to pour a glass of water from a jug on the nightstand. With a gentleness that made her heart cramp, he slid his arm behind her. "Drink. Steadily now."

Her instinct was to gulp the lot, but she took his advice and swallowed a few sips. The coolness was heavenly and she closed her eyes in bliss. A little more and she raised her hand.

He took the glass away. "Enough?"

She nodded, then wished she hadn't. Movement sent those crashing, overactive imps in her head on another rampage.

"Does your head hurt?" He set the glass on the crowded nightstand.

"No." Gradually she became aware of the details of the room. She remained at the Royal Swan. Faint traffic noise from outside penetrated the closed window. A roaring fire blazed in the hearth. Sickroom paraphernalia littered every surface.

His expression was skeptical. "I'm sure it does."

"Maybe a little." She paused. "Having you here helps."

"There's laudanum if the pain's too bad."

"No." She'd slept enough. Having come so close to permanent darkness, she wouldn't waste time in oblivion that she could spend with James.

"Don't try to talk," he said softly, setting her back on the bed.

"I want...to talk." She reached out. When he caught her hand, strength flowed through her. She managed a smile. "How long—"

"Three days. At first, Dr. Manion was hopeful, then on the second day, you took a turn for the worse."

The flatness of his voice indicated how bad that "turn" had been. "I told you... I wouldn't leave you."

His laugh was gruff, but like his touch, it fortified her. "For a while there, I feared you lied."

"It wouldn't be the first time," she said drily, closing her eyes against the light.

"Stay alive and I'll find it in my heart to forgive you," he said equally drily.

To her dismay, a couple of tears squeezed from under her eyelids. "I hate to think how I misjudged you."

"Forgiven also."

"And if I hadn't run away when you proposed, I wouldn't have caused all this trouble."

"That's harder to forgive."

Her eyes flew open in shock to find him watching her with such tenderness that she felt ready to get up off this bed and waltz around the room. "You don't mean that," she said faintly.

"No, I don't." He sighed and his grip on her hand firmed. "Eleanor, despite everything, we've come through. Let's put our mistakes behind us and just be grateful."

"I am." She tried to sit, but didn't get far. So much for dancing. "I want—"

"To sit up?"

"Yes, please."

He frowned. "Dr. Manion said I wasn't to tire you."

"From what little I saw of him, Dr. Manion is an old nag."

"Who saved your life." With more heartbreaking gentleness, James propped her against the heaped pillows.

"Yes, well, I suppose I should give him credit for that." She settled back with a muffled groan and lifted her free hand to the constriction around her head. She discovered linen bandages and nothing else. "My hair?"

"Gone, my love."

This time she shed more than a few tears. "How dare that quack cut off my hair?"

Compassion softened Leath's face. "Eleanor, sweetheart, don't take on so."

It was ridiculous to regret the trifling matter of a haircut when she'd nearly died, but she couldn't muffle another sob. "This is a tragedy of epic proportions."

She waited for mockery, but he sat beside her and drew her against him. This was what she'd wanted from the moment she'd woken, his nearness, his heat, the steadfast love in his touch. She rested her sore, shorn head on his shoulder in that special place meant just for her.

"Is that better?" he murmured, stroking her back through her nightdress.

"Yes," she said shakily without shifting.

He kissed her hand again. "It will grow back."

"In about a hundred years," she muttered into his shirt. "You loved my hair." Her tears had tested her. She was absurdly feeble.

His laugh was a low rumble in her ear and she pressed closer to the sound. "Not as much as I love you."

Her distress faded. At last he'd said the words.

"Eleanor?" he whispered eventually. "Are you asleep?"

"No," she murmured, floating between dark and light.

"I said I love you. Don't you have something to say to me?"

She smiled into his neck. He smelled so wonderful there. The glorious essence of James. That scent alone was enough to bring her back from the grave. "Do I?"

His hold tightened a fraction. "Yes, you do."

"You know how I feel about you," she murmured, surprised she found energy to tease him.

"Tell me again."

"You'll become impossible."

"Not if you have any say in the matter."

"That's true." She nestled closer. She'd always loved his big, powerful body.

"Darling?" he asked softly. She realized she drifted off again. "Does that mean you'll stay with me?"

"Of course," she said without needing to consider her answer.

Another wry laugh, full of affection. "Should we talk about this later when you're feeling more yourself?"

The hand she'd hooked around his neck tugged at the silky strands brushing his collar. "You need a haircut."

"Clearly hair is much more important than our future."

His touch restored her better than any medicine. Every moment she lay in his arms, she felt stronger. "You need to look...respectable at our wedding."

Beneath her cheek, his muscles tensed into rock hardness. He caught his breath. "What did you say?"

With some difficulty—curse this weakness—she braced to sit up. He looked completely bewildered. "You need to be tidy for our wedding. God knows, I'll look a fright so the groom must appear the part. Although I think we should wait at least until your bruises fade. At the moment, the vicar will faint clear away with terror to see such a ruffian standing before him."

"You never look a fright." He frowned, his gaze searching. "Eager as I am to marry you, perhaps we should postpone this discussion. I'm not sure you're in your right mind."

"Are you saying I've gone mad?"

Amusement sparked in his eyes. "Some would say that marrying me is the act of a madwoman. Let's talk tomorrow."

"No." She started to shake her head, then stopped

abruptly when the movement made her vision swim. "Let's decide now."

"Eleanor..."

"Please?"

For an extended interval, he stared hard at her as if he saw into her soul. If he did, he couldn't doubt her commitment to becoming his wife. Or her love for him. "Then let's do this properly. Can you manage leaning against the pillows, my love?"

"Yes," she said, and found that it was true, although she hadn't been sure.

Careful not to bump the bed, he slid off the mattress to rise on one knee. Her hand still lay in his. His gray eyes told her that even in bandages, to him she was the most beautiful creature in the world. "My darling Eleanor, light of my life, the most wonderful woman I know, my reason for living..."

He swallowed and she realized that despite her declaration at the point of death, he still wasn't sure of her. His hand tightened and he cleared his throat. Nervousness didn't come naturally to James Fairbrother. Nell's heart squeezed with love. At this breathtakingly significant moment in their lives, he was a million miles from his self-confident self.

His voice softened to the velvet that always made her ache with longing. "My darling Eleanor, I love you with all my heart. Will you do me the inestimable honor of agreeing to become my wife?"

She still marveled that such a man should love her. Marveled, but accepted. Whatever the right or wrong of it, she couldn't meet that gray gaze and doubt that he pledged lifelong devotion.

She was shaking, and not this time because of her injuries. With all the adoration burgeoning inside her, she raised his hand to her lips and kissed his knuckles.

"I love you, James," she said in a choked voice. "The honor is all mine."

He frowned. "Is that yes?"

Nell realized with a stab of guilt how she'd wounded him with her wavering and rejections and mistrust. Silently she swore to spend the rest of her life proving that he was the center of her world. She summoned a smile, although tears hovered close once more.

"Of course it's a yes. The last few days have given me a salutary lesson in sorting out what's important from what's merely trivial society nonsense." In a gesture of boundless tenderness, she laid her palm against his bristly cheek. "Nearly dying showed me that I want to live. And when I say I want to live, I mean that I want to live with you. Always."

"My darling." Radiant joy lit his eyes. He leaned forward to place a reverent kiss upon her lips. When he raised his head, he stared at her as if she'd cooked up the stars in her kitchen.

With shaking hands, he tugged the Fairbrother signet from his hand and slid it onto her ring finger. It was too heavy and too big, and she never wanted to take it off again as long as she lived. She smiled through more tears as she stared down at the rich gold. "I love it."

"It's only a stopgap. I'll get you something as beautiful as you are."

"You've turned me into a cursed watering pot," she complained thickly.

"Marchionesses are allowed to cry whenever they want to," he said, the huskiness undermining his attempt at lightness.

It was miraculous how a happy ending soothed a headache. "I wish you'd told me that before. I'd have married you weeks ago."

This time, his humor was a shred more convincing. "Well, *my* marchioness can do whatever she wants."

"In that case, she wants to kiss the marquess," Nell said unsteadily.

Gently he gathered her in his arms, his lips quirking into the smile that set her heart aflame. "My darling, I do so love it when you and I are of one mind."

Epilogue

Fentonwyck, Christmas Eve

As Sedgemoor's haughty butler showed them to the drawing room, Nell's grip on James's fingers tightened to bruising. He cast her a faint smile. "You've been here before, my love," he murmured. "You can't be nervous."

"Can't I?" she muttered.

He had to admit their surroundings were daunting. The house was huge, and not even the Christmas greenery decorating the walls made it feel cozy. It was late, close to midnight.

"Buck up, darling," he said softly, and to her embarrassment, kissed her.

For one blazing moment, she lost herself in pleasure. Then she started with dismay and wrenched away as far as his hold permitted.

Which wasn't far.

"We're in public," she whispered, eyeing the butler who

waited at a closed door, ostentatiously not looking in their direction.

"I don't care," James replied, and this time he didn't keep his voice down. He drew her back for another kiss, more thorough than the first.

She swam up from a sensual daze to a smattering of applause. At first, she thought it was her heart cavorting after James's kiss or some new aftereffect of her head injury. Then she opened her eyes to realize that the butler had flung open the door and she and James stood in full view of a room jammed with people.

"Oh, you...absolute stinker," she hissed, fighting to break free, but he caught her hand.

"Shall I announce your lordship?" the butler asked, staring above James's head while Nell's cheeks turned scarlet.

"I think we've made our entrance, thank you," James said drily and stepped into the crowded room. "Good evening, everyone."

Nell braced her shoulders, raised her chin and plastered a smile onto her face. Not before she shot James a killer look beneath her lashes. She'd get even for his antics later.

"Leath, Miss Trim." With a delighted smile, Sir Richard Harmsworth strode toward them. "We feared you wouldn't arrive tonight."

"We broke an axle outside Chesterfield." James shook the man's hand.

Sir Richard turned to the other people. "Leath, you know Genevieve, Sidonie, and Jonas. Have you met Lady Marianne Seaton, the Marquess of Baildon's daughter, and Lord Wilmott, the duchess's brother?"

Nell curtsied to a lovely woman with the face of a madonna who stood beside a tall, dark-haired man resembling Penelope Rothermere. Sir Richard continued his introductions. "That leaves Mr. and Mrs. Simon Metcalf. Lydia is Cam's sister, Miss Trim. Leath knows her from London, but I'm not sure if he's met Simon before."

"Metcalf." James nodded to the lean blond man with his arm around a striking redhead.

Another couple approached. The handsome young man bore an even closer likeness to the duchess and the pretty girl was familiar, thanks to a portrait in the marchioness's apartments at Alloway Chase.

"James, I thought you'd never get here." The girl pouted as she flung her arms around her brother. After an enthusiastic greeting, she withdrew and surveyed Nell with a hint of reserve. "May I call you Eleanor?"

"Of course, Lady Sophie," Nell said, curtsying.

After hearing so much about James's sister, she felt as if she already knew this girl. She wondered what Lady Sophie had heard about her. The marchioness remained frosty since her brilliant son had relinquished his political career in favor of country life. It was no secret that she blamed Nell.

"And this reprobate is Harry Thorne," James said.

"It's a pleasure, Miss Trim." With a genuine smile, Mr. Thorne bowed over her hand.

"There are such a lot of people here," Eleanor said shakily.

Simon Metcalf smiled too. "You'll work us out eventually. At least Lydia's the only carrot top. That makes her easy to spot."

"You'll pay for that, darling," his wife said, then looked at Eleanor. "Actually there's even more. You must meet our daughter Rose who is safely in the nursery with Sidonie and Jonas's daughter Consuela."

James's eyes searched the room. "Where are the Sedgemoors?"

Nell, overwhelmed with unfamiliar faces, hadn't realized that the duke and duchess were absent. Now it struck her as ominous that Sir Richard played host in another man's house.

"Is everything all right?" she asked quickly.

"Pen was delivered of a boy this evening. Cam's upstairs with her." Lady Hillbrook kissed Nell on the cheek with a warmth she appreciated. Now that the introductions were over, she relaxed a little. "By the way, I love your hair. Once the London ladies catch sight of it, the cropped style will be all the rage."

"Thank you." Self-consciously, she touched her cap of curls. "I hope everything went well for Her Grace and the baby."

The duchess had been so kind when Nell had arrived at Fentonwyck in her misguided attempt to destroy James. Although it was only weeks, those days seemed so long ago.

"Like a dream, I gather, although I suspect Pen mightn't completely agree," Genevieve said, behind Lady Hillbrook. "There was some concern because the baby is a little earlier than anticipated."

Her hug reminded Nell that not everyone here was a stranger. And James was by her side. She refused to turn tail and run at this, her first social engagement in her new role.

"Sedgemoor's spent most of the day skulking in his library, jumpy as a flea." Lord Hillbrook's saturnine face broke into a welcoming smile. "Miss Trim, you're here on a portentous night."

James smiled down at Nell. He looked completely besotted, she was glad to see. His grip on her hand firmed as he faced the crowded room. "Actually we've had quite a portentous time ourselves."

"Miss Trim, do tell," Sir Richard said. "Your life seems to be continual adventure."

"I think..." Nell swallowed to calm her nerves. "I think I've embarked upon my greatest adventure yet."

The guests' curiosity surged as she glanced toward James. She wanted him to make the announcement to these people she sincerely hoped would become her friends.

The pride in his eyes was unmistakable. "Miss Trim is Miss Trim no longer." He paused, and she thought what a compelling parliamentary speaker he must be, with his flair for the dramatic. "Yesterday Eleanor made me the happiest of men when she became my wife."

Leath smiled to observe Eleanor engulfed in heartfelt congratulations. Since accepting his proposal, she'd been reticent about her fears. But he knew her well enough to guess that insecurities still plagued her.

To ease her into life as his marchioness, he'd arranged a quiet wedding at the chapel at Alloway Chase. He hadn't even invited Sophie, who was regarding him with shock from a few feet away. He shrugged a silent apology in her direction. Given how she'd thrown her hat over a windmill when she fell in love, she was in no position to point the finger.

To his relief, her pretty face relaxed into a smile. He hadn't been sure of her reaction. His mother must have confided her bitter disappointment over his recent decisions. The dowager marchioness had relented enough to attend his wedding. James had high hopes that by the time their first child arrived, she'd forget Eleanor's humble beginnings and recall only how she'd always liked her.

"Have you started the party without me?" Sedgemoor asked from behind Leath.

The buzz of happy chatter faded to silence. Harmsworth approached his friend with his hand extended. "I'm so happy for you, old man."

"Thank you," Sedgemoor said, ignoring the outstretched hand and embracing his friend.

"But the spotlight isn't just on the new addition to your family, you know. Leath and Miss Trim were married yesterday."

"Good God, that man steals my thunder at every opportunity," Sedgemoor said.

Once that might have been a sneer. Now it made Leath clap him on the back. "Congratulations, Your Grace. I thought I'd save some money and have the wedding breakfast here."

"Spoken like a true politician," Sedgemoor said with a laugh.

The room erupted into cacophony. Leath's hand was wrung until it felt likely to drop off. People who hugged Sedgemoor moved on as a matter of course to congratulate him and kiss Eleanor. The ladies admired the delicate gold wedding ring and pestered Sedgemoor for details of the baby. The gentlemen called Leath a lucky dog and he had no reason to doubt their sincerity. After all, he was a lucky dog.

The butler appeared at the door and cast a cool eye over the crowd. He signaled behind him and footmen began to serve champagne.

When everyone had a glass, Hillbrook's deep voice cut through the noise. "I'd like to propose a toast, firstly to the new generation of Rothermeres. May the son be worthy of his parents, two of the finest people it is my privilege to know." He paused. "I'd also like to congratulate Lord Leath and his beautiful bride. May their days overflow with happiness and love."

"Hear, hear," Harmsworth said.

As everyone drank to the future, Leath's throat closed on a lump of emotion. He reached for his wife's hand. Eleanor glanced at him with perfect understanding and moved nearer to whisper, "I love you."

Sedgemoor smiled with an open joy that devastated his public reputation as a coldhearted automaton. "Thank you, my friends. I couldn't ask for a better way to celebrate my son's birth than to have you all here for our first Christmas as a married couple."

That boulder in his throat meant that Leath's voice emerged without its usual resonance. "On behalf of my dearest Eleanor and myself, I'd like to thank you. Words fail me when I try and say how delighted I am that she consented to become my wife."

He was a man famous for his eloquence, but that was as much as he could manage. When he looked around the room and met the warm gazes focused on him, he realized that these people knew the way love could transform a life, the way love had transformed him. The smiles said it all.

"Thank you, my darling," Eleanor said beside him. Then, to his astonishment, she rose on her toes and kissed him. He hadn't expected her to feel comfortable in this glittering milieu, but the welcome had smoothed her passage from maid to marchioness. He caught a quick taste of champagne from her lips, along with the delicious flavor of Eleanor.

Sedgemoor tapped Leath's shoulder as he released his wife. "Before you get settled here, old man, bring your bride to see Pen."

Eleanor was close enough to hear. "We don't want to intrude."

Sedgemoor smiled at her. "She'd love you to visit. She's not up to a room full of people yet, but if she finds out you've just been married and she didn't have a chance to wish you well in person, she'll curse my name." Pride lit his face. "And I'd love to show off my son."

Upstairs in the duchess's luxurious apartments, everything was quiet order. The room was elegant, made exceptional by the magnificent paintings on the walls. Leath had barely a moment to note a Titian and a Rembrandt and a Claude—and dear Lord, was that a Goya of the duchess *en dishabille*?

Dressed in a pale blue peignoir, Her Grace sat in an elaborate bed. Her head bent over the velvet-wrapped bundle in her arms. When Leath and Eleanor followed Sedgemoor into the room, she glanced up. Her eyes rested on her husband with such love that Leath felt he and Eleanor interrupted a private moment.

Before he could make his excuses, her smile encompassed them. Her shining black hair was caught in a loose knot and she looked tired but triumphant. "Lord Leath, what a pleasure. And Miss Trim, how lovely to see you, and with a stylish new coiffure. I'm piqued to miss out on the party."

Sedgemoor settled on the edge of the bed and unselfconsciously wrapped his arm around his wife's shoulders. "You've had quite enough partying today, my love."

"Yes, Christmas came early this year." She stared down at her sleeping, dark-haired son.

"We're so happy for you, Your Grace," Eleanor said. "Congratulations to both of you."

The duchess smiled. "Thank you. And given you're the first of our friends to see the Rothermere heir, you ought to call me Penelope, Miss Trim."

"Miss Trim no longer," the duke said with a soft laugh. "I know the doctor said no visitors until tomorrow, but when Leath told me that he and this lady married yesterday, I knew you'd want to wish them happy."

The duchess's smile widened. "How wonderful. We all hoped, of course."

Leath held Eleanor's hand and he felt her start. "You did?" she asked.

"Of course. We could see that you were head over heels in love and that once you'd sorted out your difficulties, you'd be perfect for each other."

"Th-thank you," Eleanor said, and Leath saw the moment when she accepted that these exceptional people had never considered her an unsuitable marchioness.

She stood with new confidence. He didn't make the mistake of thinking that everyone in society would welcome his humbly born wife, but then, these days, he was perfectly happy to enjoy the approval of those who mattered and ignore the rest. Since renouncing his political ambitions, he felt ten years younger. Ten years younger and virile as a randy adolescent.

"Come and meet my son," Sedgemoor said softly.

As Leath and Eleanor approached, the duchess held out the baby, who briefly opened his eyes on a soft complaint before closing them again. "Let me introduce Richard Peter Thorne Rothermere, Marquess of Pembridge."

"He's beautiful," Eleanor said softly. "Just beautiful."

"Yes, he is." Leath looked into the baby's face and couldn't help anticipating the day when he and Eleanor had their first child. Eleanor would wear that same proud, loving, awestruck expression as the duchess. Pray God, she also regarded her husband with the same adoration as Her Grace regarded Sedgemoor.

How he looked forward to life with this beloved woman. Every moment beckoned ahead like steps on a golden path. He couldn't wait. As if to mark the moment's significance, Christmas bells started to ring out across the fields from the village church.

Eleanor touched the sleeping baby's cheek with a tenderness he felt on his own skin, then she smiled at Leath, amber eyes aglow. "He's a gift of love," she whispered.

Leath's heart was too crammed with poignant gratitude for him to summon a smile in return. Instead he touched his wife's soft cheek with the same tenderness as she'd touched the baby. Forgetting his audience, he stared deep into her beautiful eyes and murmured, "You're my gift of love, Eleanor."

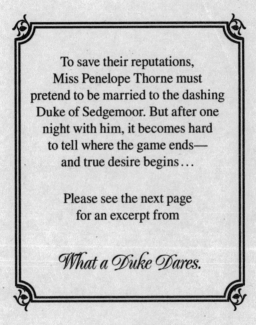

To save their reputations,
Miss Penelope Thorne must
pretend to be married to the dashing
Duke of Sedgemoor. But after one
night with him, it becomes hard
to tell where the game ends—
and true desire begins...

Please see the next page
for an excerpt from

What a Duke Dares.

Prologue

Houghton Park, Lincolnshire, May 1819

Every young lady dreamed of a proposal from the heir to a dukedom. Especially when the heir was rich, feted, in possession of his wits, and still young enough to have all his teeth.

Every young lady except, apparently, Penelope Thorne.

From the center of her father's library, Camden Rothermere, Marquess of Pembridge, eyed the girl he'd known from the cradle and wondered where the hell he'd slipped up. He straightened and summoned a smile, struggling to bridge the awkward silence extending between them.

Damn it. He never felt awkward with Pen Thorne. Until now. Until he'd spoken the fatal words.

Until, instead of radiating delight at the prospect of marrying him, Pen's black eyes sparked with the rebellious light that always boded trouble.

"Why?" It wasn't the first time this afternoon that she'd asked him the question.

Stupidly he couldn't summon an adequate answer. He'd blundered into this half-cocked. It was his own fault. Knowing Pen as he did, he should have prepared a comprehensive list of reasons for their marriage before broaching the subject.

Right now, he wished he'd never broached the subject at all. But it was too late to retreat, or too late if he hoped to salvage a shred of self-respect from this dashed uncomfortable encounter.

"Devil take you, Pen, I like you," he said impatiently. Despite her inexplicable and irritating behavior today, it was true. There wasn't a girl alive that he liked so much as the chit currently regarding him as if he'd crawled out of a hole in the ground.

He knew her better than any other girl too, even his sister, Lydia. Through their childhood, he'd rescued Pen from a thousand scrapes. She'd been a hellion, riding the wildest horses in her father's stables, climbing the tallest trees in the park, throwing herself into brawls to defend a friend or mistreated animal. Cam had long admired her spirit, loyalty, and courage.

Those were qualities he wanted in his duchess. And if she needed some guidance in deportment, he was perfectly prepared to teach her proper behavior. She was a Thorne and Thornes weren't renowned for their prudence, but while Pen might be impulsive, she was intelligent. Once she'd become the Duchess of Sedgemoor, he was sure she'd settle down.

Or he had been, until her unenthusiastic response to his proposal.

"I like you too," she said steadily, regarding him with unwavering attention.

Cam wondered why her admission didn't reassure. Inhaling

deeply, he strove for forbearance. "Well, there you have it, then."

That bitter note in her laugh was unfamiliar. He could hardly believe it, but the possibility of failure hovered. Pen was clever, determined, headstrong—he'd get that out of her soon enough—and stubbornly inclined to take a positive view of events. Or at least so he'd believed until today.

He'd also believed that she'd leap at the chance to marry him.

Clearly he'd been wrong.

He wasn't used to being wrong. Confound her, he didn't like it.

Her voice remained curiously flat. "I'm sorry, Cam. 'There you have it, then' won't pass muster. You'll need to do better than that."

From where she stood before the high mullioned window, she studied him much like a schoolmistress surveyed an unpromising student. He only just resisted the urge to run a finger under his unaccountably tight neckcloth.

Good God, this was *Pen*. She wasn't a female who put a man through hoops before she fell into harness. She'd never demand more than he could give. She'd never subject a fellow to emotional storms. She'd never lie and cheat and betray.

She was the absolute opposite of his late mother, in fact.

Cam was unaccustomed to feeling like a blockhead, especially with the fairer sex. By nature he wasn't a vain man, but he'd anticipated a better reaction to his proposal. Pen's father Lord Wilmott had been in alt to hear that his daughter would become a duchess.

Most definitely, Pen was not in alt.

And she bloody well should be. After all, she was a mere baron's daughter—and a ramshackle baron at that—while Cam was heir to the nation's richest dukedom.

The Thornes were an old family, but had always had a justified reputation for trouble. In times of political unrest, they backed the wrong side. If they managed to lay their hands on any money, they lost it, usually in some disreputable pursuit. "Wine, women, and song" should be the family motto instead of the much more staid and highly inappropriate "steadfast and faithful."

The previous generation had spawned a handful of eccentrics, including an uncle who had married his housekeeper. Bigamously as it had turned out. Lord Wilmott had squandered his wife's dowry on a succession of greedy strumpets. Pen's aunt ran with a dissolute crowd on the Continent. Peter, Cam's friend and the current heir, was devoted to the gaming tables and disastrous investments. If Cam's mother hadn't been great friends with Lady Wilmott, the families would have had little contact.

What made Pen's tepid response to Cam's suit even harder to understand was that she'd always worshipped the ground he walked on. Was he a fool to presume on childhood adoration?

A horrible suspicion struck him. Was he presuming on far too much? Despite his parents' scandalous behavior and the gossip about his legitimacy, the ton lionized Cam as the future Duke of Sedgemoor. Had endless flattery turned him into a self-satisfied ass?

If Pen thought him insufferably arrogant, no wonder his proposal hadn't bowled her over. He sighed with self-disgust and impatiently ran his hand through his hair. "I'm making a dashed mess of this, aren't I?"

Pen's slender body lost its rigidity as a wry smile curved her lips. Lips, he reluctantly noticed, that were pink and full and lusciously kissable.

As shock shuddered through him, he wondered why he'd

never noticed before. Pen had been such a constant in his life that he hadn't taken the time to mark how she'd changed.

Still unwilling to admit that Pen wasn't the girl he remembered, he looked more closely. To his dismay, the coltish adolescent hovered on the brink of becoming a true beauty. Even more dismaying, he felt the unwelcome, unmistakable prickle of desire.

"Yes, you are. But it's not totally your fault." With a grace he hadn't seen in her before, she gestured toward the leather chairs ranged around the unlit hearth. "Sit down, for heaven's sake, and stop looming over me."

Actually he wasn't looming, although with his height, he loomed over most people. Pen had always been a long Meg, closer to a boy than a girl in his mind. But in this discomfiting instant, when for the first time he saw more than his friend Peter's occasionally annoying younger sister, there was nothing boyish about Miss Penelope Thorne.

Since he'd last seen her—and for the life of him, he couldn't recall when that had been, such an ardent suitor he was—she'd grown up. The thin body had gained subtle but fascinating curves. The vivid, pointed face that had always seemed too small for her decisive features had refined into striking attraction. When had she tamed her tangled mane of hair into those gleaming ebony coils?

Apprehension tasted sour on his tongue. God help him, this new Penelope was a bloody disaster. He narrowed his eyes on the siren who had mysteriously supplanted a hoyden as daring as any of his male friends. And saw that she was blossoming into a woman who made men stupid.

Categorically he didn't want to marry a woman who made men stupid, the way his mother had made his father stupid. How insulting to his chosen bride that part of her appeal had been her lack of overt attractions.

His father's example proved what catastrophes resulted from choosing a tempestuous beauty as a wife. Cam had grown up hearing salacious gossip about his mother's affair with her husband's younger brother. Nobody, including Cam, knew who had fathered him. He was a Rothermere, but not necessarily the late duke's son.

Long ago Cam had decided to marry someone he could be friends with, not who became a challenge to every deuced roué in London. Cam wanted a wife who would help him establish the Rothermere name as one to be respected, not a cause for snickering and dirty jokes as it had been all his life.

Gossip about his parentage had dogged Cam from boyhood. School had been a nightmare, and while he made a fair job of pretending he no longer cared, he knew whispers of his bastardy still spiced the tattle whenever his name was mentioned. He'd be damned before he subjected his own children to similar torments.

He reminded himself that this was brave, honest Penelope Thorne, she who risked her neck to save a kitten from village boys twice her size. But looking at her now, he didn't see the girl who had launched a hundred escapades. Instead, he saw a woman who other men would pursue. A woman who perhaps would succumb to temptation, as his mother had done. Pen's burgeoning loveliness made Cam burn to bed her, but it beggared any chance of an unexceptional domestic life.

Feeling slightly ill, Cam accepted Pen's offer of a seat and watched her take the chair opposite. Dear heaven, when had that smooth glide replaced her eager gallop? This was Pen, yet it wasn't.

Even as he questioned his old playmate's suitability as a bride, he couldn't take his eyes off her. When had she become this intriguing creature? Where the hell had he been when the transformation took place? At nineteen, she was a little late to be approaching her first season, but he could already see that she'd set society on its ears. She'd prowl into London's ballrooms on those long legs, like a tigress set loose amid a host of pretty little butterflies.

"I appreciate that you're doing your duty by your mother and mine. A match between us was always their greatest wish." The earnestness in Pen's regard was familiar, but still he felt as if he'd been tossed high into the air and come to land in a different country. "But let's be realistic. I'm not the woman for you."

While today's misgivings hinted that Pen might be right, his pride flinched under her rejection. "We know each other so well—"

"Which is why I'm convinced that any match between us would be a debacle."

"Why?"

Her lips twisted, and he realized that her earlier bitterness hadn't entirely vanished. "Isn't that my question?" She sighed. "Cam, you need a duchess with dignity and decorum. You must have forgotten all the times you dragged me from disaster."

"You're still young. You can be trained," he said, before he recognized that such a comment would hardly forward his suit. Usually he said exactly the right thing, but this encounter rattled his sangfroid.

Her momentary softening congealed to frost. "I'm not a hound to come at your whistle."

He sighed again. "You know that's not what I want in a bride."

"Do I?" she asked, arching her eyebrows. "You've devoted your life to rising above your parents' disgrace. You've never made a secret of the fact that your wife must be beyond reproach."

He bared his teeth at her. Mention of his mother's adultery always raised his hackles. "Pen, this isn't something I wish to discuss."

She made a sweeping gesture. "Whether you want to talk about it or not, the scandals have guided your every action."

He winced under the compassion in her gaze. "That makes me sound like a complete widgeon."

"No, it doesn't."

"You can help me. You'll make a capital duchess."

"You're mistaken." He'd never imagined that worldly smile on Pen's face. His reluctant desire deepened. "I'm too independent to be anyone's duchess, especially yours."

"You can change," he said desperately, wishing he'd taken Lord Wilmott up on his offer of a brandy earlier. Cam wasn't used to being so wrong-footed with a woman, with anyone. Where had his famous social assurance buggered off to?

"Perhaps I can. If I wanted to change. I don't." She sighed with a tolerance that made his skin itch with resentment. "You'd be trading your family's scandals for mine, and the rumors would continue to dog you all our lives. I follow my heart before my head. I speak my mind. Before the ink was dry on the settlements, I'd do something to upset the old tabbies. You'd find yourself knee-deep in gossip and you'd hate that. You'd start to hate *me*."

"You're the only woman I've ever pictured as my wife. I decided as a boy that I'd marry you." He straightened in his chair and bit out each word, before remembering that he came to woo, not browbeat her. "Our families expect me to make you my duchess."

The regret in her smile did nothing to bolster his optimism. "I'm sorry, Cam. For once in your life, you'll have to disappoint expectations." Her gaze sharpened in a way that he didn't completely understand. "I know you don't love me."

He flinched back as though she'd struck him. Damn, damn, damn. *Love.* He'd thought Pen too smart to fall prey to mawkish sentimentality. "I esteem you. I admire you. I enjoy your company. You know the Fentonwyck estate. You know *me.*"

"All very gratifying, I'm sure." Her smile turned sour. "But I won't marry without love."

He surged to his feet. "We both have parents who married for love. As a result of *love*, my father descended into cruelty and obsession and my mother became a byword for promiscuity. Pardon me saying so, but your parents aren't much better. Doesn't that convince you that friendship and respect form a stronger basis for marriage than passing physical passion?"

"I doubt that either my parents or yours understood what love truly is." Emotion thickened her voice and strengthened his premonition of failure. "Love means wanting the best for the beloved, whatever the cost. Love means sacrificing everything to achieve the beloved's happiness."

"You're an idealist," he said disdainfully.

"Yes, Cam, I am." She rose with more circumspection— an adjective he'd never before associated with Pen Thorne— and regarded him with an unreadable expression. For a woman who confessed lack of control, she was remarkably controlled. "I believe love makes life worth living and nobody should marry without it. You're too young to settle for second best."

He placed a short rein on his temper. He was rarely angry, but right now, he wanted to fling one of the smug Ming dogs on the mantelpiece into the fire. "I'm twenty-seven."

She released an impatient huff. "Well, I'm only nineteen. I'm definitely too young to settle for second best."

"I hardly think becoming the Duchess of Sedgemoor

counts as second best," he said frigidly, wondering just where his childhood friend had gone.

Pen sighed as if she understood his turmoil. "It is when the duke offers only a lukewarm attachment."

Resentment tightened his gut. He didn't want to be understood. He hoped like hell she hadn't noticed his bristling sexual awareness. Having Pen recognize his unwilling desire just as she sent him away with a flea in his ear seemed the final humiliation.

"Would you rather I lied?" he growled.

She winced as though he'd hit her. "Even if you lied, I wouldn't believe you, Cam. I've known you too long. And you set your mind against love long ago."

He struggled for a reasonable tone. Blustering would only make her dig her heels in. The encounter verged dangerously close to a quarrel. "Pen, think of the advantages."

Her jaw set in an obstinate line. "Right now, aside from the obvious fact of your riches, I can't see any."

His appeal to her worldly interests disappointed her. Shame knotted his gut. With regret, he recalled the days when in her eyes, he could do no wrong. He drew himself up to his full height and glared.

"There's no point going all ducal, Cam," she said curtly, not, blast her, remotely cowed. "That look lost its power over me before you went to Eton."

She shifted closer, stretching one hand toward the mantel. When he noticed how her fingers trembled, he faced the unpleasant truth that despite outward calm, this encounter upset her.

Of course it did. She felt things deeply. More than once, he'd caught Pen crying alone after her brothers' teasing had struck a painful spot. She was proud, Penelope Thorne. Another desirable quality in a cracking duchess.

But clearly not his duchess. Pen didn't have a monopoly on pride. Cam regarded her down his long nose and spoke as coldly as he'd speak to an overweening acquaintance. "I gather that you're refusing me."

The knuckles on the hand clutching the mantel turned white, although her voice remained steady. "Yes, I am." She paused. "I appreciate your condescension."

That was so obviously untrue that under other circumstances, he'd have laughed. But pique shredded his sense of humor. Through his outrage, he knew that he behaved badly. However unfairly, he blamed Pen for that unprecedented state of affairs too.

He bowed shortly and spoke in a clipped voice. "In that case, Miss Thorne, I'll waste no more of your valuable time. I wish you well."

Something that might have been pain flared in her dark eyes, but he was too angry and, much as he hated to admit it, wounded to pay heed. She stepped toward him. "Cam—"

"Good day, madam."

He turned on his heel and stalked off.

Pen watched Cam march out of her father's library, his back rigid with displeasure, and told herself that she'd done the right thing. The only thing she could in honor have done.

Right now she didn't feel that way. She felt like she'd swallowed toads. She clung to the mantel to stay upright on legs likely to crumple beneath her.

Her anguish didn't change merciless reality. Cam didn't love her. Cam would never love her. Nothing in today's awkward, painful encounter had convinced her otherwise.

As a foolish child, she'd dreamed of him tumbling head over heels in love with her. What girl brought up in close proximity to the magnificent Rothermere heir wouldn't imagine a fairy-tale future? Especially when her mother encouraged her.

But that was before Pen had grown up and recognized the stark truth. A truth ruthlessly confirmed when she was sixteen. One summer at Fentonwyck, she'd overheard Cam talking to his best friend Richard Harmsworth about discouraging a local belle's advances. When Richard had blamed the girl's antics on love, Cam had responded with cutting contempt and said that was even more reason to steer clear of the unfortunate lady.

Romantic love has no place in my life now or ever, old chap. Let other fellows make asses of themselves. I've seen too much of the damage that poisonous emotion can wreak. It's a trap and a deceit and a damned nuisance. I'll never marry a woman who expects me to love her.

Pen felt sick to recall that self-assured pronouncement. Perhaps she might have dismissed his remarks as a young man's bravado, except that in the three years since, everything she'd seen of Cam confirmed that he'd meant every word.

Even with those closest to him—Richard, his sister, Pen—he kept some element of himself apart, untouchable. Over the years that distance had only grown more marked.

Camden Rothermere was rich, handsome, clever, honorable, and brave. And completely self-sufficient.

Pen had prayed that Cam would ignore his late mother's matchmaking, but of course, he considered it his duty to offer for Penelope. Just as he considered it his duty to inform her that his interest was purely dynastic.

If she'd harbored the tiniest shred of hope of melting the ice in his heart, she'd disregard questions of her notorious family and headstrong inclinations. She'd even try to make herself anew in the image he wanted.

But she knew Cam as she knew herself, and she'd never been a fool.

Cam wouldn't countenance a marriage based on love and she couldn't countenance a marriage that wasn't. She never went into anything halfhearted, and a loveless union would destroy her.

Pen remained trembling near the fireplace, knowing that her family awaited news of her engagement. Her refusal of the greatest marital prize in the kingdom would set the cat among the Thorne pigeons. Right now, her control was so precarious; she shied from her mother's bullying.

She fought a childish urge to cry. If she cried, there would be endless questions and more bullying. Her mother saw tears as opportunity for manipulation, not for comfort.

Pen sucked in a shaky breath and although she'd sworn that she wouldn't, she rushed to the window facing the long drive.

Cam cantered away on his magnificent bay horse. He didn't glance behind to catch her staring after him. Why would he? He'd want to get as far away from her as he could. For a famously self-controlled man, he'd verged very close to losing his temper this afternoon.

That had been a surprise. She hadn't imagined that he cared so much about marrying her. In truth, she hadn't imagined he cared at all.

But then, he'd expected her to say yes without hesitation. Despite the fact that Penelope Thorne was wrong for him on every count.

Except perhaps one.

The fact that she'd love him until she died.

Chapter One

Calais, France, January 1828

Through the bleak hours between midnight and dawn, the candles burned low in the shabby room high in the dilapidated inn. Wind rattled the ill-fitting windowpanes and carried the creaking of boats at their moorings and the reek of salt and rotting fish. The man lying in the narrow bed gasped for every breath.

Camden Rothermere, Duke of Sedgemoor, leaned forward to plump the thin pillows in a futile attempt to offer his dying friend some relief. When Cam sank into his wooden chair beside the bed, Peter Thorne's eyes opened.

Although he and Peter hadn't been close in years, Cam knew about his friend's numerous reverses. The Thornes were famously rackety, and a son and heir who gambled away his fortune was hardly the worst of it.

Cam had arrived in Calais a few hours ago and rushed straight here to find the doctor in attendance. He'd cornered the man before he left. The harassed French medico had been blunt about his patient's prospects.

At first, Peter had drifted close to unconsciousness, but the eyes focusing on Cam now were clear and aware. Eyes sunk in dark hollows in a face that carried no spare flesh. It was like staring into a skull.

"You...came."

The words were hoarse, slow in emerging, and ended in a fit of coughing. Swiftly Cam fetched some water in a chipped cup. After a sip, the sick man collapsed exhausted against the hard mattress.

"Of course I came." Anguish and outrage gripped Cam. Peter had been a companion in childhood games, a participant in university hijinks. He was only thirty-five, the same age as Cam, too bloody young to die.

"Wasn't sure you would," Peter gasped before succumbing to another coughing fit.

Cam offered more water. "We've always been friends."

"From boyhood." The response was a papery whisper. "Although you'll wish me to the devil tonight."

"Never."

"Don't speak...too soon." He closed his eyes and Cam wondered whether he slept. The doctor had said that the end would come tonight. Looking into Peter's bloodless features, Cam couldn't doubt that conclusion.

Grief stabbed his gut, made his hand shake. He placed the cup on the crowded nightstand before he spilled the water. He wasn't a religious man, but he found himself murmuring a prayer for a swift end to his friend's sufferings.

"I need your help."

Cam started to hear Peter speak. Spidery hands plucked fretfully at the threadbare covers drawn high on this cold night. If Cam thought it would do an ounce of good, he'd shift his friend to the best inn in town. But even without the doctor's warning, he saw that Peter's time was measured in hours, perhaps even minutes. Relocating him would be cruel rather than kind.

"It's Pen."

The moment he'd received Peter's summons, Cam had harbored a sinking feeling that it might be. "Your sister?"

"Of course my damned sister." Another coughing attack rewarded Peter's irritable response.

Cam slid his arm behind Peter's back to support him while he caught his breath. "The doctor left laudanum."

Peter coughed until Cam thought surely he must suffocate. The cloth pressed to his mouth came away bloody. Rage at a fate that turned a once-vital young man into a barely breathing skeleton clutched at Cam's gut.

When Peter could speak again, it was in a whisper. Cam leaned close to hear.

"I don't want to sleep." He winced as he drew a breath. Cam saw that every second was excruciating. "I'll have rest enough soon."

Staring into his friend's face, Cam recognized the futility of a comforting lie. They both knew that Peter wouldn't see the dawn.

"Pen's in trouble." Peter fumbled after Cam's hand, gripping with surprising strength. His clasp was icy, as though the grave already encroached into this room.

Cam's expression hardened. He hadn't seen Pen in nine years, since his proposal. The only proposal he'd ever made, as it had turned out. If the chit was in trouble, she probably deserved to be. "I'm sure that she's been in tight spots before."

Penelope Thorne had never had the chance to make a splash in London society. Instead, she'd joined her eccentric aunt on the Continent and stayed there. She hadn't returned to England even after her parents' death in a carriage accident five years ago. Cam gathered she'd been somewhere in Greece at the time.

He hesitated to admit that her refusal had undermined his confidence to such an extent that he only now seriously contemplated marriage again. He needed a wife to help restore his family's reputation, which was even more appalling than the Thornes', and at last he'd found the perfect candidate. His recently chosen bride was as dissimilar to his hoydenish childhood playmate as possible.

Thank God.

By all reports, Pen had become rather odd. There had been nasty rumors from Sicily about her sharing a shady Conti's bed, and of a liaison with a Greek rebel. Goya had emerged from seclusion to paint her both clothed and naked in imitation of his famous *majas*. Not to mention her week's sojourn in the Sultan's harem in Constantinople.

She'd published four volumes of travel reminiscences, books Cam had read over and over, although he'd face the stake before confessing that publicly. A man would rather be flayed than claim a taste for feminine literature.

Peter's hand tightened. The desperation in his old friend's face was unmistakable. Unfortunately. "Lady Bradford died last October. Pen's gone from disaster to disaster since. She's on her way north to Paris to meet me, but she's a woman alone on a dangerous journey."

Serves the hellcat right, Cam wanted to say, then wondered at his spite. He was accounted an equable fellow. The last time he'd lost his temper was when Pen had refused him. If she'd lost her chaperone, however inadequate, Pen should easily find alternative protection. And he meant that in the Biblical sense.

"Peter, I—" Cam began, not sure how to respond. He guessed that his friend meant to charge him with rescuing Pen from her irresponsibility. Although, hell, after a lifetime of friendship, how could he say no?

As if reading Cam's reluctance, Peter spoke quickly. Or perhaps he knew that he had too few breaths remaining to waste any. His urgency seemed to suppress his cough so he managed complete sentences. "In her last letter, she was in Rome and running out of money. That was a month ago. God knows what's befallen since."

"But what can I do?"

"Find her. Bring her back to England. Make sure she's safe." Peter regarded Cam like his last hope. Which made it damned difficult to deny him. "Elias will have his hands full inheriting and Harry's not up to the job, even if I could get him away from the fleshpots."

Peter forestalled Cam's suggestion that another Thorne brother could undertake this task. Cam rose to pace the tiny room. "Confound it, Peter. I've no authority over Pen. She won't pay a speck of attention to me."

"She will. She's always liked you."

Not last time they'd met. "I can't kidnap her."

Shaking, Peter shoved himself higher against the pillows. His black eyes, so like his sister's, burned in his ashen face as if all the life concentrated in that blazing stare. "If you have to, you must. I won't have my sister bouncing all over Europe, called a whore by ignorant pigs who should know better."

Bloody hell.

His stare unwavering, Peter clawed at the blankets. He gulped for air and gray tinged his skin now that brief vitality faded. "There's no man I trust more than you. If you've ever considered me a friend, if you've ever cherished a moment's affection for my sister, bring Pen home."

A moment's fondness for his sister? Aye, there was the rub. Until she'd treated him like an insolent lackey, he'd been fond of Penelope Thorne.

Pausing by the window, he stared into the stormy night. An endless forest of masts ranged against the turbulent sky. It was a night for making deals with the devil. Except in this case, Cam would wager good money that the devil was the woman at the end of the wild goose chase.

He caught his reflection in the glass. He looked like he always did. Calm. Controlled. Cold. The habit of hiding his feelings had become second nature. But he was sorrowing and resentful—and that resentment focused on one troublesome woman. Behind him, hazy in the glass, he saw Peter watching him, suffering stoically through his last hours.

How could Cam refuse? Futile as the quest was. Pen would go her own way, whatever her dying brother asked, whatever pressure her childhood friend placed upon her.

Cam leveled his shoulders. Duty had guided him since he'd been old enough to understand the snide whispers about his mother's affair with her brother-in-law. Duty insisted that he accept this task, however unwillingly. Slowly he faced his friend. "Of course I'll do it, Peter."

And was rewarded by an easing in Peter's painful tension and a hint of the formerly brilliant smile. The Thornes were a famously handsome family and fleetingly, Cam glimpsed his rakish old companion. "God bless you, Cam."

God help him, more like.

Fall in Love with Forever Romance

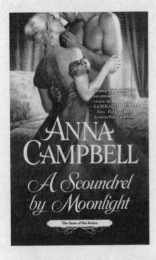

A SCOUNDREL BY MOONLIGHT
by Anna Campbell

Justice. That's all Nell Trim wants—for the countless young women the Marquess of Leath has ruined with his wildly seductive ways. But can she can resist the scoundrel's temptations herself? Check out this fourth sensual historical romance in the Sons of Sin Regency series from bestselling author Anna Campbell!

SINFULLY YOURS
by Cara Elliott

Secret passions are wont to lead a lady into trouble... The second rebellious Sloane sister gets her chance at true love in the next Hellions of High Street Regency romance from bestselling author Cara Elliott.

Fall in Love with Forever Romance

A GOOD ROGUE IS HARD TO FIND
by Kelly Bowen

The rogue's life has been good to William Somerhall, until he moves in with his mother and her paid companion, Miss Jenna Hughes. To keep the eccentric dowager duchess from ruin, he'll have to keep his friends close—and the tempting Miss Hughes closer still. Fans of Sarah MacLean and Tessa Dare will fall in love with the newest book in Kelly Bowen's Lords of Worth series!

WILD HEAT
by Lucy Monroe

The days may be cold, but the nights are red-hot in *USA Today* bestselling author Lucy Monroe's new Northern Fire contemporary romance series. Kitty Grant decides that the best way to heal her broken heart is to come back home. But she gets a shock when she sees how sexy her childhood friend Tack has become. Before she knows it, they're reigniting sparks that could set the whole state of Alaska on fire.

Fall in Love with Forever Romance

SUGAR ON TOP
by Marina Adair

It's about to get even sweeter in Sugar! When scandal forces Glory Mann to co-chair the Miss Sugar Peach Pageant with sexy single dad Cal MacGraw, sparks fly. Fans of Carly Phillips, Rachel Gibson, and Jill Shalvis will love the latest in the Sugar, Georgia series!

A MATCH MADE ON MAIN STREET
by Olivia Miles

When Anna Madison's high-end restaurant is damaged by a fire, there's only one place she can cook: her sexy ex's diner kitchen. But can they both handle the heat? The second book of the Briar Creek series is "sure to warm any reader's heart" (*RT Book Reviews* on *Mistletoe on Main Street*).

Fall in Love with Forever Romance

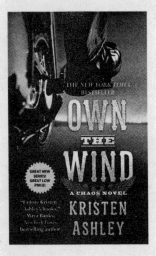

OWN THE WIND
by Kristen Ashley

Only $5.00 for a limited time! Tabitha Allen is everything Shy Cage has ever wanted, but everything he thinks he can't have. When Tabby indicates she wants more—*much* more—than friendship, he feels like the luckiest man alive. But even lucky men can crash and burn...The first book in the Chaos series from *New York Times* bestselling author Kristen Ashley!

FIRE INSIDE
by Kristen Ashley

Only $5.00 for a limited time! When Lanie Heron propositions Hop Kincaid, all she wants is one wild night with the hot-as-hell biker. She gets more than she bargained for, and it's up to Hop to convince Lanie that he's the best thing that's ever happened to her...Fans of Lori Foster and Julie Ann Walker will love this book!

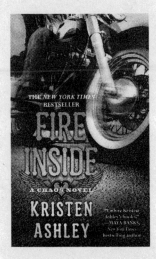